D0231776

Mistress of the Sea

Mistress of the Sea

Jenny Barden

1 3 5 7 9 10 8 6 4 2

Published in 2012 by Ebury Press, an imprint of Ebury Publishing
A Random House Group Company

Copyright © 2012 by Jenny Barden

Jenny Barden has asserted her right to be identified as the author of this Work in accordance with the Copyright, Designs and Patents Act 1988

This novel is a work of fiction. Names and characters are the product of the author's imagination and any resemblance to actual persons, living or dead, is entirely coincidental

All rights reserved. No part of this publication may be reproduced, stored in a retrieval system, or transmitted in any form or by any means, electronic, mechanical, photocopying, recording or otherwise, without the prior permission of the copyright owner

The Random House Group Limited Reg. No. 954009

Addresses for companies within the Random House Group can be found at:
www.randomhouse.co.uk

A CIP catalogue record for this book is available from the British Library

The Random House Group Limited supports The Forest Stewardship Council (FSC®), the leading international forest certification organisation. Our books carrying the FSC label are printed on FSC® certified paper. FSC is the only forest certification scheme endorsed by the leading environmental organisations, including Greenpeace. Our paper procurement policy can be found at:
www.randomhouse.co.uk/environment

Printed and bound by CPI Group (UK) Ltd, Croydon, CR0 4YY

Hardback ISBN 9780091949211
Trade paperback ISBN 9780091949563

To buy books by your favourite authors and register for offers visit
www.randomhouse.co.uk

For Mark, without whom the journey
would never have been made

'. . . O mistress mine! where are you roaming?
O! stay and hear; your true love's coming . . .'

—Twelfth Night *by William Shakespeare, Act II, Scene 3*

'. . . On that second trip [to the Indies], taken in 1571, he [Drake] came in a tiny vessel of 25 tons . . . called the *Swan* . . . the voyage no doubt had a number of financial backers. Only one name appears in the record, that of a 'merchant of Exeter called Richard Dennys,' who apparently went with other merchants in the ship with Drake . . .'

—Sir Francis Drake: The Queen's Pirate *by Harry Kelsey, Chapter 3, pp45-6 (Yale University Press, 1998)*

1

First Sight

'. . . And one especially do we affect
Of two gold ingots, like in each respect.
The reason no man knows; let it suffice,
What we behold is censured by our eyes.
Where both deliberate, the love is slight;
Who ever loved that loved not at first sight?'

—Hero and Leander by *Christopher Marlowe,*
the First Sestiad

Plymouth, England

September 1570

The chill was enough to hurry everything along, as if the season was already sliding over ice. With her hands under her cloak Ellyn tried to keep her hood over her head, and she wished Old Nan would quicken her pace. She had no wish to linger where people were crowding around the bear garden. She stamped her feet but to little effect. Nan continued to hobble, craning her head towards the ring. The noise from its confines grew louder as they neared. Howls and jeers vied with the screeching of gulls, and beneath this din rumbled a deep-throated growl.

'Is that Clouterson, would you say, Mistress Ellyn?' Nan called tremulously.

Ellyn carried on walking.

'Perhaps,' she replied. 'But I am not well acquainted with the voices of bears.'

A blood-curdling roar followed a violent thud against boards. Nan shuffled to a halt, mouth agape.

'This is no place to tarry,' Ellyn said, taking hold of Nan's arm and leading her on.

They had almost passed the ring by when one of the bear warder's touts reached them: 'A penny to see the sport, mistresses. Half price for ye. A bargain an' a privilege since the beasts be warmed up . . .'

Ellyn veered away from the man, pulling her hood over more. She glanced from beneath it, anxious to escape the growing throng. Then the glimpse of a bumbling figure made her start.

'Quick!' She turned sharply with Nan in tow.

'What is it?' Nan squawked.

'Someone I'd rather not meet. Don't look round.'

'Eh?' Nan peered over her shoulder. 'There's Master Fownes!'

'Come on!' Ellyn moved hurriedly and doubled back. Peryn Fownes was a bore she preferred to avoid, and she felt some relief when the crowd closed behind her.

The tout reappeared at her elbow.

'A ha'penny each, mistresses.' He beckoned eagerly. 'You will not be noticed,' he added under his breath to Ellyn. 'The Great Clouterson is on!' he declared in a bellow.

The bear was legendary in Plymouth. Ellyn had seen him on

parade, being marched through the town, but she had no wish to watch him baited. She tried to step aside, only to be swept closer to the gate.

Stamping feet set the tiered stands shaking; hoots and cheers rolled around bets and curses. Ellyn looked around doubtfully, wondering whether she could yet slip away. But more latecomers were pushing behind, and, for once, Nan was moving quickly. With mounting apprehension, Ellyn paid to be squeezed onto a platform, at the back of a common horde, with a view of hats and waving arms and a reek of pisspots and fish.

The Great Clouterson was chained to a stake. Two mastiffs were tearing at his haunches, another two were blood-soaked and struggling to get up from the dirt. A fifth appeared to be dead. A man was in the pit but close to the edge. In his hands was a pole tipped with a blunt piece of metal which he shoved between the jaws of one of the dogs worrying the bear.

The crowd sighed as the dog's maw was forced open. With a jerk of the pole the dog was hurled to one side. The man jumped up and out of the way. Others crouched at the top of the wall with long sticks at the ready. The crowd chanted. The bear reared up, twisted, and struck the dog still hanging from his haunches with a mighty swipe of a huge, clawed paw. A thin yelp came from the somersaulting mastiff. It was a carcass the moment it landed with a bone-shattering crack against the wall. Clouterson charged for the body, only to be whipped back, half-strangled by the chain round his neck. He shook his head, teeth flashing, showering the audience with saliva and blood. Then, with a snarl of tormented rage, he lashed out at one of the dogs, sending it flying to crash against the staves protecting the crowd.

Screams broke out.

Nan gasped.

'I cannot look.' She tugged at Ellyn's cloak with one hand while raising the other to her face, though Ellyn noticed Nan still peering from between her wrinkled fingers.

Ellyn took Nan's arm.

'We can go as soon as you wish,' she whispered.

'No . . . Oh no!' Nan exclaimed, fingers dropping into her open mouth.

Clouterson strained against his chain, head down, mighty shoulders bulging. The stake shuddered. Ellyn felt sorry for the two dogs left alive. One was bleeding badly where skin and an ear had been almost ripped from its head; the second was limping.

This contest would soon be over, Ellyn thought. The bear always won. A dog made its owner money by being the last to survive. Bears were expensive; if a dog came close to seriously injuring a bear, then a man would intervene to fend the dog off. Despite her lack of experience, she knew the rules of the sport, and she had already decided she had no wish to know more. Only the mastiff with the wounded paw was left moving around in the pit. Clouterson was dealing with the other in a frenzy of tearing.

Ellyn felt something spatter her face. Recoiling, she wiped at it furiously. She swallowed and closed her eyes, and then opened them, feeling faint. She watched the last dog alive limping warily around the pit. He had the black muzzle of all mastiffs but was smaller than most, with a striking reddish tinge to his golden coat. The dog kept close to the pit wall, nose pointing to the bear as if chances might be scented.

'Clouterson,' the crowd chanted. 'Kill 'im!'

The bear turned. With a ferocious growl he sprang for the last dog alive, driving against the chain. The dog skipped forward and raced past. A hatch in the pit wall opened for the dog to make an escape. Ellyn willed him to flee. But then Clouterson lurched, first one way, next the other, wrenching at the stake.

'God-a-mercy!' Nan cried.

The stake swung back and forth. Gasps of horror came from the crowd. People stood and fell back.

This should not be happening, Ellyn thought.

Suddenly Clouterson broke free and rammed against the wall, trailing chain and stake as if they were light as feathers. The dog leapt onto the wall, not through the hatch. Clouterson rose to his hind legs, and Ellyn saw that at any moment he would be running wild among the people. The man with the pole struck his flanks. Clouterson drew back as if preparing to jump. Piercing screams inflamed the panic. Those closest to the bear dived from him in terror, while those further away pressed forward to see more. Liveried attendants were caught in the crush. A few spectators pitched in with whatever they could use. A man in front with loose fair hair, whose cape was spattered with blood, brandished a stick, and, with a jolt, Ellyn thought she recognised him. The bear lunged as the dog sprang up. Nan shrieked.

Ellyn looked round for a means of escape. She caught sight of some steps and pulled at Nan's arm.

The bear was spraying blood. Ellyn stared over a heaving mass of bent backs and craning heads to see the dog swinging off the ground, jaws clamped around the great bear's throat. Clouterson reared to stand, forepaws flailing, while men pushed against him with sticks at his chest. For a moment the bear swayed. Then he toppled backwards into the pit with his throat torn open. The dog jumped on top.

A stunned hush settled. The bear was dead. The first to move was the fair-haired man with a blood-stained cape. He jumped down into the pit and led the dog to the hatch. Good, Ellyn thought. The man looked up, and Ellyn turned quickly; now she was sure of who he was.

'Will Doonan!' Nan said, tugging furiously at Ellyn's sleeve. 'That be our neighbour, Will Doonan!'

Ellyn pulled Nan away. She had seen Will Doonan well enough. She led Nan down the steps and fervently hoped she had not been recognised as well.

No one interfered. A thrum of astonishment drifted from the ring as Ellyn and Nan left ahead of most spectators. Even Nan began muttering in a stupefied way.

'Never have I seen the like . . . The bear running loose . . . We could have been killed. Torn limb from limb. Were it not for that dog . . . And Will Doonan, God bless him . . . To think of Clouterson brought down. And the blood. Did you see the blood?'

Ellyn did not want to be reminded of it. She was thinking of Will Doonan. Had he seen her? She prayed he had not. She had no wish for him to think less of her by association with the bear garden. But she had been at the back of the stands, under the gallery's shadow. If he had caught a glimpse, he could not have been certain – so long as he did not notice her now. Ellyn hurried on, pleased that at last Nan seemed to be making an effort to keep up, though she suspected the prospect of gossip about 'the blood' might have been the main reason.

'You must be discreet,' Ellyn said tersely.

'Have faith, Mistress Ellyn,' Nan wheezed from behind. 'As if I would be aught but mum about you. Trust my tongue not to tattle.'

This was hardly much comfort, though Ellyn accepted it would have to do. She glanced over her shoulder, aware that some of those who had been in the garden were now catching them up, but to her relief Will Doonan was not amongst them. Just then, he was the man she least wanted to see.

Will tore off his cape and threw it on the pallet in his room. He might yet have time. Old Nan walked very slowly, and he had taken a shortcut back to the house. It had been his intention to avoid another encounter, keep Ellyn Cooksley second-guessing, and not let her think he was contriving to meet her. But, since seeing her in the bear garden, he had changed his mind. He had an engagement to keep later: an appointment that could affect his whole future – but let enjoyment come first.

He wiped at his face and peered at the polished steel on the wall. Another rub got rid of the last blood spots. Flinging the towel aside, he quickly pulled on his doublet, tying up the points and straightening his sleeves. What had Mistress Ellyn been doing at the bear ring? That she would go there intrigued him. He strode to the window and buckled on his belt, looking out at the steep terraces of her father's garden below. There was no one about. The light was hazed with autumn smoke, throwing shafts through shade over the garden's tiers. He reached for a pouch, and then twisted down around the old mast at the hub of the spiral stairs. The door at the bottom led out onto steps, and on these he waited. Peering up between branches, he watched for Ellyn Cooksley's approach; then he saw her with her maid. The top of the stone staircase was the best place to intercept them. He moved that way.

'Good day, mistresses, though 'tis drawing late,' Will said casually. He could tell he had startled them.

Mistress Ellyn jumped back.

'How? . . . I'faith!' flapped Old Nan like a worried hen.

Ellyn bustled in front. When Will rose from his bow, she looked him straight in the eye.

'Good-even', Master Doonan. It is our pleasure to see you here *again*.'

Will smiled. Their game was unspoken but they had been playing it for some weeks: he would walk through the garden when he expected her to do the same. That she had not varied her ways had encouraged him. She would visit the Hoe Chapel before sundown and pass through the garden on her return. But today that had changed. She could not have expected him, and he was amused to have surprised her – and to know where she had been.

He held out the pouch.

'And I hope by this small gift to ensure that a pleasure it is.'

He moved nearer, and was gratified to see Ellyn looking back rather than away. Her eyes were fixed on him so steadily he could appreciate the subtlety of their hue: a soft nutmeg-brown, but darker around the irises, each shadow-ringed like woodland pools. The looking meant much to him; her reply was crisp.

'Master Doonan, I thank you, but in faith I cannot accept. I have done nothing to merit any token from you, and I would rather not it be supposed that I have.'

Will hesitated a moment while enjoying her attention. She was the daughter of a wealthy merchant, and he only a craftsman, yet she was studying him with an intensity that would have favoured a rich lord.

He held the pouch out to Nan.

'Then this is for Mistress Nan, whose cooking is unsurpassed in all of Plymouth. The gift is hers for the tastes she gave me when I dined with your father yesterday.' Whether Ellyn knew of the engagement, Will was not sure, but he judged it would do no harm to tell her. He pushed the pouch closer. 'The finest spices from the Guinea merchantman just docked.'

Nan gaped wider, and then snatched the pouch out of his hands.

'God bless you, Master Doonan. To think of us after what you've been through . . .'

Ellyn seized hold of her arm and spun her half round.

'I hope Mistress Ellyn will let me use them,' Nan cackled over her shoulder. She turned back to Ellyn, muttering. 'It's plain the gentleman means well, my dear . . .'

Ellyn raised her chin.

'Pah! Let *you* be wooed with spices, if to charm is his intent.'

Stifling a smile, Will bowed low. How should he proceed? He had not considered wooing with any seriousness at all. The reward of the game was in the playing, and he suspected play would soon stop if he once showed real interest. He regarded Ellyn more carefully.

'Well, perhaps we should know one another better, dear lady, since gifts should not be exchanged between strangers.' He stepped to one side to counter a shift in her stance. 'If Mistress Nan will allow us, she could rest indoors and see all is well from the window, while you stay with me and ask what you *will*.' He emphasised the suggestion with a grin. 'What say you?'

Ellyn did not look away, and her gaze told him what he most wanted to know – that she was at least entertained.

'I say you are a saucy fellow, Will Doonan. What makes you think I want to know anything?'

Nan pushed past before he could reply.

'Tush! My legs are too old to wait on banter, and my nerves all a-jangled after the calamity I've witnessed . . .'

'Hush, Nan!' Ellyn cried.

Nan mumbled and plodded on.

'I am going in, and thank you, sir.' She nodded at Will who answered with a wink.

Ellyn might have followed except that he moved to block her way. Above their heads, a medlar tree trapped a last fine trickle of gold-dust light. Around them was a battlemented wall, and below that lay the garden's lower terrace. It could only be reached by steep steps winding down. He stood at their head.

'So, sweet maiden, what can I tell you that you might wish to know?'

She stared back at him defiantly, chin raised above her ruff, since she was a good deal shorter.

'*If* I wished to know you . . . I might ask about your family.'

He broke in quickly as her eyelids lowered.

'Would you dislike me if you disliked my father?'

'What has knowing to do with liking? I might know your father to be a knave and still like your looks.'

'Do you?' Will smiled broadly.

She tossed back her head, and that set a little pendant shivering at her throat. He realised then that her skin was quite pale, and, where the sun had touched her, tiny freckles had formed, like the flecking on a swallow's egg.

She swooped on his question.

'Liking is of no account. If I were an apple I would not like your teeth.'

'You need not fear my teeth.' He made show of them as he replied. 'If you were an apple, I would not have you near my mouth; you would be too sharp.'

She left him little time to think before she rose to the bait.

'Then I am glad not to be sweet. If I was a bird I would not like your eyes, they are too much like the sky.'

He let her look into his eyes, and smiled more.

'Do not birds fly in the sky?'

'They fly, but they need to rest. I see no land in your eyes.'

What was she saying? There was jest in her answer, but her manner seemed earnest. He noticed a wave of her dark hair below the edge of her hood. When the light caught it, her hair glowed as rich as bracken.

'You should not be troubled by my eyes.' He shut them as he spoke. 'If you were a bird, I would screw them closed; you might peck them out.'

'So keep me away.' Her response was indignant.

Will smiled back, blinking happily as he saw her afresh.

'You are not a bird, but a woman.'

'A woman *you* do not know.'

'You have told me sufficient. You are a woman as fruitful as an apple with the mind of a bird.'

He laughed because she was blushing, and that became her well, he thought, checking his mirth at her pique. She raised a hand to her chest and the opening in her cloak, which drew his attention to her figure and the suggestion of her dainty breasts. She tightened her mouth, but even so he considered it pretty, perhaps better for being moulded by the feeling he had aroused.

'And you a rascal to say so,' she retorted. 'Fruitful! How dare you judge me fruitful?'

Her eyes flashed with a strength of temper he had not really meant to provoke. Again she moved to pass him but, as if they were in a dance, he mirrored her steps. Then he spread his hands as he offered her the truth.

'You have a fruitful shape, and a goodly one, too.'

'I am more than a shape, and I have more mind than a bird's!'

Will raised his brows.

'Ah! But how *much* more?' he said, attempting to soothe.

She shot him a haughty look.

'Save your questions on that, Will Doonan. You will waste your breath to ask them.'

He bowed deeply, and, as he straightened up, said, 'A pity, but no matter. I know your father and I like him. That should be enough.'

The smile he gave her was not returned. Her eyes blazed as she turned on her heel. He sensed she was no longer indifferent; that was his triumph, but it was also his loss. She did not take the arm he offered her.

'Goodbye, Mistress Ellyn. I trust you will enjoy your next dish.'

She ignored his parting words and no answer came. He watched her descending: a neat figure cloaked in mulberry red. Then he followed her progress for as long as she remained visible up to the doorway of the house. The diamond window panes revealed nothing inside – if they had he might have lingered, and seen someone behind them looking out.

He left the garden by the upper gate. Behind the Hoe, the houses nestled, overhanging like hill-lane hedges, steep gables almost touching over passageways and alley gutters that the sun never cleansed. He walked down near the harbour, not because it was the quickest way, but to escape the smell of pits and privies and catch a cold breeze from the sea, to hear the gulls and eye the ships, those spread across the Cattewater and crowding the nearer harbour quays.

He strolled on to Sutton Poole beside the narrow rope-walks where cable was made, past the tanners and salters, smithies and coopers – passing his own workshop with the caulking-mallet sign, boarded and shuttered – dodging rusting chains and abandoned nets, drunk mariners and vagrants begging, and walking under the bowsprits of the grandest ships, over cobbles streaked with visceral smears, breathing the fish-stink of the docks and the coal-smoke sinking. He moved away through the east gate, where a body turned on a gibbet like a broken vane in the wind. The ditches became deeper, though cramped dwellings remained, dirt and straw, wood and reed, mean cottages by the pack-paths to the outer quays, each ground room filled with curing pilchards, or alum-soaked canvas, or barrels of wine on which no tax had been paid.

Dusk had fallen before the watchman cried; mist blurred blue shadows around low chinks of light. He turned through an archway, one leading to a wharf, though it was a tavern he wanted, one with no stake and no sign to mark it as the 'Saracen' – only a door above a worn flight of steps that, for those who knew it, was the way inside.

A dog growled as he entered. He trod cautiously on rushes, advancing in near darkness towards a dull candle-glow. The room reeked of mouldering ale. Silence settled. An eye turned in his direction, yellowed and clouded. As Will walked closer, the man watching him stood and spat.

'What's thy business?'

The man had the arms of a mason, and a cudgel hanging against his hip. His shoulders rolled as he fingered his belt.

Will carried on, searching the far end of the room.

'I'm looking for someone. We have an arrangement.'

The dog began whining. The clouded eye narrowed.

'And who, pray, might that be?'

Will had no wish to begin a fight, but that left him with a bleak choice: to give a name or be turned away. He gave the name.

'Francis Drake.'

Will heard a voice, but it came from behind.

'Then you're looking for me.'

2

Vengeance

'. . . As there is a general vengeance which secretly pursueth the doers of wrong and suffereth them not to prosper, albeit no man of purpose empeach them, so there is a particular indignation, engrafted in the bosom of all that are wronged, which ceaseth not seeking by all means possible to redress or remedy the wrong received . . .'

—From Francis Drake's dedication to the account of his early voyages compiled by his chaplain, Philip Nichols, and presented to Queen Elizabeth I on New Year's Day 1593 (later published as Sir Francis Drake Revived*)*

Ellyn pressed a napkin against her face and rubbed at the sticky birch sap she had applied to her skin. It felt like glue, though the scent was that of a fresh spring coppice. Let it strip away her freckles and leave her as pale as alabaster. She scrubbed at the coating until it came away on the cloth, and then she could see it – balled up like mouse droppings and just as dirty: a film removed messily as from a boiled and peeled egg, and no doubt her looks would be left just as plain. She threw down the napkin in disgust.

Standing in her shift, Ellyn looked over the fire screen, and peered towards the garden through the rippled panes of glass. She blinked to clear her sight. Shadows and sunlight raced over the terraces: the signs of a strong wind dragging clouds across the sky. Memories chased with them, unfolding and changing, of the garden when she was small, and her brother, Thom, springing over the medlar when it was no bigger than a bush, just after his thirteenth birthday. She had followed and broken a branch, not because her jumping was weak, but because her petticoats had snagged. Thom had taken a whipping for that, despite her father's reluctance and her own confession.

She donned the rope hoops of the farthingale that would hold the layers of her skirts; these were clothes she had come to accept. The hoops no longer seemed like fetters, and she had lost the compulsion that had once induced her to leap. Calloused bark had formed on the medlar where the broken stump had died back, like an opening for a missing sleeve, swelling each year while the tree had doubled in height. She regarded it sombrely, remembering the tree when it had borne its first fruit. The apple was to be Thom's, Nan had announced, but it would not be fit to eat until the apple had begun to rot. The strangeness of that would never leave her. No one had wanted that first brown apple. By the time it was wizened, Thom was dead of a fever.

'Are you ready, Mistress?'

Ellyn turned and recognised that her maid Lettie was waiting. So, the time had come for her to dress for dinner, and Peryn Fownes, the double-chinned merchant who had been idly courting her, would already be discussing business in the parlour of the house. Ellyn felt her spirits sinking as she called Lettie to her side.

'Your lady Mother said the bird partlet with the blue velvet gown,' Lettie chattered, 'but which sleeves . . . ?'

Blue, red and black were held up for inspection. Ellyn shrugged. She cared less about her sleeves than she did about her freckles, but she supposed she ought to ask.

'Do you notice anything different?'

'They be different colours.' Lettie smirked.

'Look at my face, Lettie,' Ellyn corrected her. 'Do you see any change?'

'You're blushing . . .'

Ellyn glanced down to hide her embarrassment. She brushed irritably at her shift, and waited for Lettie to confirm that her efforts had been in vain.

'You look . . . a little feverish,' Lettie answered at last, with an alarming tone of genuine concern.

'I am not ill, Lettie!' Ellyn waved her aside. 'And do not fuss.' She gestured dismissively to show she had made up her mind. 'The black will do. I am sure Master Fownes will not be in the least interested in my sleeves.'

'P'haps not, Mistress, but he most certainly is in *you*.' Lettie whisked the sleeves out of sight, turning her back to work on the gown, and humming with a show of nonchalance.

Ellyn sighed. What would follow? She would dress and eat, listen to the remnants of a tedious conversation about wool prices and shipments, and then, no doubt, Peryn Fownes would expect her to join him in a game of chess, treating her to a long discourse on how her playing might be improved, since this appeared to be his idea of flattering her intelligence while at the same time paying suit. Yet she lost to him because she was bored. She was sure she could win perfectly well if she wanted to, but what would be the point? She might offend the gentleman's pride or worse: convince him of her interest.

Ellyn's wretchedness grew. Her freckles remained, and so did her guilt. She should be more grateful. Her parents had been considerate in trying to give her a choice, and within the bounds of their approval she owed them a duty to decide. Their house would become her husband's, whether that was Peryn Fownes or Godfrey Gilbert. Ellyn tugged at her bodice, tight and stiff with willow-slats and bone, as an image of sour Master Gilbert contended with that of smug Master Fownes. Neither suitor could offer a better house. Her future would be in the same place, confined within the same walls. Her children would run round the garden and jump from the steps while she, like her mother, would watch from inside, and little by little lose the desire to go out.

Lettie came over to help with the laces, continuing her babble with mischievous delight.

'. . . And Master Gilbert, too. I believe they would fight over your sleeves . . .'

Ellyn shuddered. The idea of crow-like Godfrey Gilbert fighting for her was even more distasteful than that of podgy Peryn Fownes.

'How perfectly silly that would be.' She could have said more, but held back. Any remark would be the subject of kitchen gossip, even to sweet-tempered Lettie whom she believed too slow-witted for any guile. She could no more talk freely than she could leap over the tree.

Because they were so close, Ellyn noticed that the oils in Lettie's hair had soaked through her coif. And while the farthingale was secured with a multitude of ties, she was aware of Lettie's smell: suet and onions, lavender and musk. Such physical intimacy with a gulf between their souls. Ellyn listened with a sense of imprisonment while Lettie stooped, her mouth close to Ellyn's hips, as if she was addressing the island on which Ellyn was locked in a tower.

'And I am sure Will Doonan would fight them both if they would do him the honour.'

'Lettie!' Ellyn slapped Lettie's back, but not very hard; the indignation she felt was too much to contain. Why should Lettie be thinking of *him*?

Lettie rushed into a denial.

'Though they would not, of course. And I do not mean to suggest that Master Doonan might hope to win you either. He'd be above himself even to try.'

The gown was raised with a sweep, the black sleeves fastened in place. Lettie held it before her like a robe for the condemned.

'But maybe these sleeves will taunt him as well?'

Ellyn snatched the gown away.

'I doubt it, since he will not see them.'

'I don't know how you can be so sure. Every time you come back from church, Master Doonan seems to be waiting.' Lettie darted to Ellyn's side, lifting the gown at the shoulders while Ellyn inserted her arms. 'There's another maid in this house who'd swoon at his feet for one of his smiles. *Jane* is looking forward to your walk out today.'

What relationships had been developing without Ellyn being aware? A sudden concern caused her to respond.

'I trust he's not been troubling her?'

'Marry, no!' Lettie giggled, and that did not calm Ellyn at all. 'But while he's gazing at you, we maids are deciding who'll be his real choice.'

Ellyn was shocked.

'How can you?'

'Because we women have ways of making up a man's mind without him even guessing he's not done so himself.'

Ellyn did not care to imagine what ploys Jane might stoop to use. But had she been encouraged? The question was vexing, though Ellyn had already decided to walk along the cliffs, rather than visit the chapel, precisely with the object of keeping clear of Will Doonan. His comments still rankled from their last encounter – '*Fruitful . . .*', '*Mind of a bird . . .*' – and the conviction that he had insulted her was enough to fix her resolve. She would not think of him and neither should Jane. She might perhaps meet him the next day, but most certainly not in Jane's company. If she saw Master Doonan, it would be with Nan.

'Jane will be disappointed. I have other plans for this afternoon.' Ellyn noticed Lettie's quick smile; then her mind reeled before the onslaught of a more alarming thought.

'*You* would not consider him?'

Lettie answered primly while bending to arrange the gown.

''Twould be only natural for him to wed a maid such as me.' She straightened and cast Ellyn a defiant look, but without the pluck to keep it sustained.

Ellyn stared back, and the effect was like cooling on freshly risen dough.

Lettie retreated to the dressing table with another coy remark: 'He brought me a present this morning.'

'What present?' Ellyn was appalled; she knew she should not have been, but the feeling could not be helped.

'A sweet pear. And one for you, too, Mistress,' Lettie added, with the sort of haste that left Ellyn certain she was meant to be appeased. Lettie returned with a comb. 'He said you were to have the best, and the remainder were "for the other fair maidens of the Cooksley house", a droll gallant he is, and that included Old Nan. "One apiece", he said. There was a pear for everyone.'

Ellyn sat. Did Will Doonan suppose he could win her with fruit, while at the same time pandering to all the household maids? She pulled hard against Lettie's grooming.

'He is overbold.'

'I think he has a good heart. Nan had no mind to tell you, so do not say I did—'

What new revelation was this? Ellyn's anger was rising even before Lettie had finished.

'—she means to poach yours in wine with some of his cloves so you might enjoy his gift in all innocence.'

'Pah!' Enjoy it, she would not. Ellyn shuddered to think of the servants observing and winking, assuming they knew more than she did herself.

'Jane says she will eat her pear raw and let the juice run round her mouth, thinking of his lips when she does,' Lettie continued confidently, as she stitched tight the braid she had made of Ellyn's hair. Her snickering drew a curt comment from Ellyn.

'Ridiculous!' Such licentious fancy, thought Ellyn. The girl was depraved. With an image of a pear against wet lips, she pursed her own tight, as if they had been drawn and knotted rather than fulsomely shaped. A cawle was pinned over her hair, and Ellyn gazed down at her partlet with its embroidery of birds. Most had been covered over, but two remained visible either side of an opening in which the faint shadow between her breasts almost showed as a line. She pressed her arms close to deepen the effect, but with little result; her bosom was too small. Why would a lusty man like Will Doonan be interested in a woman with small breasts? The idea was preposterous, the more so since he was unworthy and she had resolved to give him no further thought. 'A man on whom to wager, but not trust' – that was how her father had described him. They had been eating soup the previous night and the broth had been seasoned with Will's spices; because of that her mother had mentioned his name. 'I might back him with my coin,' her father had said cryptically, 'but no more than I could afford to lose. He is a venturer.'

Ellyn had been mystified by the opinion. What did her father know? They had certainly met recently, Will Doonan had told her as much, but what had they discussed? Will Doonan was a craftsman who worked with tar to caulk ships' seams; how could a caulker be considered a venturer? She had tried to find out, but in her father's baffling reply a warning had been clear: 'Will Doonan is not what he appears. Men like him are like rolling dice; they never settle. He might leave tomorrow and be gone for years. He might return a fabulous profit, or make a total loss. If he survives one venture, there will be another, and always another, until fortune turns against him and he does not come back . . .'

So he would be leaving for the sea, that had been Ellyn's conclusion, all the more reason to blot him out of her mind. She imagined Will Doonan's blue eyes looking back at her from a lighter-boat in one of those scenes she had often witnessed at the harbourside: the sailors boarding in their thick, greased jackets; the ships in the Cattewater festooned with banners and flags; trumpets blasting; drums rolling; wives weeping. It would never happen.

'Foolish,' she muttered to her reflection in the glass.

Will dipped his quill in the inkpot and added another entry to the list. The inventory continued in a painstakingly formed hand. In the quiet of his rented room he sought to take stock of his affairs. The list already filled a span-square of paper, ruled into columns like the hornbook from which he had been taught his letters at petty school. He scanned the page with a frown. His characters resembled sturdy blocks, far removed from the elegant script that distinguished the hands of better-educated men, or young ladies, like Ellyn Cooksley, with their own private tutors. Will had seen her writing in a note Jane had shown him, because Jane could barely read and wanted his help to understand it. Ellyn's hand was graceful and flowing, embellished like a vine with tendril curls and bountiful flourishes, even if her subject was wool and cloth. He put his pen down.

Had he offended her? He supposed that he had from the way she had left him, but by all that went before he believed he had won her interest, perhaps even touched her heart. Ellyn had spoken to him many times, sparred with him in wit, blushed when his words roused her, and met his eyes look for look. Give her a day or two without seeing him, and they would both be ready for more of the same. But could the game carry on? Mistress Ellyn had rich suitors, and her father would never accept him without some improvement in his prospects. Whilst the game was seductive, he could not realistically hope to win – that was the truth. He should forget her. He only played the game with ease because with her he had nothing to lose. Yet the game had taken a hold: it was the hook of first success, of small wins against the odds, and the glimpse of a glittering prize he could not measure and weigh up – though what he had seen of Ellyn enthralled him. He should quit while he could before he enjoyed the game too much.

With his elbows on the table he pressed his head against his hands; then he looked up through the open window. Leaves were blowing in the wind, and he knew from the way they scattered that a nor'easterly was getting up. Francis Drake had returned a few weeks before. His voyage to the Indies had been a success, and the investment made by Ellyn's father had delivered a handsome profit. It would be enough to encourage Nicholas Cooksley to want to back the Captain again. Already Drake was talking about making another venture, sounding out interest among the Plymouth seamen Drake knew and trusted, who had experience as well as courage. Drake had spoken of such a voyage to Will.

Will looked at his hands, seeing the ink stains on his fingers and the browning left by tar. They were marked and rough but when he flexed them they felt strong. That had not always been so; not much more than a year ago, his hands had been reduced to skin and bone, and his knuckles had stood out like galls on twigs.

He reflected on that as he clenched his fists. When he had returned from the Americas he had been close to death. He had been forced to leave his brother behind, and then hunger had almost killed him. The scars had healed, but his hatred still burned. No one knew what had happened to his younger brother, Kit. Will thought of the pictures he had seen in the *Book of Martyrs*: images of burning and torture. Will brought his fist down on the table. Where was Kit now? Was he still in the Americas, held captive by the Spaniards? That seemed most likely. Since Drake was planning another voyage there, Will owed it to Kit to go back – return as close as he could to the place where he had seen his brother last. He would have gone before if only he had been able.

Perhaps Kit was dead.

Will spread his hands over the paper, remembering his father's last words. He could hear them whenever he chose – words spoken at his mother's burial, after she had died from grief, as everyone supposed. 'There be a grave for thy mother, Will,' his father had said. They had stood side by side watching the clay thrown over her coffin. 'A place to weep over her. What place be for thy brother, Will? What hast thou brought back? Thy brother . . . Where is he?' Will could still feel the force of his father's bitter anger, see his hands trembling with the urge to smite and accuse – though there was already a rift between them, narrow but deep, and he would not cross it, even in rage.

He had not seen his father since. He had not seen his three sisters. They would always do their father's bidding. Nothing he could have said would have made any difference. He and his father had never seen eye to eye. He had been apprenticed in Plymouth while he was still only a boy. His family knew next to nothing about how he had made his way in the world. He doubted that they cared about what he had achieved: his admission to the caulkers' guild, and the lodgings he had taken above the stables of Master Cooksley's fine house; the success of his business, and his friendship with Francis Drake; or the money he had made from his last voyage with John Hawkins – the voyage which, through Spanish treachery, had robbed him of the best brother he could have wished for. All that mattered to them was that he had returned without Kit.

Nothing would deflect him from his duty to avenge his brother's fate.

A noise made him turn, the shuffle of someone by the door too hesitant to knock. He called, and the youngest of his apprentices entered, pimple-faced and bandy-legged. The boy delivered his message as if it was stinging his tongue.

'There be a meetin' at the Saracen and you're to come now, please, sir, so says Captain Drake.'

Snatching up his hat and cape, Will dashed outside. He made for the arcade leading to the front of Cooksley's house, striding briskly past the herb beds and the dark entrance to the stone staircase.

'My!'

He heard the shout too late to stop. A lady was in his path, emerging from the staircase the moment he passed it by. He raised his hands, as much to buffer as prevent her falling. The next moment he realised he had Ellyn in his grasp, and Jane was close, too, skipping behind her to one side. He felt the tension in Ellyn's arms. He could have been in a dance preparing to lift and she to spring, except that her dark eyes were wide with stunned surprise, and her full lips parted as he steadied her on her feet. Her gaze never left him while her neck arched back. For a fleeting instant he fought the impulse to kiss her, pull her firmly closer and press his mouth against hers. He felt her body yield, but then he heard a woman's cry.

'Master Doonan!'

Glancing round, he saw Jane smile coyly. He released his hold, stepped back and doffed his hat.

'Forgive me, and good day.'

Will turned and waved the boy on. Without a backwards glance he followed, launching into a sprint once he reached the arcade, running to meet Drake, and away from a temptation that could only have mired him in deep trouble.

There were ten men around the table – some Will knew well, others hardly at all. Most, like him, had sailed in John Hawkins's fleet but not on Drake's last voyage. A single candle on the table lit their faces from below. The glow threw dark shadows above brows and cheekbones, and cast looming silhouettes over the crumbling walls. Francis Drake sat with his brother, John. Next to them was Ellis Hixom, 'Hix' to those who knew him, a man with a wound so ugly it kept strangers at a distance. A lead ball had left him with a rip in one jowl through which his shattered teeth showed in the remains of his mouth. Amongst the hands on the table was another man's iron claw. The room pushed everyone close. Eyes were separated by inches, bloodshot and heavy-lidded, rheumy and patched; most were fixed on Drake. Will watched him looking from man to man, holding their silence before he began to speak, his round cheeks flushed with the same fiery red that burned in his beard, showing the humour of blood in his appearance as much as in the confidence he gave out. Will felt it as strength: the power that could hurl an order through a storm, or imbue a joke with sudden warmth.

Drake sipped from a leather tankard, and then set it down.

'I've a venture in mind that needs men such as you. It will entail a bit more than trading.' He paused and looked round. Only a slight sputtering from the candle and a surf-like breathing could be heard. 'Do you want to know what?'

Will supposed that everyone listening had given a commitment just as he had, and none knew exactly what might be involved. The men murmured and nodded, but Drake revealed nothing too quickly; instead he reminded them of a name from the past.

'I often think of my cousin, Robert Barrett. I pray that he lives, though I fear he'll be suffering. The Spaniards will torture him before they burn him at the stake.'

A chorus of 'Damn them!' and 'Bastards!' rang around the table.

Drake linked everyone in the way he continued.

'John Hawkins still weeps for his nephew, Paul. We've all lost someone close.' He turned towards a man with a livid disfigurement above a leather-patched eye. '*Your* cousin, Simon . . .'

'I saw his arm sawn off 'afore he died,' the man called Simon muttered in response.

Will realised what Drake was doing. Everyone present had suffered at Spanish hands. They had all been robbed of family or friends. He thought of Kit and others who were missing or dead. When Drake included him, he bowed his head.

'Kit among many,' Will answered softly. 'Eliseus, Harry and Job the gunner. They're just a few . . . I'll never forget them.'

Drake waited until each man had met his eye.

'We're bound by more than a thirst for riches.' He raised his voice. 'Vengeance is mine, saith the Lord, and we are but the Lord's servants.' He brought his fist down on the table. 'Are you with me?'

'Aye, Captain,' Will answered with the rest. He had burned with the desire to see justice done ever since the Spaniards' treachery off the coast of Mexico.

Drake leaned closer to the candle, drawing the circle tight, until the last traces of levity drained away from his face.

'England cannot risk war.' Drake kept his voice low. 'Our armies are no match for Spain's. There must be no hint of association between what we do and the Queen. We are on our own.'

'We understand,' said Simon.

Will muttered his agreement along with everyone else. He had never expected any levies in support but a bleak reality began to take substance in his mind, and it had the taint of piracy. They would be beyond any protection if they were caught.

In an instant, Drake's mood changed, and Will noticed a glint of devilry in his eye.

'How did David bring down Goliath?'

Hix gave a straight reply: 'With a sling.'

'With his wits,' Drake countered. He turned about, making sure of their attention. 'Spain's might is fuelled by her wealth, and we've all seen the source.'

'The Americas,' hissed the captain's brother, giving voice to Will's thoughts. Most were nodding, though patch-eyed Simon was squirming on his stool.

'But we can't attack the treasure fleet without a fleet of our own! And even with good warships, General Hawkins was routed . . .'

'Think of that treasure,' Drake insisted in a steadier pitch. 'It is well guarded once it leaves the Americas, but not before.'

'Spain controls all the ports,' Hix said bluntly.

'Does she?' Drake smiled as he threw back the challenge. 'Every inlet and every bay?'

Hix shrugged. Through the hole in his cheek, Will watched his broken teeth grind.

'There are no bays along the Mexican shore,' Hix answered. 'We know that. The Spaniards have the only safe harbour there is, at San Juan de Ulúa, where we all fought and lost.'

Drake looked pleased.

'Think further south,' he encouraged.

The candle flame wavered.

'Where?' Will asked softly.

'The land they call Panamá in Tierra Firme: the narrow isthmus between the two great seas – the land across which they take all the riches from Peru. There are reefs along the north coast forming thousands of small islands. There are hundreds of coves. I took note on my last voyage. There are many places that would make excellent bases for mounting an attack.' Drake drew out his purse. Around the candle he began to lay out coins: Spanish silver *reals* and pieces of eight, then gold doubloons. 'Imagine it,' Drake said, as he continued to spread the doubloons out. 'Every year enough silver leaves Tierra Firme to fill St Andrew's Church. Over two hundred tons.' His fingers played with the coins. 'And enough gold is shipped away to pack out this tavern.'

Will stared. He had never seen so much money, and neither had the other men, from the looks on their faces. Fingers reached for the coins. Some touched.

'This room, and more, solid with gold,' Drake continued. 'I would like to find out where that treasure is stored, how it's carried, and the route by which it's taken between the seas.'

'Aye,' someone answered. 'So would I.'

'With that knowledge we can strike, but not too soon.' One by one, Drake began to return the pieces of eight to his purse. 'We must plan carefully and cause no alarm till we're prepared. Our outward endeavour will be to trade. Let us bring back a few fancies for our ladies.'

Grins and chuckles followed while Drake gathered in the *reals* until only the doubloons remained: nine of them. Drake pushed one to each man.

'We must keep our true purpose to ourselves.' He bared his palms. 'Let us swear an oath to see our purpose through. I would trust my life in your hands, every one of you.' He looked slowly round and caught Will's eye; Will was honoured by that. Drake raised his voice. 'Your hands, gentlemen.'

They all reached out and grasped one of Drake's hands and one another's: nine pairs of hands and one alone, though even the iron claw was clasped.

Drake spelt out the promise: 'Whatever the cost, and however long it takes, we'll be avenged. Once sworn never broken.'

There was a rumble of agreement.

'Vengeance!' Drake urged, and in low unison the oath was repeated. 'Vengeance!'

Vengeance. The word rang in Will's ears and on in his mind, all the way back to the closed East Gate. And only much later, after he had paid the watchman and walked in darkness past the ships, with the rigging whistling, blocks banging and loose canvas slapping, only after beginning the climb at the base of the Hoe, his breath forming clouds, did he think of what he would leave, and then think of Ellyn.

3

O! a Kiss

'. . . O! a kiss
Long as my exile, sweet as my revenge!
Now, by the jealous queen of heaven, that kiss
I carried from thee, dear, and my true lip
Hath virgined it e'er since . . .'

—Coriolanus *by William Shakespeare,*
Act V, Scene 3

Ellyn listened as her father fastened the locks. She heard the clink of the keys on the chain round his waist, and the steward banging the shutters closed. She stared into the dark; the drapes were drawn around the bed where she lay. Old Nan would soon be snoring from her pallet behind the curtain. The house played out a rhythm that was repeated every night: the muted clatter of the candle-snuffer, shuffling in her parents' room the other side of the wall, the clinking of a chamber pot, the mumble of prayers. Her father would be propped up by pillows and chewing angelica root to ward off the plague. Somewhere far off an owl began hooting. Then the watchman's call reached her, muffled by distance from the front of the house:

'Eight o'clock, look well to your locks,

Your fire and your light, and so good night.'

He would call again later and Ellyn was sure she would hear him. It had been dark for over an hour but she would not be able to sleep. She was too alert to the sounds, too aware of her mother's cough. Ellyn's tension rose even after the rasping ceased, leaving a restless calm in which the house settled, as if, in minute clicks, the weight of daub, timbers and brick were interminably marking the degrees of time.

Ellyn covered her eyes. She twisted until the coverlet was bunched in a knot and her mouth was pressed against hard stitches. Unwanted, an image of Will Doonan came to mind. She thought of him at the bear ring, blood-spattered and leading the dog away, and then she thought of him outside her house, catching hold of her after almost knocking her over. His face had been very close; she remembered feeling that he might kiss her, even fleetingly *wanting* him to kiss her. She had never known a man's kiss, not a kiss of the kind lovers shared. The coverlet was rough. Would Will's lips be soft? Banish the idea. She screwed her eyes shut while sheets and blankets became tangled with her nightclothes. Her limbs felt weak as if weighted with chains. Drawing breath, she stilled. She could hear footsteps. Twice already she had tiptoed to the window after hearing passers-by below. On the last occasion she had spied the water carrier heading home. His steps had been slow, but these were quick. Who would use the way through the garden so late? Who except

Will Doonan, returning to his room above the empty stables that her father let out? She got up from her bed.

Ellyn peered from the window and then immediately jumped away. He was there and gazing back. She looked again and kept motionless. The man below was also still, his face upturned like a pale statue's in the moonlight. It *was* Will Doonan, but what could he want?

She began to worry that Will might shout and wake her parents; if she did nothing then she was sure he would. That must not happen – she had to stop him making a noise. Hastily she pulled on her cloak and crept down to the parlour to see what he was about.

The stairs were dark. Ellyn stumbled blindly before her hands found the balustrade. She groped past wall-hangings and wainscoting, cold plaster and rough beams. Familiarity guided her towards the oak of the parlour door; then wan light from the window helped her pick her way inside. She reached for the latch and opened the casement wide.

All she could discern were falling specks: a moonlit haze and spots of rain. The shadows were misty and the path was glistening. A buttress leaned against a high blank wall, the box disappeared in a maze; the shrubs crouched. She could see no one. She was too late, she decided, as she retreated from the cold, securing the window and feeling mildly foolish.

Then she heard a sound. A step? Little was clearly visible through the diamond panes of glass. Trembling, she lifted the latch again, opened the window and peeked outside. He was watching.

Hurriedly she pressed a finger to her lips, because her parents' bedroom was directly above, and the sound of talking could easily disturb them. She leaned out and he stepped closer. The window was waist-high before her, though the garden outside was considerably lower. She would have to bend over to speak quietly. But if they held their faces near enough, they might whisper and not be heard. They almost touched. She could feel his warmth and caught the smell of his clothes: wood smoke mingled with something earthy. Where had he been? She noticed the workman's width of his shoulders and that beneath his cape he was wearing an old, stained jerkin. His hair was damp; it hung in loose locks that bunched around his neck. In the deep shadows beneath his brows she caught the gleam of his eyes.

The ridge of the window frame dug under her stomach. Her hands were cold against the sill. She had to grip hard so as not to fall out. A droplet of icy water found its way round her neck and then trickled down within her shift. She squirmed while trying to keep her hold. Suddenly they were together. His arms embraced her: rough hemp in creases, hard leather under his cape. His stubble brushed her cheek and his lips pressed against hers; heat coursed through her body to her most private places. His kiss was a wave that drove against her then pulled away, soft as water and with the force of the tide. It was over in moments. Her eyes opened as he let her go. She drew back and stood straight, though her heart was pounding and her balance unsteady as if she was trying to adjust to the motionless floor.

He remained by the window in a way that suggested he wished to speak.

She glanced around guiltily, half expecting at any moment to see her father marching towards her. When she turned back, Will was gone.

She stood in a daze, staring at the place where he had been. Whatever he might have wanted to say to her, she would not hear it that night.

Once again on her bed, Will's kiss overwhelmed her thoughts. She could still feel his touch, setting her tingling from head to toe. Did the kiss mean he loved her? She pressed her wrist against her lips, curled over and hugged her knees. The kiss had inflamed her; she would never have confessed as much to anyone but she could admit it to herself. Will had been audacious, but he must have desired her intensely to have risked what he had done. If her father had seen him kiss her, he would have been banished from the house – lost his lodgings at the least and probably his good name in Plymouth. She remembered the gifts Will had brought, and the compliments he had paid, his persistence in meeting her, and the passion of his hold, reflecting on each in no order until they were deliciously mixed in her thoughts. A wave of pleasure flared through her again. She had a handsome admirer; the kiss proved his devotion. Then a cold stab of anguish made her tense.

Will could not presume to be seriously considered a suitor, so had he taken advantage? She buried her face in the pillow. Had he kissed her out of devilment? She had given him no encouragement to be so forward. Peryn Fownes and Godfrey Gilbert had both courted her ardently without coming close to such a favour. The thought of intimacy with either made her shudder with revulsion, yet whichever one she married she would have to kiss without reservation – and more. She would have to surrender to her husband completely; she knew what would be her duty.

She felt suddenly degraded. Burgeoning tears stung her eyes. Who did Will Doonan think he was to imagine he could kiss her without offence? He should know she was not a common wench like Jane who might drool as she dreamt of his pear-sweet kisses. Would he boast about what he had done to his friends? Her stomach lurched. Was the reality that he had abused her? She stared into the dark. How could she face him with self-respect when she saw him next?

The questions multiplied in her mind, on and on throughout the night, and when sleep came at last, her dreams brought no rest.

The following morning, Ellyn approached the kitchen in a daze. She barely noticed the clear sky outside, or the sparkling light that made the autumn colours glow. She shivered. The fire had gone out in her room, and her porridge had been served cold – or perhaps she had dozed off after being called to break her fast – or . . . she could not remember. The porridge had been tasteless and she had been left with no salt – not that she was hungry. She hurried on while hugging her sides. Even the dining chamber was chilly, and she felt sure this should not have been so. Her vague recollection was that Godfrey Gilbert was expected for dinner. A growing certainty about the arrangement was enough to throw a shadow over the day. Had any preparations been made? Probably not. She tried to consider what would need to be done, but in vain. Her thoughts kept returning to Will's kiss the night before. She was agitated and distracted when she found Old Nan in the kitchen, feet up on a stool, with her back to a roaring fire. Ellyn rubbed at her temples and then succumbed to the impulse to join Nan by the hearth.

'Where is Jane? My porridge was flavourless and cold.'

Since Jane was responsible for the porridge, Ellyn instantly suffered some contrition for complaining to Nan unfairly – and that only made her feel worse.

Nan sighed and lumbered to the cauldron, rather ungraciously, thought Ellyn. The pot was stirred and the porridge sampled, actions which Ellyn took to signify that she was making an unnecessary fuss. Nan smacked her lips and drew them in over her gums, with the result that her chin was left very close to her nose. Her expression matched the 'Humph!' that followed.

'She will be told, Mistress Ellyn. But seeing as you be here, and she be drawing water, perhaps I should give you a fresh bowl and you season it to your liking.' Nan sniffed. 'Did you not have salt?'

Ellyn rolled her eyes in response, since the answer should have been obvious.

'I expect Jane's mind is in another place, with another person,' she said, while liberally sprinkling salt over the new helping she was served. She was sure she did not need to be more specific; they both knew who that person was. 'These distractions must stop—'

Her exhortation stopped first, interrupted by the arrival of Lettie carrying a bucket of plucked birds. Lettie marched in sullenly, bobbed a scant curtsy, hefted the bucket onto a side table, and beheaded a thrush.

Ellyn decided to press on for Lettie's benefit as well as Nan's, aware that everything she said would be passed on to Jane. Though Lettie set about gutting the little carcass with fury, and Nan began beating a sauce no less intently, Ellyn was too familiar with them both to doubt they would be listening.

'Jane should know that the object of her fancies most certainly is not preoccupied with *her*. If she does not believe that, she should ask herself whether she was with him last night, or knows what he was doing.' Ellyn hoped that the correct inferences would be made by the maids, at least enough to suggest that her information was better than theirs. 'Jane must accept what I can tell her: that she is wasting her time even thinking about him. This silliness must stop.' The passion of conviction brought a flush to Ellyn's face, a sensation heightened by the welcome effect of heat. She felt the time had come to be direct. 'The influence of Will Doonan is interfering with the proper running of this house.' She sat straight on her stool, confident that she had made her points well, thus she was surprised by the reproach in Nan's look.

'There may well be no more chance of anything of the like very soon,' Nan said while whipping her mix.

Ellyn nodded, though she was puzzled by Nan's remark.

Just then Lettie made an odd noise, as if she had acquired a tongue from the mounting pile of little birds' heads, only to have it strangled in her throat.

Another thud on the chopping board made Ellyn reflect. Was anything being hidden from her that she should know? She turned to Nan.

'What do you mean by *no more chance*?'

'As if Master Doonan would be able to have anything more to do with us once he goes back to sea,' Lettie broke in petulantly without turning round.

'Back to sea!' Ellyn gaped. She stared at her porridge while Nan answered sombrely.

'He's been talking to Francis Drake, and the Captain is rallying men for another Indies voyage. They've been seen together on the *Swan—*'

'That's Francis Drake's ship,' Lettie chipped in.

'—and Will's 'prentice said his master was with Captain Drake last night . . .'

'So we know where Will was,' Lettie added. 'He was with Francis Drake, and that means he may soon be leaving us.'

Ellyn took a spoonful of the gruel and raised it to her lips.

'Oh . . .'

She had never felt less like eating, but she put the spoon in her mouth. The porridge tasted vile; she had added too much salt. She was mortified by the thought that her worst suspicions might be true. Will had kissed her without sincerity, simply to satisfy a passing fancy. She swallowed with a gulp. Did he care for her at all? Did *she* care? She stirred her spoon around the bowl. Why should she care when men of much greater rank and prosperity were vying for her attention?

She gave a start as Lettie decapitated another bird.

'I remember Will Doonan after his last homecoming over a year ago,' Nan continued with bleak gravity, her chin as pronounced as the plucked tail of a roasting fowl. 'I knew his mother well, God bless her, and she could scarce recognise him, so wasted he was. He lost his young brother to the Spanish and that broke her heart. Within a month she was dead.' Nan shook her head. 'Over four hundred men set out in John Hawkins's fleet, and only a tenth came back. I dare say you'll have heard all about *that*, Mistress Ellyn. Many mothers and wives have been left weeping in Plymouth.' She raised her chin towards Lettie. 'And maidens, too.'

Ellyn's response was muted.

'I didn't realise he had been involved.'

Nan sighed.

'That he was. But since, until latterly, he lived outside the town walls, there's no reason you should have known or shown interest. His father has the Orcheton Mill, and by rights that mill should have been Will's one day, except that there ever was some strife between them. So the mill was to have passed to Kit.'

'That's his younger brother,' Lettie blurted. 'But Kit ran after Will to sea.' Her voice became shrill and ended in a wail. 'Now he's dead or in a dungeon.'

Nan sucked in her lips and muttered darkly, 'May God's mercy be upon him if he lives, and his soul, if in Heaven – to think of the barbarities that might be visited upon him . . .' She raised her voice. 'Kit was left as a hostage, held by the Spaniards, and after the attack on John Hawkins's fleet, nothing's been heard of Kit since.'

Despite the heat from the fire, Ellyn felt suddenly cold. Will had lost his brother just as she had lost hers, and that must have been even worse for him than the death of Thom had been for her; at least she had known Thom's fate. The torment for Will would still be continuing, made worse by uncertainty – he could not even grieve properly.

She bit her lip.

'But why was Kit taken hostage?'

Nan stopped beating her sauce.

'Surely you know what happened?'

Ellyn cast her a beseeching look. She was familiar with the story of the defeat of John Hawkins, but she wanted to learn more about Kit's loss and what Will had been through.

Nan clicked her tongue.

'They were near the land called Mexico that yields the Spaniards much gold, and John Hawkins had to repair his ships after they'd been blown off course, so he sailed into the nearest harbour. Then, the very next day, the Spanish treasure fleet arrived, and there were still storms raging which could have dashed it to pieces—'

'A good thing, too,' Lettie declared.

'No, child.' Nan wagged her finger. 'That would have meant war.' She eyed Ellyn sagely. 'If the treasure fleet had been wrecked, then we would all have been in peril. Under truce, Master Hawkins and the Spanish Viceroy agreed to berth both fleets side-by-side. They swore not to attack the other, and as surety for that pledge, they each gave up twelve hostages.'

Ellyn nodded eagerly, though she had heard nothing new. She did not want Nan to stop. She wanted more about Will and Kit.

'Kit volunteered,' Lettie trilled. 'He stepped forward boldly after Will tried to hold him back. That's what I've been told.'

Nan cleared her throat, looking grave.

'A few days later, the Spaniards reneged. They attacked without warning after sneaking an army onto their ships. General Hawkins was trapped. The Spanish fleet was twice the strength of his. Our Plymouth men fought bravely, but only two ships got away. Francis Drake commanded one, and Will escaped on the other, though the voyage back almost killed him.'

'There was not enough food, even after half those aboard had been set ashore in the wilds,' Lettie whispered, 'left to take their chance in Mexico.'

Nan shook her head.

'Kit never returned.' She gave a deep sigh. 'He had the face of an angel. Blond hair and blue eyes, just like Will's, and with a sweetness of temper that was enough to melt your heart.'

Lettie looked wide-eyed at Ellyn.

'What if Will tries to find him?' She stifled a sob. 'We might never see Will again.'

Ellyn turned from Lettie to Nan, and then reached out to them both.

'Let us not be downhearted over what may never happen.' She projected as much confidence into her words as she could muster, though it was with an effort that drained her. Was Will really about to leave? Just then she was acutely aware that she most wanted him to stay. She heard Lettie snuffle and patted her arm. 'Activity best conquers melancholy and we have much to do. A dinner . . .' She faltered. 'A guest . . .' She rose hastily and took a deep breath. 'I shall attend upon my mother.'

Moving back through the house, she thought of Will as she had seen him last, with his moonlit face and his damp-darkened hair. Then climbing the stairs, she thought of Kit, imagining the effect on Will of leaving him as he had. She clutched at the banister and pictured Kit being led away, and Will having to watch – the two of them forced apart – Will's face, twisted in anguish, and Kit, just a boy. She looked across the stairwell and tried to think of something else: the dinner in prospect, what her mother might need. But the idea of the boy was still in her mind. He was like Will, only younger, and he looked like an angel.

She wondered where he was.

4

Threat

'. . . The day being come we were espied by the Spaniards, and pursued, and taken, and brought before the Vice Roy and head justices, who threatened to hang us . . .'

—From the account of the imprisonment by the Spanish in Mexico of the English survivors following the battle of San Juan de Ulúa as recorded by Miles Philips, one of the captives (in The Principal Navigations . . . *by Richard Hakluyt)*

The City of Mexico, the Americas

'I am next.' Kit felt the length of the reed in his hands. He held it up towards the light for all to see.

The response was hushed.

'May God have mercy on you . . .'

'No prayers.' Kit put an end to the muttering. 'Say no prayers for me.'

The five men with him fell silent. Someone shuffled and coughed, then only breathing could be heard.

Kit pressed his back to the wall and clasped his hands round his knees. The others must not feel him shaking. He sought to be free from their touch, and that was possible now if he hunched up small. He had been close enough to his companions over the last few months, forced to rest in turns because there was so little room on the reed strewn floor. He had to find peace.

He looked up at the light. It entered in slender rays through tiny holes set in stones that were too high to reach. The rays were his link to the world outside. His eyes fixed upon them. If he was taken to his death, then the light would fade and be gone, and later return with a dawn he would not know. But he could not accept that his death might be near. He could not conceive of a world continuing in which, for him, everything was over. Perhaps he had not lived long enough to come to terms with that idea. At only seventeen, how could he be reconciled to the end of his life? Heaven was not Earth, and it would be stranger than the difference between the Indies and England. He could not think of dying. He clenched his teeth.

He had made himself brave in front of his friends, and he must not fail them now. They were all much older. When the time came to leave, he would have to show courage because they would be watching him. This was why the lots had been drawn: to give the next man chance to prepare, so that when the moment arrived he could be calm in going – to prove that Englishmen were not cowards.

But he was afraid. After the first prisoner had been taken, the Spaniards had soon returned to drag another away. He might not have much longer. Sweat trickled down his sides. The air was motionless in the dark at the bottom of the cell. He bowed his head and gasped.

What would happen? he wondered. All that was certain was that he would not be set free. He could be taken to another prison somewhere else in Mexico. He might be tried before one of the Viceroy's courts, questioned again by the bishop, or marched back to the coast, all the way from the great city, to be delivered to the Inquisition in a ship bound for Spain.

Someone groaned: a small quiet sound, but enough to make him think of other sounds he had heard.

He might be tortured.

For weeks on end he had listened to screams, cries that could have been made by anyone: sick or wounded, or deliberately hurt. But one man calling had been begging for his mother, that word had been clear. Who had he heard? Someone among the English prisoners that the Spaniards still held: any one of a hundred or more. Did it matter who he had heard? It mattered that he had not heard his brother crying out. He had not heard Will.

He pressed his thumb against his teeth. It was something he knew he should not do. 'Better way not,' as his mother would say. 'And thee be blessed with an angel's face,' she would add, as though that made any difference. But he took his hand from his mouth since she had entered his mind, and he imagined her nodding in an approving way.

He should be praying.

'Mother. Father,' he mouthed without speaking. He named his sisters in the way he had always done in his private prayers: a name to ask God's blessing for each. 'Will.' He prayed that his brother would be safe at home, and that the men with him in the cell would find freedom before they died.

There were footsteps approaching.

He prayed for his best friend: 'Hal.'

'Yes, Kit?' Hal answered.

He must have spoken out loud. He stood up on trembling legs. The footsteps were very close, reverberating rapidly along the passage outside. Three guards had hauled the last man away, knocked him down when he struggled, then trussed up and gagged him. He would not go like that.

Kit peered at his companions in the gloom and sensed that Hal was squinting at him in a way he remembered from days at sea, one brow down, the other raised quizzically under a shock of black hair.

The footsteps stopped. Rattling and banging came from the other side of the door: the sound of bolts being drawn. Hal stretched out his hand and Kit clasped it in both of his.

'Pray for me now.'

The door was thrown back and yellow light flooded in. With it came a draught like a gust over warm marsh, cutting into the stink of stagnation in the cell. Kit moved to the opening. A sword was pressed to his throat.

'*Ahora usted.*' The voice was surly.

Kit held out his hands, but he was seized and turned as his arms were wrenched behind him. His wrists were lashed together. A helmeted Spaniard came close and held a noose before his eyes, then a black sack was pulled down over his head, and he felt the noose digging hard into his neck. The rope tightened until he staggered forward. He tried to slow and was choked. He could see nothing inside the hood. The floor was sloping. He was sure he was walking down. The walls seemed to narrow, to close in and strike his arms. Jibes rang loud in his ears.

'Perro inglés, enemigo de Dios . . .'

The rope tugged him roughly, bumping him about from side to side. With every breath he gagged as the hood was sucked into his mouth. He tried to concentrate on where he was, not succumb to the panic that was welling up inside him. He thought of his arrival months before. He must be somewhere beneath the Viceroy's Palace; he had seen the buildings when he was paraded as a captive, and the ruins of an Indian temple overlooking a great lake. He was stumbling through a passage: a long twisting tunnel. He tripped, cracking his head. His knees and shins struck the sharp edges of steps. Against his ribs, he felt the point of a sword.

'Marchad! Luterano . . .'

He had to get up. He lay sprawled against stairs, and the rope tightened so hard it was easier to crawl than climb on his feet. But he would not slither on his belly. He shuffled to a crouch and staggered up towards a voice – one that rang out into space and was answered with a thrum: the muted babble of a watching crowd. Then he could feel the sun beating down. The noose fell slack. He stood and swayed.

Nothing touched him.

He tried to keep still and not shiver or faint – only listen to the droning voice.

'. . . Cristóbal Doñan . . .'

The voice stopped. None of the words had made sense, except that at the end he had heard the semblance of his name. Someone took hold of his shirt, pulling it wide and baring his chest. The noise increased: the clamour of a baying mob. A blade dug into the small of his back. But he leant against it and kept his balance, only wavering slightly in spite of the pain.

He wanted time before he took a step. He had climbed, so he could tumble, and then his fall would be broken by the noose round his neck. The Spaniards had threatened him more than once with hanging. Terror weakened his legs.

He had to be brave and not think of dying. He imagined the crowd and their upturned faces, the shimmering white of the Indians' tunics, the Spaniards looking on from the windows of the palace, the city of Mexico spread out with its streets of water and reed-roofed houses, the snow on the peaks that could be seen from the lake, rising from haze, glinting with light – and the sun shining down across the other side of the ocean, breaking through mist, reaching his home. The welcome light of the sun: it was what he longed for most – and home – his home.

He was jabbed again and teetered on his toes. The next push would give him no choice. This was his ending.

His eyes watered. He could not see. But suddenly he could.

The hood was yanked from his head. He was rammed forward to a surge of yelling. Everything blurred as he looked into the sun. Nothing was distinct except for the noise and the nakedness of his shoulders as his shirt was torn away. Then he saw the people, not so far away and not so many. No one was clad in white or looking up. They were all on his level, and mostly in the shadow of buildings around a courtyard. At last he recognised what all the shouting was about.

They were calling out bids.

5
Silence

'. . . Except the gravity of some matter do require that she should speak, or else an answer is to be made to such things as are demanded of her, let her keep silence. For there is nothing that doth so much commend . . . a maid, as silence . . .'

—The sixth Duty of Maids and Young Unmarried Women, from the New Catechism of Thomas Becon, *Chaplain to Archbishop Cranmer in the reign of Edward VI, first published in 1559 shortly after the accession of Queen Elizabeth I*

Ellyn found her mother in her room. Her hair was made up elegantly, braided in coils under a cap trimmed with lace. Fine lines crazed her skin, like the cracking over an old varnished panel, but her eyes were bright, and the turn of her head was swift. A perfumed pomander hung from a silver girdle at her waist, and, from her ears, trembled little ruby tears.

She was sitting near the fire, embroidering a stomacher with a pattern of strawberries and ladybirds, curling stems and variegated leaves. There was nothing to suggest that she should not be moving about the house or enjoying the garden, going to market and church, or walking along the cliffs. But Ellyn knew her mother would stay where she was as she had done since Thom's death; her life had become bound within the threads of her handiwork: unthreatened and ordered. Her journeys would be of her own devising while her imagination guided her needle, each stitch taking a small step into a beautiful, tranquil world. It was a world Ellyn could not enter with problems of her own.

At the moment her cheek was kissed, Ellyn's mother put down her sewing.

'My sweet,' she said to Ellyn.

Ellyn knelt at her side.

'Are you comfortable?'

'Quite comfortable as I am, where there is not a draught to trouble my poor throat.'

The response was a whisper that Ellyn would never have heard had she not been so close, yet she was used to her mother's voice, and it did not alarm her.

'I came to enquire whether you have given all the instructions you wish. I believe Master Gilbert is expected for dinner.'

'That he is,' her mother answered while stroking Ellyn's hair. Ellyn felt the gentle weight of her mother's hand, moving with the kind of soothing that might be used to calm an excitable pet. 'Your father is with him now,' her mother went on. 'They are at the new warehouse inspecting cloth. Then they will dine here. And you, dear Ellyn, should join them after that.'

It was a mystery to Ellyn, one that had never been properly

explained, how her mother, in self-imposed seclusion, could keep abreast of events outside. But this was a fact – she always appeared to know exactly what her family and acquaintances were doing. Her mother was rarely mistaken, though she never became involved and abhorred any confrontation. Ellyn had long ago given up appealing to her for help in her personal battles, especially those with her father; her mother would never oppose him. So she kept her feelings about meeting Master Gilbert to herself – they were not what her father would want to hear. She tried to look pleased. At least she would not have to talk with the gentleman while she ate.

'Your father was particular,' her mother continued: '"Be sure Ellyn joins us after the last dish", he said. I fancy they may have something of significance to put to you.'

Ellyn's heart sank. What could be *of significance*? She stiffened as one obvious possibility loomed large in her mind. She might have pulled away without realising. Her mother patted her head.

'Do not be concerned.'

Ellyn was even more alarmed. Had she betrayed how she truly felt? If her mother once suspected that she was determined to resist marrying Master Gilbert, then she would probably alert her father who would only attempt to coerce her. Better to appear dutiful and play along with their plans. She let her mother take her hand.

'Nan knows precisely what to prepare,' her mother said softly, while kneading Ellyn's fingers as if she was trying to smooth them. 'Venison pastry with honeyed mustard, turbot with Dutch sauce, marchpane dainties, maced cider and sack . . . It will be quite singular. But you must take your portion later,' her mother added.

'While they are dining, you should be making yourself ready. I shall have Lettie bring you your dress – perhaps the lily partlet and green sleeves? I must think upon't.'

Ellyn considered suggesting that she might make her own choice with a mind to colours that were much more drab, but acquiescence was wiser. She kept quiet.

'Be sure to whiten thoroughly and line your eyes,' her mother advised. 'Your father will expect you to be looking your best.'

Ellyn bowed her head, foreseeing a trying morning and, beyond it, nothing pleasant.

'Will you come, too?'

The response was predictable. Her mother put a hand to her mouth and her voice became hoarse.

'No, no. I would only be a hindrance, and my cough a trial.'

'I am sorry.' Ellyn meant what she said. She pitied her mother and felt guilty for considering, in private, that perhaps she could fight whatever disabilities confined her. Though her mother was little use as an ally, Ellyn sensed her kindness. She looked up and caught her mother's eye, discerning a depth of sadness that gave her the impulse to confide in her fully – she yearned to do it. But then her mother turned to her sewing and peered at the stitches, and Ellyn bit her tongue.

'The occasion is for *your* enjoyment,' her mother said, as she matched a new thread to the design. She was emphatic, though no louder; Ellyn strained to hear her. 'Have no concern for me, rather be mindful of your father. The gout is but a symptom of a greater malady.'

'What?' Ellyn frowned, astounded.

Her mother slowly shook her head.

'The physician has said he must stay calm. He must not be agitated or vexed.'

Was her father truly sick? Suddenly Ellyn was thrown into a spiral of worry. It had never occurred to her that, as between her parents, her father might have the more serious affliction. She had never really accepted that her parents were not immortal. Her father could be insufferable but she wished him no ill.

'So, my sweet,' her mother continued in a fading whisper, 'I trust you will ensure that nothing *in you* will give him cause to be distressed.'

'Of course not!' How could her mother even think it? But Ellyn realised that assurance was what her mother needed; strong emotions only disturbed her. With an effort, Ellyn softened her tone. 'Be at ease. I promise I shall give him no offence.'

Her mother's trust was confirmed with a kiss.

The box was very fine. Its lid was inlaid with a chequered veneer, and around its sides was a pattern of tooled ropes with roses. If she could have been sure the box was empty, Ellyn might have happily admired it. But she knew that inside would be a present from Godfrey Gilbert, and about that she was miserably ill at ease.

She prayed the gift would not be too precious or personal, nothing that might be used to seal a betrothal – not a poesy ring in interlocking bands each inscribed with a motto of love, *'I am yours, you my choice . . .'* Let it not be that. Gingerly she placed her hand on the lid and made a wish as she closed her eyes – not a portrait in miniature to be worn on a sash. (How romantically could Master Gilbert be painted, with his bald head and waxbill nose?) The gentleman was watching, so was her father. Ellyn breathed deeply, conscious that she had to be guarded. She steeled herself, opened the lid, looked down, and smiled.

'A carcanet. How delightful!'

The choker Ellyn removed was made of enamelled gold flowers supporting a pendant of pearls cleverly fashioned in a gold setting. The pearls and the surround made the form of a lamb; it was really quite exquisite. Ellyn hooked the chain round her neck, suspecting that her mother must have known about the gift all along, since her partlet and high collar left her throat wholly exposed.

Master Gilbert turned to her father.

'Does she like it much?'

Ellyn shivered with distaste. One of the gentleman's most irritating habits was that of addressing her indirectly as if she was an object incapable of speech. But her father beamed approvingly.

'Assuredly, Godfrey, though blessed if I thought she could be made prettier. Yet you have done it.' Her father clapped his guest on the shoulder and raised his glass. 'A toast to that!'

Ellyn watched them both from across the table.

Master Gilbert narrowed his eyes as he faced her, drawing in his chin to give a ferret-like prominence to the length of his nose.

'The fairest maid?' he suggested.

'A maid nonpareil!' roared her father.

Ellyn was left with the impression that the fortified wine the physician had prescribed for his gout was having too beneficial an effect on his choler. She worried about him less and smiled more.

'I thank you.' She looked at Master Gilbert and wondered what he and her father had been discussing. If their plans involved her, then she preferred to know. She decided to try a little probing. 'I hope your business ventures will be successful.'

He responded with a laugh.

'You speak of ventures lightly, as though the outcome might never affect you. But I can tell you, my dear—' he looked pointedly at Ellyn '—that your father and I have been considering an enterprise that may well concern you as much as it does us.'

Ellyn tried not to frown.

'Truly,' her father joined in, then turned to his guest and murmured, 'I think we may disclose this, Godfrey.' His eyes twinkled in Ellyn's direction. 'If this enterprise yields even half the return of the last, there will be a *date to be fixed*, one that *you* may look forward to.'

Master Gilbert fiddled with his glass. Her father stifled a belch, and Ellyn's hopes plummeted further. She was sure the 'date to be fixed' must be that of a wedding, but what was the enterprise that her father expected to be profitable? Suddenly a disturbing possibility occurred to her – perhaps it involved Francis Drake's next voyage. It could do. Will had told her he had dined with her father, and Nan had said that Will had been seen on Drake's ship. She thought quickly.

'I wonder whether this enterprise might concern a ship called the *Swan*?'

The response was clear astonishment. Her father slapped his thigh and chuckled loudly.

'By my faith! However did you arrive at that?!' He entered a muttered exchange that Ellyn had no difficulty in hearing. 'I swear, Godfrey, I have not breathed a word to anyone. Have you been putting ideas into her head?'

The coolness of Master Gilbert's answer did not escape Ellyn's attention.

'I would never discuss business with a woman.' He looked towards her and offered a buck-toothed leer. 'But she is, perhaps, rightly curious, and the sailing of the *Swan* hardly secret. I have no objection to her being apprised of the essentials.'

Her father raised his glass again.

'She has the mind for it, to be sure.' The face he turned to Ellyn was ruddy and supremely merry.

'Kerseys for the Spanish Main, my dear, and a very handsome gain! Ha!'

Ellyn strove to give an impression of happy interest while trying to make more sense of his remark. A kersey was a locally woven cloth, so she presumed her father and Master Gilbert had pooled resources to make a shipment (and no doubt Master Gilbert had advanced the credit since her father was notoriously tight-fisted). She could understand the trade's attraction: the kerseys would be smuggled to the Spanish Main in the Americas and sold free of duty, to the mutual advantage of both suppliers and buyers, at the expense of the King of Spain. Such schemes were the basis of almost every undertaking from which the Hawkins family had amassed a considerable fortune, and her father was always trying to emulate their success. Her conclusion was that Will and her father's cloth might both soon be heading west across the ocean. She touched the pendant at her neck and tried to remain outwardly cheerful.

'I suppose the lamb is representative of the wool to be shipped?'

Godfrey Gilbert gave a nod, and Ellyn's fingers moved to the links supporting the tiny animal: two fine chains each ending in two larger rings.

'And the bonds may suggest a blackamoor's manacles,' Gilbert added.

'Ah!' Ellyn made a greater effort to preserve her smile. Would slaves be involved in the next enterprise they planned? Certainly John Hawkins dealt in slaves; a bound Negro was prominent in his new coat of arms. Was there a connection? But of more concern to her was whether Will would be in jeopardy.

'I pray the enterprise does not meet with any difficulties such as those that beset the last voyage of Master Hawkins.'

'That sorry catastrophe!' her father exclaimed, with a wave of his hand. 'Have no such fear, my sweet. The Spaniards will not be concerned by a single ship. The *Swan* returned from the last venture without any trouble at all.' He thumped the table with renewed jocularity. 'So be in good cheer! Excepting the wildest storm, you may begin to think of the date to be fixed. And no doubt Master Gilbert will be thinking of matters more material!' At this he emptied his glass and chortled, while Godfrey Gilbert smiled thinly and rose to take his leave.

Ellyn had no choice but to allow Master Gilbert to drool a kiss over the back of her hand – something that reminded her of the trail of a slug. As soon as he was gone she picked up a napkin and vigorously rubbed at the wet of his touch.

Her father slumped in his chair, loosened his ruff, produced a voluminous handkerchief and mopped at his brow. Ellyn settled beside him and quickly dismissed the steward when he showed his head at the door; she wanted a few moments with her father undisturbed.

Ellyn had not the patience for sweet-talking him at length and launched straight in with the subject that concerned her most.

'I trust, Father, that if you were to receive an offer for my hand in marriage, then you would discuss the matter with me first before intimating I might accept.'

He appeared flustered. His face was so battered by the effects of smallpox and corpulence, marked with pits and lumps, burst veins and blotches, that by all objective standards he was ugly. But to Ellyn, his looks meant nothing; his response was what mattered. She kissed him and he smiled.

'Of course, Lynling.'

He used the pet-name he had given her from the time when she played on his knee. Ellyn suspected she was about to be coaxed and felt a little happier.

'But if an eminently worthy man were to make such a proposal—' he gave her a hug '—and if, in turn, *I* might be inclined to pay an appropriate dowry to that man's father, one able to offer *you* a good jointure, why then, would it not be reasonable to expect you to look favourably upon such a union, most especially if it was desired by both families?'

Ellyn's answer was crisp.

'Most certainly, if the man be not Godfrey Gilbert.'

Her father threw up his hands in exasperation.

'Then let him be Peryn Fownes!' His face became redder. 'But I wish you had made your preference plainer – 'twould have saved everyone much trouble.'

'Nor Peryn Fownes!' Ellyn retorted, bridling instantly. Why must it be either? A sudden recollection of the promise she had made her mother constrained her from further protest.

She continued in a milder tone. 'Dear Father, I have not yet decided . . .'

'You must!' he bellowed. Too late, Ellyn noticed his colour darkening and the fresh beads of sweat that appeared across his brow. His anger broke like a thunderstorm with violent noise.

'Since you clearly cannot decide, then I will decide for you. A wedding *must* be arranged, and this dithering ended.' He hurled his words at her. 'You are twenty years of age and might by now have given me four grandchildren or more, if you had not been so obdurate.'

'I ask only for a little time . . .' Ellyn began to plead.

'Your time has run out!' Her father railed, his eyes started as he glared at her. 'Do you suppose you will attract suitors for ever? A maid must be wed young if she is to bear a good crop, since not all her fruit will last a season, as you should know.'

She gasped and clutched at arguments like collapsing steps, desperately and without forethought.

'There may be others, better—'

'What others?'

'The Queen is not yet betrothed,' she threw out, but instantly regretted the remark.

His rage only worsened.

'Might England go to war because of your choice?'

She shrank from his shouting but he leaned over her.

'Am I besieged by legions of wooers? No and *no*! You must know your place, your bounds and your duty.'

She hung her head, though he only heaped more admonishment upon her.

'You will wear Master Gilbert's gift with pride, and await the day when good commerce persuades him to enter a commitment that is closer.' Her father staggered to his feet, swaying while he leaned on his stick.

Ellyn caught his arm, but he shrugged her away.

'Say nothing more!' He thumped his stick down. '*I have spoken.*'

Aghast, Ellyn watched her father lumber to the door, banging into a cupboard before lurching and marching out, hose sagging around his swollen ankles. She was left in the company of abandoned trenchers and spilt salt, a dish from which a turbot head stared flatly back at her and the basin of water in which fingers had been washed. Its surface shone with a greasy film. She had not eaten but gulped at the sensation of something sticking in her throat. Awareness of the broken promise to her mother made her dejection more acute. Since she was a child, her father had never chastised her so forcibly. His censure stung deep, bursting the bubble of her pride, and reminding her of everything that constrained and oppressed her.

She was chill with the realisation that she would *have* to wed Godfrey Gilbert, and, if not him, then Peryn Fownes. What silly daydreams had she entertained? Her reveries of a knightly courtship, of being wooed like a lady in a classic romance – even the most agreeable of her musings about Will Doonan – all these fancies had been crushed at a stroke. Her only hope of reprieve was if some calamity befell the *Swan*: fire, storm, or attack – a total loss at sea. But how could she wish for that if Will was as much at risk as the cloth on which Master Gilbert expected to increase his fortune?

Ellyn gazed at her ringless hands, at her sleeves the colour of lush meadows and spring leaves: green for fertility and passion.

Her cuffs were edged by the stitches her mother had sewn, neat and measured, each pulled perfectly tight – so passion was finished. How fitting.

She shook her head. Her father was a tyrant and she hated him. Didn't he care about how she felt? Surely he could see that she loathed the idea of marrying either of the suitors he had encouraged for his own selfish ends? But that was an unworthy thought. She trembled with frustration and put her hands to her face. A fresh wave of guilt coursed through her. Her father was only acting with her best interests at heart. It was his duty to ensure she wed well, and hers to accept the guidance he gave her. She took a long breath and sat up straight. She would not sink into self-pity; she must not. She would pray for her father's health and she would pray for Will. Next she would find out whether Will was actually sailing on the *Swan* – she did not know he was for certain, and how could she assume anything on the basis of Nan and Lettie's gossip? She resolved not to tolerate any more tittle-tattle about him. There would be no more rumouring, and she would talk to him as soon as possible. Only then would she know the truth. But what if he was going? She stared at the window.

What if he had kissed her only to leave her with Godfrey Gilbert?

6

God and Saint George

'God and Saint George, upon those traitorous villains, and rescue the Minion, I trust in God the day shall be ours.'

—The words of John Hawkins on leading his men into action at the battle of San Juan de Ulúa, 23rd September 1568 (as recorded by Job Hortop, gunner aboard the Jesus of Lubeck, from Volume 6 *of* The Principal Navigations . . .*)*

Will walked quickly towards the docks, only slowing once he reached Sutton Poole, and there he paused at the quayside, looking at the ship on which he might soon be sailing. At just twenty-five tons, the *Swan* was not much more than a bark, but she looked neat and nimble, and had served Drake well on his recent voyage. Will hooked his thumbs in his belt and eyed the hull below the waterline, peering down into the shadows to scrutinise the timbers for trailing weed. He was satisfied with what he saw. If Drake got the backing he was after from Nicholas

Cooksley, then she could be provisioned and ready within a few weeks. But how would Mistress Ellyn react to that? He supposed she might not wish him to go.

Their kiss the night before had told him more than a host of words. She had not been unwilling; he had felt it as soon as they touched, and the pleasure of that revelation had changed the way he beheld her. She was more hot-blooded than he had supposed, not such the strait lady as her quick tongue had suggested. Was there a chance he could win her if he stayed?

He tipped back his head and looked at the mast tops of the *Swan*, and those, much higher, belonging to the other ships beside her. He saw brightly painted crows' nests against the crisp blue sky, and faded weathered rigging that was almost white in the glare of the sun. The day was frosty but fair. It would have been a good one for getting underway. What he saw was a reminder of the last time he had sailed.

At San Juan de Ulúa, on the morning of the battle, the sky had been as clear and the ships had been as close – but it had been hot. He stared at the dancing light on the water – that had been much the same – but in the Gulf of Mexico, the sea was greener, and so clear he could see the sand at the bottom of the harbour, fathoms below.

He had been with his friend, Eliseus, in a small bobbing boat, caulking the stern of the Queen's carrack, the *Jesus of Lubeck*. He had been labouring to seal the leaks in the great ship's seams, clinging to the hope that a Spanish Viceroy could be trusted and that the hostages would be returned as soon as the *Jesus* was ready to sail. His faith had been in that – they would get Kit back.

Then he was there, hearing the blast from the trumpet that had signalled the start of the Spanish attack, and General Hawkins shouting, 'Treachery!' before rallying the men with his battle cry. The Spaniards had swarmed over the *Minion*, grappled and boarded her from a hulk. By the time he and Eliseus had got back on the *Jesus*, Hawkins was in armour and leading the repulse. The episodes flashed by in his mind, shuddering with gun blasts and blurred by smoke, only slowing in clear distinction around the memories that were worst: Eliseus smiling, though part of his skull was gone. Will had looked round for his friend's helmet, unable to see it for the press of men fighting. Eliseus was still warm. He had crouched behind the bulwarks while shots whistled overhead, hearing the Spaniards cry, 'Santiago!', conscious that he could smell hot blood. The skin was black where the ball had entered behind Eliseus's jaw. Beside him, a Spaniard writhed, clutching at a broken pike-shaft left sticking in his groin. Near the man's foot he had found the helmet – it was filled with gore.

They had re-taken the *Minion* and saved the *Jesus*, fired guns all day at the Spanish fleet, blasting a great man-o'-war until her magazine exploded and masts, men and rigging were blown skyward in a ball of flame, but the *Jesus* was trapped, and most of Hawkins's ships were crippled.

Another memory overwhelmed him. He was treading in blood . . .

. . . The wounded filled the gangway behind the gun deck below. Screams merged with the screech of sawing. When the sawing stopped, the surgeon emerged. His expression was granite.

Will lowered his eyes as the surgeon pushed past. Someone clawed at his ankle: a burly-framed man who would not let go, whispering his name. He knelt and saw Harry; his face had a sheen like raw egg-white.

'Sew me up, Will. My needle's gone.'

'How's this?'

Harry's leg was wrong, as if a giant had taken a bite. Harry circled it with his hands.

'A piece of iron . . . Never trust an iron breech.'

Will realised what had happened as he looked at the bone in Harry's leg: a gun had exploded in firing. He was kneeling in Harry's blood and there was nothing to stop the flow.

'The surgeon's coming soon. I'll get some rope.'

Harry grabbed at his arm.

'Thread's what I need. Not rope, nor the barber. Keep my leg . . .'

'Steady, Harry.'

Go. Will ran at the double but found nothing he could use. The guns were pounding. Men were calling.

'We're holed, Will. Get below.'

'You're needed, Will.'

'Lead and tar . . .'

Quick. He had to get back to the gunners, help Harry, stop the leaks. Again and again he felt the *Jesus* being struck. He slid down a ladder and squeezed into the powder store. He dragged out a barrel. *Rope.* He climbed into the forecastle, barrel on his shoulder, and dodged around the cannon. The deck was like a slaughter-house, blood strewn with straw, crowded and steaming, the guns liable to kick. Will heard tackle crashing down, shot rolling and weights dropped, curses and screams. He reached his friend Job, loading a culverin. Job's face was black with powder. Young Paul was holding the match, shaft shaking in his grip. No one stopped.

Will put the barrel down. Over the bulwarks near the culverin were myriad flecks like drying mud: Harry's blood.

'They're firing from the end of the quay,' Will yelled. 'Harry's hurt . . .'

Job turned without speaking. Will caught his look and stumbled away. Where the foretop lay, more rigging was down; the main was damaged. Will knew the *Jesus* was doomed. He stepped over bodies, and stripped a belt from one, shot full of lumps like the warts of a toad. A cannon-blast shook him. *Run.* He hurtled into the sterncastle and got back to Harry, looped the belt around the big man's thigh, and braced to pull hard. Rope would have been better.

'Will?'

'I'm with you, Harry.'

He pulled, but the belt was stiff and Harry's thigh was massive. Harry's breathing had the rush of waves over gravel.

'Are you sewing, Will?'

'The best I can.'

The breathing became softer. Will bent closer to hear.

'Harry?'

'I can ne'er feel it at all.'

Harry made no sound; his eyes were motionless, staring up towards the hatch. Will saw the opening and moved fast. He climbed out into pandemonium: seething confusion beneath the sinking red sun. Men were lugging boxes, kegs, weapons and silver – a brass globe from General Hawkins's cabin, bags from the treasure store, skins and crystal – all were being lowered to the *Minion*; what was not lowered was thrown.

Will spotted the general and the bo'sun struggling with a chest.

The *Jesus* was listing. She rocked and men fell, one against another. They dropped what they held: guns, sacks and biscuit drums.

Will pushed through the crowd. Suddenly men were scrabbling for the rail, climbing over the bulwarks, leaping for the *Minion* and throwing off the ropes.

'Hold!' the general was shouting. 'Back to the *Jesus*. Stand fast till we're ready.'

Few obeyed. Men leapt between the gunwales of the ships.

'Hold!'

It was too late. Sails unfurled on the *Minion*. She was moving away. Then all at once Will understood the desperation to flee. A Spanish fireship loomed blazing in a sulphurous halo of light, flames crackling, smoke billowing. Moments later, the general jumped; he had no choice. Only the *Minion* had any chance of escape. Will followed, almost falling. The heat from the fireship was carried nearer by the wind, and the stink of its burning. The gap widened.

'Jump!' The general called, holding out his arms.

Young Paul was left on the *Jesus*, clutching a goblet and jewelled plate.

'Drop them!'

Paul stood paralysed with fear. Will could see that he was crying; the fireship roared nearer and lit up his face. He dropped what he held, but it was as much as he could do.

'Jump!'

Will looked down at the sea that separated the two ships. When he looked up, the wind blew straight into his eyes, fire-hot and keening, carrying thick smoke and ash.

'Jump!' the general yelled.

No one did. There was no turning back.

Will would never forget.

The wind was cold. Will felt it, looking up. He saw the prow of the *Swan* and her furled spritsail swaying. A whistling thrummed around him: the sound of the breeze in ropes and rigging. He heard the grinding of rubbing strakes and the creak of masts and yards. Waves slapped against the quay. He turned and stepped away. Only when he resumed walking did he notice the people around him: mariners and merchants, pedlars and lightermen, and a portly gentleman whom he recognised ambling along in the opposite direction. Will raised his hat as he neared.

'Good day, Master Fownes.'

Peryn Fownes inclined his head, and smiled with a look of mild confusion.

'Eh! Good day.' His waddling gait did not slow.

Will supposed Fownes had forgotten him, though they had been introduced by Nicholas Cooklsey only a few weeks before. Indeed, he wondered whether Fownes was on his way to Cooksley's house. That was certainly possible; Fownes was known to be courting Ellyn. The thought made Will change course. He drew closer to the gentleman.

'I have news that might concern you, good sir. I serve a man who knows Mistress Ellyn Cooksley.'

'Verily?'

Will could tell that he had struck a spark of interest; Fownes gave him a sharp look, and then tucked his chin against his ruff.

Will kept alongside him.

'My master thinks very highly of the lady.'

'As does everyone, I am sure,' Fownes responded drily. He veered away.

Will followed.

'He is a veteran of wars and an accomplished swordsman.'

'Ah . . .' Fownes hunched his shoulders under his cloak and carried on walking, but Will noticed the gentleman's hand moving unsteadily towards his sword hilt, and his eyes flickering wildly, from Will to the narrow alleyways, to the people passing by.

With a few easy strides Will drew ahead of Fownes a little, just enough to be sure Fownes could hear him as he lowered his voice.

'My master brooks no rivalry and has a great passion for duelling.'

'O! Oh . . .' Fownes flinched. His mouth shut like a trap then opened as he gulped for air.

Will looked Fownes up and down, from his fat calves to his fluffy hair, to his white-bowed shoes.

'His temper is quick.'

Fownes looked round and edged away.

Will nodded and smiled.

'I thought I should warn you.'

At that Will stepped aside, and watched Fownes continue in a meandering circuit like a ponderous beetle temporarily stunned. When eventually Fownes settled on his course, Will was satisfied. The gentleman doubled back, away from Cooksley's house.

'Are you coming in to get warm, Mistress Ellyn?' Nan poked her head round the parlour door. 'You'll catch a chill in those damp things.'

Ellyn pulled at her gloves in a show of removing them and looked back through the window towards the steps to Will Doonan's door. He was nowhere to be seen. In fact, for almost two days since the incident of the kiss, she had failed to make any contact with him, and she was still none the wiser as to whether he would soon be leaving. She kicked off her overshoes, conscious that her stockings were wet and her toes were cold; then she saw a blur of movement outside.

'Yes!' Ellyn announced, hurriedly putting the shoes back on. 'Though I thought I might pick some quince. I noticed there were a few ready when we came through the garden just now.'

'But it's pouring!' Nan protested while Ellyn slipped away.

No sooner was she in the garden than Ellyn saw Will striding towards her.

'Master Doonan!' She tried not to look flustered in the midst of pulling over her hood. It was drizzling hard. Rain dripped from Will's hat and down his oilskin cape.

'Should you not be within, dear lady?' His blue eyes glittered as he looked at her. It was enough to make her almost forget what she meant to say.

'I shall not be long . . . I merely wished to say . . . how much we have all enjoyed your spices.'

He smiled broadly behind a trickle of raindrops.

'I understand you may be leaving for the Indies.' She wiped the rain from her face, unsure how best to continue.

Will leaned towards her, but all Ellyn heard was Nan's cry from the house: 'For the love of Jonah, come inside or you'll both be drowned!'

Ellyn sensed Will was behind her as Nan gestured frantically for them to take shelter. Huddled up and dripping, they were bustled into the kitchen.

'I'll leave you two to dry,' Nan said, with a conspiratorial hush to her voice. The latch clicked, and next they were alone by the crackling fire.

Ellyn untied her cloak and Will lifted it from her shoulders.

'Let us speak directly,' she said, shivering. 'We may not have much time.'

His answer was to draw up a stool and beckon for her to sit.

'You are cold,' he said. 'Come close to the fire.' He took off his hat and cape and spread all the outer-clothes across the end of the table; then he joined her by the dancing flames.

'Your hair curls when it is wet.' He looked at her intently. 'It becomes you.'

Without thinking, she reached for a ringlet that had sprung into a tight coil by her cheek.

'I wish my hair was straight.'

'I do not.'

'I wanted to say . . .' Why was Will talking about her hair? She tugged at the sodden ringlet and tried to tuck it back behind her ear, though by a brush of dampness, seconds later, she knew the strand had bounced out of place. Two days ago Will had kissed her, and now they were together again – and alone. She wanted to ask what he felt for her, but how could she in all modesty?

'Is it true you are sailing for the Indies?' she blurted out at last.

'Yes.'

'Yes,' she echoed softly, suddenly hurt – hurt so much she was lost for words.

Will gazed at her steadily.

'Once Captain Drake has provisioned his ship, then we'll set sail. Your father may help with that. He's backed the Captain before. But we may not be ready for another month.'

'Only a month?' She looked at his strong, solemn face, and the sandy stubble over his firm chin. 'I thought your business was here, in Plymouth.'

He gave a nod.

'I have a journeyman who can manage my affairs while I am gone. My business is caulking ships, and there's a need for such skills on a long voyage.'

What was going through his mind? Why had he kissed her when clearly he never meant to stay? She felt wretched. Were his blunt answers meant to tell her that she did not feature in his plans, as if they had never shared any intimacy, as if there had been no kiss? Did she mean nothing to him?

He half closed his eyes.

'I have to go. I swore I would, for my brother's sake. On my last voyage to the Indies, he was taken prisoner by the Spaniards. I'll probably never find him. But I must try, and if I fail, then at least I'll have a chance to be avenged.'

'For the loss of your brother?'

'For the loss of Kit, and many others.' His face darkened. 'For what the Spaniards did at San Juan de Ulúa.'

She thought back to what Nan and Lettie had told her, sensing both anguish and rage deep within him and that, whatever had happened at that place, it was driving him still. She watched him open his hands, palms uppermost, and rest them on his knees.

'I hoped that by explaining you would understand,' he said.

'I do,' she whispered, stunned by the glimpse of vulnerability she had seen in him, wanting at once only to show that he could trust her.

He moved his hands towards hers, gently covering them.

'There are gentlemen who will pay court to you, but I hope you will not rush into accepting anyone.'

She bowed her head.

'I must do as my father bids me.'

'Wait for me.' He leaned towards her and raised her right hand to his lips, catching her eye as he did. 'Be strong and patient.'

It was too much. When he placed his arms around her, she gave way to his embrace, and the soft press of his lips, and the passion of his hold. Before the heat of the fire, hearing the hiss of burning wood, smelling damp wool and leather, she succumbed to a temptation that had been irresistibly gathering strength: to kiss him again – longer and harder. His hands were in her hair, on her throat, and hers were around his waist; then he was drawing her closer and she clung to him as he murmured, 'Wait for me.'

Wait. She would wait . . .

Suddenly she broke free as tears welled in her eyes.

'Wait for how long?' She pulled away. 'I may have no choice . . .'

He reached to soothe her, kissing her again, but she cried out the truth.

'*You* are leaving – not I!'

As she pushed him back, she heard a rattling at the latch. Instantly they both sat straight.

She raised a hand self-consciously to her neck, and she felt the heavy links of the choker around her throat.

7

Beginning

'. . . There must be a beginning of any great matter, but the continuing unto the end until it be thoroughly finished yields the true glory . . .'

—From a dispatch sent by Sir Francis Drake to Sir Francis Walsingham

Plymouth, England

October 1570

'Plymouth will not have seen such a spectacle since Catherine of Aragon first came here from Spain!'

Ellyn cringed. She shuddered to think how Will might take her father's boasting, particularly since he was bragging about the prospect of her marriage to Godfrey Gilbert, and in front of the gentleman, too. She glanced surreptitiously across the table towards Will. They had hardly spoken for a week. After the closeness they had shared on the afternoon of the downpour there had been little opportunity for anything more than exchanging pleasantries. For days she had agonised over his behaviour, deciding one moment to forget him, and the next thinking of nothing else but him. But what would his opinion be of her now? He had been invited to dinner, along with John Drake and Master Gilbert, and her father was talking about her marriage as if she was already betrothed. She was anxious to assure Will that was not so. She searched his expression for a look of understanding, but he regarded her as impassively as moon-faced John Drake beside him. She prepared for her discomfort to grow worse. Her father was enjoying himself.

'Would you like two little blackamoor pages to carry your train, my dear?'

She would not, but he would not want to hear that. Indeed, it was plain her father expected no response from her at all. He addressed Master Gilbert sitting beside him, while she, on his other side, could follow everything he said.

'We shall have pages, and maids in matching colours scattering enough tussie-mussies to make the streets around St Andrews smell like a pomander!'

By way of emphasis, he pulled a rose from the nosegay that adorned the table, sniffed it theatrically, and threw it down to join the other scented flowers carefully scattered over the floor, an action that set the dogs squabbling with low frustrated growls.

'Ha!' her father roared. 'The people will not know themselves.'

Ellyn winced. What really worried her was that Will might assume her father's ambitions regarding her marriage had been nourished with her support. Will's coolness was unsettling. She expected him to show some hint of being concerned, instead of listening calmly, as he was, while she was the one blushing hot. She longed for a draught of cold air. She was burning with discomfort and powerless to prevent her father from embarrassing her even more.

'If this venture meets half the promise,' he boomed, 'we shall have a pageant of liveried musicians playing hautboys and flutes!' Her father downed his drink and stifled a belch. 'So, gentlemen, you should know that much more than my purse is committed to your success. My daughter's happiness depends on it also!'

Ellyn looked away, as if the daughter he spoke of had not yet been seen in the room.

But the remark was not lost on John Drake. He responded drily, 'The wedding will await our return?'

'Most certainly, sir,' her father confirmed in good humour. 'The wedding will *require* your return.'

'I shall look forward to it.' John Drake added.

'And I.' Will glanced towards Ellyn, but she turned aside.

She could not accept that, truly, Will might have meant what he said. Was he really looking forward to her marrying Master Gilbert? She prayed he was merely being polite.

'I am sure you will be prepared to wait, my sweet,' her father said, squeezing her hand, 'for the prospect of a more glorious conclusion.'

She stiffened while Master Gilbert smiled, head on one side like a jackdaw that has spotted something shiny to steal. At least her father was not planning on her marrying very soon, but that was little comfort since her betrothal seemed a certainty.

Her father turned to his guests.

'My Ellyn is blessed with the patience of a queen. She will wait like Penelope weaving her endless web to preserve her purity for the one to whom destiny has joined her—'

Ellyn groaned inwardly, and breathed a sigh of relief when he tailed off.

'—but we will pray for the voyage to be swift as well as prosperous.'

John Drake offered him reassurance.

'We should be back before next winter, given favourable winds.'

Ellyn cast Will a desperate look, but he did not meet her eye. With her spirits sinking, she guessed that Will meant to go as he had told her. He had not changed his mind. He would be sailing on the *Swan* and, when the ship returned, her wedding with Master Gilbert would be arranged.

'A spring wedding!' her father said. 'What could be more propitious?'

The smile he gave her revealed the decay in his teeth; it stretched the pox scars over his nose, sent blood rushing to burst vessels, and wrung the bags under his watery eyes, but it tempered her frustration. She kept quiet and thought fast. Why was her father so keen for her to be married *after* Francis Drake's return and not before? There could be only one motive, she reasoned: money. Her father was plainly intent on making the wedding an occasion to impress the whole of Plymouth, one that would advance the names of Cooksley and Gilbert, and bring both houses to the attention of the most distinguished and powerful. He must be expecting a considerable profit, one much greater than the gain he had already made. Yet how? She assumed an air of guileless interest and fished lightly for an explanation.

'Might the trading on this next voyage be any different to the last, Master Drake?'

John Drake regarded her blank-faced, then answered unhelpfully, 'Aye, that you could say, Mistress Ellyn, the trade will be different.'

'Most delicately put!' her father guffawed. 'Yes, verily, it will be a *man's* trading, a more *lusty* trading!'

The substance of what he meant was a mystery to her, but Ellyn was used to her father's bombast, knowing that he liked to hint at matters that he believed were beyond the understanding of women. But she was not stupid.

'And more hazardous?' she suggested, hoping that Will would not be in danger, but at the same time wondering whether her marriage was such a certainty.

Master Gilbert was dismissive.

'You need not concern yourself, my dear.'

Her father waved his hand limply as if his rings were heavy weights.

'There will be little risk. Be content to know that we have an opportunity to improve on the methods that the Hawkins brothers have found useful.'

'Involving no slaves?' she asked quickly.

'No slaves,' Will replied.

'And no danger to your father,' John Drake added, not to be outdone in enlightening her. 'Though he stands to receive no less than if he accompanied us.'

'Accompanied you? Surely not!' Ellyn made the comment lightly, but she noticed the frown that began to draw John Drake's brows a little closer. She looked boldly back at him, confident he would not be so rude as to ignore her. 'Are any who are not mariners to sail with you?'

John Drake shrugged.

'Richard Dennys has asked to come.'

'Dennys of Exeter!' Master Gilbert exclaimed. Ellyn thought he sounded petulant.

John Drake nodded.

'Aye.'

'The folly of that does not surprise me,' Master Gilbert went on. 'He is young, loud-mouthed and hot-headed.'

Will ended the awkward silence that followed.

'We advised against it,' he said. 'There is no need for any merchant to make the voyage.'

Her father blew out his cheeks.

'Ah! But Dennys has a nose for commerce for all his wind and frivolities. He has proved it. The young man made a ransom salting in pilchards for France before the fish laws were tightened . . .'

Ellyn guessed her father was ruminating on the possibility that Master Dennys might be stealing a march. She detected the rumble of anxiety in his bluster.

'How can men of the sea be expected to understand the subtleties of commerce?' her father said, becoming louder. 'They may trade for profit, but will it be the best? Will they be ambassadors for future dealings when relations may become . . .'

Ellyn held her breath.

'Strained,' he said at last.

Ellyn hoped he would end there since she could see that his argument was close to causing offence, but he swaggered on.

'Dennys will have good reason for going, I know it. He will be intent on establishing contacts, he will be monopolising, fraternising—'

'*I* will not go,' Master Gilbert cut in, as if he felt the sting of some personal challenge.

Her father huffed, puffed and made Ellyn so alarmed she took hold of his arm, but he pulled away.

'Zounds, sirrah! No one has suggested it!' He thumped the table. '*I* will go!'

'No, sir!' Will exclaimed under his breath.

'No! You cannot . . .' Ellyn pleaded, stunned.

At the same instant, John Drake began a dogged reasoning.

'Pray, consider, Master Cooksley. It may not be possible . . .'

With a louder thud on the table her father silenced them all.

'Unless it is possible, I shall be unable to offer my support. An investment requires confidence.'

'This is madness,' Will murmured.

John Drake looked uneasy.

'There are few above thirty years who will sail with us.'

Her father's response was visible fury. His hand shook as he clenched it in a fist. His face turned livid.

'Are only the young fit for endeavour?' he railed. He brought his fist to his chest. 'My heart beats as strong as yours, my head is as sound and I have the stomach for the task.'

'Think of dear Mother.' Ellyn tried desperately to deflect him but was ignored. She appealed to Will. 'Master Doonan, please tell my father he cannot go!'

'Good sir,' Will said, though without the severity she would have liked, 'you should allow yourself time to reflect.'

Her father shook his head and fixed John Drake with an obdurate look.

'Let me suggest a new proposal. Take me with you, and I shall double my advance, enough for all your provisioning. Put that to your brother, sir. Francis Drake should be satisfied.'

John Drake was satisfied, Ellyn could tell. She heard some talk about discussing the matter, and the limitations of space aboard one small ship, but there was no attempt to argue further. Will looked grim and said nothing more.

When both men rose to leave, Ellyn realised that her father was determined upon sailing with them, and that it would be well-nigh impossible to make him change his mind. He would do it, however grave his own misgivings, because he was proud and stubborn and he would not be seen to back down. She knew him. He was obstinate and vain – and selfish, too. He had plainly not given a thought to the effect of his recklessness on his family, or anyone else who cared for him.

Who would look after his business while he was away? The answer was smiling at her. Ellyn watched Master Gilbert take his leave with the pitying grace of a triumphant champion. John Drake followed, and Will made his departure in a way that left her feeling as if she had been slapped. He was abandoning her, and her betrothal to Godfrey Gilbert was almost a certainty. Worse still, her father was now determined on joining Drake's voyage.

Her father breathed heavily, leaned on his stick, and grimaced when he bowed. But she wanted to seize his stick and bring it down over his rump. He was a capricious old fool, yet she could not say that to his face. There was only one suggestion she could think of making that might have the effect of weakening his resolve.

As soon as they were alone she flung her arms around him.

'Dear Father, do not go.'

He shrugged her off.

'I have decided!'

She held him again.

'If you insist on accompanying Francis Drake, then I must go, too. You will require a companion – someone who understands your needs. I will—'

'Nonsense!' He pushed her away, and waved his hand at her crossly. 'What idiocy! Vex me no more with your foolishness; the idea is preposterous. Drake would never allow a woman aboard. You must remain here with your mother where Godfrey Gilbert can see you are safe. I am going, and that is *that*. Enough of your meddling! So help me, I must rest.' He lumbered wheezing towards the door. 'Try me no more!'

Was she trying him? She bit back the urge to shout at his back.

He was trying *her*.

And Will had wounded her heart.

Will peered through the gateway in the garden wall. There was no one there. Should he wait? Imperatives crowded his mind: the need to confer with his journeyman; examine the books of his business; make more arrangements for his departure; buy the sword that he wanted; visit the cobbler and tailor; sort out what he was taking; and mend his chest. He turned and squinted through the gaps in the golden foliage. He was impatient to be gone, but he was also eager to talk to Ellyn. That prospect held him back.

He ran a hand over his rough beard, not that his appearance would matter now. The talk of Ellyn's marriage had come as no surprise, and the preparations for his sailing had made his desire for her more manageable. He still cared about what she thought of him, but what concerned him most was how she might help his plans.

Snatching a fruit from the medlar, he turned it idly in his hands; it felt as hard as a stone. How much longer would she be?

Speaking to her was as important as the other tasks that awaited him, and all were incidental to his one overarching objective: seeing through his sworn enterprise with Drake, striking where the Spaniards were weakest, securing the resources for that purpose and leaving soon while the weather was good.

He squeezed the fruit in his fist. He knew the venture could succeed; his faith in Drake gave him confidence in that. With success would come riches, perhaps rank and prestige. The mission might make him, and Kit would be avenged. The venture fired everything he did. He had packed the work of weeks into days with little sleep – it energised and consumed him and deprived him of rest. Waiting was difficult. He glanced again towards the gate, and then he let the fruit drop: two ladies were approaching.

Will greeted Nan and Ellyn courteously, and a few words with the old maid gave him the promise of privacy that he wanted.

Nan nodded and turned.

'I shall watch from the kitchen,' she announced in parting.

Will moved closer to Ellyn, struck afresh by her loveliness, despite their meeting only the day before. Even her freckles looked delightful, though he knew most women tried to mask them. While he was still taking her in, she spoke up.

'I meant to thank you for your present, but wanted to do so by letter, since I thought that might be best.'

'Good!' He tried to put her at her ease. He had left her a token that morning, since soon he would be departing: only a few threaded bells, each no bigger than a pea. He had acquired them from a mariner in the hope they would appeal to her, and he could tell that was so.

She took a step closer.

'I fear my father spoke rashly.'

He smiled.

'Yes, I hope so.'

Her eyes lowered, and Will watched her soft lips meet, and then part in hesitation. The desire that had once impelled him to kiss her came close to seizing him again, but he checked it.

Her lids flickered.

'Please understand. Nothing is arranged between Godfrey Gilbert and myself. My father likes to air his wishes, that is all. I am not betrothed.'

'Ah!' Will smiled more broadly, and held her gaze when she looked at him. 'I am glad.'

She looked at him expectantly, but he could not disregard the issue that was most urgent. It could affect everything.

'I hope your father's declared intention to make the voyage was similarly wishful. I am concerned that he should not see it through.'

'Yes,' she answered quickly. 'I have urged him to re-consider. Most strongly,' she added.

He sensed she was disconcerted yet, having raised the issue, he was determined to press his point home. If her father suffered some catastrophe on the voyage, it would be devastating for her and could wreck the whole enterprise.

'You must prevail upon him not to go.' Will took hold of her hand to emphasise his plea. 'He cannot fully appreciate the dangers he would face.' He saw bewilderment in her look and wrapped her hand in both of his. He could not easily spell out the risks since Drake had sworn him to secrecy. Violence was likely; if there was fighting with the Spaniards, then Cooksley would be in peril. He was an old man, plainly unfit for action. Drake would not refuse him because he needed the merchant's backing, but perhaps Ellyn could persuade her father to see sense. 'The voyage would be too much for him.' That was as much as he could say. He trusted she was alert to the gravity of his warning. 'He will listen to you,' Will said, kissing her hand before stepping away. There were sounds of people walking through the arcade, and he could see Nan hovering at the scullery door.

As he left, he hoped that Ellyn would prove him right.

There was a room in the house that no one used. It was tucked below the roof and had timbers that showed inside the walls, with a ceiling that sloped and a low window jutting out over the garden. The room was not neglected, it was swept and cleaned, but even when guests required beds they were never shown to the door: the one that Ellyn now entered and closed quietly behind her. She moved like a trespasser, with slow footsteps and a racing heart, taking in air unmixed with smells from the rest of the house, those of wood smoke and cooking. This air had the taint of old secrets buried deep.

Ellyn looked around her. The room was filled with the furniture of her memories: the fire irons with frog handles by the hearth; the joint stool on which she and Thom had played jacks; the canopied bed where he had slept that had been a palace in their games, as well as a dungeon and an island, a ship and a carriage, with turned posts to which the horses of their fantasies had been tied; and an elaborate headboard inscribed, they were sure, with magician's spells. Thom used to touch the carved patterns whenever he had nightmares, but they had been no help when he lay dying, shivering with cold and drenched in sweat, his breath wheezing as from broken bellows.

She saw the bowl Thom had used for washing, the pitcher from which he had once tried to drink and so chipped his front tooth, and the little boat he had made with sails cut from an apron. Thom had told her he would one day be a captain with a fleet of ships like Old Man Hawkins, and she had envied him that ambition. In their play, the boat was a great carrack with a gilded prow, and fortified castles in its bow and stern, and she had longed to be its master instead of the princess always waiting for the ship's return. She had admired, emulated and been hopelessly jealous of her brother.

The room was quiet, but she tried to summon up the sound of Thom's talking, and from somewhere distant in the house she heard a faint murmuring. All night there had been noises, needlessly hushed since no one had slept. In a few hours' time her father would be leaving.

Thom would have gone with him, had he lived.

She listened, and for a moment she believed she could hear Thom calling in his unbroken boy's voice, but then that faded, and she became aware of others in her mind. Will Doonan was exhorting her: '*You must prevail upon him not to go . . .*'

How could she? She had tried every stratagem but her father overruled all argument. What chance did she have of asserting her judgement over his? Yet Will had mortified her with his urging, and the worst of it was, when he had approached her at first, she had assumed it was because he was interested in *her*, that he was dismayed by the prospect of her marriage to Godfrey Gilbert. She had even thought he was hoping for another kiss. So vanity had made her blind. In the darkness of the room she could see more clearly.

Will was leaving as well. He would soon be with her father aboard the *Swan*, gone on a journey of excitement and adventure, while all she had to contemplate were months of avoiding Godfrey Gilbert, and if not him, then Peryn Fownes. She would pray for Will and her father to return safely from their voyage, but after that only misery awaited her. Once the venture had secured Master Gilbert's fortune, he would be intent on claiming her in marriage. She sighed and tensed. From deep in the house came the unmistakable tones of her father's speaking: the voice that had comforted her as a little girl, as well as frightened her when she had misbehaved. Suddenly she felt a stab of acute guilt, not for being where she was, but for being the child who had survived . . . for being a woman . . . for not being what her father most wanted. She caught her breath.

She looked at Thom's clothes chest with his initials studded in nails. The heavy iron clasp was fastened but ready to be drawn back. The key had been left in the lock. She crept closer.

One by one she took out Thom's clothes and laid them flat on top of the bed. Shirts, doublet, stockings and loose-fitting breeches; she spread them all out. The moths had not spoiled them, but they looked shabby and small: thin, limp garments that were not much larger than her own modest size. Yet she remembered Thom as tall: her strong, big brother who could pick her up easily. She raised a shirt to her face and tried to believe that the essence of Thom was still inside, but she could not. The odour was not his and neither was the touch. Belt and dagger joined the rest, cap and jerkin. She took out a pair of wide, blunt shoes. And suddenly there he was, in their shape she saw his feet: his moving, living feet. Running her fingers over the leather she felt the press of his heel and the push of his toes. She put the shoes on the floor and looked at her own feet beside them.

Thom's shoes were much larger.

Then she smiled, though she had thought she might cry.

Her mind turned to her father's voyage. He would need someone to nurse him; without proper care he was liable to become intolerable. She nudged the shoes with her toes. She could have been of use as his travelling companion. Was it not her duty to protect him now that he was ailing? Her mother required attention, too, but her father's need was greater. She considered what she might do, going over steps that seemed more plausible the more she thought them through. All she wanted was resolve, the sort of brave, bold fortitude that Thom had always shown. Was it really so impossible? She might keep close to Will, too . . .

She picked up the shoes.

Ellyn did not see her parents' parting, but their farewell was gentle, she was sure. She had no doubt that loving endearments were exchanged. The house fell quiet for a while and, in the aftermath, her father was subdued until he realised that someone had let a chicken into the hall and he could not find his best ash stick.

The departure was chaotic. Her father had been allowed three chests, but they were not enough. The result was that he carried too many possessions. Sword and scabbard, jewelled chains and an enamelled flask, silver tankard and knife, all were hung about his person. He even had an account book attached to his girdle, and he wore a fur coat so heavy that he had to be carried in a litter down to the quay at Sutton Poole, since his gout-swollen legs could not bear the total burden.

At the dockside the lighter was ready, the bo'sun waiting and the goodbyes brief, constrained by the crush of a swelling crowd. The maids offered their parting gifts, mariners jostled to take charge of the chests and Ellyn heard her father demanding assistance before summoning Godfrey Gilbert to a last urgent counsel. In the thick of the commotion most speech was drowned. The maids never stopped weeping, and Ellyn lost patience with them all.

Huddled in her cloak, Ellyn searched in her bag for the miniature of her mother she had arranged to have painted. The locket was small and light, and she hoped that her father would find it a comfort on the long voyage. The portrait had been made at her insistence, and after two unexpectedly painless sittings (painless since neither subject nor artist had wanted to speak), a fine likeness had been produced with a simple linear purity. Ellyn considered the gift more suitable than those her father had already received, though she had been too charitable to pass comment. She glanced at his stooped shoulders, and noticed the heavy cape lined with rabbit fur that Nan had draped on top of his gown, so making him stagger even more. She thought of Jane's present: the strong, plum brandy that her uncle had distilled with an infamous reputation for the headaches it could induce. And somewhere on her father's person would be the amulet that Lettie had said was a proven charm against the evils of the sea, containing part of a mermaid's tail that would always float, though it stank like something rotting.

She thrust the locket in her father's hand as he embraced her, and she wanted to speak but the words would not come. The hubbub rose around her, good wishes merged with calls to board, the blast of trumpets and the beat of drums.

'Sweet Lynling . . .'

Her father kissed her in a fug of smells, those of the press of people, the sea and fish, his fur-lined gown and the rabbit-skin cape, the sack that had fortified him and the ale that had washed it down and perhaps even the odour of the mermaid's tail. Ellyn held him; then he was gone. She moved to the quay's edge, but he was already in the boat sitting next to Richard Dennys. She turned to Godfrey Gilbert and noticed he was deep in conversation with the younger merchant's associates. Will was nowhere to be seen; she supposed he was already aboard. The *Swan* lay at anchor in the Cattewater, almost invisible behind the teeming craft around the harbour mouth, and soon her father would be joining the ship. Old Nan, Jane and Lettie were clinging to one another as though they were in the midst of a raging storm.

'I shall watch from the Hoe,' Ellyn said to them crisply, though she doubted they heard her.

She pushed through the throng, trusting that the maids would understand she needed to see more clearly – to appreciate (when they noticed her absence) that she would want to be alone to follow her father's departure. She hoped they would not rush after her. Other people were arriving, while a few, like her, were making for the cliffs. Children raced for the Lambhay, squealing, and behind them came the peddlers and conjurers, the quacks, mystics and ballad-mongers, who were drawn to any crowd. She passed street-sellers and loiterers before entering the back alleys, almost deserted, that led up steep slopes to the old castle towers.

What should she do? She looked at her feet and held her cloak wrapped tight as she climbed. This was the way in which decisions were made: not in fantasy, but reality – so she thought as she watched her own steps; decisions were made by proceeding in a certain direction, following a course until there was no going back. She could continue to the Hoe and later return to her home, retrieve the letter for her mother she had left in her room, and destroy it by burning. That would be easy. Or she could dodge inside the next empty passage, and go back by another way down to the docks. Her steps quickened. No one was about. She came close to a dark gateway in which she could see no sign of life.

She darted into the shadows and whipped off her cloak, revealing the clothes she had kept hidden beneath.

From her bag she pulled out a cap, hurriedly placed it on her head, and tucked her hair up inside. Stumbling and fumbling, she kicked off her slippers, rolled them up in the cloak, and stuffed everything in the bag, ignoring the fact that the cobbles were wet. The shoes she stepped into were flat and wide.

They were Thom's.

With burning cheeks and panting hard, conscious of the dagger bouncing awkwardly at her hip, Ellyn raced down the hill. Her running was reckless in shoes that were too large for her. She tripped and almost fell. She pushed out at anything that appeared in her way: people and posts, buildings and barrels. At the waterside she called out.

'Can someone take me to the *Swan*? A shilling for the *Swan*. Will anyone take me? A shilling to get me there . . .'

Jeers and laughter followed as she picked her way around the quay, together with a few comments she had no wish to understand clearly.

'What ho, lad! Sheathed thy sword late, eh?'

'Nay, he was all night long trying to find where't should go!'

'Yea! And he'd 'ad such a skinful that once 'twas in, he forgot where he was!'

Ellyn shrank inwardly, but continued her erratic progress along the ranks of moored boats, calling out with mounting desperation, until she heard a phlegmy voice.

'The *Swan's* crew left at daybreak, lad. Best look lively!'

The man who had spoken was already casting off. Ellyn saw him throwing a rope from the stern of a little boat that could only be reached by climbing across three others. She hesitated, looking round for a helping hand or some support, but of course there was none.

The man barked at her.

'Quicken thy sticks!'

She almost fell as she scrambled down. The first boat rocked, and she lurched. She staggered like a drunkard and clung like an infant. Laughter rang behind her until she reached the last boat, and there she quailed at the sight of the choppy sea. The man leaned across, grabbed her shoulder, hauled her over, and sent her sprawling at his feet. While he rowed she avoided his eye, but busied herself by looking in her pocket and finding the shilling she had offered to pay. She pulled a face to suggest she was indeed feeling tipsy, in the event quite easy. Once a sail was raised to catch the sharp wind, the boat bobbed violently in the waves further out, but the craft was fast. She reached the *Swan* in good time, while the lighter with her father was still lashed to the leeward chains.

Ellyn was taken to the other side feeling sick.

'I thank you, good sir,' she mumbled, paid the boatman, stood, toppled and was unceremoniously shoved into a sling that pulled her up to the deck as effectively as cargo.

Fear set her shivering. She had hoped she might sneak aboard unnoticed, but plainly she would be seen as soon as the winch set her down. What would she say? Her legs felt naked without the wrapping of skirt. She was conscious of looking ridiculous. In wide-eyed panic she stared at a scene that twisted and rolled as the sling was raised then lowered. Everywhere she looked men were moving about, climbing rigging, setting sails, and gathering round to properly receive the important merchants who were boarding on the other side. Ellyn caught a glimpse of her father's new rabbit cape, and the sort of outlandish hat-plumes she associated with vain popinjays; she had no doubt that Richard Dennys was sporting them. Only one man was close as she put her feet on the deck. But she had to speak.

'Good—'

Her greeting was cut short.

'Gurt below, thou clay-brained scut!'

A stinging blow to her ear sent her tumbling to her knees. The pain was so intense that tears filled her eyes. She was faint with shock. But then she became aware that whoever had hit her was probably approaching. She saw boots near her hands. She pushed up unsteadily, as startled and terror-struck as a field mouse in the open. Glancing round wildly, she tried to take in where she was. Then she did what field mice do: she made for the nearest hole her size and disappeared by squeezing inside.

8

Discovery

'. . . They are ill discoverers that think there is no land, when they can see nothing but sea . . .'

—*From* The Advancement of Learning, *Book 2, Chapter 7, by Francis Bacon, 1st Baron Verulam, adviser to Elizabeth I*

For days Ellyn cowered in the darkness after burrowing mole-like into the deepest nook she could find. She did not dare show herself. The mariner's blow had made her realise the enormity of what she had done. Nothing in her upbringing had prepared her for the predicament she faced: the isolation and disorientation, and the relentless physical discomfort. Her original, rather nebulous plan had been to play the role of a galley boy who might be accepted as useful before a joyous revelation. But the viciousness of the mariner had shattered that fantasy. She was ruled by terror: the dread of brutality should she be discovered, and the fear of condemnation should she make herself known – she could barely conceive of her father's wrath on finding out she had stowed aboard the *Swan*. Her objectives contracted down to the simple necessities of sleeping and eating, and trying to stay hidden.

Ellyn discovered where she was mainly by touch at first. But even far below the main deck, with no portholes or lanterns to give any illumination, somehow, obliquely, light found a way inside. It suggested details haphazardly, either in splinter-sharp points or a vague shadowy haze, and from these fragments she made a picture of the place she inhabited.

She was in the sections of a ship, inside another that was whole.

There were timbers that arched over her and others that were stacked up, or made inaccessible by heaps of canvas and rope, planks and huge poles. Mingled with the odour of rot and festering skins was a foul and acrid vermin stink. She came across nets and anchors, blocks and chains, sacks of bolts and wooden nails and something she identified eventually as a rudder, cut in one piece from a massive block of oak. It was the rudder that made her realise she was amongst the parts of another vessel, though she had no idea why the *Swan* would be carrying such a load. She had expected to find cloth.

Her nausea settled slowly. She found it a comfort to sniff her sweet-pouch of herbs. The bag of posies that used to hang from her girdle proved just as invaluable as her looking glass and comb. She came to know the safest times for scavenging amongst the stores. With increasing desperation she searched for the food she found palatable as slowly but steadily it began to run out. She could not abide the hard biscuit or salt beef, and subsisted mainly on carrots and cheese. The thudding of feet was a warning to take cover, and she soon linked this with the changing of the watch. She made an effort to gauge what was happening elsewhere on the ship, and she began to develop an understanding of the daily routine. In particular, she listened out for her father; sometimes she was sure she could hear him on the deck above her lair.

Her father's gait was distinctive, as was the tapping of his stick, and one night, after nine bells had sounded, she heard him lumbering about almost directly overhead. His steps appeared firm, and the thump of his stick had a regular beat. That was reassuring. Peering up through the grating that covered a hatch, she spotted a pile of firearms, secured by a net, obscured in part by a large moving shadow – one that could only be his.

The tapping became louder then, after a thud, it suddenly stopped. She listened with alarm. All she could hear was faint moaning. Who was there to help? However much she dreaded discovery, she could not leave her father alone and lying injured. She shinned up a ladder, pushed the hatch open and wriggled quickly out.

'Alas, good sir!' Ellyn called while picking her way to him. The words were forced between gritted teeth in an effort to rouse him without alerting anyone else, though in her anxiety she rather mangled the attempt to sound like a boy. 'Are you much hurt?'

'Ellyn?' her father groaned, and so did she inwardly. He raised a shaking hand. 'Can that be you?'

She noticed the lantern he must have been carrying, lying on top of a sack and still alight. Hastily she set it on the decking behind her, and then blew on her fingers since she had scorched them in the process.

'Sir?' she asked, managing to wince with a hint of enquiry.

With a trembling hand, her father traced the contours of a growing swelling on his balding scalp.

'Where am I?'

Ellyn drew closer in consternation, but quickly shrank back in panic as he clutched at her sleeve.

'Marry, boy! Me-thought I heard an angel!' Eyes glazed and rolling, he gave a beatific smile and sank back onto the floor.

Ellyn made an effort to lift him but merely succeeded in bending his neck.

'Be not troubled, uncle,' she gasped. 'Only try to get on your feet.'

In an endeavour to raise him further she moved her hands under his shoulders. His head fell back on her knees. She made another attempt but his head slipped between them: one of the drawbacks, she realised, of wearing breeches and not a skirt.

'Get up, uncle, please!' she pleaded.

The response was a bewildered gasp.

'I'faith I hear my Lynling!'

Ellyn froze.

He looked up from her lap and gave a rapturous gap-toothed smile.

'Is she not with you?'

Ellyn averted her face, momentarily at a loss as to what to do next.

Her father groaned again and writhed.

'What place is this? I must be damned to be hearing her . . .'

In a few awkward movements, Ellyn extricated her knees. Then, by rolling up the fur cape that Nan had given him, she was able to put it to good use at last; she settled her father's head on the makeshift pillow. What more could she do? She rose unsteadily and picked up the lantern.

'Stay awhile, sir. I will fetch help.' She backed away. 'Do not move!'

'Do not go!' he called after her with a wail.

But she was already making for the nearest ladder. Ellyn climbed to the next deck and hailed the first seaman she ran into.

'Aid and mercy! Prithee come quickly! Master Cooksley is hurt!'

The mariner's shadowed torso loomed menacingly nearer, like a fantastic creature from a navigator's chart: a fish-man with no arms, and eyes in his chest – until Ellyn realised that he had a blanket pulled over his head.

'Where, boy?' The fish-man's question bubbled from a growl in his throat.

'Here!' She turned away and beckoned hurriedly. 'Follow me!' She dashed back, hoping that the jolting might help disguise her voice. 'I would have carried him if I could . . .'

By swinging lantern-light her father became visible as an unmoving mound under a large fur cloak: a kind of tumulus, emitting ghostly moans, that blocked the narrow passage beyond the foremast of the ship. The fish-man discarded his blanket and pushed past her.

''Ods me, Master Cooksley! Taken a tumble 'ave 'ee?' the fish-man exclaimed. Then he yelled so loudly that Ellyn jumped. 'Ho! Help here!'

The response was immediate, as if a bee had signalled a threat to a hive; assistance came rushing from every direction. Ellyn sensed she was about to be trapped. She put the lantern down near her father's feet, edged away and began to squeeze past the men just arrived. But, before she could bolt, a gurgling snarl from the fish-man reached her.

'Hey lad! Not so fast. We 'ave need of thee yet. Light our way and show willing.'

Ellyn had little choice since she was hemmed in by men with the look of scoundrels and rogues. The fish-man and three others had her father in their arms as if they were about to wield a battering ram. She retrieved the lantern and turned her back on them quickly. Hunched over, in an attempt to be less conspicuous, Ellyn led the procession with the aid of ear-burning abuse at every possible wrong turn. Curses directed her to her father's cabin. Eventually, and with an audible sigh, her father was laid on his pallet.

Ellyn shrank back.

'Is my angel still with me?' her father gasped.

'Angel?!' one of his bearers muttered, to which another replied, 'Ee's 'ad a tap on 'is pate.'

A thick-browed seaman put a heavy hand on his breast.

'Be at ease, sir.'

Her father slumped down. He could hardly argue.

'Some rum'd 'elp 'im,' someone suggested.

Ellyn began to slink away. If she could only slip out of the cabin, she might stand a good chance of making an escape. Then she heard a familiar growl.

'Stay, lad!'

She pushed on, but was impeded by more men at the door. A hand grabbed her from behind.

'Let me see thy face.' The fish-man dragged her towards him.

She recognised his smell. His grip was like a hook that dug into her collarbone. 'Do I know thee?'

She became conscious, despite trying to keep her head down, that his gleaming eyes were peering very close. His questions were surly.

'What be thy name?'

'D . . . D . . .' she stammered, on the point of pleading, 'Don't hurt me!'

'My angel!' her father croaked feebly.

The fish-man took hold of her ear and pinched with the ferocity of a shark taking a bite.

'Thy name, angel.'

Ellyn squealed. Tears filled her eyes. Her ear was being torn apart, and the pain was so great she could hardly speak. But she had to.

'D . . . Daniel, sir.'

Another voice snarled.

'I aint 'eard o' no Daniel aboard, hast thou, Gillon?'

'No, Lucas,' came the cold reply. 'I ain't neither.'

The fish-man twisted and then jerked her ear hard, sending Ellyn's head into a dizzying turn that ended, in agony, with a vision of his thick, glistening lips curling as he spoke.

'I believe we 'ave a stowaway. A little thievin', fen-spawned, base-crawlin' stowaway.' The lips were licked and his words became meaner. 'Oh, what we will not do to you, boy . . .'

Desperately, Ellyn tried to reach for his hand, but the pinching became worse.

'For pity, sir . . .'

'Oh, how we will wring you and skin you and string you out on a line—' the fish-man seized both her ears and forced her head back until she caught a vile view of the roof of his mouth ' —but only after we 'av dangled and drawn and made yer sing and dance.'

Gasps were wrung from her, though Ellyn bit her lips and screwed her eyes shut. She could not take any more. She cried out. But just as she thought her torment could get no worse, a gentler voice brought it to an unexpected end. A voice that she knew.

'Easy there. Let me look at him.'

Ellyn was certain, even before she opened her eyes, that Will Doonan's hands were cradling her head. He took off her cap and loosened her hair. Relief washed through her. She would throw herself on his mercy and Will would protect her. As she blinked away tears, sounds of astonishment rose around her.

'Fie on me!' someone exclaimed.

'A woman!' the fish-man gulped.

'A lady!' said the man called Gillon.

'Mistress Ellyn!' Will sounded incredulous, but his tone was soft, and she was aware of the gentle way in which he was smoothing out her hair. She supposed she would find some tenderness in his face, but she was wrong. As her vision cleared she saw disappointment in his look.

'Dear lady!' His voice was suddenly icy and his expression as hard. 'Shame on you for a fool,' he whispered.

Her spirits plummeted. His blue eyes wounded her more than the assault on her ears. In the set of his mouth, there was only stern reproach. Ellyn gazed back at him in despair and then rushed over to her father before tears could betray her.

'Father!' She threw herself against his bosom.

'It is you!' he mumbled from beneath her, managing eventually to prop himself up.

Ellyn buried her face in his chest, stifling the urge to sob in the folds of his shirt.

He wrapped his arms around her and she felt him kiss the top of her head. That gave her a glimmer of hope. Her father would stand by her. Then he tensed.

'By Jove, what madness is in you?' he sputtered. 'What churlishness do you show me by this . . . this *mischief*?' He held her away but, with his hands on her shoulders, he did not let her go. He shook her. 'What have you done?'

Ellyn lowered her head. A stinging patter of muttered comments came from those looking on.

'She will 'ave to go,' gurgled the fish-man.

'T'will bring ill fortune to 'ave a woman aboard,' said someone else.

'Child, how you provoke me!' Her father vented his anger with more shaking, though she was shuddering anyway with each thunderclap of denigration. 'Wilful, headstrong, wayward ingratiate,' he boomed and rumbled. His eyes started. 'How can any man control you?!' he raged.

'Father, please . . .' Ellyn pleaded forlornly.

'Perverse and ungovernable . . .' The rant continued.

'Father!' She tried to interrupt him, but the only respite he gave her was when he drew breath. Then, in that momentary pause, a small commotion occurred, and the cause was soon obvious when Ellyn looked round. Two gentlemen, whom she had never met, emerged from the throng around her father's bed. One had the same reddish hair and complexion of Master John Drake, though he was shorter and looked brighter, with eyes that appeared to take in much very fast. The other man, who stepped towards her, was as handsome as Narcissus and expensively dressed. As he took the liberty of staring closely at her face, she noticed the silver buttons down the front of his stuffed doublet.

'Ah ha! What pretty boy is this?' he asked, without any introduction, and next had the effrontery to place his finger under her chin. 'A *very* pretty boy . . .'

Ellyn would have been more piqued if she was not so upset. The man looked over her and towards her father.

'One you forgot, eh, sir? Ha, ha!'

Before she could think of a cutting response, the red-haired gentleman bustled forward, plainly amused.

'How now, Master Cooksley? You appear to have brought more baggage than you thought!' Narcissus laughed loudly at this – witlessly, thought Ellyn – and chuckles broke out elsewhere that left her blushing even deeper.

'But I trust you are not hurt?' the red-haired gentleman asked him.

'No, no,' her father answered in a downcast manner, his temper evidently deflated. He let Ellyn go. ''Tis nothing. My daughter, Mistress Ellyn . . .' He waved his hand limply from her to the gentlemen. 'Captain Francis Drake, and Master Richard Dennys.'

The Captain bowed low.

'Honoured, sweet maiden.'

His companion bent slightly after making a ridiculous flourish.

Ellyn's discomfort became more acute. Should she curtsy? Yet she was not wearing a dress. Surely she was not meant to bow? She glanced down at the breeches that were too baggy on her legs, and the shirt that was showing between ties that had come loose. In the midst of this dilemma she heard the fish-man pass comment.

'A damned inconvenience. We shall 'ave to take 'er back to England.'

'Two weeks lost and northers getting up,' another man grumbled.

'Tush, gentlemen,' her father broke in, to Ellyn's relief, though that soon faded. 'My Ellyn has surprised me, but she will not put us out. We will continue and she shall not trouble you.' He punched out a promise, looking crossly at Ellyn. 'My word on't. I shall keep her out of harm's way.'

'Good, sir,' Captain Drake declared, with the manner of someone used to jumping at opportunities, 'then we are decided.' He turned and addressed everyone. 'It is not for us to interfere with anything in Master Cooksley's custody.'

Ellyn's heart sank further. She was uncomfortable with Drake's wit, and even more with what he implied.

'But my advice to you, sir,' the Captain added on catching her father's eye, 'is to keep what is most precious to you out of sight.' To Ellyn's chagrin he gave her a wink, and then added loudly, 'T'would not do for it to become a temptation!'

Master Dennys chortled, and so did a few others, though the levity soon ended with the departure of the Captain. Everyone followed, except for Ellyn and her father, who were left sitting on the pallet, in stony silence, side-by-side.

Ellyn felt as if a pit had opened up under her feet. She was falling into an abyss and no one was prepared to help her. She had been berated and belittled and now she was shunned. Will had left without even giving her a glance. She stole a look at her father who glowered straight back. She had hoped for some sign he was just a little pleased to see her. Instead, he stood up, marched over to the door, locked it with a clatter and pointedly hung the key on a chain around his neck. She tried not to show her unhappiness, but the assault on her ears had been excruciating. She wiped her eyes.

'Weep, but it will do you no good,' her father shouted.

'I am not weeping.' Instantly she regretted having spoken at all.

'Your punishment shall be imprisonment!' he railed at her. 'Take good stock of where you are.'

She kept her head down and drew a sharp breath.

'Here . . . you . . . shall . . . stay!' His voice rose and shook with rage.

She stared at her shoes and wished he would go so she could give way to the tears she was determined not to show him. She looked up to a small window. At least she could see the sky.

And she was bound for a new world.

9
Brave

'O brave new world . . .'

—The Tempest *by William Shakespeare,*
Act 5, Scene 1

Panamá, the Americas
April 1571

It was scorching hot. Ellyn's nose and cheeks stung though she had only been ashore a few hours. She considered wearing Thom's cap, but had no wish to spoil the effect of the dress she had spent weeks sewing. In any event, the feel of the sun on her face was welcome after being confined for so long in a tiny, dark cabin. She was acutely self-conscious – concerned about what others might think of her after her unjust incarceration. She was also thirsty and tired, while her vision swam as if she was still out at sea. There was nowhere for her to sit, other than on the washed up palm trunk from which her father could be heard complaining. The mariners milling about were giving far more attention to off-loading provisions than to their passengers' needs. Where would she sleep? The island appeared remote from any human habitation. She had been told they were near Panamá but she had no real idea where that was. Suddenly she longed for a house, somewhere with rooms and beds, proper chairs and a privy. She looked at the tangle of vegetation behind the white, sand beach. What might crawl out to confront her if she spent a night by the shore? Then a deep voice startled her.

'I'd wear a hat, if I were you.'

She turned to find that Will was proffering his cap. The sight of him made her heart leap. For too long she had been shut away from good company, particularly his.

'Thank you,' she replied, 'but I am enjoying the sun, and I have a hat if I wish to use one.' Raising her chin, she wondered what he made of her looks in her new clothes. As it was, at that moment, she would have much appreciated a hat, but her appearance was more important. She wanted Will to see she was unbowed by her father's treatment – more than that, she wanted him to find her attractive.

Will put back his cap.

'As you wish.' He smiled. 'I hope you like this place. We shall be here for a while, out of sight of the Spaniards.'

She considered telling him that the place was too hot and full of insects, but decided against complaining. She had no wish for him to think she was not game for the challenge.

'It is pleasant to be off the ship,' she said, 'but my father and I require proper shelter. What if it rains?'

'You may get wet.'

She considered Will askance. Was he teasing her? She shot him a reproachful look.

'My father must be kept dry.'

'Our priority is to find fresh water and victuals. Once we have those, then a hut will be made for you.'

'A hut?' Her apprehension probably showed. What did he mean by that? 'A hut' did not sound like the kind of shelter she had hoped for.

'If a storm gets up,' Will carried on blithely, 'you can always go back aboard the *Swan*.'

'I am *not* going back in that cabin!' How could he suggest such a thing when he must have guessed she was heartily sick of being cooped up on the ship?

Will inclined his head.

'That will be your choice, dear mistress. Your father, at least, will be offered a bed aboard.'

'But . . . Master Doonan!' she called after him as he strode off, and she understood why he did not stop when she noticed Francis Drake not far away. Will's behaviour still rankled. She brought her fingertips to the bridge of her nose and the contact was painful.

'Ellyn!' She heard her father's fractious summons and wheeled round.

'Yes, dear Father!' she answered cheerfully, and hoped Will would hear her. Let him believe she was in high spirits and pleased with everything she found.

Will looked past Francis Drake to the curved oak braces that the carpenter was shaping. One lay like a whale's rib on the white coral sand, the other was being planed beneath the scant shade of palms.

'There will be more work needed when those riders are fixed: caulking the bolt heads and tarring within . . .'

He spoke of his concerns once the hull of the pinnace had been strengthened. Putting two heavy guns in front of a deck for twenty oarsmen made bracing the bows a wise precaution. The sections of the little *Kestrel* had fitted together nicely; her assembly had been quick, but her design was based on a galley's, and not a fighting ship's. The conversation turned to the practicalities of installing the two bronze half-culverins. The discussion absorbed him, but his eyes still turned towards the rough frond shelters that had become a tiny hamlet over the past few weeks. He had caught sight of Ellyn walking by, and she was not a person he could notice then instantly dismiss from his mind. He watched her strolling along the beach, wearing the pretty cream-coloured dress she had made herself from her father's kersey cloth. Looking back at the *Kestrel* did little to restore his concentration.

The *Swan* was in hiding off the coast of Panamá, at least a day's sailing from the nearest city, Nombre de Dios. The ship was tucked away amongst the uninhabited islands that trailed to the east like a stream of sparks. They had made a base on an islet named after the pinnace they were building. Will was anxious enough for Ellyn should they be discovered on Kestrel Island, but he was troubled more by the idea of her being with them once they left. She would be a hindrance if there was any action, and that was likely once they put the pinnace to use. With the *Kestrel* they would do as they had planned: attack the Spaniards by surprise using the boat's shallow draught to sail close to the mainland shore, perhaps even venturing inland along the deeper rivers. He did not want Ellyn with them for that.

Why had she come? He could not understand her motives. It was simpler to picture the tackle needed to shift a culverin's weight. Her actions made no sense to him. He accepted that Cooksley was in poor health, and that she believed he might need her, but plainly he disagreed. She had defied him flagrantly in a way no father could condone, especially in a daughter. She had been headstrong in the face of her father's bullying, and he could equate with that. He might admire her pluck, but he could never approve of what she had done. The waywardness of her behaviour left him wondering about her good judgment. Sneaking aboard the *Swan* must have taken some courage, but it was also reckless. Her presence was a threat to the whole enterprise. The men would be constrained by having a woman to protect. How could they strike at the Spaniards and be sure to keep her safe? And he did not like the way she was always attracting lusting glances. Even amongst the crew her reputation was at risk. He enjoyed the sight of her no less than any man, but that did not mean he wanted her on the mission. She was already spoken for in her father's mind, and the enterprise with Drake was no place for lovers' games.

Yet he desired her no less; he felt it whenever he saw her.

The fact was he was annoyed with her, but he felt responsible for her, too. He could not easily dismiss the possibility that he might have unwittingly encouraged her to come – or perhaps that was to assume too much. Her hot-headedness could have been prompted simply by misguided loyalty to her father. Whatever the explanation, it did nothing to address the problem, and the only solution he could think of involved some cost to himself. The issue was vexing, but it had to be faced.

'Concerning Mistress Ellyn, Captain . . .'

'Ah, yes,' said Drake with alacrity, as if a sudden switch from talk of loads to a lady was quite natural to make. 'Mistress Ellyn, our mistress of the sea. I also am concerned about her, but let us not be *too* concerned, eh?'

Will ended Drake's chuckling with the simple truth as he saw it.

'She would be safest left here.'

'For so long as any French privateer or Spaniard does not find her,' Drake replied.

Will nodded; Drake had voiced the fear that troubled him most.

'I would like to ensure that does not happen, with your permission, Captain.' There – he had said what he did not want to, but knew he should. He would give up the chance for vengeance and riches to watch over Ellyn Cooksley, a woman promised to another man, who had disappointed him deeply. He would even give up another small chance of finding Kit.

Drake raised his hand.

'No, Will, I have need of you. I have already discussed the matter with my brother and he will stay with the lady. She will be well protected.'

Will was wrong-footed. Having prepared himself to make the sacrifice, he had not anticipated that someone else might see it through. But of all the mariners who could have been chosen to safeguard Ellyn, he could think of none better than the Captain's brother. He could not imagine John Drake being any threat to her virtue. Even so, he preferred not to leave her.

'Allow me then to assist him. One man alone is not enough—'

'No, Will, as I have said,' Drake cut in, and Will stopped short of persisting. It was plain the Captain had decided.

'Six men will stay with him,' Drake added by way of concession. 'I have already chosen them.'

Will nodded, as satisfied as he supposed he could hope to be, and broached another subject that he considered almost an equal difficulty, and not far removed. It was possible, for the time being, that the same solution might serve both.

'There is her father also . . .'

'Master Cooksley and Mistress Ellyn, and Master Dennys *as well.*' Drake gave a short laugh. 'We are concerned for all three. We have a triangular uncertainty with the points yet to plot. But I have no doubt a course can be navigated.'

Will's brows rose as he followed the Captain's meaning, though he had no idea of the 'course' Drake had in mind that would involve both Cooksley and Dennys, and no time to speculate.

'Hello!' Drake exclaimed with a look of surprise. 'Here comes a point now.'

Will turned to see Ellyn, to whom Drake immediately bowed.

'Dear mistress,' said Will, bowing also, though Ellyn appeared indifferent to the deference he showed her. She shaded her eyes and peered up at the *Kestrel*, beginning a circuit around the hull in just the same way that Will and Drake had done moments before.

'Your little *Kestrel* looks almost ready to fly.'

'She is,' Drake responded. 'I hope we shall sail her in a few days and see how the land lies.'

Ellyn scrutinised the pinnace keenly. She took off the high, crowned hat that Will was sure he had once seen her father wearing, though without the parrot feathers that now adorned it. She tipped back her head and eyed the bows, and there her focus settled: on the low forecastle at the beak, near the point where the bowsprit was lashed to the prow.

'Will she be carrying canon at those gun ports?' she asked with an edge to her voice.

'Gun ports?' Drake cocked his head to examine the same place. 'Ah, yes,' he said, as if the openings had only just been brought to his attention. 'The usual purpose of a gun port is to accommodate a gun.'

Ellyn frowned. She caught Will's eye and immediately looked away. To Will, she seemed to be wrestling with a worry much as he had done earlier, one that she wanted to share, though she was uncertain whether she should.

'I am troubled for my father,' she sighed. 'I fear that if he is put in any danger, or if there is any threat . . .' Her words tailed away and closed with a simple fact. 'He is not a young man.'

'Just so,' Drake confirmed.

'He needs rest and must not be made anxious,' Ellyn added. And Will was sure of her sincerity, though he could not help but recall the moment that 'Ellyn, the cabin boy' was revealed as 'Ellyn, the daughter', and he did not remember Nicholas Cooksley being particularly calm on that occasion.

'Captain,' Ellyn addressed Drake in a tone close to beseeching, 'I wish to suggest that my father remains on this island and is not taxed so soon with any more sailing.' She put her argument with conviction, though Will sensed it was also with an effort. 'I shall watch over him until you return, and I am certain your enterprise will fare no worse for being without him at this juncture.'

'Yes, Mistress Ellyn.' Will threw in his agreement before she could vacillate. This was an appeal he most wished to encourage.

'I am sure you are right,' Drake replied, and his whole manner conveyed earnest sympathy. 'But will your father be content with such an arrangement?'

Ellyn raised her head and eyed Drake sharply.

'You must convince him that he will be.'

'Ah!' Drake acknowledged, with a frown that suggested deep thought.

'Please, Captain Drake.' Ellyn touched his hand, at which Drake took and kissed hers before she could object.

'Be at ease, sweet mistress. I shall do my utmost to see your wishes are carried out.'

Will could see that Drake was flirting but assured himself that nothing was meant by it. The Captain had shown a skill he esteemed, though Ellyn might yet be sailing on the *Kestrel* unless her father could be persuaded to stay as well, and Will was in some doubt as to how that could be achieved.

Drake resumed his perambulation around the little ship, and Will followed after watching Ellyn depart. The talk returned to practicalities, this time concerning the materials they would take should the *Kestrel* need repairing, at worst should she be holed. They were so deep in conversation that Nicholas Cooksley was only noticed once he was close to approaching. He appeared as if battling through quicksand, arms flailing and scarlet-faced. Will rushed to help him to the strip of shade beside the hull. Once there, Will and Drake had little choice but to hear him out.

'I trust that my Ellyn has not made it her business to interfere with yours,' Cooksley puffed. 'I noticed she was with you, and I hope she has not intruded. Women can never stop meddling, but she is my daughter.'

Cooksley waved a hand amidst a profusion of lace: a boon for keeping the sand flies at bay, Will thought, though of little use for cooling. He wondered what Cooksley might be working up to.

'I am accountable for her, answerable and duty-bound to care for her,' Cooksley went on, 'to say nothing of my love as a father which remains steadfast, no matter how much she may shake it with her maid's silliness. I must constantly watch over her, and this burden is compounded by my duty to others. She is all but betrothed to Godfrey Gilbert, you know.' At this, he shot Will a grotesque smile and, despite all his inclinations, Will forced a grin back. 'What would *he* say if she were to come to any harm?' Cooksley did not wait for a reply. 'She must be shielded and protected, despite my desire to engage in bold commerce at the earliest opportunity, I can neither desert her, nor allow her to be put in jeopardy.'

Will and Drake exchanged bemused glances.

'For certain,' Drake interjected.

'She must remain here,' Cooksley said, at last coming to a conclusion, 'and I have no alternative but to stay with her. She must be safeguarded.'

Will exhaled.

Drake assumed a concerned expression.

''Twould not be right to attempt to dissuade you,' Drake admitted with an air of gravity. 'However much I might wish to.'

'My only reservation is that if there is any trading . . .' Cooksley began a peevish counter-argument, but Drake cut it short.

'Most unlikely at this juncture.'

'All to the good.' The relief in Cooksley was obvious. He put a finger between his neck and his ruff, as if to let out the heat that had been building beneath. 'But I would be more comfortable if that fact could be made known to Master Dennys, and if he were to appreciate that at present there could be no possible advantage in his going with you, and much possible disadvantage if he does.'

'A case could well be made,' Drake said, managing to give an impression of mulling over a difficult task while ardently wishing to help.

'Make it, Captain,' Cooksley demanded. He slapped at his neck and then examined his hand with disgust, took out his kerchief, mopped his face and nodded. 'I shall place my faith in you to do that. Adieu!'

With Drake still beside him, Will watched the old man shuffle off. They looked again at the pinnace, and then back at the vegetation flanking the beach. Will hesitated to refer to the last vague assurance that Drake had given, though he very much hoped that Drake was not intent on leaving Richard Dennys behind as well. He preferred to have Dennys where he could see him.

'About the stores,' Will began, wondering how he could broach the subject of Dennys without stepping out of line, but when he glanced round he realised he had already lost Drake's interest. The Captain was staring at something beyond Will's right shoulder.

'Ah ha!' Drake chortled. 'I believe I can see the third point on your starboard side.'

'Good day, good sirs,' came an airy greeting.

Will recognised the cultivated court English that Richard Dennys persisted in using. He considered it affected, since everyone knew that Dennys had been raised in Devon. Will scowled as the merchant returned a cursory blow.

'You will be sailing soon?' Dennys asked lightly.

'The day after tomorrow, most probably,' Will answered tersely.

'Will you be joining us, sir? Drake enquired.

The question put Will more at ease; it was not what he considered 'persuasive'. But then Dennys narrowed his eyes, and held his well-made face motionless, much like a ferret sniffing a promising scent.

'That rather depends on who will be going. I assume you will not be taking our fair Venus revealed?'

If the description was meant as a homage to Ellyn, or to demonstrate some sophistication in learning, then Will considered that Dennys had failed on both counts. He had no tolerance for the sly smile that played across the merchant's lips, and would have ended it with a curt remark except that Dennys spoke first.

'It will distress me to see her put in any danger.'

'Be not distressed, Master Dennys,' Drake assured him. 'Mistress Ellyn will remain here under her father's protection.'

'Ah!' Dennys broke in as his fine black brows shot up (it would not have surprised Will to find that they were plucked). 'So Nicholas Cooksley will not be bargaining with the Spaniards just yet?'

Drake gave a nod.

'I doubt any of us will be bargaining for a while. We must scout first.'

Dennys responded with a quizzical look, and it was plain to Will that the prospect of scouting was not what absorbed him most.

'But surely Age is a poor guard for Beauty,' Dennys observed.

Will drew away a step; the man made him feel ill at times.

'Master Cooksley might be found wanting,' Dennys continued, 'if there is any real jeopardy—'

'Master John Drake will remain with them,' Will broke in. 'They will be safe enough.' He did not want Dennys left under any misapprehension that his presence might be valued as a guard.

The Captain's eyes flashed sharp as steel towards Will, and light as sunshine at Dennys.

'I hope they will,' Drake said blithely. 'But I would have no fear for them at all if *you*, Master Dennys, were to offer your brave protection.'

Will swallowed hard, bit back the urge to protest, and watched Dennys stroke his scented beard with hardly a suggestion of wavering. He had an urge to kick him.

'Truly, to go with you and leave the lady without a fit champion to defend her would be both self-serving and ignoble. I shall stay,' he concluded resolutely.

Drake bowed.

'I am in your debt.'

Before Dennys could leave, Will took him to one side. He spoke under his breath.

'Do you know how to discharge a firearm, Master Dennys?'

Dennys gripped the hilt of his rapier and gave a disdainful sneer.

'A gentleman fights with his sword.'

Dennys moved to leave, but Will blocked his way.

'If anyone threatens the Cooksleys, he will not be a gentleman, sir.' Will's response was deliberately muted. In a sudden fluid movement, Will pulled out his knife and threw it, turning, to stick blade-first in a barrel. Dennys jumped back. Propped against the barrel was a firearm: a caliver. Will paced over, retrieved his knife and shouldered the caliver along with the cartridge belt and powder horn that he had used earlier in the day for target practice.

Someone called out, but Drake's voice silenced whoever it was.

Will pushed caliver, horn and belt hard against the merchant's chest.

'You had better learn,' he said. He strode away. He would make the best of it. John Drake would keep Ellyn safe, and he trusted she had more intelligence than to be taken in by Richard Dennys; the man was patently a buffoon. She had shown selflessness in wanting to remain with her father (someone whom Will privately considered a cantankerous old bastard) and that had raised her in his esteem. The thought of leaving her made him feel uneasy, but at least he would have a chance to begin searching for Kit. That was why he had come.

Will looked out to sea, half closing his eyes against the sun. Perhaps Kit was hundreds of miles away, still near San Juan de Ulúa in the Gulf of Mexico – if he lived. Why should anyone in Panamá know anything about him? Will paced on along the shore.

But perhaps Kit was close.

What does a dying man see? He sees his past in vivid, bright passages: episodes that are portals to the whole of his best experience, but jumbled and filtered so that all the vile parts are faint, and all the goodness rises up. This is what Kit believed. It explained why he thought of his boyhood often, moved like a sleepwalker and remembered little from the time he had been held as a captive. He was sure he was dying, but that prospect no longer frightened him. He had witnessed enough in the last few years to no longer care about staying alive.

The river swirled around his legs. Through the vermillion surge he could see the pale suggestion of his feet, but they were so numb he could barely feel them. He knew his lips were chapped and his hair was lousy. Where his skin was bare it was blistered and scabbed. The rags that he wore gave scant protection from the sun; they held no warmth since they were soaking.

In a gleam of sunlight he looked up at the thunderclouds that threatened to drench him afresh, watching them thicken and darken, while steam rose from the river and the dense forest of the gorge. A fresh downpour stung him and, at almost the same moment, he was kicked in the side. Unbalanced by the chains round his ankles, the blow pitched him against planks. A shout followed that he ignored. He was bent double above a sluice, head close to slats, and he could see the glint of gold in amongst the grit that was trapped.

Kit picked out a tiny bead and put it in a pouch round his neck. This was the second place near the river's source where the Spanish had found the 'pleasure' as they called it: the *placer* that produced gold, though it was no pleasure to him. He had been discovering the little nuggets all morning, but the finds had only inflamed the greed of Lázaro, the half-blood *mestizo* who had been left in charge. It was why the gang of slaves upstream were being whipped by the two native hirelings, made to dig out the river bank faster with their hoes, and shovel the grit into the feeder channels until they ran red with soil. It was why he could not gaze any more at the clouds, but had to sort through the stones with his thin, deadened fingers. So he listened to the river's rush and tried to forget all the other sounds: the groans of the Negro on the gravel downstream, whose spirit was running out with the flux from his bowels, the cries and curses and the squawking of the parrot that Lázaro had netted and was plucking alive for his warped entertainment.

He welcomed the rain. If the rain continued the river might flood. Let it rise and carry away all the boards, posts and tools, the canoes and flimsy fern-frond shelters, wipe out the trenches, and sweep away everyone, himself included. And he would drown, of course, since he could not swim with his feet dragging chains, but he accepted that prospect. He had seen worse deaths.

On the road from San Juan de Ulúa many of the injured had died slowly. They had been starved and stripped of most of their clothes, driven across deserts and forced to climb icy mountains, beaten for stumbling, half-strangled by ropes, unable even to scratch with their hands trussed behind their backs, those that had two hands left. Some had lost limbs or were badly burnt. He would have remembered them better, except for the blurring that settled like mist over his memory, pushing the worst thoughts further back. He thought of his own burnt hand after the skin had healed, and his pride in the scar that was proof, so his father said, that he was both brave and blessed.

'Thou hast fortune's mark, if e'er I seen it, and thou bist manful to have borne it well,' his father had said while tracing the print of the horseshoe's curve. Then he had made Kit raise his hand as if in a signal to stop. 'Hold thy hand up so, and thy luck will ne'er run out.'

Ever afterwards Kit had used the gesture in the best of his games: the duels he had fought with Will in their make-believe wars. Though Will was bigger, Kit had rarely lost. If ever he came close to being forced to submit, the power of the mark would always protect him, or so he believed – but only Will knew its secret.

He raised his hand from the water and stretched it flat, the scar remained, a pearly white. Its shape was like a crescent moon, and twinkling near it was another gold nugget even bigger than the last. He placed the find in his neck pouch and held his hand before his face, thinking of all his luck that must have fallen out to leave him indifferent, even to gold.

He had tripped over Will – that was how the burn had been caused, and at first, to his shame, he had blamed his older brother. Will had been running about in the village, and he close behind. They had been chasing in and out of doorways on the way home from dame school, but Will had stopped inside the smithy, sensing the danger too late, and Kit had plunged on regardless and taken a tumble near the forge. He had fallen with his hand against a searing shoe, just as the blacksmith was about to hammer it to shape, and only narrowly had he escaped with his fingers still whole. That was his luck, and to be chided, not beaten; Will's punishment had been worse. Then his pain had eased with his hand in a bucket, thrust under water, cooled just as now.

Kit bared his palm in the foaming stream. He was prodded with a stick, but did not react. He bent his head and stared down. The water was frothing like the flow in a leat, and rushing with it were memories of home: the smell of Orcheton coombe, its mud and grass, the heavy boughs of the walnut tree that skimmed the surface of the upper pool. And he imagined walking the worn-down drovers' track, hearing the pounding against the waterwheel, and the muffled rumble of the grinding stones. His mother was there in the kitchen, offering him a taste of freshly made jam: raspberry and apple, tart and sweet. Then he was with his sisters, collecting eggs from the coop, and his hand was deep in the warmth under the breast of a hen.

If he shed a few tears, no one would have known; the rain was falling in torrents.

He glanced round and saw one of the hirelings furiously scrabbling around a sluice upstream.

'*Oro, oro! Aqui! . . .*'

The man's shouting was lost beneath a sharp clap of thunder that ripped loud and rolled on. The deluge increased until all Kit could see was rain-streaked and greyed. It was lunacy to continue, but the gold had overwhelmed Lázaro's sense and his helpers' as well.

The Negro slaves toiled, almost naked, hacking away at the riverbank, causing great sections of earth to fall into the flow. The channels overran as they shovelled in grit. Even Lázaro was madly searching, lank hair dripping, bent over a trap. But watching the frenzy, Kit felt at peace, and the Indian who struck him made little impression. Kit did not turn or try to move. If he did not struggle, the shackles hurt less. He knew who was beating him: a small, wizened hireling with a beaded collar of seeds and bones, whose smile revealed the blackened stumps of teeth. The smile was one he preferred not to see. There was a time when he had held the man's whip, but such power as that had given him he had thrown away. He had lost his small liberties by trying to escape.

It had felt like flying: that moment of running, tearing through the jungle. Though he had known the risk, there had been joy in his blundering. His downfall had been the freeing of the slaves, and that was not from any noble motive – he was honest with himself – but because he recognised he could never last alone, and then he had wanted to live. Lázaro had been alerted by the smashing of the chains; noise carried far along the river valley. There had been no way to soften the sound, and Lázaro's dogs had soon hunted him down. Only one man managed to evade recapture for a while, and then the search had become a game, deliberately prolonged, while the Indians made sport with their tracking skills, driving the man down the valley, hemming him in against the river, until exhaustion overcame his will and eventually he dropped.

Kit hung his head. Lázaro made no secret of what had happened to his quarry; he wanted everyone to know, and to know the fault was Kit's. The man had been bound with vines, dragged bleeding to the water's edge, weighted with rocks and abandoned for the lizards to find: the alligators and caimans. Days later, all the slaves had been taken to see the little that was left, and Kit had shuffled with them, his ankles in fetters. But he did not remember *what* he had seen, the mist settled over that. Instead he thought of friends he had known much longer ago.

Why had he not been executed in Mexico? He should have died then. Some things were clearer, looking back. There were too many English prisoners to put to death all at once. The sanction of the Inquisition would have been needed for that, and the Inquisition was in Spain. Had anyone been taken there? He did not know. He remembered the crush of men in the Viceroy's dungeon, the last Englishmen he had seen. What had happened to them? Maybe they, too, had been auctioned off in the Viceroy's

Palace, then taken to places far away. The Spaniards probably thought that they would be no threat, scattered wide, and worked like slaves.

He had heard of no Englishman since the day he was sold, bought for his strength to row in a galley. And perhaps, afterwards, the Spaniards had supposed his spirit would be broken, and that was why he had been freed from his bonds, and sent out with Lázaro to find river gold in Panamá. Kit knew the way the Spaniards thought; it was beneath their dignity to be seen to work, and every settler needed overseers for his slaves. What better job for an Englishman to do? They believed he would not bolt because he was alone in a strange land, with no possible sanctuary and nothing to gain by running away, so why would he try?

But he could not live the Spanish way, he could not forget his English tongue, worship the saints in Latin and defer to peasants who had won titles through murder and pillage. He had been captured but not tamed. And now he understood why some of those Negroes that General Hawkins had taken had died on the *Jesus* for no clear reason. He was dying, just the same.

The lash struck him again but he did not care. The river was rising and he did not move. He stared at the commotion around the upper sluice.

Through the driving rain, beyond Lázaro and the slaves, he could see earth sliding fast down the side of the valley; it fell in scarlet streams. Cloudbursts sometimes caused the land to slip, and Kit imagined that might be happening, except that a man dropped down behind the tumbling dirt, and he was armed with a bow. Kit saw him clearly, and another, and another, some with clubs. The men crept closer, in the shallows, along the river's course. Who were they? Kit stood and watched, waiting to be shot by one of the archers. They were all African blacks and daubed with dyes, half-armoured and clothed in strange trappings and rags. Those without helmets had locks like manes or heads that were shaved. He had heard of bands of escaped slaves who lived wild in the mountains: *cimarrones*, the Spaniards called them – 'mountain-top dirt', the name implied. He supposed the marauders were *cimarrones* but no one else appeared to notice, until Lázaro turned and pelted screaming downstream.

The screaming ended as Lázaro was struck: a blow to the head made by a giant with a cudgel. The crack echoed once above the river's roar. The mess was like the spurting earth, and then Lázaro was gone beneath the bubbling flow. The slaves scrabbled round, dragging their chains. They lifted stones, and hurled them on top. Nothing remained visible beyond the water spouting up. But Kit saw one of the hirelings. The river carried him bobbing near the bank, banging against the boards not far from Kit's feet, turning the water even redder with the blood from his throat.

Kit looked up to see an invader drawing a bow, taking aim at his chest. He stood where he was and the ending was silent, drowned beneath the water's rush. He was surprised to still be standing. Then he looked round. A canoe was drifting away downriver, but rocking, unbalanced and half-hanging from it was the other Indian hireling. Everything paled. He did not want to die with his brains smashed out, or his neck half severed. He had hoped for an arrow clean through the heart. But another of the *cimarrones* was charging straight for him, wielding a sword. Kit seized the pouch from the cord around his neck and held it out, palm flat.

'Kill me quickly.'

He supposed that if he did not flinch it would soon be over. The man stared at his hand, seized the pouch and looked inside. Laughing, he threw it wide into the river. A raider approached. He had a club at his hip, and his lips had been disfigured by the scorch of a brand. He took Kit's head in his hands and held it close, so that Kit could see nothing but the scarred face of the man, and the brown flecks fraying in the whites of his eyes. But Kit sensed that the African with the sword was walking behind him. Voices were raised in a language he could not follow, though he imagined what was meant. He would get the sword in the back, and he prayed the strike would be high, not a thrust below the ribs that would leave him to die over days.

It was all he could do to stand and not struggle, breathing deeply to fight his dread, inhaling the smell of the man who would not let go of his face. Then he heard a sharp, loud, ringing blow – the sound of rock striking metal: the iron of his chains. He pitched forward freely and fell against the black man's chest, warm and wet with rain and sweat.

The man's arms were around him, tight and strong, and there was no pain at all.

10
Danger

'. . . As to danger, and the damage and destruction done by corsairs along the coast, and by outlaw negroes on land, the situation grows worse daily, for neither the barks of the Chagres River trade to the House at Cruces nor the overland pack-trains have been able to make their journeys without being assaulted and robbed . . .'

—From a plea for assistance made by the factor Cristóbal de Salinas, officer of the Crown, to King Philip II of Spain, written at Nombre de Dios, 20th May 1571

Ellyn looked out from her hut. Surely an enquiry about dinner would give her reason for walking along the beach? She could make certain that a broth was prepared to her father's liking, and, in the process of seeking out the cook, she might come within view of those at work on the *Kestrel*.

She put on the hat that she now wore everywhere outside, and chose a course by the provisions destined to be ferried to the newly launched pinnace. Her route would bring her to within a few yards of Will, and, if he wished to speak with her, then he could, and at the least he would be bound to be aware of her. She walked on and responded politely to the mariners who stopped and hailed her, keeping her face turned towards the cooking area, while catching sight of Will out of the corner of her eye. He had seen her, she was certain; she could tell by the turn of his head, though she made sure not to show it. Then, with a pang of frustration, she realised he was not about to come after her. But she would not show any concern. As she made her way along the beach she could hear him giving orders.

'Bring up that keg.'

'Aye, Will.'

'Let's have the water skins next . . .'

She expected Will to hail her at any moment, and was left disappointed when he did not. Why not? He should have been attentive. John Drake had announced that Richard Dennys would be remaining with her and her father on the island, so whatever the exploits that required guns on the *Kestrel*, Will would be able to pursue them without being impeded by the gentlemen. She would occupy the merchants and leave Will to do his adventuring – he owed her some thanks.

Having neared her objective, a cursory search convinced her that the cook was not to be found. So she retraced her steps, deciding that a visit to John Drake's hut would be in order, while at the same time taking her past Will once more. She needed to speak to John Drake about the leaks in the roof; her father had said as much that morning. She looked back along the shore while heading circuitously for her next destination. Will was conspicuous because he was tall. With his loose shirt untied at the neck, and the broad belt he wore at an angle over his hips, he looked far more lithe and vigorous than ever she could have imagined Peryn Fownes or Godfrey Gilbert. In the context of the enterprise, she was beginning to see qualities in Will that had passed unnoticed when they had both been in Plymouth. She saw how the men followed him, except for Francis Drake, of course, who was an experienced captain and older than most. Captain Drake must have been about thirty years of age, whereas Will was not much above her own age of twenty. Even so, the Captain conferred with him, and Will commanded the respect of the mariners; she thought more highly of him as a consequence.

She sensed he was watching, and she walked with deliberate poise, but he did not even acknowledge her. Instead, he picked up a rope as she sauntered by. She could not pass him again and say nothing.

'Master Doonan, I need to speak with you.'

Will put down the rope and strode towards her.

'What is it, Mistress Ellyn? As you can see, we are very busy.'

'This will only take a moment.' Her indignation rose at his hint that she was interrupting him. After the advances he had made towards her in England, she felt he owed her more consideration. She could not believe he was no longer interested – even if she was with him on Drake's enterprise when clearly he didn't want her to be. His coolness was galling. She spoke tight-lipped. 'My father is not in the best of health, and there are leaks in our roof.'

'Are the leaks over your beds?'

'No, but the damp makes the hut smell, and the floor is becoming muddy; my father's cloth is getting wet.' Will frowned, and that encouraged her to go on. 'Please do not suggest that we move aboard the *Swan* since the ship is about to be careened and we have been told it must be cleared.'

Will cocked his head.

'Is there anything else?'

'Since you ask, we are also short of water. One small barrel a day is not enough for us to clean and wash, as well as drink.'

'Mistress Ellyn.' Will took her arm and guided her a few paces away from the nearest men. She allowed him the liberty since the contact was pleasurable. It suggested a desire for more intimacy, just as she had suspected – a desire that she shared. What would he do next?

When he spoke again, his voice was low.

'If you require a roof without leaks and water for washing then you should have stayed in England.' He made to turn from her but she caught hold of his arm.

'That is no way to answer! The fact is I am here, and we cannot live in squalor!'

'You can live with smells and a bit of mud, and you can live without washing. We need fresh water aboard the *Kestrel*. Once we are gone, you will have more water from the mainland.'

'That is not good enough!' She sensed her voice rising and tried to moderate her tone. 'The roof needs to be repaired.'

'The roof will have to wait.'

'Are you refusing to help?' She looked at him incredulously. Surely he did not mean to brush her grievances aside? But he simply gave her a nod.

'Good day to you. I must be going.'

She drew a sharp breath and swallowed the urge to respond

curtly. Turning, she walked away as sedately as she could. Not long afterwards she became aware that one of the mariners was in her wake. Glancing round, she saw the man called Simon. Despite the patch over his eye, he had features she found appealing: soft, brown curly hair, and a bashful smile. He drew alongside.

''Tis a fine day, Mistress Ellyn.'

She was still smarting after the hurt of Will's rebuff, but she kept her reply light.

'Indeed, yes, though rather hot.' The fact that such a rough seaman should want to exchange remarks about the weather had the effect of making her feel much better. She beamed at him. 'I hope the calm will aid your sailing.'

'Aye, thank'ee. We should be goin' soon . . .'

'Simon!' An abrupt shout brought the young man's patter to a halt. 'Over here.'

She knew immediately that Will had called him away. With a mumbled apology Simon left her alone, but she resisted the temptation to look back over her shoulder.

She smiled and carried on walking.

One cannon shot was all it took – one blast from the fortified bulwark that protected the treasure house at Nombre de Dios, and Will knew that the Spaniards were not interested in peaceful trade, even trade kept secret. The warning confirmed what everyone aboard the *Kestrel* suspected: the Spaniards along the coast had no more need for English supplies; the treasure fleet had arrived bringing goods from Spain. There would be no more selling of smuggled Devon kerseys.

None of Drake's men were dismayed. It suited the Captain's

purpose to have the Spaniards show their colours. Hostility would be met with hostility. Will was glad to have left Ellyn at their hidden island base, even with Dennys as her companion – though whenever he reflected on how she might be faring, he was needled by an urge to return to her fast.

'The Chagres!' Drake had declared, jabbing his finger against a stolen chart at the point where that river met the sea to the north-west. 'Since the Spaniards will not invite us to their table, let us see what pickings we can find.'

'Rich pickings, I'll wager,' one of the mariners remarked. 'All those fineries and fancies from Spain for Peru.'

The Captain chuckled, and the rest grinned. They all relished the prospect of hunting for booty.

'Here, somewhere—' Drake made a sweep with his hand around Cartagena to the east '—Captain-General Flores de Valdés waits to entertain us with his Indies fleet.' Drake glanced up, and there were nods of understanding from those gathered round, Will included. It was a risk they all accepted. With the treasure fleet would be protection, perhaps as many as five Spanish warships to guard both shipping and the coast.

'We must show General Valdés that we can provide amusements of our own.' Drake smiled as everyone else laughed. They would have sport with the Spaniards, and it would be on Drake's terms. They would come to be feared, but not as barbarians. The Captain required discipline, and they were all agreed: they would not use violence unless given good cause. Provided the Spaniards acquiesced, then no harm would come to them, but if any resisted, they would be shown no mercy.

At the first opportunity, Drake cautioned the Spaniards. On the way to the Chagres, a frigate was taken, but only after a trumpet-blast had called the ship to parley, and the Spaniards had erred by trying to stop the English boarding. Defiance carried a price; it had been met with gunfire and a hail of bolts and arrows, enough to bring a few Spaniards down and put the rest to flight. And since the Spaniards had chosen to scuttle away, Drake made certain their return would be equally inglorious. He ordered that the frigate be stripped and gutted, its sails spoiled and its boat stoved in. Then he wrote the Spaniards a polite note:

> *'Done by the English, who are well disposed if there be no cause to the contrary; if there be cause, we will be devils rather than men.'*

They had triggered alarm along the treasure coast, and they would strike next where they were least expected.

Will heard the cry: an owl-like screech. It meant Drake's group had surrounded the warehouse and were set to attack. That left the Spaniards inside the inn to be dealt with, and he hoped they would be sound asleep, lulled by the belief that they had little to fear so far up the Chagres, deep inland. He opened his covered lantern a slit, enough to see that a bar had been left beneath a window nearby. The Spaniards had been careless. The window was open in the sweltering heat. He gently closed the window shutters, and then slotted the bar across. He looked round. Behind him, Hix beckoned with a shadowy fist. Now only the inn door could be used for escape, unless the Spaniards tried to jump from the balcony above, and Hix would be waiting for them if they did.

Will gave his answering call: a sharp whistle between his teeth. With lantern flashes he signalled to the men by the corral, further on up the path. Glints flashed back. The three others sent with him were huddled by the door, and in their shadow-shapes were the traces of match cords glowing: pin-pricks of light – signs that their firearms were primed and prepared. He knelt beneath the window, and set the darkened lantern down.

Everyone was ready.

Cicadas thrummed. Frogs along the riverbank made strange clinks and whines. Somewhere in the jungle an animal howled. The forest was black – a vast blank wilderness in which Kit could be near or far or nowhere at all.

Will breathed deeply.

Suddenly a shot cracked out, sharp as a thunderclap, triggering a frenzy of flapping in the treetops above, and then a rush of stamping from the direction of the corral. The drum of hooves rumbled towards him along the path. He reached for his cresset: a fire pike topped with tar-soaked rags. Shouts rose from inside the inn. He heard a mule galloping past, hurtling down towards the river jetty. Others followed, milling wild. There were rattling sounds, becoming louder, behind the inn door. The next instant it swung wide, releasing a glaring stream of orange light. Mules flashed by him. A Spaniard dashed from the inn wearing only a shirt. The man brandished a sword, shouting as he waved to try and slow the stampede. '*Mira! Las mulas! . . .*'

'Go!' Will yelled.

His three friends roared and charged for the doorway. Another shot cracked out, hammering against stone. Will heard broken cries and the clang of metal. He opened his lantern and lit a rag end from the cresset. The fire pike flared as he swung it round, both hands on the shaft, to see the Spaniard outside the doorway turning, and Hix running to head him off.

Will lunged, sweeping the cresset up and then down at the moment the Spaniard weaved to get past. The man slashed out at Hix, but the fire-head caught him, glancing across his legs. The Spaniard staggered and Hix struck, knocking the sword from the man's grasp. Hix wheeled. Will ran nearer. The Spaniard sprawled in the dirt with his shirt tail in flames.

'*Dios! Socorro!*' The man screamed and writhed. He jumped up, then fell again as Will thrust at him with the pike. Hix jabbed his sword against the Spaniard's chest, pinning him to the ground. The man's wailing became a piercing shriek. Despite the pressure of the sword he beat dementedly at the flames. Smoke rose from his hips. Hix laughed.

'*Socorro!*' the Spaniard screeched.

Will threw the cresset down, kicked dirt over the man, trampled on his shirt and rolled him over with his boots – and if he trod on the Spaniard it was more than he deserved.

'He's roasted enough,' he muttered.

Then Hix joined in the stamping with a few hard kicks.

'Damn him.'

More shots sounded from the inn's upper rooms. Will held his knife to the Spaniard's neck.

'Get up,' he commanded.

The man stood and stumbled. He winced and clutched at his ruined shirt, eyes rolling towards Will.

'*Inglés!*' he gasped.

Will pushed the man towards the inn, past the flaming cresset on the ground and a toppled candle-stand inside the entrance, over broken pots and strewn baggage.

'Move!' He forced his prisoner along the hallway, pressing the knife-blade flat against the Spaniard's neck. When he reached an open door, he craned round to peer inside. Beyond was darkness and an evil stench, one that he knew: the *Jesus* had carried such a smell from Africa, deep in her hold.

He threw a word into the darkness – a word loaded with faint hope.

'Kit?'

The clink of a chain sounded close to his feet. He stared down.

There were people on the floor. He could sense their breathing, feel their heat But there was no answering voice. No response from anyone.

The Spaniard hung back. Will pushed him away and towards another doorway that was glowing with light. Inside, he found Glub the quartermaster with his caliver levelled at a dozen or more captives. They were huddled beneath a large table. Most were servants by the look of their skin. All were male. Will shoved the Spaniard down to join them. The man groaned.

'Sit quiet,' Glub barked, and aimed his matchlock at the Spaniard's belly.

Will glanced round.

'Where are the others?'

In the corner of the room was an open staircase. A heavy thud shook the ceiling. Glub raised his brows and jerked back his chin.

'Up there.'

Will ran up the steps. He could hear a Spaniard shouting. At the top was a passage with arched openings off; drapes were hanging from most, hacked and ripped. Through one of the arches he saw patch-eyed Simon and the bowman, Morrys. They were both crouched down. Facing them was a Spaniard with an arquebus in his hands.

'*Quédese!* . . .' The Spaniard yelled while edging away. Will saw everything in an instant: the window near the Spaniard and the firearm he held, the open chest by his friends, the scattered pearls on the floor. He darted along the passage, through the next archway, and dived inside the adjoining room.

At the end of the room were shuttered doors – beyond would be the balcony. Will hurled himself at the doors. At the moment he crashed through there was an explosion of noise. Then he heard Morrys howl, 'Bastard! Bastard! . . .'

Will staggered, veered and saw the Spaniard at the next window in the midst of tumbling out. The man landed on the balcony, and then leapt for the balustrade. Morrys roared from the window behind. As Will reached the Spaniard, Morrys sprang out. Will grabbed the man by the shoulders and wrenched him hard back. Morrys punched the man in the face, again and again.

'He's shot Simon.'

'Let me at him.' Will drew his knife and held it to the man's throat, feeling rage surging inside him. He turned to Morrys. 'Go to Simon,' he rasped. 'Help him.'

He marched the Spaniard back through the shattered doors, across the room and into the passage, treading on pearls as he made for the stairs. Then he saw Simon coming close, dragging a chest with a broken hasp. More pearls were spilling out.

Will stared at his friend.

'Are you hurt?'

'Only a knock.' Simon grinned.

Morrys joined them, bent under the weight of full saddlebags over his shoulders. His brow was bleeding, but he managed a smile.

'That shot at Simon were dismal-bad.' He lurched up to Will's prisoner and slammed his fist against the man's ribs. 'Lucky for you, Spaniard.' He turned to Will. 'Bastard was hiding under the bed.' With a kick, Morrys sent the man sprawling. The Spaniard finished in a heap at the bottom of the steps.

Will bounded after him and called back.

'Take everything. Empty the place.'

He forced the Spaniard towards the table while sounds of destruction rang out: smashing and clattering as objects were tossed down the stairs.

The prisoners were quiet. None of them looked at Will. They watched the muzzle of Glub's caliver, and the mounting pile of their plundered possessions. But from the hallway someone was calling.

Will made for the shouts. A lad ran up to him, a youngster from Drake's party. The lantern he carried was shaking in his grasp.

'The Captain's finished and asks that you leave, sir.'

'Has he found much?' Will demanded.

'Rich cloth, wine and spices . . .' The lad's eyes widened. 'There be oil and soap, too, but we'll be leavin' that since the *Kestrel* can't hold no more . . .'

'Has all the cloth been taken?'

The youth appeared puzzled.

'Aye, sir. All the silks and linens.' He spoke urgently. 'The Captain says you should come right away and leave the lodgers comfortable.'

Will's smile was grim.

'He said that?'

'I'sooth he did.'

Will nodded.

'Then help us do it.' He called for Hix, strode back into the room and beckoned to the others. The pile had grown. 'Heap the lot outside: curtains, bedding, everything. We'll take the best and leave the Spaniards a fine bonfire. So they won't catch cold,' he added, to a chuckle from Glub.

Morrys and Simon set to work, their belts bristling with the weapons they had seized. Will marched up to the prisoners and drew his sword.

He searched for the Spaniard who had shot at Simon. The man's head was down, but Will recognised his lank hair. He held the sword blade under the man's bruised chin, bringing it up until the Spaniard raised his face. The man's eyes were puffed up and screwed closed; his teeth chattered though his jaws were clamped tight. Sweat glistened in his stubble. Will thought of what he might do. He snarled as he pressed the blade against the man's skin.

'Do you know of any English prisoners? *Presos ingleses?*' He had learnt what to ask. '*Dónde están?*' He pressed the blade harder. Then he let the man speak.

'*No, no!*' the man screamed, eyes rolling. '*No ingleses!*'

He heard Hix very close.

'Shall we tie 'em up?'

Will stepped back and shook his head. He had made up his mind.

'Strip them.' Will looked round the room, at a broken lute on the floor and the hangings dragged from the walls, smashed crocks and the rifled belongings. 'Burn all their clothes.'

His eyes settled on a large ring with a multitude of keys. It hung from a hook on the damp-stained wall. He grabbed the keys and strode out. Through the chaos in the hallway he made for the dark doorway he had peered into first. He threw the door wide. By the dim light that streamed in he saw a score or more faces looking up: all were black.

He weighed the keys in his hand. Then with a shout he threw them inside. 'Free yourselves!'

Morrys staggered by hauling a blanket bulging with plate.

A fire already raged on the path beyond the inn. It cast a brilliant light into the hall that shone from points across the floor; Will bent towards one and picked up a pearl, then as many others as he could quickly reach. He charged outside.

Sheets and mattresses were going up in flames – every item of fabric from the upstairs rooms. Morrys and Simon had hold of the chest. Hix dashed past with his arms full of clothes, and then cast them all on the fire. The messenger lad was on his way, staggering bent double with a box on his back. Will took weapons and the blanket stuffed with silver. The rest would burn. The Spaniards would be left naked with nothing but oil and soap.

'Let's go!' he called to his friends.

Will ran with them down to the jetty, and his spirits soared with every step. They had shamed the Spaniards and made themselves rich. Drake would be well satisfied.

The pearls in his pocket would be for Ellyn.

11
Sounds

'. . . The isle full of noises,
Sounds and sweet airs, that give delight, and hurt not.
Sometimes a thousand twangling instruments
Will hum about mine ears, and sometimes voices
That if I then had waked after long sleep
Will make me sleep again . . .'

—The Tempest *by William Shakespeare,*
Act III, Scene 2

Panamá, the Americas
May 1571

What was he doing? Ellyn's attention had been caught by the sight of someone twirling about on the beach: a man possessed of an elegant shirt, a sword and good legs – a man with dark hair fetchingly tied back with a red ribbon. Richard Dennys was engaged in a duel with an invisible opponent at the edge of the sea. He was showing off, she decided, while bending her head once more over her sewing, and she would not be distracted by the performance.

But his calves were very fine.

She stole another glance at him between stitches. From her position under the shade of a straggling tree, Ellyn was confident he could not see her clearly, so what could be the harm in taking an occasional peek? Master Dennys had the sort of physique it was difficult not to look at. A few ostentatious leaps drew her gaze back to his legs. Were he not so vain, she might have considered him more seriously. But what sort of man would wear black crossed-garters over bright red hose? She pondered on this, until she realised to her consternation that he was walking towards her.

Master Dennys proceeded with an expression of happy astonishment, as if he had only just become aware of Ellyn's presence under the tree (something she very much doubted). His approach sent her into a flurry of stitching, though a few surreptitious glances informed her that he was striding energetically across the sand, and next that he was almost beside her, chest heaving and breathing deeply. She bent her head, conscious that this small show of indifference was hardly likely to be convincing; so it proved.

'Ah, Mistress Ellyn!' he addressed her heartily. 'I am pleased to find I have an audience, and yet more delighted that my observer is the lady to whom my practice is dedicated.'

Ellyn made an effort to continue with her needlework without any hint of having been distracted. Threads were pulled and examined diligently.

'I hope that is said in jest, Master Dennys, since I can assure you I was not watching. What practice?'

Master Dennys drew his sword again with a flourish. The action was so quick that Ellyn flinched.

'This, fair mistress,' he said, slashing his blade repeatedly above her head. The result left her cowering beneath a shower of sliced leaves.

He laughed.

'The cut and thrust of the *spada da lato*, as I am sure you must have noticed since your fair visage was turned towards me while I was rehearsing my principal attacks.'

Squinting up, Ellyn was perturbed to see the knowing look on his face. She might have been keen for Will to think she found the gentleman diverting, but she certainly had no wish for Master Dennys himself to suppose the same.

She brushed away the leaf parings, shook her sewing and took off her hat, tipping it up and smacking it vigorously in a way she trusted would make plain her exasperation.

'I may have been resting my eyes. I was not aware of any attacks.'

With some alarm, she saw Master Dennys raise his sword once more, but it was in the manner of a salute, blade upright before his face. And then, to her relief, he sheathed it and dropped on one knee beside her. She ignored him and searched for her needle.

'The lady feigns disregard,' he proclaimed, somewhat theatrically, thought Ellyn while pulling her sewing about, convinced that she had pinned the needle through before brushing the fabric clean of leaves. How tiresome.

'But the courtier understands her meaning,' he went on. 'A knight can expect no display of interest from the object of his devotion. He must be content with the slightest acknowledgement.'

Having located the needle at last, Ellyn stabbed it into the cloth, brows raised and shaking her head, in a manner which she hoped would convey her disdain. She had a suspicion that Richard Dennys was mocking her, and that did nothing to lessen her irritation. As his pronouncements continued, she became aware that he was peering ever more closely at her face.

'The arch of a brow,' he said.

Ellyn lowered her brows and shot a contemptuous sneer in his direction. It elicited a smile.

'A glance,' he added.

Ellyn scowled as she made a misplaced stitch. Now she would have to unpick it. She pulled the sewing closer to her eyes, and at the same moment Master Dennys took hold of a corner as if to admire it. The result was a stretched piece of fabric that neither could do with as they wanted. Ellyn jerked the sewing from his hands.

Master Dennys appeared unperturbed.

'The knight remains true regardless of reward,' he asserted, gripping his sword hilt instead. 'This is your privilege as a lady: to receive loyalty and give nothing.'

He shuffled nearer while Ellyn jabbed at the offending stitch. She hoped that her sigh would convince him that this was not the way either to amuse her, or win her regard. Her vexation was increasing, but the only discernible effect was to make Master Dennys more insistent.

'My sword is your protection because my allegiance is to you.'

Her response was crisp.

'I am sure you need have no concern for my protection, Master Dennys. I have the *Swan's* guns, Captain Drake's brother and six other men here to safeguard me.'

'Ah, but these men are not true gentlemen,' Master Dennys

countered, without any hint of having registered a rebuff. 'They are not knights in spirit. They have no proper training in the art of combat. The arquebus and musket are their weapons of choice. They would rather trust to firearms, though these weapons are as likely to blow powder in their faces as to hit a target by design.'

Ellyn frowned, and this was not conducive to her attempts to re-thread the needle. Why was Master Dennys blathering about firearms? She was not in the least interested. Then he startled her once more by whipping out his knife. The thread shook just as she had it in the needle's eye.

'*Fie!*' she muttered under her breath, then lowered her hands and glared at her tormentor.

Master Dennys had hold of a round, plum-sized green fruit, and was toying with his knife as though he was about to peel it. He waved the blade in the air.

'I prefer to be certain that when I engage, I strike.' Suddenly he stuck the knife in the fruit's skin. 'And when I cut, I disable.' The blade must have been sharp; in a relaxed stroking motion he cut the fruit clean in half. It was full of moist seeds which he nonchalantly proceeded to scrape out. 'So be not afraid. You are at no risk while I am by your side.'

Ellyn snorted. She was not afraid, and she was certainly in no need of protection by a man whose valour was proven in combat against fruit. When Master Dennys offered her one of the halves, she declined dismissively.

'I would recommend you try this,' he persisted. 'The flesh is soft and delicate. And behold its colour!' He held the half before her eyes. 'I would liken its tint to a maiden's blush.'

It was a striking pink, Ellyn acknowledged, and willed herself not to redden.

Master Dennys moved the fruit under his nose and then sensuously near to his lips, closing his eyes, allowing lips and flesh to touch in the action of a delicate kiss.

'Are you not tempted?' he asked.

Ellyn could not stop the heat from rushing to her cheeks, though she was trying hard to remain aloof. She fiddled with her sewing while Dennys continued in a deep, honeyed voice.

'No? Then I shall describe the taste.'

He had taken a bite; Ellyn knew it, though she was determined not to watch. She could hear his murmurings of satisfaction.

'Ahh . . . It is ambrosial . . .'

Out of the corner of her eye she caught his lascivious look.

'I believe this might be to your father's liking,' he said, and immediately he had her attention.

She turned, and he stared back.

'I hear he has lost his appetite,' he said.

Ellyn blanched. It was true that her father had not been eating properly for weeks, and her concern made her reconsider her choices. She could keep Master Dennys at the distance she would have preferred, or she could be more agreeable and accept what he was offering. She saw that he had more of the fruits in a small bag. Perhaps they might appeal to her father. Yet how would she know if he had no opportunity to try?

'I might take one of the fruits after all, if you have another,' she said graciously.

Master Dennys smiled.

'If you will hold out your hand . . .'

Ellyn did so, but he merely scrutinised her palm as if he was expecting something more from her. She steeled herself.

'Thank you, Master Dennys.'

'As you *desire*, Mistress Ellyn.'

Ellyn struggled against the impulse to pull back. He touched her palm like a fortune teller and stretched out her fingers as if he was measuring them for a glove. Slowly he brought one of the fruits close, and lingeringly wrapped her hand around the skin.

As soon as the fruit was in her grasp Ellyn snatched it away. Master Dennys might have good legs but she found his manner quite repellent. She looked up at the beach rather than face him again. Then her mouth opened.

'Master Drake!'

John Drake was about sixty paces away, beside the great beached hull of the *Swan*. The ship had been heeled over in shallow water to allow for her cleaning, and Ellyn had been vaguely aware of the men working on her all morning. But she had not expected to see Master Drake among them, particularly not looking as if he had been there for some time. He should have been with her father. She stared harder to be sure. But there was no doubt: John Drake's build was distinctive – he was as square as a block – and he was the only man with red hair who had been left behind on the island.

Guilt added to Ellyn's vexation. She should have been watching. She had promised her father she would return as soon as John Drake left their hut. Ellyn stood hurriedly and wrapped up her sewing. What if her father had been calling for help? With barely a glance at Master Dennys, she dropped a small curtsey, offered a curt farewell and left.

*

Prickling with heat under the weight of her kersey dress, Ellyn turned away from the *Swan* and strode in the opposite direction along the shore. Her shoes filled with sand in her effort to make haste, and struggling with her footing did nothing to improve her temper. She made for the largest hut amongst the small group of palm-frond shelters – one she shared with her father on Kestrel Island, and which had recently been distinguished, at his insistence, by the positioning of a breech-loading gun near the opening that served as a door. This was her father's 'house'. On approaching, she eyed the pile of round shot next to the gun's box-carriage. She could have sworn it had grown larger in the hours since she had left – on her father's orders, she assumed. What if he had asked for black powder as well? She prayed none had been provided – she did not relish the prospect of her father attempting the art of gunnery.

Ellyn flapped peevishly at a few biting flies, small as dust but more troublesome than fleas. She was beset by trials beyond her control: heat and sand, guns and insects, her father's diet and the drivel of Richard Dennys. Could the day get any worse? She prepared to duck under the sackcloth that screened the entrance to the hut. There was no sound from inside. Her anxiety increased; so did her pique at the prospect of being chastised. What would she say? She bit her lip and frowned.

Then she saw her father, and smiled.

Nicholas Cooksley was bent over his account book, wearing a dressing gown, sitting at a table improvised from planks and barrels. Surrounding him were bales of tarpaulin-draped cloth, stacked up from the sand almost as high as the palm-thatch roof.

He had the aura of a relic set in a strangely padded niche, faded, tattered, but still requiring veneration.

Ellyn's first view was of the top of her father's head; it was blotched and ringed by cobwebby wisps of bedraggled grey hair. Then, when he looked up, she noticed that his colouring was high in patches over his cheeks, becoming most intense at the end of his bulbous nose. The rest of his face was mottled and sallow. His eyes were yellowed and glazed, widening as soon as they settled on her, and then quickly narrowing as she approached.

'What foolishness is this?' he demanded. 'You have been gone over an hour!' The greeting ended on a querulous note. 'Where have you been?'

Ellyn put her sewing on a box. She noticed a pike and halberd stacked nearby, along with a sword and mace, breastplate and helmet. The armour was for her father, she presumed, though she doubted whether it would fit, even given his recent loss in weight. The weapons worried her. She sat opposite him.

'I was only sewing,' she answered with as much casual ease as she could muster. 'And I am sure I was not that long. You asked me to go, if you recall, so you could speak to Master John Drake . . .'

Her father waved his hand.

'Yes, yes. I cannot remain silent when I have been *robbed*.'

What did he mean by that? she wondered. She sighed inwardly and made an effort to appease by asking, 'Robbed? How?'

'Blatantly robbed.' He riffled through his book and flicked at the pages. 'This is the proof. There are two bales missing: forty yards of Cullompton kerseys dyed gallant yellow. Look. Appraise. Read for yourself . . .' Dramatic gestures made it plain that she was expected to be convinced. His manner became more whingeing.

'I should have been vigilant. Yet how can I safeguard anything when you keep wandering off?'

'But you told me . . .' she began in defence.

'Do not argue!'

Ellyn's indignation was drowned beneath a burst of violent shouting.

'Be silent when I am talking! How often must I remind you? I should be watching over my goods, not worrying over you.'

She took a breath. She would not rise to him.

'But you need not be concerned . . .'

'Need not! Go to!' He huffed and puffed.

Ellyn listened, determined not to be provoked. She would allow his bluster to blow itself out.

He thumped the table, making everything on it bounce: book, inkwell, jug, bowl and trencher. A candlestick toppled over.

'Tush! There . . .' Suddenly his eyes rolled. He looked shocked, and that alarmed her. He stood unsteadily and shuffled round, seizing her arm. 'Do you not hear the Spaniards?' he whispered.

All that Ellyn could detect was a sound typical of most afternoons on the island: the distant roll of thunder.

''Tis only a storm, dear Father, somewhere far away.'

He lurched from her towards the gauze-covered window and wrenched the fabric aside.

'If that is thunder, where is the lightning? Where are the clouds and rain? No. No . . .' He stared wildly at her. 'The enemy is close, and you must stay here where you are safe.'

'I am always near,' she said with a smile, but it disguised her concern. What was he talking about?

He took hold of her by the shoulder.

'What use is near if I cannot see you?'

She touched the puffy hand that was digging most painfully into the base of her neck, though he did not lessen his grip.

'I heard one of the savages screaming only paces away from this place,' he muttered against her ear.

Ellyn turned to face him, holding his watery gaze.

'A bird, most probably,' she said with deliberate levity. 'One of the creatures that make such noises. The trees are full of them.'

'Do not question me!' He leaned over her and bellowed. 'How can you know what I heard?' Stumbling, he leaned on the planks for support, and Ellyn willed him to sit down while stifling the urge to suggest he should. She knew his moods. In a rage he became perverse. What could she say?

He shook and raved.

'Always contradicting. Never heeding . . .' Then he stopped and gazed at her intently. Had his fury broken? She believed she could detect a return to lucidity in his look, but that hope soon faded with the shifts in his expression. He appeared bewildered, then fearful. His eyes bulged as the blood drained from his face.

'There are threats all around.' He held her again, not painfully this time, but with a trembling grasp. 'We must have a palisade and sentries. I have told John Drake, but he agrees and does nothing. Who will take action? Who will dig the defences? Must I do everything myself?'

'Of course not.' Ellyn struggled not to be curt. 'I am sure Master Drake will help as soon as he is able, but he is breaming the *Swan*. The cleaning is necessary.'

'I know what he says! And do not tell me again.' He began another rant. 'What use is this burning of barnacles if we need to escape? What if we are attacked? We should have a fort and a moat . . .'

Ellyn twisted round. She would not confront him and see his fury grow worse. She cast about for any distraction. On the table, the fallen candlestick lay embedded in the congealed remains of his dinner. In fact, as she realised when she looked more closely, the meal had hardly been touched.

'Oh, Father, you have not eaten!'

There was no need to exaggerate her concern; she had never known her father show such a sustained disinterest in food before. What was wrong with him?

'Would you like something else?' she asked, and remembered the fruit that Richard Dennys had given her. 'I have this.' she added, and held out the green offering.

'A fruit?' The reaction was not promising. Her father wrinkled his pitted nose, turned his back and hobbled over to his stool, slumping onto it with a wince.

'A pox on all fruit!' he growled. 'My bowels have been scoured by a surfeit of pips.'

Ellyn lowered her eyes. Was there anything she could do that would not start him railing? Now he was shouting so loudly she was tempted to cover her ears.

'I need meat!' He yelled. 'I am a man, not a slug!'

She picked up the candlestick and examined the mess left behind.

'But this was fish!'

'It was not cooked.'

She had no wish to contradict him, but this inaccuracy was so great she felt compelled to correct it.

'This fish was charred over a fire!'

He shook his head with a shudder that set his sagging chin quivering.

'I like my fish poached in milk, as you well know.' His lips puckered with petulance.

'But there is no milk!' How could he expect milk? What sense was there in such thinking? She tried to reason with him. 'We are on an island . . .'

'Excuses! Evasion!' His bawling cut her short. 'Everyone talks. No one listens. I am surrounded by idiots and thieves.'

Ellyn was stung. What had she done to warrant such denigration?

'Oh, Father, do not say that of me.'

'You may not be a thief, but you have shown yourself a dolt. All the rest here are knaves. Look at this.' The account book was thrust towards her. 'Read it!' he commanded. 'Go on!'

Ellyn stared blankly at the columns of figures while her father's muttering rumbled on.

'Why is it always so cursed hot. Has someone stolen the breezes as well? Where is the air?'

She looked up to see him lumbering over to one of the piles of cloth. He began poking at the bales, peering at the lead seals, sputtering like a smouldering firework. 'Swindlers and cheats. Vermin . . . Lice . . .'

Ellyn wondered whether she should intervene. Amidst his grumblings were shrill exclamations: 'Gone! . . . Purloined! . . .'

She moved nearer to him and sat on his bed, patting it invitingly.

'Please rest, so that I may better study these records. Perhaps I should read, while you indicate what is missing?'

With a pronounced sigh he turned about, gesturing in a display of irritation. But then he dropped down heavily on the pallet, leaving Ellyn with the impression that he had actually been longing to rest his legs. Shaking his stick at the cloth he answered her gracelessly.

'Do so then. Declaim the whole cargo if you must. Make an oration of it! 'Twill put nothing right.'

Ellyn plumped up a pillow behind his back, and tried to ignore the unsavoury odour she noticed once he was close to her. What was it? Decaying shellfish? Before his grunts and mumblings could find better expression, she started to read from the book aloud: 'One half-bolt tawny coat-weight fustian two and one half yards . . .'

A snort and a prod at a bale confirmed that this item was present. The process was repeated with several more entries, and soon his noises and gesticulations became less frequent. His head drooped, and his breathing assumed the grinding rhythm of shallow snoring.

Ellyn hummed. Her eyes settled on his neck and on a large swelling clearly visible, along with a rash of angry blotches and folds of sagging skin. Beneath the dark smudge of a purplish vein she believed she could detect the quiver of his pulse, but there was no steadiness to it. She fell silent.

She knew her father was ill, but not seriously sick, surely? He was not feverish, after all. She worried about him, but she doubted the wisdom of alerting anyone else. The *Swan* had no physician, and the mariners would be apprehensive if there was any suspicion of disease, not that she believed he had any threatening contagion. His maladies were gout and bad humour, compounded by the climate and poor diet. But what could she do? He should never have come. He was so irritable, he was impossible. And why did he constantly berate her? She was blamed for everything he found wrong, however unreasonably. Did he want her to leave him? Let him stand sentinel alone over his precious cloth, and dig his own moat if he chose to. Since she annoyed him so much, perhaps he would be happier for that.

She fumed silently while his snores deepened, becoming interspersed with gurgles and wheezes. Her duty was to care for him, though she was in the grip of an urge to turn her back on him totally. She got up and looked down. He had not stirred, and with his chin on his chest, and his soft wisps of tousled hair, he looked as defenceless as a nestling. Like that, he troubled her conscience. She slipped out in a fit of defiance.

Ellyn was in no mood to talk to anyone. She walked away, leaving the huts far behind, and the *Swan* further off. Towards the end of the beach was a fringe of mangrove trees, and she made for this place, where at least she could hope for some solitude in peace. The sea was turquoise, and the sky slate-blue, while the small humps of other islands feathered across the horizon in a streak. The view was soothing.

At the edge of the sand she stopped, having picked her way among the usual detritus: bleached branches and husks in a thin tide-line of weed – there were coral fragments and many small, pretty shells. She collected a few and thought of a likeness. Was she not like a sea-creature inside a shell much the same? She had been encased by her upbringing, tossed by the world's currents and now she was washed up, all but alone on a desolate shore. The profundity of this musing pleased her at first, until she recognised it as self-pity, overblown and conceited, and that made everything worse.

When would the *Kestrel* come back? What had happened to Francis Drake and his men? She had tried to suppress her fears about Will, but at that moment she fervently prayed he was well and safe. He had been gone for too long, and she regretted the petty friction that had developed between them. She could barely remember what had been the cause – something about leaks in her shelter and a shortage of water. How had that discord come about? She should never have allowed it. When he returned they would be reconciled. She would welcome him warmly and try to make amends. Ellyn reached for another shell, only to see it covered by sudden deep shadow.

The shadow's shape was startling, like the spectre of a man . . .

She looked up, and reeled in horror.

A giant stood near her; another man was not far away. They were fearsome, black and hideously strange: dark angels as she had imagined them from pictures of the Apocalypse, but manifest, real and drawing closer. She froze, petrified, wanting to run but simply staring – at their frayed clothes and peculiar armour – at the gleaming gorget over the nearest man's throat. His bare chest was scarred in long puckered lines, and she could see the muscles of his lean, flat stomach. His cheeks were daubed and his hair half-shaved. He had something writhing in his hand that he was holding out, as if for her to take. What was it? A lobster. Her impulse was to turn and plough through the sand. But where could she go before they caught her? And then. What then? She could not think. What if she screamed? No one else would hear. She was too far away from the huts and the mariners. The man with the lobster was approaching. She took a step back. The creature's thrashing appalled her. Should she speak? He would not understand. But she should try. She must try. When she found her voice it sounded strong, though she did not know how – inside, she was quaking.

'What do you want?'

The giant with the lobster dropped it into a crude open-weave basket, and then he dangled the basket from a length of twine. He extended his arm as he advanced to a point where the thing almost brushed against her dress.

Ellyn spread her hands, hoping that he would understand her confusion. What did he want? She took another step back and stopped. She would not run and encourage them to chase her. The man moved his free hand closer to her skirts. The gesture was shameful. What did he mean by it? She could barely believe that he would actually dare touch her. She stared at his hand as he pinched a fold of her dress, knowing that now she could not get away; he had her in his grasp. She should have run, but it was too late.

He rubbed the fabric between his fingers, stroking it slowly. She was faint with shock. No man would ever seize a woman's skirts, unless . . . *unless*. She would not consider it. Let him do no more than feel the cloth, if that pleased him. She looked at his face searching for some compassion with which to plead. His eyes were depthless; she could see no pity in them. She glanced again at his hand, and he let go of her. Her breathing was sharp. She tried to control it, not to show relief. She would not bolt. Not yet. He pointed at his chest. What did he want? She trembled as dread possibilities sprang to her mind. But at least he was no longer touching her. He gestured afresh, from her skirts to his chest: his bare chest. She did not know what he was asking, but she could recognise something he needed. She looked back into his eyes and kept her terror contained.

'Please wait.'

Ellyn turned and walked briskly away. She kept her back straight and made no attempt to run. She did not look round, or shout, or try to catch anyone's attention. Her object was to demonstrate that she was not afraid, and once she reached the group of huts, she gained in confidence. What had she to fear? The black men had done her no harm, they had even offered her a lobster – the recognition of that determined her actions. She made direct for her father's house, and crept behind the canvas screening off her own room. Her father remained undisturbed; she could hear his loud snoring. She gathered up a length of kersey: the remains of the roll she had used for her own dress. It was as much as she could carry. With the cloth in her arms she began to retrace her steps. No one challenged her or appeared to notice. Before she had gone far she saw the two wild man approaching. Then she heard shouts.

Some of the mariners were running towards her; there were others further behind, she was conscious of their calling. She glimpsed the men from around the *Swan* pelting headlong across the shore. She kept going. If she could reach the black men first, a crisis might be averted. They were quite close, though standing still. From somewhere behind her back, she heard Richard Dennys yelling madly, 'Stop, dear lady! Get back! You are in the way!'

In the way of what? She turned and saw him crouching behind

a palm trunk with a caliver in his hands. It was pointing unsteadily in her direction.

'Hold your fire, Master Dennys,' she said curtly. 'And put that weapon down lest you injure me!'

Unperturbed, she continued walking. She was sure even Master Dennys would not be foolish enough to attempt to shoot past her.

The giant with the lobster laid the basket on the sand. Ellyn drew near him and set the cloth alongside. Instantly the man bent to examine what she had brought. His companion had a bow, she observed, and an arrow ready to fire, as if that would be any use against loaded matchlocks. The giant who had felt her skirts was now rubbing the kersey – smelling it, pulling and twisting the cloth. Apparently satisfied, he slung the roll over his shoulder.

A gruff bellow made Ellyn turn. She did so without thinking, without even realising it was her father until she saw him staggering along the beach. But she knew him straightaway, despite the helmet shadowing his eyes, and the bouncing breast plate half over his belly. He was brandishing a pike, and for a harrowing moment she supposed he was about to attempt a charge. The weapon wavered as he thrust it forward. He hunched his shoulders, head down. His legs moved. But Ellyn was the one who began to sprint.

'Father!'

She dashed towards him as he collapsed.

Two weeks later, the *Swan* was back afloat. Ellyn sat near the opening that formed a window in her hut, and saw the ship at anchor a little way off from the beach. Thunderclouds towered in the sky. Waves sparkled and were shadowed in patches. The elements seemed very close. The house had so little substance that, even inside, Ellyn felt nothing was shut out. The sand and the sea – the gusts of fresh air, and the fiery light of the sun – they all touched her senses, and yet all seemed remote.

In the lee of the *Swan*, a much smaller craft was moored alongside.

The *Kestrel* had returned only a few hours before. Together with Richard Dennys, John Drake and the few mariners left with them, she had rushed across the sand to witness the event and join in a welcome that had been overflowing with joy. But now, in the aftermath, her happiness was subdued, and the sight of Will approaching only deepened her wistful mood.

He walked briskly, with conviction, wearing the white shirt and leather jerkin that he had worn when the *Kestrel* arrived. But she noticed, as he came nearer, that his beard was newly trimmed, and his fair hair tied back. His head was down for the most part, as if he was engrossed in contemplation, deliberating on issues that involved difficult decisions.

She envied him his choices since she had so few left.

When he reached the hut, he touched the little gold bells he had given her in England and that she had hung inside the doorway. Their tinkling was a sound she linked with calm: the period before her father had decided on the voyage and she had followed him on the adventure that had led to where she was.

As Will entered, she stood.

'Mistress Ellyn,' he addressed her brightly, rising from his bow. 'Captain Drake, the officers of the *Swan* and I would be honoured if you and your father would join us for dinner.'

He looked around after delivering the invitation, as though he was expecting to see both his intended guests, but the distinct sound of snoring must have convinced him that he would not. Her father was sound asleep behind the screen that partitioned off his bed. Will took a step nearer, and she was suddenly conscious that they were completely enclosed, albeit that the walls were made of canvas and sticks. They were alone in a place with a semblance of privacy, and, within the flimsiness of the house, his physical presence was very strong. He exuded vitality. He was so deeply tanned that his eyes, by contrast, were a piercing pale blue. Around them were small crinkling creases that deepened as he smiled.

'We shall be eating soon, Mistress Ellyn,' Will said. 'Our appetites are hearty.'

Ellyn gestured for him to sit, and did the same. They faced one another by the plank table, on small log stools, surrounded by piles of faded and sagging cloth. She answered him levelly.

'Thank you, Master Doonan. I shall be delighted to attend, but my father is resting and would be best left undisturbed. So I ask you, please, to keep your voice low. I hope the Captain will accept my apologies and that my father will be excused.'

'Is he unwell?' Will frowned as he put the question. 'John Drake said that there had been an incident involving escaped slaves – the brigands they call Cimaroons. He said that Master Cooksley had not been seen about much since.'

'My father supposed a threat where there was none; that was all. The shock made him faint, though he was soon revived.'

'The Cimaroons did not molest you?' Will leaned forward and eyed her steadily.

'Oh, no! There were only two, and we have seen no more of

them since. They gave us a lobster, and took some cloth in exchange. It was nothing but a barter.' She made an effort to appear indifferent and changed the subject without ado. 'I am sure your voyage must have been much more exciting. Did you do any trading?'

Will looked pleased.

'Ah yes! I have these for you.'

The little bag he offered her resembled a nobleman's brocaded purse. It was adorned with an elaborate heraldic crest, and inside were a good number of large and perfect pearls.

She held her hand flat and placed one of them on her palm. 'This alone must be worth a small fortune.'

Where had the gift come from? She suppressed her curiosity so as not to appear ungracious. Moreover, she suspected, the truth might prove a burden, and she had no wish to induce Will to lie. She tipped the rest of the pearls into her hand and examined them in awe.

Will grinned.

'They will be enough for you to begin your married life in comfort, without the need to beg your husband should you want for any luxury.'

The talk of a husband perplexed her. She had almost forgotten her father's plans for her marriage, and it upset her to suppose that Will might be content for her to wed. But perhaps he was being considerate. It did not matter. She would not marry anyone insofar as she could see ahead.

'I cannot . . . ' she began hesitantly.

'Yes, you can.' Will wrapped her fingers around the pearls. His movements were tender and swift. When she looked up at him, he drew his hand away. This was not the way that Richard Dennys had obliged her to accept his pip-stuffed fruit. Will's gesture in touching her was impulsive, she realised, and ended by self-constraint. She returned the pearls to the bag and held it in her lap.

Will sat back.

'You must keep the pearls, dear Mistress Ellyn. We shall be leaving tomorrow, all of us together. Before three months are out you will be in England, safe with your father, and he much richer, having made such a profit with this enterprise that he will no longer be interested in selling the Spaniards' cloth.'

By keeping her attention on the purse she hoped to hide her concern. She had supposed that Francis Drake would want to leave the Americas once his trading was finished, but not straightaway. How could his business have been concluded so quickly, and without a single bolt of her father's kerseys being sold? Will continued enthusiastically, as if he thought she could not accept that he was bringing her good news.

'Think of green England, where the rain is gentle and the sun is kind. You will see her again soon. You will be home, free from danger, with your mother and maids to look after you, wearing your pretty dresses, enjoying music and dancing.'

His smile was encouraging, and beneath it she could sense his sympathy, but that made her melancholy more acute. Will believed she had been unhappy and that his tidings would give her heart. But she could not anticipate the prospects he described – she could not even contemplate how she might begin talking about her father. She felt the weight of the purse in her hands.

'You must have achieved much on your sailing in the *Kestrel* for the Captain to be content to return to England now.'

'We have begun a fair exchange, and collected a little of what we are owed – enough to sting the Spaniards and make it prudent not to linger.' The vehemence of his answer surprised her; then he beat out his words. 'But this is only the beginning. Next year we will come back to finish the reckoning, and when we do, we will be stronger—'

What 'reckoning' was this? She listened in a daze, beginning to accept that Will must have been engaged in activities more dangerous than simple trade and more questionable too, though she had always suspected that piracy would be involved. Why else had the *Kestrel* been so well armed?

'—so let King Philip wring his hands when he learns that the English have plundered the shipping along this coast, raided his best warehouse inland and captured a frigate bearing his precious dispatches.'

Ellyn raised a hand to her mouth. This was even more audacious than she had supposed.

'Did you dare do that?'

'Aye, and more,' Will chuckled. 'We watered down his orders and fed his letters to the fish! We threw them into the sea!'

Ellyn looked at him in amazement. She was thrilled by what she was hearing, but troubled, too. She cared for the Spanish no more than any subject who was loyal to the Queen. But King Philip was sovereign over the greatest power on earth; to provoke him was reckless.

'I have been afraid for you. Had I known all this, I would have feared much more. What risks have you taken? The Spaniards must be searching. If they find you they will be merciless.'

'They have set a fleet on our tail but they will not catch us hidden here. So do not worry, though we must leave soon.' He smiled at her, then his brow furrowed. 'I do not fear them. Since the Spaniards took my brother, they can do me no worse harm.'

While Will fell silent, she remembered Nan's words: 'The Inquisition have him, 'tis said.' She reflected on what Nan had told her. Will's brother might be dead. Will had said he did not know where Kit was. How should she respond? To her relief, Will continued blithely, 'I was more anxious for you, left in the care of Master Dennys.'

'You should not have been concerned. The gentleman is a knight as brave as St Michael, and this has been proven by his displays of swordsmanship in plate corselet, his valiant challenges to the waves and his wearing of spurs in the absence of a horse.' If there was mischief in her reply, then it was because she was pleased to lighten Will's mood, and even before she had finished, Will was chuckling. But as she signalled for him to hush, her father called out in alarm, 'What ho! Someone is about! Ellyn come – I hear him!'

With a despairing glance at Will, she hurried behind the screen.

Though the air was sultry and trapped by canvas, her father lay shivering under a heap of blankets and clothes, topped by his gown and rabbit-skin cape. His face was yellowed and blotched. When Ellyn crouched beside him he turned towards her with a groan, his sunken eyes flicked open to reveal a glassy and jaundiced gaze; then with a shout he raised a hand.

'Get back, you ruffian!' He fixed a manic stare on Will, and gripped Ellyn's arm. 'Give me my sword! The enemy is in our midst!'

She sighed, stroking his thin hair, and beckoned for Will not to get too close.

'Do not touch him,' she whispered, and next raised her voice. 'Not an enemy, dear Father, but the best of friends. This is Will Doonan.'

'A friend?' her father rejoined in a quavering voice. He squinted at Will with a befuddled expression. 'Ah, yes, I remember you, sir.'

It was apparent to Ellyn that her father was attempting to grin, though the result was as attractive as a gargoyle's leer.

'I have the baize you ordered,' he announced. 'The wool is fulled and dyed, felted for hats, as you asked, and thicker than any other you might find here about. This is no plain, steamed wool, this is a Barnstaple, sir – a Barnstaple baize, and they are the best!' With this he shuddered, his words slurred and ended in a drawl. 'Come back in the morning and I will show you in good light. It is too dark now to see what is yours.' After a few heavy gasps he made another effort to speak. 'Ellyn . . . Has he gone? O have pity and keep the bed still,' he moaned.

Ellyn clasped her father's hand and placed it back against his chest.

'No one will disturb you, Father. Try to rest.'

A breeze swept through the hut; then thunder rumbled somewhere far off, and suddenly rain hammered down and began to drip through the roof.

'Lo! A tempest strikes this house,' her father bellowed. 'Close the windows and bring all in. Tell the steward!'

'I will, Father,' she reassured him.

'Is your mother in her room?'

'She is.' Again Ellyn held his hand, but he was shaking and brushed her away. She stood and stepped back while he whined and wheezed.

'Now stop your rocking and let me alone.'

'I am still, Father, and I do not touch you.'

'So leave me,' he sputtered.

Ellyn watched him subside as his breathing rasped into a rhythm that suggested fitful sleep. She gestured for Will to follow, and they left with less noise than the downpour outside.

They sat as they had before, near the window on opposite stools. The rain trickled around them, dibbling over the stacked cloth, spattering the table and muddying the sandy floor. Ellyn watched drops fall like shot to land on Will's jerkin, darkening the leather in slowly spreading patches. Their eyes met and locked; then she glanced down.

'I will stay here with my father.'

Will shook his head.

'You cannot do that. Your father is ill and we must leave.' He gave her a sad but kindly smile. 'He needs to be back in England.'

'He cannot be moved!' she protested. 'Any disturbance makes him sick. He can barely raise his head. You have seen how he is. The slightest motion distresses him.' Unwittingly her voice rose. 'He could not cope with the rolling of a ship. The voyage would kill him.'

'But there is no other way!' Will's look was hard when he caught her eye. Ellyn bowed her head and she heard him sigh. He continued with more moderation. 'Your father will be cared for on the *Swan*. We can strap him down.'

'No!' She was horrified. How could Will think of doing that? Was her father to be handled as if he were a beast? Ellyn glared back. Then she stared at the purse that she had left on the table, lying sodden in a small pool of water.

'There is another reason for my saying he must stay.'

'What reason?'

She sensed compassion in the way he spoke to her, but the explanation was still difficult. She bit her lip.

'The mariners shun him; I know it. Since my father has been confined to his bed, they have not come near our hut. His appearance repels them. They dread infection and with good cause. I have no doubt they will be pleading with the Captain for the *Swan* to be spared from the threat of contagion. Let there be no division because of that. My father would not wish it, and he would die in any event if he was subjected to months on a ship at sea.'

Now Will knew, and she had felt shamed by the confession. She had more pride than to hope that Francis Drake would risk the disaffection of his men and command them to sail with her father aboard.

Will was quiet for a moment. When he spoke, he was solemn.

'I cannot abandon the two of you here alone.'

'You will not abandon us; you will come back. My father is diseased and cannot be moved. My wish is to remain here also since I have already been exposed to whatever it is that ails him.' She gazed at Will as he pondered, his handsome head on one side, and suddenly she wanted him to hold her as he had done once, to shoulder her worries and take them away. But of course that would not happen. What must he think of her? She was never going to be his lady and now she was his problem – more so than ever she had been before: part of a difficulty in which her presence alone was trouble enough. She had done no one any good, and she anticipated his response, because, as she knew, he would feel obliged to help.

He looked back at her.

'If you are determined to remain, then I will stay here also.'

She gave a faint smile.

'No, though I thank you. What would happen should you be discovered? The Spaniards are in pursuit as you have told me. And, if they find you, then your life would be finished and the Captain's plans ruined. He could not return.'

Will seemed hurt.

'Would you prefer that another man stay with you – Richard Dennys perhaps? He is not involved in our design.'

'Lord, no!' She forced a short laugh. 'Spare me from the protection of Master Dennys!' What was Will thinking? Did he suppose she had declined his protection because of an objection to him rather than anyone else? He could not have been more wrong. She tried to explain her reasoning, aware, as she did, that she was also convincing herself.

'I have considered this carefully and I am sure that a single woman and a sick old man would cause the Spaniards no real concern. We are plainly not corsairs. Our very isolation would be our best defence.' With what she hoped was a cheerful expression she switched her gaze from the purse to Will's grave face. 'My father should be fully recovered by the time Captain Drake comes back. Then we will sail to England with you.'

'But this place is too remote!' There was entreaty in his

argument, and insistence as well. 'You might be attacked by Cimaroons. You might need a physician's help.'

Ellyn sighed.

'Then leave us nearer to Nombre de Dios. Are there no other islands that are closer to the city?' She did not care where they were left, provided it was not so far away.

Will gave a nod, and from the way he winced she could tell he was at war in his own mind. He shook his head and then seized hold of her, sweeping her close to him, his voice swollen with feeling.

'I cannot leave you.'

'You have to.' She pressed her fingertips to his lips as his face contorted in anguish. 'For Captain Drake and his men and for our own sakes, too; this is the best way.'

'No . . .' He screwed shut his eyes, and then opened them to look long at her.

What was he thinking? she wondered. Did he really want to stay with her? Or had he concluded there was no more point in trying to persuade her to leave? He could already have decided to appeal to Francis Drake, supposing, perhaps, that she would follow the Captain's orders if she would not take his advice. He might believe she would have to be overruled, since a woman could not manage without the aid of a man; if that was so, then she could do nothing.

He got to his feet and she rose also, standing with her hands clasped like someone accused awaiting judgement.

'I shall speak to the Captain,' he said.

She bent her head.

'I thank you, God yield.'

The next instant he took hold of her hands, stepped very near and pressed her fingers back to his lips, then he folded her hands in his and urged her fervently under his breath.

'Come with us.'

'I cannot,' she answered softly. 'Go back to England and speak with my mother, I beg you. Explain what has happened as gently as you can. Affirm our love for her.'

He kissed her hands and nodded, pulling her closer until their faces almost touched, and she realised she had set him an almost intolerable task. In his expression she saw regret with none of the acclaim that she heard in his murmuring, 'My brave lady.'

She was not brave. She would have happily set sail for England immediately, if only she had believed that her father could endure the crossing, and she might have felt more worthy except for the drops of water that dripped unbecomingly over her head.

But Will seemed not to notice. He addressed her in low tones.

'I left my brother in Mexico, and good friends, too. The Spaniards have them all.' He paused so very close she felt his sigh on her cheek, and the warmth of his whisper against her ear, and the touch of his lips as he spoke. 'Now, must I leave you?'

She regarded him in silence hoping that he would accept she was not upset, and not wiping away tears, but only dabbing at the water that was trickling around her face, and believe it was this that made her snuffle as she watched him bow and walk to the door.

12
Reasons

'. . . Reasons are not like garments, the worse for wearing . . .'

—From a letter by Robert Devereux, 2nd Earl of Essex and favourite of Elizabeth I, sent to Lord Willoughby

In the middle watch, at the dead of night, Will crept below the waterline in the depths of the hold. He was alert for the odour of marsh gas and rot. He felt for sacks stretched to bursting around wet and swollen beans, for bulging barrels, and timbers sprung from nails. Occasionally, with his lantern held high, the light would reach past stanchions and braces, heaps of equipment and tight-packed provisions, to reveal a section of the planking that lined the ship's hull. Then he would eye the seams for the glistening of water aware that, even if he saw it, he would next have to find the source. There were three layers of timbers between the hold and the sea, and those were like a labyrinth for any water seeping inside. But he did not stop. He probed and searched, listening to the creaking of the masts, and the hollow booming echo as the bows broke through the waves. The *Swan* was dry but he could not relax. He found it easiest to sleep in the light of day – to close his eyes to the ocean slipping by and to the distance that was increasing from the place where Ellyn remained, left with her father at the ends of the world.

From the time he was a boy he had thought of the Americas as forsaken; they were as distant from England as it was possible to sail. The only language in those lands was that of the stars, the sun and moon, day and night. He could remember the Psalm that had nourished such ideas, read from the Great Bible, by the vicar in the village church: '*The heavens declare the glory of God . . . Their sound is gone out into all lands and their words into the ends of the World.*' As he climbed the companionway that led above decks, he thought of the mystery of those words. In the furthest places, at the ends of the world, there was no language but the sound of the stars. He had believed that once, when he had longed to escape his home, and believed so still. Perhaps Ellyn could hear it now.

The stars were a constant that linked them both, those of the Little and Great Bear, and even the constellation of the Swan could be seen from Panamá, a land now far away. And it pleased him to observe, when he stepped outside, that the sky was clear, the ocean calm and that the officer of the watch was on the upper deck, taking a reckoning by astrolabe with his sight on the North Star. Will looked to the same point, past the line of the foremast, beyond dark billowing sails, into a space crossed by rigging but brilliant with light, crammed so full with stars that there was no blackness between, only the gleaming of other lights that were fainter and smaller. In the firmament were the patterns that gave him some peace: the proof of a greater order in a world beyond man's control.

But the comfort was brief. In a surge of frustration he smacked his fist against the gunwale. Nothing was certain. With the passing of each day he felt his power to help becoming less. Firm plans had been made to return to Nombre de Dios, but for that they would need backing, more men and at least two ships. It was little reassurance that, on the Captain's orders, they had stowed supplies for the next voyage at another secret base. Almost three years ago his brother had been left as a hostage with more surety for his safety than sequestered provisions, and Kit was still lost.

Too much was at risk. He gazed at the fathomless sea. What could he do? He owed the Cooksleys no fealty. He was not part of their household, and it was not his place to interfere. But their fate depended entirely on an English ship going back, and he was involved with that. Who else would care about a young gentlewoman of no great birth, and her witless sick old father, for all his dealings in Plymouth? He had no doubt that Cooksley's wife would mourn their absence, and weep in private, and that the maids would weep in public and gossip, too. There would be debates behind closed doors in the Plymouth Mercers' Hall, and Godfrey Gilbert would make a show of loyalty; he could use Cooksley's capital to finance the next voyage. Then, for certain, Richard Dennys would invest as well, since he would not have the nerve for another voyage with Drake. Perhaps the Cooksleys would be mentioned before the Mayor and Corporation – but, if they were, it would be in confidence. And if Master John Hawkins were to report secretly to the Queen, then he also might let her know of the English lady with a courageous heart who had been left in the Americas for the sake of her father.

But there would be no campaign or speeches. Drake's enterprise could not be sanctioned. No one would commit the Cooksleys' plight to accounts or record books. They would soon be forgotten, and he was under no illusion. In the affairs of the world, the Cooksleys' part was as noticeable to most as the gleam of faint stars. His own significance was less. Should Drake not succeed in carrying through his intent, then the Cooksleys might remain forever an ocean away from England, and sweet Ellyn would fade like a flower uprooted and left on sand. The thought stirred his guilt.

He had acknowledged that Nicholas Cooksley was too ill to make the voyage; that much was obvious, and the crew did not want the risk of contagion on the ship. So Ellyn's reasoning had made some sense to him, and he had understood her contention that he should not stay with them. If the Spaniards had found him with the Cooksleys their position would have been much worse, and he would certainly have jeopardised Drake's plans – the Spaniards would have tortured every last secret out of him. But had he made the right choice? Had he allowed Ellyn to persuade him, only for Drake's chance of seizing a fortune – and his own as well? He was tormented by the idea. The stark truth was that he had left the Cooksleys in the Americas while his chief ambitions remained intact. But was that really so? What did he want? He wanted to find Kit or be avenged, and in the process secure some riches. He had thought riches might help him court Ellyn as he wanted. He had never imagined having to choose between them. Is that what he had done?

Leaping onto the ratlines, he climbed them fast, trusting to instinct as he scrambled above the mainsail to the top. From the platform he looked down, seeing a shifting view with a pendulum's swing, while the mainmast yawed with the roll of the ship. He saw the decks diminished below bulging grey sails, the great swaying yards and the lines of rigging before countless stars. But while all else moved, the stars remained still.

He gripped the rope to the topmast, as fat as his fist, and thought of the days of labour ahead, and all the preparations that would need to be made before he could set sail on the high seas again, perhaps on the same ship, but on a voyage westward, going back. And he wanted to close the future up and seal it like a seam, hammer in oakum and cover it with tar. He wanted to plug all its gaps, and stopper them till he was spent, and not see it, as he did, like a void he could not shape.

Through a gap in the trees Kit noticed a patch of distant sea. He knew he was somewhere west of the Chagres, heading away from the coast and into the mountain wilds. He could make out the flecks of white sails, but he did not linger to try and study them. There would be no point. They would not be English. In the three years since he had lost his liberty to the Spaniards, even after his rescue by the *cimarrones*, he had learnt not to cling to false hopes. Let the sails fade into the ocean and not disturb his small contentment; merely the glimpse had induced a pang of loneliness.

He looked ahead to his friends climbing the jungle-clad slope, and his gaze returned to a young Negress. He could see her clearly from a bend in the trail. She had aroused his interest earlier, perhaps because her clothes were thin, clinging like new leaves to the buds of her breasts. Her dress was still wet from her capture by the river. She was pretty and smooth-skinned, with a figure of supple curves. Already he had smiled at the girl on the way back from the raid, and she had returned the same moist-eyed look of a trapped doe that had first aroused his sympathy. Kit believed he could understand her feelings. She would be bewildered, just as he had been after the *cimarrones* had found him. She would have no sense of liberation, only the fear of a worse slavery.

He watched her carrying a large gourd full of fish. The thing was difficult for her to manage as she scrambled up the track, but it showed that the girl had been claimed, Kit supposed. He would not interfere, though he wished that the girl could have been shown a bit more kindness. From his position near the end of the file, Kit saw her struggling, feet sliding in loose mud, while thorny creepers snagged at her torn and bedraggled clothes. The gourd belonged to Alaba, the man striding out in front of her, and Alaba was strong; he had no need of help with his carrying.

Kit looked aside.

A green lizard caught his eye, one with the miniature frame of a thin plated dragon. It remained perfectly motionless on a sun-dappled branch, but he would not shout that he had spotted fresh meat; he would leave the creature in peace. He breathed deeply, inhaling the pig-stink of tapir, while around him water drops shone like jewels on moss, and bright waxy flowers trailed their roots into the air. He thought of rest and food, together with the pleasure of drying his feet. A spot itched on his back that he suspected might harbour a grub, and he wondered idly who he might ask to dig it out.

His gaze returned to the girl. She had been stopped by a man called Sancho whose ears had been mutilated during his time as a captive. Sancho proceeded to tie a bundle of vine stems to her back; then he placed himself in front of her and continued walking. The girl was left to trudge behind with the gourd balanced on her head and the stems bouncing over her shoulder.

Everyone kept moving, until a howl of raw rage brought the line to a sudden halt. Kit saw the blur of a lunging man. Head down and roaring, Alaba pitched at Sancho and knocked him sprawling. Next, Alaba was on top, punching and kicking, butting Sancho in the face. The men wrestled savagely, rolling almost off the track before Sancho drew his knife and Alaba grabbed a stone. At that moment the nearest *cimarrones* pulled the fighters apart.

'*Ella es mío*!'

'No! Woman mine!'

Sancho and Alaba shouted at one another in the bastard speech that had become their common tongue – Spanish mixed with some of the English Kit had taught them, though there were other words Kit heard with the ring of African abuse. The knife was forced from Sancho's grip as he was pinned back, snarling. Blood bubbled from his nose. Alaba spat and writhed. Three men held him with his arms in a lock.

'Thief!' Alaba yelled.

Kit marched towards the commotion. Men stood aside to let him pass. The girl pressed into the damp vegetation until she was half-covered by leaves despite the ants that crawled over her. She still had the gourd on her head and the bundle on her back. He smiled and signed for her to put them down. In obeying, she looked terrified.

One of Sancho's torn ears was bleeding, and Kit wondered whether Alaba had used his teeth as much as his fists. Sancho's long shins were clad in greaves and circled by shells below the knees. His bare chest was heaving. He panted, open mouthed.

'*Juzque*,' he gasped. 'You judge.'

Kit raised his right hand and recognised the ripple of murmured approval as every man around him responded in kind. This had been the way since the day the *cimarrones* had split his chains. They had called him the bearer of *Ifá*: wisdom. They said he was marked by iron with the sign of mother Mawu. Before every raid they would touch the scar on his palm, his hand on their heads. If ever a decision had to be taken they would ask his advice, and each time they moved camp they would search for one he liked. Whenever a man was sick or troubled it was always the same – they would seek him out. Their faith in him was a mystery, though plainly it was linked with his horseshoe scar.

Kit looked up. The action gave him a chance to reflect, and it settled his mind to fix on something remote: a fragment of sky beyond a lofty tree. What did his friends expect? They would want him to order a combat to rules, watch over the fight and then proclaim the final victor. But both men were massive; he could not award the girl to either without wounding the other's pride. He spread his hands and stared at his palms, calloused and stained, with the scar like a sickle island in the cracked dirt of a dry lake. What would Will do in his place? Will was always fair. Kit remembered how his brother would sort out the squabbles he had with his sisters.

'We will hunt again tomorrow,' he said. 'We will find more women. Some may be prettier.' He looked at Sancho and Alaba in turn. 'You must each agree that if you win the girl, you will keep her.'

Several of the onlookers grinned. Sancho and Alaba looked less confident, but they raised their hands to receive the press of his palm.

'You must accept my decision.'

They made plain that they would, muttering, '*Be ni*,' and '*Sí*'.

Kit had not expected otherwise, though he often found their meekness puzzling. He was so much younger and slighter, and they could easily have killed him, but he had learnt to speak boldly, and they had never yet opposed him. He turned back to the girl, leading her forward to stand between them.

'My decision is hers,' he announced. 'Let the girl choose.'

Alaba scowled while Sancho gaped. Kit could feel the astonishment of the rest gathered round. He took the girl's chin and directed her head towards the men, first one, and then the other.

'Choose,' he said.

Her eyes rolled helplessly. Did she understand? He held her hand up for her to point. She must know, he thought, her arm wavered as if she was making up her mind. Both men eyed her darkly. Kit stood aside, but then she moved towards him, hand outstretched. She touched him firmly on the chest.

Kit recoiled. What did she mean? By knitting his brows, he tried to alert her, to show she must not touch him and had made a mistake. But she reached for him again, clasping the rags of his shirt, and Kit would have shrugged her off except that the men around him were pushing the girl closer, while Alaba and Sancho, no longer restrained, were roaring with laughter and pummelling his back.

*

The island was a whole varied landscape compressed into the crescent shape of a fennel seed, with steep hills for mountains, small streams for rivers and a white beach for a bay that Ellyn had traversed from end to end in eighty-three steps. This was the place where she and her father had been left, set down from the *Swan* one night, before the ship sailed for England.

From the beach, looking over the sea, when the view was not obscured by spray or rain, the suggestion of a settlement could be seen in the distance: Nombre de Dios. The city was less than a league away; it appeared as a break in the line of lush mainland forest. She often saw ships, yet none came near. The island had small fertile fields, and a coral-stone shelter that she and her father soon made their home. But the domain was tended by people like ghosts.

On the sole occasion when Ellyn saw others on the island, they must have left by boat as she hurried to greet them, though she noticed no one actually go; she never caught them up. Yet the evidence of human activity was everywhere around: lines of drainage channels and pits in the soil left by the harvesting of roots, piles of weeds pulled from plots of strange plants – some like rushes with giant spikes ten times the size of ears of wheat. In nine days of exploring, her modest garnering had seemed like stealing, and she was further constrained for fear of being poisoned by the food. Whether to boil or soak, peel or deseed were all unanswered questions. As a consequence her diet was largely confined to old ship's biscuit. She might have been more concerned about the effect of this on her father except that, since their arrival, he had eaten hardly anything. This was why she felt so frustrated as she crouched among the rocks at the end of the beach. She tugged at the net she had left in a coral pool, but it was snagged. The harder she pulled, the more it tore, while around her hands, taunting her in their abundance, twirled glittering shoals of bright little fish.

She should not have been vexed by her failure with the net, but the idea of catching some food had become a fixation. It was as though netting a fish would allay all her worries – cure her father's disease and ensure their preservation. Yet she accepted this was nonsense, so why was she troubled? She squeezed her eyes shut, blinked and swallowed, trying to calm herself with reason, while knowing the answer full well: a netted fish would have been proof of her ability to manage.

Sitting back on her heels, she turned to the cliffs where parrots squabbled in the treetops over fruit too high to pick. And this was the nub of her quandary – she was hungry in a place of plenty, surrounded by dainties beyond her reach. With mounting exasperation she yanked harder at the net, only to pull it out at last, stinking, ripped and empty, except for pieces of broken coral and something that resembled a prickly chestnut. It was while she was deliberating on whether this catch might be edible that she became conscious of voices coming from somewhere out of sight.

Instantly she dropped the net and scrambled for the hut.

A musketeer was by a galley on the beach. Not far away, another half-armoured man was beating at the undergrowth around the coral-stone shelter. Ellyn dashed closer as fast as she could with her skirts held up and her feet sinking in the sand. Panic tightened her chest. She breathed in gasps, trying to run, thinking only of her father whom she had left alone. Shouts assailed her that she ignored.

'*No se mueva!*'

'*Señorita!*'

A man with a drawn sword strode rapidly across her path. But the plaintive sound of her father's wailing impelled a surge of strength so desperate that the soldier trying to stop her only succeeded in tearing a sleeve. She bolted past him and through the door.

The chaos inside confused her senses. Shadows coalesced around the hunched shape of a man pulling linen from a chest, while light streamed through dust picking up glints from points and links. She glimpsed the shimmer of steel and the pale pages of a book amongst up-ended articles and things jumbled in the dirt. Amidst all this, the taint of her father's sickness and the earthy smell of the shelter were somehow mixed with the odour of oil, suggesting a lamp spilt, or weapons greased; she did not know. The only clear perception she had was of her father's strident moans, though all she could see of him was the mound of his legs. The man's wide shoulders obscured the rest. Then, as the man turned, she was startled by the sight of something white over his mouth, and this was all the more striking because his hair was black and so were his clothes, but he did not speak. She heard her father calling out.

'Put that back! The walls will fall down! Desist, sirrah, and do as you are bid. Pull off my boots!'

The sight of her father's locket in the man's grasp finally triggered the release of her rage. To witness her father scorned in his incapacity, and their belongings treated with such disrespect, was an affront and violation that was too much to bear.

'Stop that at once!' she shouted as she rushed closer, glowering down at the man's masked face. He had a handkerchief held under his nose. His hooded eyes widened slightly as his arched brows rose – brows that were so thick there was no true gap between them. But he kept the cloth in place and straightened smoothly to stand before her. The man was short, though the cut of his doublet gave his stature some distinction. When he threw back his head she glimpsed the frill of a ruff above a high, tight collar, and all this coupled with the rings on his fingers, and the elegance of the rapier at his hip, was enough to convince Ellyn that the man most probably had some rank. And then, too late, she feared for what he might do. With the handkerchief still pressed to his mouth, the man raised his free hand and snapped his fingers.

'*Váyase, señorita.*'

The precise meaning of what he said was lost to Ellyn, but his gestures were clear. She watched him wave at her dismissively, and then nod to a soldier who moved menacingly towards her. She ignored him and flung herself down at her father's side, pulling a sheet over his bare feet, wondering why it was that he had complained about boots, though nothing he said any longer surprised her. With her arms wrapped around him, she tried to soothe as he whined.

'This tavern is a stink-hole! The lackeys here are imbeciles. Come here, man, and ease my feet. Fetch me my pumps.'

'Father, hush, for pity.'

She stroked his wisps of hair and looked down on his half-closed eyes. In the dim light his skin appeared yellow. Strong hands pulled her away, but she did not struggle, she knew resistance would be futile, and a commotion around her father would only distress him more. So she turned in the hope that the man behind her, too fastidious to breathe the same air that she did, would have some compassion if she beseeched him with a look. But his response was a scowl, and to address her in words, which to her amazement she could understand, albeit that they were ponderous with a thick Castilian accent.

'Come outside, *señorita*.'

Orders were snapped that left her released. The man who could speak English barked more commands behind her. He sent soldiers scurrying who had assembled near the shelter, and others from the beach then followed them into the trees. She was left in no doubt that they were searching for anyone in hiding. They advanced up the slopes, hacking and slashing, probing as far as the heights above the cliffs and the rocks below them. They would find nothing, of course, except perhaps a torn and useless net. But while the man turned aside, having taken the silk away from his mouth, she was surprised to see him shut his eyes. He breathed deeply, lips trembling, before again covering his nose and inhaling with a shudder. She was left staring at his hand with its jewel-encrusted rings, and the black hair that grew on the backs of his fingers, until he settled enough to put the handkerchief away.

He had an animal look that repelled her, animal because he was so hairy, but he was also quite handsome in a haughty way. His features, in profile, were like a heavily buttressed wall. He had a hooked nose, and a jutting chin that was further emphasised by a neatly clipped beard. The effect was of an expression that was fixed in disdain, something she noticed most when eventually he faced her. She felt belittled by his regard, though he bowed to her quite courteously.

'Capitán Gonzalo Callejón de Bastidas. I serve His Majesty at Nombre de Dios. It is a pleasure to find an English lady here.'

Ellyn curtsied and clasped her hands to hold them still.

'My name is Ellyn Cooksley, daughter of Nicholas Cooksley, master merchant of Plymouth. It is an unexpected pleasure to meet a Spaniard who speaks English.'

'I was taught by slavers—' Bastidas gave a scornful smile '—but my English is poor. I have little use to speak it. We do not trade with foreigners. You understand? They cause trouble.' He extended his arm towards the sea, encompassing the spread of the whole horizon in the way he swept his hand. 'This coast belongs to Spain. It is Spanish since my grandfather, Rodrigo de Bastidas, came here to discover and conquer for Aragon and Castile. The whole sea of the Caribs and the land, everything – these islands and bays – all belong to Spain. The Empire supplies what we need.' He turned and fixed his black eyes upon her. 'So why are you here?'

'My father is sick,' she said as steadily as she could, 'and I am caring for him.'

'Alone?'

'Yes.'

'Where are your friends?'

'On their way back to England.'

He gave a hollow laugh.

'You expect me to believe your countrymen have abandoned you?'

'They have not.' She was bold because Bastidas had offended her. He should know the reality. 'I have chosen to remain'

Bastidas snorted.

'Perhaps this is how Englishmen treat their ladies: like dirt. I am not surprised. Your friends show no concern for who they hurt. In their barbaric attacks they wound women. They abuse priests. They have killed.' He lowered his voice in a way that alarmed her because it was so intimate. 'Do you trust these men to return for you?'

She looked away and clasped her left arm with her right, not realising what she was doing until she felt the rip in her sleeve. She did not trust Bastidas to have told her the truth, but neither had she detected any hint of a lie in his account.

'I know nothing of any attacks.' She gazed at the sea, and her manner was more diffident because the best reply she could give was an admission she found upsetting. 'I cannot be certain my countrymen will return for me, I put no faith in that.' She turned to Bastidas and saw his lips curl in an expression of derision, small evidence that at least he appeared to have recognised her sincerity.

He glanced towards the shelter.

'Your father is ill in the body and head—' he sniffed and grimaced '—so he may stay here. This is a good place for . . .'

In the pause that followed she wondered what he meant to say. Her fears brought no words of comfort to mind.

'*Segregación*,' he concluded, and then edged a step back. She noticed he was careful to keep a small distance from her, and she found that demeaning because of what it implied. 'Do you know where you are?' he asked.

'I must be near Nombre de Dios, since you are a captain of that city.'

He smiled thinly.

'The name of this place is *Bastimentos*. We call it the "Isle of Victuals". It is like a garden for us. Some of the people of the city grow food here. They told me that strangers had arrived. But I see you are helpless.' He waved his hand towards the fields on the slopes behind the house. 'You will not starve. I shall send someone to bleed your father and tell the workers to keep away.' As he continued he became more assertive. 'In time you must come to Nombre de Dios. You will learn how ladies are treated by the gentlemen of Spain.' He gave a crisp bow. 'With honour.'

Ellyn stiffened. The suggestion was one of the possibilities she had feared most: to be separated from her father and taken to live with the Spaniards. She could not countenance that.

'I shall stay with my father on this island. Send no one to treat him; he would not allow it.' She lowered her eyes and forced a polite acknowledgement. 'But God grant you mercy for the kindness you have shown.'

'Yes, *Señorita*, you *will* stay here for now. We do not want disease in the city. But if you live, you leave.' He tipped back his head. 'It would be a kindness to imprison you,' he added meanly.

'I have done no wrong.'

He snorted and stared at her.

While he scrutinised her face she looked at his doublet, concentrating on the fine slashing and padded bands that suggested a refinement out of place. She had no wish to meet his gaze lest he expect her to plead.

Abruptly he swept his hand away and gripped the hilt of his sword.

'You should not be here.'

'But I am, and I shall stay.'

'So be it,' he snapped, and turned sharply on his heel. In a series of rapid commands he summoned his men. Ellyn saw the nearest come running as a shot rang out from the trees. Then he turned back and his voice was tight.

'I shall send you a priest. As a Christian, you will wish this.'

She was being watched, she realised, and she could not refuse. Any hint of impiety would be enough to condemn her.

'I would be pleased to receive a man of God.'

'I pity you,' he sneered. 'You will soon ask for my help.'

The Spaniards left quickly. Ellyn noted about twenty men assembling around the low galley that had brought them. A forked pennant flew from its mast. As Bastidas clambered aboard, a striped sail unfurled that was marked with the great cross of Spain. While the craft was being pushed away, she made a dash for the shelter. Her relief in being allowed her freedom was suddenly overwhelmed by apprehension, and this was made worse by the sight of the devastation all around: vegetation cut and trampled, tools and baskets left broken where they had been thrown, kegs forced open and sacks slit. Some of her hand-stitched clothes were strewn inside the entrance, along with a mess of scattered tinder, dried beans and her father's robes. The damage was a humiliation that made her too angry to cry, though this was tempered by relief on hearing her father calling out, and on finding the pearls Will had given her, untouched above a rafter.

'They have gone!' she called brightly as she ran to her father's side. 'All is well!' She stroked his brow to reassure him, but he continued to call loudly.

'Go! Be gone! Out upon't and good riddance!' His face was contorted with pain.

She took his hand. What had been done to him? Surely they would not have hurt a helpless, sick old man?

'Oh, Father . . .'

He gasped. But suddenly his hideous expression transformed into a look of delight as he rolled his eyes and released a sonorous fart.

'Now let us sleep,' he murmured while beaming back at her.

She tucked him up with a smile, but in her heart she was in despair. What would happen to them now? 'If you live, you leave,' the Spanish captain had said. Her greatest fear was for her father's health, but she also feared for their continued liberty. What if they were taken away? Will could not yet have reached England, and already she longed for him to come back. But would they still be on the island when he did? And, if not, then how would he find them? The arrival of Captain Bastidas had angered as much as disturbed her. She had taken an instant dislike to him. He had said he did not want any disease in the city, and she supposed that was why they had not been removed forcibly, but it unsettled her to think she was beholden to him for their freedom. His arrogance had been insulting, and his men had behaved disgracefully. He had claimed she would ask for his help. She resolved she most certainly would not. But what if she had to beg him to leave her and her father alone?

13
Alone

'. . . In solitude she lived,
And in solitude built her nest;
And in solitude, alone
Hath the Beloved guided her . . .'

—*From* The Canticle of the Soul and The Bridegroom, *stanza 35, by the Spanish Carmelite mystic Juan de la Cruz (John of the Cross), composed during his imprisonment*

Panamá, the Americas
July 1571

Ellyn held the spoon to her father's lips.

'I have made you a potage. See how good it is! Please take a sip.'

He had been asleep, and his head lolled against her arm but, while his mouth remained closed, his eyes flickered open. The smell was working its magic.

She had caught a bird. It had happened quite by accident after her abortive attempts at fishing. She had slung her broken net over bushes, thinking she might as well throw it away, only to find, after a night of crashing thunderstorms, that a large pheasant-like fowl had become snared in the mesh. The bird was not one she particularly wanted to trap, since she enjoyed the greeting of its kind with their loud clacking every morning, but the catch was providential. She had made a stew.

Dealing with the bird had not been easy. She could not bring herself to wring its neck, and anyway she did not know exactly how; it was something she had never done before. So she had picked up the net and swung it hard against a rock. The desired result was instantaneous. The decapitation and cleaning had been attended to in the way she had seen Nan do, but the handling of the entrails, and the flies gathering as she had pulled them out, had troubled her enough to take the gloss from her triumph. She had buried the offal in the sand, under the place where she had lit a fire. She remembered Will's advice: 'The Spaniards will see your smoke,' he had told her before he left, 'but they will find you anyway, so let them. You must cook for the comfort it will give you.'

She was sure Will would have approved of the way she had used his tinderbox, arranged the brushwood on the beach, and set the fire burning brightly; then in its embers she had placed a crock containing the fowl chopped in quarters, and water from a stream, together with pieces of ship's biscuit. And she felt he would have been doubly impressed by the means she had found to flavour the stew. Inspiration had come after she had decided to reward herself with a little grooming. While searching for her looking glass, she had found her sweet bag of posies, and in this, she realised, were all the herbs she could wish for. The dried leaves and blooms meant to protect her from infection had been picked from the garden of her father's house in Plymouth. So she had removed as many of the tiny grey lavender flowers as she could distinguish, knotted the remainder in the linen bag, and left it to steep along with the meat in the pot. It was the homely aroma of this infusion that rose from the spoon she held under her father's nose. Mixed with the smell of cooked fowl was a redolence of violet and thyme, rosemary and sage: the best of seasoning, and more than a hint of perfume as well.

Her father's lips trembled as she held the spoon near his lips.

'What goodly fragrance is this? Oh, my sweet Lynling, that taste doth bear me away.'

'But you have not tasted anything yet,' Ellyn protested, though in truth she was delighted by his reply. He appeared more alert than he had done for a long while. She dabbed with a napkin at his pockmarked chin, and listened as his voice strengthened.

'In that fragrance is the taste. Let the broth cool. Do you touch my feet?'

She frowned. What was he saying? Only a sheet touched his feet. She saw the hump that they made and squeezed it.

'I do so now.'

He closed his eyes.

She squeezed again, harder, first one foot then the other, but they remained inert.

'Can you not feel this?'

She heard a faint sigh.

'Oh, mercy!' In consternation she reached for his hand. It was cold and limp. But his mouth was moving, and there was awareness in the way he kept his yellowed eyes upon her.

'Be at peace,' he whispered. 'You will not have much longer to wait.'

'Do not speak in such a way!' Letting go of his hand, she patted the mound of his knees, and wondered whether he was conscious even of the gout that used to pain him. 'You are weak, but you will recover if you will only eat. Oh, Father, please try.'

She continued with her coaxing, eager to keep him awake lest he again lapse into delirium, conscious that for weeks he had only sipped at water. Why, when he must be hungry, would he not swallow wholesome liquid that was placed in his mouth? She watched more of the potage dribble uselessly round his chin, and mopped it up as from a baby.

'You must try,' she insisted.

'Enough.' He groaned and turned his head. 'So help me I am finished,' he gasped.

She placed the spoon in the bowl at her side on the ground, resolving not to pressure him any more, but to be cheerful.

'Your fever is gone and your look is brighter. And now the broth is cooled,' she added, with what she hoped was a note of happy surprise. 'So you must taste it.'

'Be still and let me rest,' he muttered. 'You have been a good daughter.'

She felt humbled.

'Not so good, truly.'

'That is a comely dress, and you have made a home of this hovel.'

Since entering the shelter, her father had proclaimed himself to be in many places, but she had never once heard him describe his whereabouts as a hovel. She followed his lead and let her focus drift over the walls – across the rough coral stones, and the dark space beneath the low roof in which creatures scurried, though she was not sure what.

'Do you see everything?' she asked.

'Yes . . . but not my jewel . . . where is that?'

Instantly she knew what he wanted. His 'jewel' was his locket: the ornament containing the miniature likeness of her mother that she had given him before the voyage. She found the pendant and brought it to him.

'Here, Father.'

'Ah . . .' He opened the locket, and kissed the image inside.

'You have given me comfort.'

He seemed lucid. Could this be the opportunity that she had hoped for all along?

'Will you try a taste now?' she asked.

'Yes.'

She sighed and stood, silently giving thanks, saying nothing lest he change his mind.

'Put out two bowls,' he wheezed as she turned to go. 'One for Thom as well.'

'But . . .' She would not distress him more by reminding him that Thom was dead, instead she nodded and smiled down at him.

'Fetch another,' he mumbled, 'and we will sup together. Thom is waiting for me.'

Crouching beside him once more, she brought her face close to his.

'If I bring another bowl, do you promise to eat?'

His ugly features contorted in an expression of pathetic appeal.

'Oh, Lynling, I am hungry.'

She dashed to the fire still smouldering on the beach and hurriedly ladled out another helping, then returned to set a second bowl beside the first. Both were placed where her father could see them, though she could tell he was no longer watching. She spoke to wake him up.

'Here is your bowl, and the other as well. If you are ready, I shall serve you.'

He gave no response. She bent nearer to peer at his eyes. They were not quite closed, but they were focused on a spot that did not change as she moved.

'Father?'

She placed her hand on his brow and swept it back over his wisps of hair. She watched his lips for the tremor of his breathing, and there it was, but very slight. Then a trickle of blood ran from his nose. He coughed suddenly, and she saw another bead of blood swelling in the corner of his mouth.

'Oh, God!'

She raised his head and pushed up the pillow behind. He must not choke. His eyes did not move. She wiped his nose and left the napkin under his chin.

She raced outside to stare at the distant outline of Nombre de Dios. The sea was empty. Who would help her? No one could see if she waved or hear if she screamed. The she remembered Will talking. 'The Spaniards will see your smoke . . .' She had not wanted the Spaniards to come, but now she did. They had to come quickly. She pulled ferociously at the piles of tinder that were stacked near the shelter and dragged everything she could to the fire: sticks, branches and dry fronds. She heaped up the lot until flames leapt skyward in shimmering heat. She dashed back inside.

Her father was motionless. She crouched beside him. She tried to settle her own hoarse breathing so she could listen for his, though there was not even a trace of a tremble in his lips. Blood was drying under his nose and glistening below his ears. With her hands either side of his face she kissed his cool brow. She had fought with him all her life, but she did not want him to die. *Let him live.*

She got up and reached for his broadsword, and then darted back onto the beach. The fire raged, though the flames were lower. Wheeling round, she hacked madly at the undergrowth nearby. She cut and chopped, throwing vegetation onto the blaze, stems and vines, anything green. Smoke billowed and rose, making her splutter while her eyes streamed. The smoke became thicker. It spiralled at an angle in a sickly white plume to fade against the darker clouds that loomed overhead. A fat raindrop splashed her face. She let the sword drop and ran back. Huddling down by her father, she pressed her face against his chest.

When she was a child, walking with him in the garden, she would hide her head in his gown; she would bury her nose in the wool of his clothes and breathe their smell mingled with that of their home. And in the summertime, if the sun was shining, then this was the fragrance: violet and thyme, rosemary and sage.

'Oh, Father . . .'

He had left without giving her a chance to make her peace, or say anything meaningful, or even goodbye, or that she loved him.

For all his faults she loved him. Her tears ran into his shirt.

His jewel was in his hand. She pressed his fingers around the locket, and then placed his hand over his heart.

It was pouring now, the rushing of the rain muffling the pounding of the sea, and the shelter was filling with smoke. Ellyn got up unsteadily and wandered out in a daze.

She could see nothing but smoke, it was like a mist all around.

But in this there was light, shifting and swirling, and the shadow of the water before which other forms were darker: the suggestion of a boat and a man in robes, who had his arms held wide and was walking towards her.

The man was a Blackfriar – a Dominican. Ellyn knew what he was by his white hood and black cloak. His head was shaved and a crucifix hung round his neck. She accepted this. There was nothing about anything that could have shocked her any more. She stumbled towards him in a daze and clutched at his hand, then by gestures tried to show him that he should go with her to the shelter. He spoke, but she could neither understand nor answer. Her voice was lost in her throat. What could this man do? He looked too slight to be of any help.

Through the drizzle and haze, she made out the suggestion of others moving about, but further off, near the boat that must have brought them all to the island. None of this surprised her. She only cared about getting the friar to the shelter and close to the pallet on which her father lay; then all she saw was her father's face when she fell by his side. His eyes were closed, but his mouth was open with the defenceless serenity of a newborn's sleep, nose upturned and lower lip drawn in.

His colouring was like a husk around a dry grain of wheat.

The friar began intoning; she did not know what. She could see what he was doing: holding the crucifix to her father's mouth, then bringing a vial to his half-closed eyes, wiping the lids with a cloth, so drawing them shut.

'Per istam sanctam Unctiónem . . .'

Her father was still. She watched as a wail swelled to bursting in her throat, caught and would not come. That his end should be like this – reduced to ignominy in such a place, far from her mother and his home, cut off from everything that gave him pride, blessed in Latin by a Spanish priest. But there was no one else to ease his journey, and this time, for certain, he was leaving her behind.

She tried to pray, but her fingers curled and tightened into fists.

The friar was kneeling at her side. She heard only the fuzz of noises outside the house: the pattering rain and soughing sea. Then in a voice that rumbled as if turning over stones, the friar led her with words she had learnt as an infant and used long ago.

'Pater noster, qu es in caelis . . .'

'Our Father, which art in heaven . . .'

They prayed together, and in time he must have left, because she found herself alone with her father, and so drained of passion that she entered a strange calm. She knew what to do, and she began without hurry, and with a singular strength, first to undress, then clean, and lastly to clothe her father in his best shirt and hose, his finest breeches and satin doublet. She drew Nan's rabbit-fur cape around his bony shoulders, and buckled his girdle round his waist with his account book attached, together with his tankard and knife.

The friar returned. She looked up once and saw his face clearly. It was the shape of a gourd: wider at the eyes with a long narrow jaw, swarthy and smooth-skinned, save for two deep lines either side of his solemn mouth. Though lightly built, he managed, with her help, to move her father to the kersey cloth she had spread out over a sheet of canvas on the ground. While she knelt by her father, she heard the friar leave.

She saw Thom, too. He drew close beside her, and pushed back his hair when he pulled off his cap. His cheeks were flushed as if he had been running for a while, but he did not look upset to see their father on the cloth, neither did their mother who carried on sewing. Ellyn saw her better when Thom crouched down. She was sitting nearby, working with her needle on a pattern of birds and leaves, her head tipped to one side in an attitude of listening, though no one spoke until the friar returned and began reading.

'Amen,' he concluded, and closed the Bible in his hands.

So be it, Ellyn thought. The friar addressed someone else at the door. Who was that? She saw a small, black-skinned boy whose only clothing was a loin-cloth of red calico. Where had he come from? Had she seen him by the boat? She could not remember. The friar wrapped her father in the kersey and then took the corners of the canvas at the end above his head. The boy grasped the canvas below her father's feet, but he was only a child, and so she helped him. Together they shuffled to the doorway with the burden slung between them. She stretched out her hands to shield her father from being knocked.

They were in a clearing, surrounded by brush, on a shelf of higher ground behind the mangroves that fringed the beach, and beside the friar were several Indian men and the small boy in red calico. Everything was finished. The earth was piled up, and the friar had made a cross from branches that the boy had found. She would have stayed, but the friar and the boy led her away, and she did not resist since she had decided to return for her father's hat, certain he should have that on the cross, since she had forgotten to give it back. When the friar tried to lead her to the boat, she shook free of his grasp, making clear her choice with the only word she knew that she was sure he would comprehend.

'No,' she cried. *'No!'*

His eyes were full of pity, and she believed he meant well – he had helped her, after all. But she turned away and made for the shelter. Low voices receded behind her, together with thuds and splashes and the slap of oars. She knew the friar and his men were leaving, and she did not mind.

She found the hat, but in the quiet of the shelter sudden exhaustion overcame her. Curling over on her pallet, she dragged the sheets into a knot and buried her face in the folds. She did not want to be alone. She wanted someone strong beside her. She wanted Will. Then she became conscious of someone's touch, and she realised, through her tears, that a child's hand was clutching her sleeve, one that was small and black, and that close to her face was a child's warm, bare chest. So she supposed that the boy in red calico must have been sent back to stay with her. She could feel the boy trembling and she took him into her arms.

Pressing her cheek against his, she surrendered to her need for someone to hold.

14

The Web

'. . . For falsehood now doth flow,
And subjects' faith doth ebb,
Which should not be if reason ruled
Or wisdom weaved the web . . .'

—From The Doubt of Future Foes, *a poem by Queen Elizabeth I, assumed to have been written in 1571 following the discovery of the 'Ridolfi Plot': a conspiracy to betray her involving Mary Queen of Scots and King Philip II of Spain*

'Master Cooksley was alert when I last saw him.' Will glanced from Mistress Cooksley to the black velvet cap he was turning in his hands. What could he say of Cooksley's illness that would not cause his wife great distress? 'However, he took any disturbance badly. Your daughter insisted he should not attempt the voyage, and I believe she was right in her thinking. He was too ill for a long journey. To recover he needed rest.'

Will swallowed and crushed the pile of the cap beneath his fingers, smoothing it as soon as he realised what he was doing. How could he explain the fact that he was in Plymouth, in Cooksley's house, in the lady's chamber, while her husband and daughter had been left in the Americas?

'He could not sail with us; neither could we remain with him. The Spaniards were looking for us. We were not strong enough to oppose them directly.'

'Was my husband strong enough?'

Mistress Cooksley looked up from her sewing. The intensity of her gaze made Will pause; her question struck straight at his conscience.

'No . . . no, he was not,' he answered quietly. He shook his head. He had imagined the meeting would be difficult, but that had been poor preparation. He felt accused by what he was saying. 'The Spaniards were looking for Captain Drake, not Master Cooksley; that is the point. It was Drake they wanted, and those who sailed the *Swan*.'

Lowering his eyes, Will began turning the cap in his hands again, watching the colour of the velvet changing through shade after shade of black. Ellyn had charged him with explaining gently, but how could he?

'If any of Drake's men had stayed with your husband and been found, then your husband would have been counted with them. Mistress Ellyn understood this. She knew that the Spaniards would see her and her father alone as no threat, so bravely she chose to remain with him, though I entreated her not to. Heaven knows, I did not want to leave them.' He sighed. The explanation had seemed like an excuse, and a weak one at that.

'And now you regret that you did,' Mistress Cooksley said softly.

'Yes,' he confessed. He could not deny it, and somehow, improbably, she appeared to understand. He had expected her to blame him or weep, but instead she resumed her sewing, pulling through a tiny needle that trailed a fine crimson thread.

'My husband knew the dangers of the enterprise. It was his choice to confront them, though perhaps he believed he could still act as a young man.'

She looked saddened, but she preserved an air of calm. Her hands did not shake, and she continued with her stitching methodically. The pattern was very large: some sort of counterpane, Will imagined. Where the embroidery was complete, it made an elaborate intertwining of stems and leaves, with fanciful birds amongst other details he could not place. But he noticed that the part she was working on was stark. All he could see were stems, as if winter had come and all the life had died back.

He had done as Ellyn had asked. He had assured Mistress Cooksley that her husband and daughter loved her; perhaps that accounted for her fortitude. She seemed to accept everything else with equanimity. When she spoke again she did so without any hint of the reproach he was expecting.

'My daughter's case is different. I believe she had little understanding of what she would face in running away.'

'That is true. No one told her.' Will thought of the banter he had exchanged with Ellyn before the voyage. He had never meant to tease her into risking her life to join him, but perhaps that was the reality. 'No one thought she might stow away.' He regarded the lady steadily, hoping for an answer to the mystery he could not conclusively explain. Why had Ellyn hidden herself on the *Swan*? Mistress Cooksley lowered her head over her sewing. What did she know? It surprised him that she appeared to be aware of the true nature of the enterprise, or at least its dangers, yet he was sure that Ellyn had been in ignorance; she seemed to have believed she was stealing away on an exciting journey, nothing more. He smoothed the pile over the crown of his cap. 'But we will bring Mistress Ellyn back. We are preparing for another venture, with two ships and more arms . . .'

A disturbance at the door made him glance round. Then he saw Old Nan enter, bearing a tray set with a jug and glasses, and behind her were several maids lingering in the shadows beyond the frame: Lettie and Jane, if he was not much mistaken. Nan shuffled towards her mistress stoop-backed, with a wobble to her carrying that set the glasses lightly clinking. Both ladies looked as if they had aged by more than the year since he had seen them last. He supposed the worry had taken its toll. Nan put the tray down with a wince of discomfort.

'Here be some wine, Mistress, warmed as you like it.' She craned round to peer at Will with a crumpled and toothless smile. 'Oh, Master Doonan, forgive me but I could not help but hear your talk of arms. Pray that you deliver good Master Cooksley and poor, innocent Mistress Ellyn from those devilish, murderous Spaniards. Since we heard they were not come back with you, we have been sleepless with worry . . .'

'Nan, please.' Mistress Cooksley stopped the outburst mildly.

Will stood up and put on his cap.

'I have said all I meant to, and I must be going. We will be sailing again very soon.'

Mistress Cooksley set aside her sewing, but he gestured to keep her from rising. She looked up.

'Bid John Drake see me. I will give whatever help I can.' She frowned and took a few laboured breaths. 'God grant my husband and daughter still live.'

'Oh, mercy, yes!' Nan blurted out.

'Aye.' Will nodded. 'God grant that, and I'll not return without them, not again.' He meant it, from the bottom of his heart and the core of his soul. 'I swear it – I'll bring them back.'

The talk had helped clear his thinking, and had made him realise what he had not fully admitted to himself until that moment. Making his fortune was no longer important, not before finding Ellyn and ensuring her safety. He would go on the next voyage for her above all – to fetch her home, and her father, too, if he lived.

He should never have left them.

He kissed Mistress Cooksley's hand, and she touched his cheek. 'God be with you.'

Kit lay slumped on the track, one side of his face pressed against mud and stones, the other caked with blood and crawling with flies. When the horseman came near enough, that was when he would shout, but he would cry out in Spanish: '*Tenga cuidado!*' The warning was the signal that had been agreed with his friends, and it should make the Spaniard freeze – it meant 'Look out!' The call would spring the trap.

With a single eye he peered at orange toadstools on a rotting branch. Creepers glistened in the gloom around giant roots folded like curtains by his head. He heard the clattering of hooves and the ragged tramp of men, though he sensed it more as a shivering in the ground. His left arm was crushed beneath the weight of his chest, and when he tried to flex his fingers they felt deadened and swollen. But he remained as he was, with his blood-soaked shirt slowly sticking to his back, and it comforted him to think of the blood as his shield. His appearance would protect him – the blood was not his.

He would wait. He would silently breathe the sour air, and not scratch at his scalp where it itched under the helmet, or brush away the insects, or wipe his stinging eye. As the noises became louder, he fixed his stare. He did not blink. The horseman was a blur at the edge of his vision, but he heard the ill-tempered voices and the changing beat that told him the column was slowing, and next that the Spaniard had dismounted and was striding towards him. He kept motionless. When the Spaniard's boot pushed under his chin, he did not flinch. Then he screamed, '*Tenga cuidado!*'

The Spaniard staggered back as an arrow shot into his face. Kit rolled over and saw him swaying. More arrows struck the man's breastplate, his thigh and his shoulder. The Spaniard's wails soon subsided, drowned by the blood spilling from his mouth. The forest rang with howls and shrieks, the whinnying of the horse and the war cries of the *cimarrones* – the clang of machetes hitting steel – the chop of blades against flesh.

The Spaniard's horse bolted and thundered by.

Kit crawled away. He glanced back once over his shoulder to check that no one was following. What he witnessed was half-hidden by showers of falling leaves. The Spaniards were snared by stems across the path: the trap that had been laid in front and behind them. As they struggled to get away, more stems tightened and caught their feet. He closed his eyes to the frenzied blows, and the glimpse of something bloody that wheeled like a cudgel thrown up into the air, and dropped trailing cloth to be lost in the vegetation. What was it? An arm? He looked again as he turned his head, and noticed the Negroes who had been captives cowering half-naked in a huddle. They were still roped at the neck. He had seen enough. He got unsteadily to his feet.

Walking along the path, he came to a place where light broke through the trees. Then he lifted his face to the sun, feeling the blood around his mouth tightening and cracking as he smiled. But his smile was a grimace between joy and despair, something that twisted between anguish and relief. Everything around him was green, and through the slits of his lids that colour was all he saw. He thought of sycamore sprigs gathered to welcome the best season, and drums beating loud in rowdy celebration. The sounds around him were much the same, though he knew what would be happening: the Spaniards who had escaped would be fleeing towards Nombre de Dios. Those left wounded would be killed. The fighting was almost over.

Kit pulled off the helmet that had hidden his blond hair, and raked his fingers over his scalp. Soon he would be back with the girl who had made him a home. He yearned to be with her. Ololade would wash the animal blood from his skin, and bring him clean clothes that once other men had worn. She would feed him choice meats, and give him drink to dull the worst memories. With oiled hands she would rub his body, from his neck to his feet, until he relaxed and curled against her, nuzzling at her breasts like a baby, and she would give him a mother's comfort, stroking his hair and singing to him gently. Then afterwards he would be proud to have planned for what the Spaniards would do, to have understood their thinking, and so help free their poor captives. He would have no regrets, and his sorrow would be less.

He clenched his hands to stop them shaking. It was as much as he could do to live for each day.

At a sound Kit turned round. His friends were approaching in file along the track, together with all the Negroes no longer bound. The procession was led by Sancho: the giant with torn ears who had once fought over Ololade.

'*Ìyá* Kit, we salute you!' Sancho bowed from the waist and Kit returned the courtesy.

'These men give thanks,' Sancho said. '*Gracias*.' Kit watched as the freed men sank to their knees. He gestured for them to rise, but none did; they touched their heads to the ground.

'They honour you,' Sancho explained.

Kit walked up to the first man; there were half a dozen in the line. He stopped and touched the man's shoulder. 'Tell him to get up.'

Sancho and the man commenced a brief exchange that Kit could not follow until Sancho spoke again.

'They ask you to go with them. They have a village in the mountains. They want you to join them there.'

The first man looked up and reached for Kit's right hand. Kit did not resist. He let the man stare at his scarred palm and press the mark to his brow. Then Kit understood. He stared at Sancho.

'Have they heard of me?'

Sancho conversed with the men rapidly.

'*Sí*. They look for you, but the Spaniards catch them. They seek "*el inglés de la luna*" – the Englishman who bears the mark of the moon. It is you they want.'

Kit looked askance at the row of naked bent backs. He shook his head.

'Tonight you must eat in my house.' Speaking quietly he moved along the line, allowing each man in turn to do the same as the first – to touch his hand. What did it matter?

'Then tomorrow go back to your people.' His voice hardened as he went on. 'Tell no one where I am. I will not go with you. This is my place.' He glanced up at the trees that rose sheer above his head. '*Este cerro.* This hill.' From his hut, not far from Nombre de Dios, he could look out to sea – it was all he had left.

'I will stay here.'

After months of rain and overcast skies, tempest-lashed days, and nights that languished in sultry stagnation, the clouds cleared at Christmas time, and, barely a week into the New Year, the fleet from Seville arrived at Nombre de Dios. Ellyn saw the white sails of the galleons and caravels as they entered the bay. Days later she saw them go. Since being left on Bastimentos, she had taken a keen interest in any ships passing by.

Marco had stayed with her: the small, black slave boy of the Spaniards who had worn red calico when she had seen him first, the day her father died and her world changed for ever. Marco had not left her since. With the exception of occasional visits from Friar Luis, the Dominican who had administered her father's last rites, she and Marco were left undisturbed and untroubled by the servant gardeners who tended the island's crops. Perhaps the Spaniards of Nombre de Dios feared she might give them her father's disease. Perhaps she alarmed them, as a foreign lady, in a way they could not easily address. Whatever the reason, they left her alone, and that suited her well. She learned to be self-sufficient.

With Marco's help she came to appreciate the bounty the island offered. She discovered what could be eaten and how best to prepare the food. By watching the labourers on the island, she taught herself how to cultivate her own small fields. Life on the island was hard, but it was not unpleasant; the climate was tropical, often stormy, but never too cold. Though she longed for Will's return, her loneliness was not unbearable. Friar Luis had become a friend; he left her a Bible in Latin and a book of chivalric romance in Castilian, and she loved little Marco as if he was her own dear child. She had no wish to leave Bastimentos; only by remaining on the island could she hope to be found by Will.

Every once in a while, she would go with Friar Luis to the city, and make the crossing, about two miles distant, in a boat with a sail rowed by ten strong men. She would hear Mass and make confession in the large church beside the monastery, and try not to notice the people pointing her out, or turning their backs to huddle and whisper. Afterwards, she would leave the church with the friar, her face veiled by a mantilla, and make her way to the harbour front by the fastest route past the timber houses. Then, reassured of her piety, Friar Luis would return her to the island in the boat by which she had come.

She never stopped believing that Will would come back. When that happened, she expected, he would want to know as much as possible about the city, and the ships and mule trains that sustained it. So she made an effort to be observant, and master some of the Spanish language, too. At the same time she schooled Marco in the rudiments of English, thus, in a halting way, they could both converse quite well. All this meant that she could follow Marco's explanation, as they watched the ships leaving Nombre de Dios, standing together on the island's beach.

'*Ellos van a Cartagena.*' Marco waved a thin arm to imply that the place lay far to the east. 'They go to Cartagena,' he translated and smiled. 'In March they come back. Sometimes April.' He flashed his white teeth again, plainly proud to have been able to impart this in English. 'Then they go to Havana. After Havana, to Spain.'

'Why do they come and go like that? Back and forth,' she asked, making a similar movement with her hands.

'Back and forth,' Marco repeated, as if he was feeling the words with his tongue. 'They do that because Cartagena is *bueno*. It is big city.' He made an expansive gesture with his arms. 'The ships come to Nombre de Dios. They bring things from Spain. Then here everyone is happy. The ships go to Cartagena. *El trajín* comes here from Panamá. *El trajín* has things for Spain. So the ships come back.'

'*El trajín*? What is that?'

'It is *las mulas y la carga*.'

'Mules? The ships come back for mules?'

'No, no.' Marco grinned and wrinkled his nose.

'The mules bring *la plata*.'

'Plate? Silver? The mules bring silver from Panamá?'

'*Sí.*' His eyes bulged as he blew out his cheeks. '*Mucha plata y mucho oro.*'

'I see,' she said, nodding. 'The mules bring a lot of silver, and they also bring much gold.'

On her next visit to the city, Ellyn remembered what Marco had said about the mule trains. She smelt the dung from the beasts even before she disembarked from Friar Luis's boat. There must have been two hundred beasts outside the counting house, lined up four abreast; she saw them when she reached the market place. Yet this was only one *trajín*, Marco assured her, the latest to come from Panamá. In the event she was not much interested since there was so much else to attract her attention. Friar Luis encouraged her to spend a few hours in the market, and she accepted the suggestion gladly. Tents and stalls filled most of the plaza displaying a wealth of fabrics in brilliant colours, and not only were there lengths of cloth hanging like flags in the bright sunshine, but taffetas made into gowns and lace into ruffs; bodices stuffed with busks and the bell-frames of great farthingales; painted fans and ornate headdresses; gilded leather girdles and mantles of fine lawn. These were just some of the things from Spain that were making her feel happy, not least because, through brave bargaining with Marco's assistance, and the use of one of the pearls Will had left her, she had managed to purchase a few of the items she most wanted. She conversed in Spanish from behind her veil and, despite her awkwardness with the language, she was not rebuffed. Indeed, she felt something approaching comfort in the midst of so many people: gentlefolk and servants, women and children also, since many of the Spanish men had taken Indian maids as wives – and there were even a few ladies who by their look had come from Spain. After many quiet months on the island, she had come to miss the company of a crowd. And she missed having ladylike shoes – the sort of soft dainty slippers faced with blue watered silk that she glimpsed among many others arrayed in the centre of the square.

'Marco, stop. I must look at these.'

Marco's eyes rolled when she tugged at his sleeve, pulling him to a halt in the thick of the throng. Piled in a basket, balanced against his chest, was a stack of glazed dishes, topped by a bird cage that was clamped beneath his chin. This made it difficult for him to talk. But he looked the epitome of the perfect page, with his hair neatly clipped to the shape of a ball, and dressed in the boy's clothes she had once worn herself – except that his feet were bare. Since the pumps that had been her father's were much too large to be made to fit, she had been left with little choice but to continue to wear Thom's shoes, though they had split and were most ungainly. So in an instant her heart was set on buying the slippers, while she privately resolved that Marco should be treated as well. It also occurred to her that there had been a time when to have something respectable to put on her feet would have seemed the most ignoble of lowly ambitions. But that did not lessen her delight.

'*Cuánto?*' she asked, and made clear her interest by pointing. The trader at the stall held up the slippers in response, then launched into a stream of gabbling that Marco interpreted by extending three fingers. Her excited conclusion was that she might afford the price, so she offered two *pesos*, supplemented by a *real* when the merchant shook his head, though Marco's expression left her wondering whether she had been overgenerous. The merchant's jabber continued in the midst of the clamour. This was so much better than the ostracism she had felt on her previous visits to the city. No one was glancing at her furtively, or making her feel like a leper. So she could not understand why the trader holding the slippers suddenly fell quiet and backed away. She only sensed real shock when she heard the dishes fall and smash. Then someone behind her grabbed hold of her arms.

The soldiers who seized her marched her from the plaza alone. They took her to the side of the market square that was nearest the sea. From there she was escorted through an archway, and along an arcade by a courtyard where men were training with pikes. It was difficult to take much in or keep her sense of direction. A soldier paced in front, while another marched behind, driving her into shadow and up a steep flight of steps. She emerged on the veranda of a large timber building. This was part of the garrison barracks, she realised at last, yet she was surprised to have arrived on an upper storey, when her apprehension led her to expect some sort of descent into gloom, certainly not the bright airy room that she finally entered.

The room had a tall open window that overlooked the market place; she knew this by the hubbub that rose from below, and a glimpse in the distance of the roofs of the government houses. But that was soon obscured. Standing by the window was a man dressed austerely in a black silk jerkin over a wide-sleeved white shirt. A tremor of alarm shot through her as he turned. Immediately she recognised the buttress features of Captain Gonzalo Bastidas, and the solid black line of his thick arched brows. He bowed and beckoned her to a solitary chair. There was no other furniture at that end of the room. She sat uneasily while the soldiers stood beside her.

'Welcome, *Señorita* Cook-esley.'

In his accented speech, even her own name sounded strange. She pulled the veil of her headdress more securely across her cheeks. It was a meagre shield. Bastidas fixed on her eyes.

'I am glad you are well. I thought that on such a hot day you might like to drink.'

She bowed her head. The heat was stifling in the room, trapped by the wooden walls and ceiling. She felt her skin prickling beneath her shift.

He filled a silver goblet from a pitcher, and offered it to her in a way that seemed strange until she realised he was proffering it left-handed. She shook her head but he pressed the goblet into her grasp. There it remained. The guards were dismissed. She heard the door click.

'Do you like our market?' Bastidas asked while pacing around her.

'I did, until your men took me away.' She could not quite keep her voice as steady as she would have liked, and that added to her humiliation. She glared at him.

'It is better than the market in Plee-mouth?' he went on.

She bit back the urge to deny and correct.

Bastidas continued to circle her.

'You may buy all you want here: silks, jewels, perfumes, things for the hair . . .' He paused, and his lips twitched into a sneer as his gaze travelled down towards the hem of her skirts. 'You may buy shoes.'

Conscious of her colour rising, she quickly tucked her tattered footwear out of sight under her petticoats.

Bastidas walked closer, and then hooked her veil to one

side, leaving her with a snaking image of his dark-haired fingers.

'Please drink,' he urged, and guided the goblet to her lips.

She sipped to end his harrying, inhaling a sharp metallic smell when she brought her face close to the wine.

Bastidas carried on with his stiff-backed pacing, occasionally turning and unsettling her with a stare.

'Perhaps now you think you would like to be here, not the Isla Bastimentos. Your father is dead, I have been told.'

She did not speak.

'I am sad with you.'

There was no warmth in the remark, and she saw condescension in his look. She averted her face.

He circled her again.

'Why go back? There is no need to stay alone.' He stopped and peered at her. 'Do you still believe your English friends will return for you?'

'It will make no difference, whatever I believe.'

By keeping her attention on the goblet, she blanked Bastidas from her sight, until he took the vessel away and placed it on a table.

'I do not want you to be . . . disappointed,' he said. 'So I wish your friends to come. We are ready to greet them.'

'Have they been seen?' she blurted out, as a faint possibility triggered a sudden thrill of hope.

'Not yet.' Bastidas regarded her with hooded eyes. 'But we know where they will go. They left provisions in a place we found – the same place they left the good people they captured. But fortunately these people did not die. They got away.' His tone softened.

A shiver passed down her neck when she heard him murmuring close behind. 'Are you glad?'

'I wish for no one to die, English or Spanish.'

The reaction was a short hollow laugh.

'Your friends are stupid. If I had been your Capitán Draque, I would not have left prisoners.'

She watched him move towards the window. She supposed he could only have meant Francis Drake by what he said. In Spanish, '*draque*' meant 'dragon'.

'What would you have done?' she asked, hoping he would say more about Captain Drake.

Bastidas bowed his head, looking down at his feet in an attitude of intense scrutiny. Then he brought his heel down before a dark spot on the floor: a beetle, she realised when she saw it suddenly crawling. But then he rocked his foot forward until, with a tiny crunch, his boot was flat on the boards. Stepping back, he pressed his handkerchief to his nose and inhaled with a snort. That was all the answer he gave. His back was turned to her as he looked out over the balcony. After a while he spoke. 'This place disgusts me.' Stepping aside, he walked to the table, and filled another goblet from the pitcher. 'I hope your friends come to visit us this year. If they do not, then I fear you will never see them again. Shall I tell you why?'

Ellyn kept quiet; she expected to hear nothing that she wanted to.

Bastidas raised his goblet, drank and smiled.

'Your country and mine will be united in faith, very soon. The Pope and the king of Spain are cleansing heresy from the world. They have destroyed the fleet of the Turks. They will destroy your queen. And when Mary, Queen of Scotland, is Queen of England also… *Vaya*! English pirates will have nowhere to hide. They will be finished – *Terminados*. You wait on Bastimentos, but you wait for nothing. So, I think, we should help one another.' He drained his goblet, set it down and folded his arms, half turning as he did, head down, as if he was rapt in contemplation. 'Do you agree?'

She did not answer, and he resumed his pacing, drawing gradually closer until he ended behind her. She jumped when his hand brushed her neck. The shock was worse for the touch being so light. But he merely swept back her veil, pushing it away so that she felt his breath on her ear when he whispered, 'Do you agree, *señorita*?'

With a shudder she twisted away from him, conscious of his smell all around, as cloying as ambergris, but powerful and sharp. A shiver of apprehension coursed across her shoulders and back, induced by anticipation as palpably as if he had stroked her, though he did not. His hand hovered by her cheek. She saw it when she started, and in that instant he withdrew.

She tried to keep her voice level.

'I have no need of your help, Captain. Friar Luis looks after me, and that is enough.'

'Ah, yes. You are fortunate to have the protection of a Holy Father.'

He walked to the table and proceeded to wash his hands, drying them scrupulously with a napkin. It made her think of what he had touched. She felt defiled.

'I would like to go to Friar Luis now. I wish to be taken back to the island.'

'Go then.' His tossed the napkin onto the table. 'And if your friends come back, I will invite you here to see them.'

The abruptness of the dismissal made it seem like an insult, though she had feared he might not let her go. The sting made her snap, 'I doubt they will stay here because you wish it.'

His response was a smile as thin as a cut.

'I disagree. I think they will stay.' He walked to the window and pointed outside. 'Their heads will be in the plaza, over there.'

Rage and disgust overwhelmed her, made her stand on impulse and speak at the same time. 'I beg leave.'

Bastidas bowed.

'*Adios, señorita.*' He strode briskly to the door and opened it for her. 'I hope we will have cause to meet again very soon.'

She walked out, meeting his eyes as she passed, though she felt demeaned by his parting. In the cloud of her thoughts were the hailstones of guilt, because she had been tempted by the prospect of quitting the island for the city, exchanging degradation for comfort and isolation for society – but only for a moment. The heat of shame was now burning her back, made worse by the soldiers who marched her away, so denying her any show of leaving because she chose to. She kept her head held high, but she wanted to run, she was so desperate to be gone – to return to her island freedom, and as far from Bastidas as it was possible for her to get.

15
Fortune

'Captain Drake, if you fortune to come to this port, make haste away, for the Spaniards which you had with you here the last year have betrayed this place, and taken away all that you left here. I departed from hence, this present 7th of July, 1572.
Your very loving friend,
John Garret'

—The message inscribed on a lead plaque and fastened to the trunk of a great tree at 'Port Pheasant', the secret cove so named by Francis Drake where he had left supplies in 1571, and to which he returned on 12th July 1572, from Sir Francis Drake Revived, *compiled by Philip Nichols*

Tierra Firme, the Americas
July 1572

Will stood on the ridge with a commanding view of the bay, taking his turn as lookout, scanning the sea for sight of ships. He knew the Spaniards had been alerted and would be on the watch for Drake's return. The white smoke rising was the first warning they'd received, the second was a caution left by another Plymouth captain. The message had been scratched on a plate left nailed to a tree. And, perhaps they should have moved on and found a better place to hide, but Drake had been against that because Port Pheasant suited them well; the cove offered fresh water and the fowl for which it was named. Moreover, as the Captain put it, 'There's no port more convenient for the building of our dainty pinnaces,' and since the Spaniards called him 'the Dragon', he had to uphold his reputation. Drake would show no fear. But if any Spaniards came close, then the news would be out; what Drake was up to was plain to see.

A fort was being built: a huge pentagonal structure, hard against the shore, fashioned from tree trunks shifted by pulleys and hawsers, with one side open to the water, and the rest as high as a house. In this their three pinnaces would be assembled: the *Bear*, the *Lion* and the *Minion*. It was a mighty undertaking, one that left the forest cleared for fifty feet round about, but it was eating up time. While the slopes echoed with the thud of logs, tackle squealing, blows and shouts, Will's mind teemed with questions, and most of those were centred on Ellyn – Had she been found by the Spaniards? Was her father alive? Were they still on the island near Nombre de Dios? The questions buzzed in his head with the persistence of drunk wasps, and were stirred to a frenzy by the Captain's arrival, though Will's greeting was calm.

'All clear, Captain. I have seen no sails.'

As Drake shielded his eyes to search the horizon, Will looked down at the craft moored up in the bay. The *Swan* was dwarfed by the *Pascoe*, a carrack of seventy tons from the Hawkins fleet. Beside her was a ship brought in by Captain James Raunce, another seafarer in Drake's confidence, who had arrived at the cove only the day after they had entered. Raunce was now allied with their venture, so his prizes were theirs as well: a caravel from Seville, and a small shallop little bigger than a fishing boat. This shallop was the vessel to which Will's attention was drawn, for precisely the reason that it was wholly unexceptional. He could conceive a good use for it.

'We said we would return for the Cooksleys.' Will eyed Drake cautiously, and when the Captain remained silent and continued to gaze out to sea, Will decided to say more. 'I could take the shallop with a few men and fetch the Cooksleys now, if you will allow it.'

'No, Will, I do not allow it.' Drake did not even turn. He stood, arms akimbo, with his stocky legs astride, while Will's frustration rose. Drake's ruddy face was impassive, fixed like a figurehead's staring into the distance. Will clenched his jaw. What did Drake know of the debt Ellyn was owed? She had risked her life for the sake of her father and, in the event, that had spared Drake much trouble. But Will could tell she barely featured in the Captain's thinking.

Drake took off his cap and ran his fingers through his hair.

'We will return for the Cooksleys, but not yet.' He narrowed his eyes. 'Which way blows the wind?'

The Captain would know, so why had he asked? Will studied a pennant on the *Pascoe*. 'Nor-westerly, quite brisk, sir.'

Drake nodded.

'We are fifty leagues from Nombre de Dios. With a strong headwind, and the drift against us, it might take more than a week to get near the city.' Drake gave Will a hard look, as if this statement alone was explanation enough. 'The slowest of our ships will set the speed for the rest.'

Will thought of the pinnaces under oars, fighting both the current and the wind to crawl slowly west, and he supposed he understood Drake's reasoning: it would take them long enough to reach Nombre de Dios without waiting for the Cooksleys to be brought from the island first. He still argued.

'But once we are nearer, a boat could be dispatched to remove the Cooksleys from danger should we need to leave quickly—'

'No,' Drake said, cutting him short. 'The boat might be seen so close to the city.'

Will frowned. What sense could there be in fretting about a boat's detection when Drake's fleet would soon be obvious to every Spaniard along the coast?

'The ships will be seen first . . .'

'They will not,' Drake barked. He paced around the small hilltop clearing, looking out to sea, and then again at Will. 'We are close to the weakest link in the flow of riches from Peru: the source of Spain's wealth. You know where that is – not at Cartagena, or along the Chagres – but over there.' Drake pointed to the west. 'At Nombre de Dios, the treasure house of the world, and it's ill-protected and unwalled. Now I have the hammer to break it open: ships and pinnaces, all the provisions I could wish for, the arms and ordnance, enough men united in heart.' Passion rose in his voice and lit up his face. 'God smiles on us, Will, so let us seize the advantage and jeopardise *nothing*.' He clapped Will's shoulder. 'The Cooksleys have waited a year; they will wait a little longer.'

That was an afterthought, Will recognised. Drake was set on his purpose. Will stared at the empty horizon much as Drake had done before, imagining their own ships passing over it. What then?

Drake gripped Will's shoulder hard before letting go.

'We swore an oath together. The time has come to see it through.'

Drake was calling on his loyalty, and Will realised only then that his questioning must have hurt; he sensed it with some remorse. He had the honour of being valued by the bravest man he knew, and how had he repaid that? Drake had given him his trust and this was the test. He would not fail it. Ellyn could be in no more danger now than she had been before. The island where she had been left was not far from Nombre de Dios. Once their mission was complete, he would fetch her away.

He met Drake's eye.

'I want vengeance as much as you.'

With an air of getting down to business, Drake hooked his thumbs in his belt.

'Success will depend upon surprise. If Nombre de Dios is prepared for anything, then it is an attack from the sea. The Spaniards have discovered the supplies we left here; they will be expecting English carracks. We know that at Nombre de Dios they have guns along the harbour.'

Will gave a nod.

'Aye.'

'So we will not use our ships.' Drake swept his hand over the bay. 'We'll hide them away first on one of the islands a few days hence, then we'll approach in the pinnaces and keep close to the shore, with our weapons in barrels and so concealed. Away from the city, a few boats under oars will not arouse much suspicion, even if they are spotted. But before we round the headland we'll wait for darkness to give us cover . . .'

*

Morrys turned to Will from the bench in front.

'We'll be sitting ducks in that haven.'

Will nodded in the gloom. He had sensed the shift in the mood. Morrys was not alone in his muttering. The wind was changing, whipping up waves that made the boats at anchor roll uneasily above the reef. Thunder growled over the sea. Will shuffled and rubbed at the fresh calluses on his hands. Even John Oxenham joggled his knees. He was known as 'Ox' for his mettle; he was not lightly unnerved. No one dozed, though they'd been rowing without rest all day. Probably most were thinking about what the Negroes had said: those they had found on the island where they'd left Raunce with the ships. Nombre de Dios was expecting reinforcements – attacks by Cimaroons had put the place on the alert. What would they face? Drake had seventy-three men in his three pinnaces and the shallop, but the city was protected by a whole battery of guns; they knew as much from the previous year's venture. Everyone was on edge. And when the moon broke through cloud to film the sea with wan light, Will was pleased to hear the clink and thud of anchors being weighed. He was keen to be moving.

It was a release to channel tension into powering fast across the bay, unlocking cramp, making for the low silvery buildings below the quiet black hills, and hear only the steady slap of the sweeps hitting the sea, then drawing through with a sloosh, driving the boats over the rip, tholes grinding as the oars turned. There was no talk. The helmsman called the stroke to grunts and hoarse breathing, the focus in the union of body and mind, pull and push, each man intent on working his oar in the race to reach the harbour before the guns came to life.

The pain in Will's hands merged with the ache in his back, but both sank beneath the aim repeated in his thoughts, marking the same beat, echoing the stroke: *seize the treasure, avenge Kit, seize the treasure, find Ellyn.* They were all one in a mix with what needed to be done, and in the heat of exertion his qualms disappeared.

From the single tall ship moored in deep water in the bay, a tender was lowered. But the city still slept. Will glanced over his shoulder. Nothing moved along the sheen that marked the line of the shore. No lights appeared above the black harbour wall. One of the pinnaces changed course to chase the tender to the east. The rest continued south, making for a knoll at the city's edge. Will bent his back to the stroke until they were close enough to see surf and smell the stink of dung and spices.

'Heave!' Ox called, and those with him all pulled, straining to drive the pinnace up the sand and onto the beach. Then the hull scraped and they ran aground.

'Out! Take your weapons.'

They scrabbled for crossbows and swords, strapping on what they could and jumping into the shallows. Drake had drilled them to wait while weapons were passed down, and most grabbed what they were meant to, but some ran from the water as if terrified of drowning. In the darkness, all were clumsy. Will almost foundered before he took the arquebus Glub handed him. Morrys had his quiver and the bow across his back, while Hix shouldered a pike. The three of them joined the others who were preparing near the knoll.

Will worked by rote, feeling for his powder horn, priming the pan of his matchlock and snapping it closed, dropping the butt to charge the barrel, tipping more powder into the muzzle and placing a ball in the bore, then some tow, packing them tight with the rod, fingers fumbling though he knew what to do. The shore remained quiet, but that could not last. Will lit his match cord from one of the slow fuses passed round. Morrys and Hix were already charging along the beach. It was plain where they should go: above a platform, at the end of the harbour, the barrels of heavy guns stuck out over the sea.

Shouts rose from those who reached the battery first.

'Spike them!'

'With what?'

'The pikestaffs.'

'Are you crazy?'

One man tried his knife-hilt in a vent, while others hacked at the axle ropes.

'That's the way, lads,' Drake bellowed. 'Dismount the beasts!'

He bent to a gun carriage trail, and Will stooped with him.

'Up!' Will heaved, pushing with the rest to tip the barrel on its trunnions until the muzzle pitched down and the colossal weight crashed, clattering to the ground. They let the trail drop while swinging it round, smashing it over the parapet. Another shattering crack followed, and a third soon after to a ripple of muted cheering.

'Spoil the lot!' Drake called.

With aching arms they set about disabling the whole battery, hauling at the carriages, grunting their exultation when the last barrel crashed loose, but satisfaction was cut short by the tolling of a bell: a knell from the city that sent a shiver through Will's spine. They had not advanced far, and already the Spaniards were being roused. He looked up at the knoll. Was more ordnance up there?

Drake began calling and pointing to the same place.

'Dickon, Jack Harris, Morrys, Will . . .'

They were the fittest and youngest, and Will guessed why they had been chosen. He picked up his caliver as Drake shouted above the clanging.

'Those named, come with me. The rest of you take ease and listen to the music.'

Fire pikes were lit; even so, they stumbled. The path was rough and steep. But Will climbed fast, only slowing near the top to peer into darkness and hear the alarm incessantly tolling from the city spread out below.

Drake charged first, running out into the open. That was all there was: a cleared site for ordnance, and a view down to the bay where all their boats could be seen, while away to the south the city square was bright with torches.

'There they are.' Drake pointed to the square where the Spaniards were gathering. The houses around it were arrayed in neat patterns like blocks. Drake traced a few lines with his finger. 'We can use those streets to meet them.' He turned and raised his voice. 'Back down, fast!'

Will dashed after Drake.

The beach blazed with light as more fire pikes were set flaming, and Drake had drums sound a beat while he divided his force: a dozen men to guard the boats – sixteen to follow his brother, John and Ox – the remainder with Drake to storm the city from the harbour. Will stood with Ox, as he was bid, and saw from the Captain's gestures that they were to march round from the east.

Drake held up his fist, rousing everyone to the same cry. This would be their vengeance.

'For England! God and St George!'

They were an army, ready and cheering. Will advanced behind Ox, and in the midst of the din the tolling of the bell was almost drowned. Heading back towards the knoll, they veered right between some beachside shacks and joined a street that was deserted. Will marched into the city shoulder to shoulder with his friends. His blood raced, senses opened. He could taste the smell of war – burning tar, match cord smouldering, sulphur and sweat. Their shadows leapt over shuttered windows and doors. They bayed like wolves, while ahead came the sound of their main force approaching. The way was clear to the square, where a glow appeared as at the end of a tunnel, and then movement – a commotion. Drake's company was there, drums beating, trumpets blasting, shouting in triumph. Will glimpsed them from the side: men kneeling with pikes, others levelling firearms. Ox wheeled and yelled.

'Ready your weapons!'

Will pulled up sharp. He checked his primer then heard a volley – a succession of sharp cracks that kicked up dust in the square. Men from Drake's force were on the ground, others falling back. That was all he could see beyond those in front along the street: nothing of any Spaniards, only the damage they had inflicted. The drums were still beating.

'Go!' Ox shouted, while up ahead John Drake and a few pikemen were already lumbering towards the square.

Will broke into a lope.

'Charge!' Ox roared behind him.

They ran as Drake's company fired: a volley of shots and crossbow bolts – cracking reports and the whistle of vanes.

Much was lost in an orange haze. Drake's main force was charging south when Will joined them from the east. He veered behind the men with fire-pikes. The Spaniards were massed straight in front, some trying to reload, or firing in thick smoke – a turmoil in which men were writhing, brandishing lances and slashing with swords.

He sprinted ahead and took aim, heedless that he was panting so much he could not steady the barrel. He had a clear line of sight. He cocked and fired.

He ran on, sudden elation heightened by the thrill of the chase. The city was theirs. The Spaniards were taking flight. Some were cowering but most were running away. He joined the pursuit, dodging muskets discarded, fixing on a man amongst the stragglers who thrust at Hix with a sword. Will turned the caliver in his hands, shifting his grip from stock to barrel. Ahead, the Spaniards were pouring through a gate. He pelted forward and swung, watched the man topple as he struck. Then he saw Hix sprawled in the dirt.

Will reached for his friend.

'You alright?'

Hix took Will's hand and stood, spitting while he cursed, 'Craven curs drop their arms like shit . . .'

They turned as a great cheer broke out from the square. Then, as one, they made for the noise. Behind them came the thud of the city gates slamming shut.

*

'Where's the gold?' The question was bellowed, over and over. 'Where is it?'

Too many people were yelling all at once. The captured

Spaniards gabbled madly. They were herded towards a tree in the centre of the square, firearms held to their heads. They stammered and begged, talking in a rush that few could follow.

'What's he saying?'

'He has a wife and six children . . .'

'Can't someone shut up that bell?'

'Cap'n says no. He'll not 'ave us storm a church . . .'

Ox tried to interpret: 'The treasure house is over there.'

Will saw the place meant: a stone edifice on the harbour side, with only a few small windows high up. Then hands began pointing towards an elegant building with tall doors.

'What's that?'

'The guv'nor's house where they count the gold.'

Will took the chance to reload. In the flickering light he scanned the windows around the square. His eyes settled on the Governor's house. Suddenly the great doors flung open as Drake and a file of men charged them. Then Will glimpsed a flash behind the balcony of another building. He aimed and fired. Wood splintered as his bullet struck, while in front of the grand house men were pressing forward in a mass. Few got past the crush, and it seemed to Will that, once he had loaded, the Captain was back within moments and standing on the steps.

'Silver! Enough to fill our ships!' Drake raised his arms in triumph. 'Silver!' He silenced everyone with the word; his voice filled the square. 'And we'll touch none of it. We're in the hornets' nest, and no time to waste. We want gold!'

'Aye. Gold!' The men roared, crowding round him.

'Follow me!' Drake bounded down and across the square, a stocky figure brandishing a sword, with a tight-rolling stride that to Will looked unnatural. Was he limping? Will tensed, his euphoria gone.

Another shot cracked loudly, and Will saw the tell-tale puff of smoke. He took aim at the place and fired. With his back to the tree he almost turned a complete circle, staring uneasily at the buildings that enclosed them on all sides. The treasure house looked impregnable, a great stronghold with a nail-studded door. Men began ramming it with a hitching post, but while the door shivered, it held. Will moved closer, training his caliver on the windows above him. He caught sight of Morrys kneeling, bow drawn, but they could not cover every building. He felt his scalp prickling. There was no protection. The square was an open target range for any marksmen in the houses.

The thuds of the battering ram jarred with the clanging of the bell. Shouts drew Will's attention. Two men were racing up from the harbourside: men who had been left with the boats. They were calling for Drake.

'There be troops coming . . .'

'Have you seen them?' Drake shouted.

Will trained his matchlock back on the buildings, trying to listen while he watched.

'A slave told us,' one of the men answered.

The muttered reaction swelled to an ominous thrum, but Drake cut through it. 'Might be nothing. John, go and look. Take Master Oxenham.'

Will made sense of little else. He looked at the ground and the hump over which he had almost tripped: a body, he realised, when he knelt in the shadows, the body of a boy. The face stared at him open-eyed. The boy's neck had been half shot away and his head was at an angle as if, like a wrung chicken's, it had been twisted from his trunk. The sight turned Will's stomach.

A great shout came from the men ramming the door, but Will kept staring at the boy. In his hand was a trumpet. The boy had no weapons save for a knife at his belt. When Will bent closer he saw a fat drop of rain fall on the trumpet like a tear. Then suddenly he became aware of a myriad sharp noises: pattering and plinking, tapping and drumming. More drops bounced over the metal. As his pity gave way to fury a clap of thunder tore open the sky. The square pulsed with blue light. Rain fell in a sheet, a torrent that drowned everything: washing out mortar, turning earth to mud. Will was soaked as if drenched by a wave. Powder was useless. He darted back through the downpour to join the rest by the treasure house.

They all pressed against the stones but the high eaves gave little shelter. The light was brilliant, then gone. Another explosion made Will duck. The sky quivered and pulsed. Shots cracked sporadically. Amidst the stink of sulphur he smelt the sharp tang of resin. Stretching out his hand he felt thumb-fat holes between mangled nails in the battered door. Somewhere under cover there were Spaniards still firing. The light of the fire-pikes was gone, doused by the spate. In the darkness a man slumped and splashed prone to the ground. Muttering rose.

'Can't do nothing with wet bow strings.'

'Nor muskets.'

'Ox is back. He says the boats be safe.'

'For how long?'

'We're done for if we linger . . .'

'Will?'

He turned to the whisperer, and the awareness that somehow Morrys had found him. In the gloom, figures took shape at the edge of the crowd, and Will knew with a sinking heart that many were on the point of creeping away.

'Stay where you are!' Drake's voice rang out as the rain stopped falling. He thumped the door with the pommel of his sword. 'I have brought you to the mouth of the treasure of the world! Would you run from it?'

Will could hear him very close, rousing and fervent, but there was also pain in Drake's voice, and Will felt shamed that the Captain had been reduced to entreaty. Or was he hurt?

'You only have to take what lies inside,' Drake shouted. 'If you have not the nerve, then blame no one but yourselves. Ready your weapons!'

'Aye, Captain!' Will answered with all the spirit he could muster, and he grabbed one of the burning fuses, re-lit his match-cord and set about priming his caliver afresh, facing the dark square when he was done. And when he wiped at his brow with the back of his hand he felt the shake of his own exhaustion, but he was fixed in his resolve. They could not give up, not so close – they would stand together. They must not fail.

He blinked to clear his eyes, and saw the next instant that Drake was moving into the open. The Captain had hold of an arquebus and he was yelling as he swayed.

'Break down the door!'

Will fired above Drake's head, aiming blindly across the square, a shot to distract while he ran. And others were rushing forward on either side, crowding round the Captain, because they too must have seen, as he did, that Drake's legs were buckling and he was about to fall.

'Hold the Captain!'

More shots flashed, spewing smoke: shots from both sides.

'He's bleeding bad.'

'Get him back.'

Thick blood pooled over the mud. Will saw it in the flare as another firearm discharged: a spurt of orange light, grey dirt, shining puddles and bright red blood. Even with a scarf twisted tight round his thigh, Drake bled while they carried him. In the moonlight his blood spattered black across the beach, all the way to the boats.

'Let's get him to the island where we left the Cooksleys,' Will said as he helped lift Drake aboard. 'It's not far.'

'Aye,' Ox answered. 'We can tend him there.'

The boat was hauled into the waves and pushed away.

'Heave!' Ox called. 'To the Cooksleys' island.'

Will prayed that Ellyn would be there.

'Ellyn. Prithee. God speed! . . .'

Ellyn knew she was asleep. A voice was hurling her name through her dreams. Someone was calling for her over and over, yet she could not find the door that would allow her to get out.

'Open up, Mistress Ellyn!'

She had to wake, and her hands were searching the walls for the door, then suddenly it was open, and she realised she had been in Thom's room in her imagining, aware almost at the same moment that there were people trying to reach her. She heard them when Marco screamed. Who were they? Sitting bolt upright, she stared at the first light of dawn breaking through a small high window, and the shadowy figure of Marco, jumping up and brandishing a stick.

'*Vete! . . . Vete! . . .*'

The boy was shrieking and there were men yelling outside. She was chill with shock, supposing that soldiers had come to seize her, suddenly certain she was on the island, in the shelter she shared with Marco, though she could hear cries from another place, and friends: Will. She was sure she could hear Will calling.

'Rise, dear Ellyn! . . .'

But there were other voices mixed with his.

'Get it open!'

'Hold there, he bleeds.'

Bleeds? She struggled to pull on her robe, trying to reason while the pounding on the door shook the sense from all she heard.

'We're losing him.'

'Quick! Bear him up.'

The door flung back as she neared it, and a mass of men barged straight past. They were carrying a body; she recognised that when they lowered their burden to her bed: a man covered in blood. She tried to see who it was in the dawn light from the open doorway. The talking quickened.

'Who'll search the wound?'

'I'll do it.'

They were all intent on the injured man, or was he dead? She caught sight of his leg bound tight with a cloth, like a scarlet cord around a scarlet curtain, and when she glimpsed his face she knew that Francis Drake was lying senseless, with his head on the pillow where moments earlier she had been dreaming. But he was alive;

she saw his chest heave as someone tore open his shirt. The jabbering became more urgent.

'Here's stuff for bandages.'

'Rip it up.'

She searched for Will and spotted him bent over the Captain, seeing first his hair, pale and matted, then the stubble of his beard as he angled his head. Stains deepened the set of his features: blood, earth, soot – she could not tell what. Some of the marks might have been bruises. He seemed different, older and leaner, changed from the image she had preserved of him for a whole year of waiting. When he glanced up, their eyes met. She edged towards him, behind the men. As soon as she was close, he took her hand. No one else could have noticed.

He spoke in an undertone.

'Your father?'

'Dead.'

His frown darkened.

'The Captain needs help.'

'I'll get hot water.'

She left quietly, her mind teaming with thoughts of what might be needed: water and kindling; she sent Marco to fetch more. Which was the best pot? She had to set a good fire, clean whatever might be used: knives and tongs, she had tongs. Where were they?

Marco was leaving when she passed the doorway. She saw the beach, and three large boats drawn up onto the sand with the sun rising behind them. All across the shore were dark bundles, strewn as if washed up above the line of high tide: Drake's men, she realised – men, spent and asleep, lying where they had dropped – men dead to the world – men who could take her back to England.

16

With Great Store

'. . . the Isle of Bastimentos, or the Isle of Victuals . . . is an island that lieth without the bay to the westward, about a league off the town, where we stayed the two next days, to cure our wounded men, and refresh ourselves, in the goodly gardens which we there found abounded with great store of all dainty roots and fruits; besides great plenty of poultry and other fowls, no less strange than delicate . . .'

—From the account of Drake's movements following the raid on Nombre de Dios, on 29th July 1572, as recorded in Sir Francis Drake Revived, *compiled by Philip Nichols*

Ellyn had to concentrate on the slicing, which was hard. The problem was that the block was running with juice, and so the fruit slid, and it was covered with bits of the husk she was paring. She saw everything in a blur; she had been awake most of the previous night following Captain Drake's arrival on the island. But the men were hungry. She had to take them what was ready: some of the produce of Bastimentos that was easy to eat, such as the delicacies called bananas, soft and sweet, and boiled Indian corn, together with the fruit she was cleaning. So she put what was prepared into a bowl, and left the shelter for the beach, scanning the groups of men for those she should go to next. Straight away she was aware of Will, though she tried not to show it, just as she tried to ignore the bawdy remarks as she passed.

'A taste for me, Mistress, right starved I am . . .'

'Yea, a kiss, fair lady . . .'

There was a ship nearby that Drake's men had captured, and it must have been carrying wine; she had seen the skins passed round eagerly. She would not be offended, and she could better understand since she'd learnt about the failed raid on the city. She would not mind that Will had barely exchanged a few words with her alone, and those about her father. Will would talk to her in time, and his reticence would not upset her, not when men were hurt, and all that really mattered was to get everyone well enough to set sail for England. She reminded herself of that as she weaved along the beach, and took comfort in hearing her own language, however roughly spoken. Soon she would be sailing homeward, and she looked out to sea, only to spot Will again and feel her heart race. But she also noticed a galley: a vessel approaching under oars, with a striped sail bearing the cross of Spain, and a forked pennant that was all too familiar.

'Will! That galley. There . . .'

She was running with the bowl and spilling fruit, seeing Will preparing to fire along with others by the shore. Men dashed over the sand, grabbed weapons and loaded matchlocks. Someone stopped her from approaching, though she could still see the galley and the man who disembarked once it had grounded on the beach. He was short and dark haired, with a wide-shouldered doublet. She was in no doubt as to his identity as she watched Drake's men surround him. While Captain Bastidas was marched away, more of Drake's crew trained their firearms on the soldiers left in the galley. A crowd milled about, setting out crates under a canvas awning, planks for a table, food and drink, her linen and plate. Men ran back and forth, and she would have joined them. She made to dart behind Drake as he was carried out of the shelter. But again she was waylaid. With rising frustration she was led back inside, knowing that Drake and Bastidas would be intent on a parley while she was left excluded.

Even Marco was set to waiting, and she considered doing likewise. But how could she, without appearing to pry? While racking her brains for a solution, she caught sight of a few large leathery leaves of the kind that Marco liked to set smouldering. It was an Indian custom that some of Drake's men enjoyed. She thought of the wounded she had noticed with the leaves smoking in their mouths. Those leaves might aid her also. She grabbed what was there and smiled at the mariner stationed by the door. She darted past him. The crowd was easy to squeeze through, since everyone was watching the visitor. Murmurs swelled as she passed, but no one restrained her, not before Bastidas had singled her out.

'Ah, *Señorita* Cook-esley! Your friends have visited Nombre de Dios, but for a stay too short. I invite them back, and with you, dear lady.' Bastidas gestured with a languid all-embracing wave.

Ellyn supposed Bastidas had come to assess Drake's strength. The Spaniard was arrogant enough to believe he would be safe, and that Drake would treat him with respect, since he was a gentleman.

Captain Drake beckoned her closer.

'I see you are acquainted.'

Ellyn edged forward to the place where Drake sat with his bandaged leg stretched out on a barrel. Bastidas, to her consternation, shot her a brazenly familiar smile. What should she say? She could hardly deny knowing him.

'Captain Bastidas and I have been introduced.'

Her response felt like a betrayal, more so when she caught sight of the faces in the crowd, and Will among them, frowning. She regretted having made herself conspicuous, though Drake gave no indication that he desired her to go. Instead he took one of the leaves she had almost forgotten she was holding. At this, out of politeness, she proffered another leaf to Bastidas. His reaction surprised her. He turned aside, took out his handkerchief, and pressed it to his nose.

Drake nodded with evident satisfaction, and proceeded to make a show of enjoying the scent of the leaf, inhaling from it deeply before favouring Ellyn with a grin.

'Please sit, both of you.'

Only one seat was visible, and that opposite Drake. While Bastidas moved towards it, she moved well away. She had no wish to appear in league with the Spaniard. As if her reaction had expressed her wishes, one of Drake's men answered by standing. She took advantage, since that brought her closer to the Captain. At the same time Bastidas was being challenged by the smoothing of the leaf on Drake's leg. It kept him leaning well back. She detected devilry in Drake's response.

'We accept your invitation, Captain, and thank you for it. When we are ready we will visit Nombre de Dios again.'

Bastidas gazed around him, eyeing everyone keenly.

'But a host must know his guests. May I ask whether any *corsairs franceses* will honour us also?'

Drake laughed as he rolled the folded leaf.

'We are all English, sir, and I hope without need of any Frenchmen to escort us. You should know my reputation by now.'

'Of course. I have been much looking forward to meeting Capitán Draque. I thank you for your greetings – the bullets and arrows you leave in my city. Perhaps there is something we can give in return?' Bastidas paused and cradled his chin while his eyes settled on Ellyn. 'I am pleased you are not with the French,' he went on. 'Your arrows will not be . . . *Venenoso* . . . How do you say?' He angled his head.

Drake licked the rolled leaf and raised his brows.

'We do not use poison, if that is your concern. If any who resisted us are injured, they may be treated with plain surgery, and let their wounds be a reminder that we should not be opposed. We will harm no one who yields to us.'

In the pause that followed, Drake twisted towards Ellyn, and she realised, to her consternation, that he was expecting her to set his rolled leaf smouldering. She was saved by the intervention of a mariner with a glowing match cord. Drake touched the end to his leaf and drew, breath by breath, until smoke issued streaming from his mouth and his nose. The smell of it swamped the stink of sweat under the canvas. Bastidas coughed.

Drake exhaled in a pungent cloud.

'As for what you might give us, there is nothing that will satisfy, except that commodity which you get from the earth and send to Spain for the greater trouble of the world. Until we have enough of that, we will keep returning.'

It was clear to Ellyn that Drake was talking about gold and silver, but Bastidas seemed intent on misunderstanding; he made a dismissive gesture.

'Naturally, you will return because, for you English, Nombre de Dios has much to interest. We did not know why you left in such a hurry last night.' Bastidas craned his neck in an exaggerated display of staring at Drake's injured leg. 'But now I think I see.' Again he smiled, and it made Ellyn want to shove him hard away, though another stream of smoke did that for her well enough.

Bastidas sat back with his jutting chin thrust forward above his collar and ruff. 'Come back whenever you want. Be my guests. Mistress Ellyn will speak for my courtesy, yes?' He peered at her, and seemed satisfied when she looked away. He went on with easy confidence. '*Vaya!* She is my witness. Her company enchants me. I hope you will not take her away.'

Ellyn stared.

'But I am . . .'

'For certain.' Drake cut her short. He breathed smoke towards Bastidas. 'I would not wish to subject the lady to any more hardship without cause.'

She turned to Drake, barely able to take in what she was hearing, but he raised his hand to her while keeping his gaze on Bastidas.

'Since you have been so courteous, Captain, I see no reason to unsettle the lady further. But I require your assurance that she may remain here undisturbed.'

'No!' she gasped, on the point of arguing vehemently, but she bit back the objection that would have openly defied Drake's authority. Bastidas was already answering.

'*Sí, sí*. I swear it. Leave the *señorita* without concern. I will respect her as if she were a Spanish lady.'

What could she say without challenging Drake in front of everyone? She turned her eyes to Will, beseeching him with a look. But he said nothing, and his face revealed no more.

'Good,' Drake concluded. 'Nombre de Dios shall be our surety until such time as we return for her. If she comes to any harm, or is interfered with in any way, we will burn your city to the ground.' His eyes glittered as he fixed on Bastidas. 'Therefore treat her well. You will dine with us?'

'I would be honoured.' Bastidas inclined his head, and the satisfaction in his expression brought Ellyn close to crying out.

'If I may speak with you . . .' she said to Drake under her breath.

'Later, dear lady.' Drake took her hand and kissed it, as if that was what she wanted. He smiled, seemingly oblivious. 'Let us eat first. What best can we offer?'

Ellyn regarded him askance. There seemed little doubt about the Captain's none-too-subtle hint that she should be attending to their dinner. But she was reeling from the shock of what he had arranged, with no regard for her wishes, or any consultation or debate. She searched the faces in the crowd, hoping for a last chance to appeal to Will, but in the crush she could not see him. She stood unsteadily and walked away. Then hurt struck her afresh. Why, after everything she had endured, why did her own countrymen not want her to be with them? And she was deeply disappointed in Will, who had made no effort to intervene in her cause, as if he cared nothing for her. Yet she had been sure of his affection. She had believed he had come back to rescue her. How could she have been so wrong? She wanted the sand to swallow her up. She stumbled on, head down, not thinking about where she was going until she found herself back inside shelter.

The next moment someone thrust a half-plucked fowl into her hands.

Will watched Bastidas pacing towards his soldiers in the galley, one hand on his sword hilt, elbow out, the other arm swinging with his pompous stride. The man was a coxcomb in a far outpost whose soldiers had fled when his city was attacked. He would probably be intent on retribution, however mean and petty. Will did not want Ellyn at risk because of that. He walked over to Drake and, at a nod from him, sat close.

'A word with you, Captain.'

'I'm listening, Will.' Drake half-closed his eyes as he puffed on his leaf, but Will did not doubt his concentration.

Glancing round, Will kept his voice low.

'We cannot leave Mistress Ellyn here alone.'

'Why not?' Drake blew a stream of smoke into the air and watched it rise. 'She's been here alone for almost a year without mishap.'

'As soon as we move against the Spaniards she'll be seized. Then we'll be held to ransom to get her back.'

'That could help us.'

'How?' Will put the question bluntly. The coolness of Drake's response had shocked him – it was as if Ellyn's plight meant nothing to the Captain, though he was sure that could not be true. 'We can't play games with her safety,' he added.

'This is no game, Will.' Drake's eyes followed another trail of smoke then flicked towards Will. 'The Spaniards will be watching her. This island is close to the city. As long as she remains here, the people of Nombre de Dios will feel safe. They'll expect us to return for her before we strike at the city again, and to do that by sea. They'll prepare for a sea attack – and they'll leave her be.'

'Her life will be at risk . . .'

Drake stopped him short.

'The life of every man in this enterprise is at risk, and Mistress Ellyn's life is no more at risk here than with us in the thick of action, or left somewhere else with scant protection. She will be a hindrance if we remove her, and a boon if she remains. Leave her on this island, and we'll be able to take the Spaniards by surprise. They'll be looking out to sea while we move on them inland.'

Will frowned, even more anxious then he had been before. Drake's reasoning made sense, but it held no assurance for Ellyn's safety, neither did the threat made to Bastidas that the city would burn if she was harmed. In that event, it would be too late.

'But if we attack the city again,' he said urgently, 'her life will be as good as forfeit, as you said . . .'

'That's not what I have in mind.' Drake grunted and took hold of his injured leg, lifting it from the barrel and resting it stretched out, heel on the ground. Will had almost forgotten that only hours earlier Drake had been fighting for his life, but there was no hint of weakness in the way he argued.

'She will be in no greater peril here than she would be in our midst. Do you think I would do anything to deliberately jeopardise a lady's safety?' Drake looked Will in the eye, and Will slowly shook his head. He could not believe Drake would leave Ellyn in imminent danger.

Drake turned to face the sea.

'We'll strike next along the Royal Road – the road between Panamá city and Nombre de Dios. We know that's the way by which the gold and silver goes. It must be. We've found no bullion along the Chagres.'

Drake looked at Will, and Will nodded, remembering the raid along the river that had yielded only pearls and silk the year before.

'The slaves who joined us last night,' Drake went on, 'have said the Cimaroons will help us. We'll attack inland where the road is ill-guarded. We'll bleed the Spaniards of their riches, and Mistress Ellyn will be taken to safety before they even have chance to cry out.'

Will bowed his head. The plan had much merit. But how would it help Ellyn?

'In the meantime she'll be left defenceless,' he argued.

'She will be safe.' Drake bent forward, meeting Will's gaze when he looked up. 'Trust me.'

Leaning back, Drake settled his leg on the barrel again as if to signal that the meeting was over. So did it come down to trust? Will rubbed his brow. Was that all he had to rely on?

'We swore an oath, Will.' Drake inhaled deeply. 'We came close to seeing our purpose through last night.' He looked hard at Will. 'You fought well.'

'No more bravely than you.' He could not deny Drake his bravery. And he trusted him.

Drake smiled.

'We won't fail again. Thank Mistress Ellyn for her loyalty, but tell her none of this. Tell no one. The lives of seventy men depend on that.'

'I'll say nothing.' Will stood, his commitment given. 'I'll go to her now.'

'If Mistress Ellyn would care to dine with us, I would be delighted, but I think she may not.'

Drake's eyes narrowed again as he smoked, and for the first time Will noticed the sheen of sweat over his face; perhaps that was the proof of his pain.

Drake inclined his head and grimaced.

'See how the cooking fares. I like my bird tenderly done.'

Feathers rolled around Ellyn's feet as she walked inside. Men were tearing at carcasses and busy with knives. Her little house had become a kitchen, while fowl were being plucked and gutted, made ready for roasting over the great fire on the beach. She wanted privacy, and her only hope of sanctuary had been denied. She coughed. The air was thick with dust. She found a bowl and moved to a corner, hoping to hide her face, because she was trying not to think of Drake's decision to abandon her, or the conversation she had left, or Will, or what lay ahead. For a long while she stood still because the sounds of chopping, and the feel of the dead bird she held, reminded her of her father's end, and then of a fateful morning when Lettie had been beheading thrushes, and that put her in mind of England and her dreams of returning there with Will. So she thought of him anyway, which caused her eyes to fill with tears.

She drew quick breaths and raised a hand to her face, caught in the realisation both that she was making herself look dreadful and that a man had moved very close: someone who was talking while tossing feathers into her bowl. It was Will, speaking softly.

'We will come back for you.'

She wanted to shake him and cling to him all at the same time. If they were going to come back, why did they not take her away now? She could barely bring herself to respond.

'Then why leave me?' she eventually asked.

'We have to. Be strong for us. We will not be gone long.'

'Strong . . .' she whispered, shaking her head. The word caught in her throat. She could have been strong enough with Drake, able to cope with any danger, bear any hardship. Had she not proved as much? She struggled against the urge to break down and weep, scream out her grief, or throw the dead bird at Will very hard, but instead she pulled at the quills that remained in its breast.

'Why must I stay?'

'By staying here, you will help us most,' Will answered gently. 'It gives us advantage. Unless we outwit the Spaniards we'll have no hope of seizing the treasure . . .'

'What treasure?' She turned to him. In the dull light she saw his handsome face brighten.

'The bullion from Peru,' he explained, as if he thought she did not know. 'The bullion that is taken to Nombre de Dios.'

'There is no treasure left in the city, and none on the way.' She forced the words out. Had the decision to abandon her been made on such wrong reasoning?

Will looked at her askance.

'That can't be so.'

'It *is*.' She glared at him.

'How can you be sure?' Will moved nearer to her.

She met his gaze, her jaw tight with anger.

'I've been watching what goes on in Nombre de Dios, and my boy, Marco, has been telling me about the traffic in gold and silver . . .'

'What traffic?' Will's whispering became urgent. 'Answer me fully but let no one else hear.' He glanced round and resumed plucking, bending his head to the task, though she could tell he was also listening.

'The armada left a month ago,' she said plainly, 'and all the treasure went with it . . .'

'Where?'

'To Spain. There will be no more now until after the next fleet arrives.'

'When?'

'Around Christmas . . .' She tried to explain, wanting to help him, though she knew what she said would be no help to her, and all the while she was playing out the action of pulling at feathers and moving her hand over the bowl. But nothing fell out when she opened her fist. She was concentrating on what she had discovered about how the fleet moved back and forth, bringing goods from Seville and then spending the dry season in Cartagena, before returning for the treasure from Nombre de Dios and heading back for Spain. She squeezed all the information she could give into a few terse sentences. It was as much as she could do.

He frowned, looking round.

'So we will have to wait . . .'

No one was near them, the shelter had emptied while they were talking, and only two men remained who were standing by the door. The aroma of roasting fowl wafted in on fumes of smoke.

Will placed his hand on her back.

'Thank you for this. Find out more if you can. I will return for you.'

'Take me away. Please.' Her voice cracked. The few feathers she had managed to pull out tumbled towards the drifts around her feet, together with a knife caught by her sleeve. She bent unsteadily as she scrabbled to retrieve the blade, knowing that if Drake acted on her information he would probably be gone for at least another six months, and what would happen to her then? She could not bear so much more waiting, subjected to the attentions of Bastidas or stultifying isolation – abandoned because she was an encumbrance, an unwanted burden, a woman in the way of the enterprise of men. Even Will was not concerned enough to protect her.

'I thought you cared . . .' she mumbled. It was too much. She shuddered as she fumbled, not minding if she was cut, or that Will was murmuring while he stooped, crouching down at the moment she decided to rise, so her head struck his chest. Next she was swaying, close to falling, except that he caught her, silencing her cry, first with a hand, then with a kiss.

He held her tight, and the kiss was everything she wanted for as long as it lasted. But in a moment he drew back. 'I have put your case to Drake, and he will not change his mind.'

'No!' she burst out. Surely he could not kiss her and then simply go? She pulled away from him, but he took hold of her again.

'Getting you away from here depends on the whole enterprise. We are bound in this together – not only you and I, but Drake and every man with him. So you must believe me when I tell you that we will return for you as soon as we can, before you are put in any more danger . . .'

'Believe you?' She cried out as she struggled free. 'How can I believe you when you leave me?'

'Sweet Ellyn, please understand; this is not of my choosing.'

He reached for her again, but she backed away.

'No!'

What was he thinking? That he could settle her with another kiss, or by calling her 'sweet'? She spun round to see the two men at the doorway with their heads turning as she faced them. Had they been watching? Will had shamed and hurt her enough. When he took her arm, she shook free of his touch.

'Get away from me!'

Let the men hear and stop him if he tried to follow her, though she knew he would not.

She walked out alone.

With his hand spread wide Kit blocked out the sun, watching the rays break between his fingers. Then he raised his right arm, joining thumb and first finger together to make an 'O'. Through this ring, by looking up, he could see nothing of the forest but only a circular patch of sky, and clouds swelling and shifting shaped by a wind he could not feel. The sky. The same changing sky from wherever it was seen in the world: his for a moment. Suddenly he ducked, dodged and pulled the knife from his belt, wheeling round.

'Sancho!' Kit held the blade poised to strike, but he laughed at the same time. 'You'll have to wash if you want to surprise me.'

Sancho was also crouched to spring, his great arms held wide, skin gleaming like polished jet, and Kit guessed that if he had not moved first then his friend would have pounced, and taken pleasure in giving him a shock. Out of the corner of his eye, Kit glimpsed more of the *cimarrones* rising up from the undergrowth. Sancho drew his own knife, the size of a cleaver, and held it quivering, close to Kit's face.

'If you were Spanish, then I cut off your nose.'

'But because I am English I am favoured with your smell?' Kit sheathed his knife calmly and tipped back his head. 'Is there a reason for this just now?'

'The Spaniards are on the road to Nombre de Dios. Many of them.'

Fast as a snake's tongue, Sancho slashed at something by Kit's side, slicing the blade back and forth, then holding it flat to display what he had caught: a giant black worm with a multitude of legs, rippling wave-like as it writhed. He grinned.

'They travel in a long line, north from Panamá.'

'How many?'

'*Ciento* – a hundred. Maybe more.'

With a nonchalant flick of his wrist, Sancho threw the worm aside, but Kit followed his black eyes and knew, when another man yelped having been struck by the creature, that he had taken aim with some care. Sancho feigned bemusement and scratched at his neck beneath a silver gorget and a tattered silk cord.

'They have *cañón* and *armas*,' he added. 'Muskets and bows.'

'Soldiers?'

Sancho nodded, shaking his matted locks. He spat.

'*Soldados*.'

'A hundred more soldiers for Nombre de Dios . . .' Kit murmured, reasoning aloud. 'Have we frightened them that much?' He looked from Sancho to the others, all still and watching him closely. 'Show me.' He glanced up; then he smiled. 'Since I have a good nose for a bad smell, I would like to sniff them out for myself.'

Ellyn tugged at another weed below the spindly yucca plants in the furrow. A tremor of pain ran through her back. She straightened and gazed towards the shore, beyond the tops of the mangroves that grew below the level of the fields. The horizon was as empty of anything unusual as it had been whenever she looked. When would Drake's men return? Surely after four months, and near the end of the worst rains, they might be expected any day? She bowed her head and saw her clod-caked shoes, her mud-spattered skirts and the thin sleeves she had rolled up because she was sticky and hot. She looked like a churl. Suddenly she was troubled by the thought that, if Will could have seen her just then, he would not have wanted to kiss her as he had before they'd argued. She wished their parting had been better. She wanted him back.

She bent again, wiping her hands on leaves still dripping wet from earlier rain. Apart from Marco, she had no one to talk to. Friar Luis only visited rarely, and the labourers on the island behaved as if they had been told she was a witch. Perhaps they had. Such tactics would be consistent with the guile of Bastidas, if his strategy was to drive her to seek companionship in the city. What was happening? Were Drake's men in any trouble? Sometimes she feared her spirit would break – that news was her sustenance, and she was dying of starvation. Couldn't she ask Friar Luis to take her to the city, just for a day? And if Bastidas intervened, couldn't she face him? She would, she resolved. She might even send a message to the friar with the next fieldworker she saw.

Rubbing the small of her back, she stood and turned to cast a fond eye on Marco at the end of the plot. He was knocking dirt from a yucca root, scraping the tuber with a stick. He was a small scrawny urchin, but her heart went out to him. His arms were still stick-thin as she saw when he waved. His quaint manners puzzled her. Why was he waving? Without comprehending she began to wave back. Then with a shout he was gone, over the edge and down the slope.

'Marco!'

She stumbled after him, hearing him calling from a distance but unable to make him out. What was wrong? At the side of the clearing she came across the sword they kept to deal with snakes. She picked it up and sped after him.

Vegetation closed around her, and the stink of hot swamp. Insects whined past her ears. Marco's cries became louder. Suddenly she was out in the open, on the shore, not far from the shelter. Before her were two giants with Marco pinned between them.

'Stop!' She brandished the heavy sword. The blade wobbled as she thrust it forward. But she marched straight at the men. 'Let him go!'

The men were tall and black, wild-haired and daubed, garbed in pieces of armour and the remnants of fine clothes. They had bows and arrows with quivers on their backs. She recognised their scars as she neared them, and the tattoos of one that ran in lines down his chest: the giant who drew his knife as he pulled Marco to his side.

'No!' Ellyn cried and dropped the sword. She ran towards Marco, arms outstretched, while the giant with the knife began shouting, stepping back. His companion, by a canoe, hurled something out onto the sand. But all that concerned her was taking hold of Marco. She did not look up until the men had jumped into their boat. They began paddling furiously away. Then, as she hugged Marco, she saw what they had left.

The men had given her fish.

17
Unrest

'. . . Such is the state of affairs and the great unrest which the French and English have created here, as the *Audiencia* of this kingdom will report to Your Majesty. As soon as I arrived on this coast I manned the remaining brigantine with thirty men . . . and this vessel is escorting the barks which leave this port with merchandise which must go forward. Up to the present no mishap has befallen them, nor do I think any will befall them while I am here . . .'

—*From the report of Diego Flores de Valdés, Commander of the Indies fleet and armada, to King Philip II of Spain, written at Nombre de Dios, 20th February, 1573*

Nombre de Dios, the Americas
January 1573

'Ah! *La señorita* Cook-esley. You look enchanting! I wish you good cheer this Twelfth Night.'

Captain Bastidas bowed from the far side of a long table resplendent with fine plate and sumptuous food. Though the sun still streamed through half-shuttered windows, glass and silverware glittered under clusters of lit candles. Ellyn held her head high as she walked into the room. But while the starched lace of her ruff was tight around her neck, the cut of her bodice left her feeling exposed – a reminder that the clothes were not hers, and she had been given no choice but to wear them. Soldiers had accosted her without warning as she was leaving church with Friar Luis. Then, despite his protests, she had been marched away, taken to the Governor's house, and left with Indian maids whose instructions must have been to pamper her whether she liked it or not. She had been washed, changed, powdered and perfumed, dressed magnificently and had never felt so abashed. All this left her rueing ever having asked for another visit to the city. She should have stayed on the island, out of sight of Bastidas. Now he could see her too clearly. She had no veil. Her chest was bare above her breasts, and only the fan that she held could provide any concealment. So she made use of it as she entered, with her other hand on her skirts, conscious of the farthingale like a cage around her hips.

Bastidas waved his hand and the guards either side of her left the room. He proffered a thin smile.

'This is the Eve of the Epiphany, the day we call in Spain "*El Día de los Reyes*": the day of the kings who found the baby Jesus. Please share with me this feast to honour them.' With a sweeping gesture he indicated the lavish display, and then beckoned for the servants to help her sit.

'Surely not alone?' Ellyn let her affront at the suggestion show. To dine alone with him would be unseemly, and she wanted him to know that the invitation did not appeal to her.

Bastidas inclined his head, and she noticed how sleek his oiled black hair looked in the sparkling light. His expression formed the suggestion of a sneer as he watched her.

'I am sure you would not wish for public show? No?'

'I wish to be shown respect,' she said crisply. 'I would like a duenna.'

By way of response he snapped his fingers, at which two Negro page boys took her arms and began guiding her down to a chair. She considered resisting, but then allowed herself to be seated, deciding that nothing could be gained by making a scene. A footman poured out wine, while Bastidas took his place facing her along the length of the table.

'Alone is better for talking.' With another wave of his hand he dismissed the servants. 'I have good news,' he announced as she heard the door close.

'Indeed?' She tried to conceal her apprehension. Christmas had passed by and Will had not come back for her. She had heard nothing of Francis Drake and his men since the day they had left the island following the attack on Nombre de Dios, and that was almost six months ago. Did Bastidas know what had become of them? But if Bastidas considered he had good news, then it was hardly likely to be good news for her.

His answer was to push several dishes along the table.

'Let us eat. Try this. It is *olla podrida*. The meat is like pig,' he added, indicating a dish containing a stew-like mix of meat and fruit. 'And there is *perdiz con chocolate*,' he went on, gesturing to a silver platter on which joints of roasted fowl lay under a thick brown sauce. 'You know chocolate?' he asked. 'The taste is bitter-sweet.'

Something about the dish reminded her of the birds she had

plucked when she had been with Will last. She ignored it and placed a small piece of 'pork' on her plate.

Bastidas helped himself and proceeded to eat with a show of relish.

'You like the dress?'

He stared as she cut up her meat. She was conscious of his eyes roving over her while with each restricted breath her chest rose and fell. She speared a morsel with her knife feeling a surge of anger she could barely contain. The dress might have cost a fortune, but she did not care for the way in which it had been foisted upon her. Yet he had hinted at news, and she wanted to know what that was; she could not ignore him.

'The cloth is rich,' she answered coolly.

'It is *brocado* from Seville. I had it cut and sewn specially for you. Please accept as my gift for *Los Reyes*.'

She put down her knife and picked up her fan.

'I prefer the English fashion in cut. It is more genteel.' She watched his face twitch.

He gave a stretched smile and raised his glass.

'We have reason for celebration.'

She forced a smile back, certain that he was hinting at more than the festival for the holy day.

'The Day of the Kings?'

'Better than that.' He drank deeply. 'The fleet from Spain has reached Cartagena. Soon it will be here. Perhaps tonight.' He spoke in a way that showed the jut of his lower teeth. 'We will have a great fair and market. You must enjoy it.' Beneath the thick line of his brows his eyes gleamed darkly. 'I hope you are not upset because your friends have not returned.'

Ellyn looked down at her plate.

'You have not seen them at all?' he asked.

She raised her eyes, wondering what he knew.

'Not since the day you saw them also on the island.' She took a deep breath. 'Do you have any idea where they are?'

Bastidas turned his gaze towards a pile of papers on a side table. He nodded.

'I have reports.'

'Please tell me.' She clutched at the napkin in her lap, screwing it into a knot as she waited.

Bastidas pushed aside his plate and reached for the documents.

'Your friends have been troublesome around Cartagena,' he spoke while placing the documents in front of him. He picked up the first letter.

'"On the thirteenth day of August in this year of . . . "' With a supercilious wave he continued reading. '"There appeared before this city and coast two ships and three boats . . . English corsairs who sought to land, but . . . " How do you say it? They were spied. "They did not dare to come ashore . . ."' He lowered the letter and looked at her. 'I read from the report of the officer who had the defence of Cartagena when your Capitán Draque arrived.'

'The officer thinks much of himself.' She met his gaze, wondering what Drake had been about. Why had he chosen to attack Cartagena? With so small a force he could have had no real hope of success.

Bastidas angled his head.

'Shall I go on?'

'Yes,' she said stiffly.

'"The corsairs were more than two months by this port,

capturing and burning coast traders and doing much damage . . ."'
Bastidas riffled among the remaining papers, going through the motions of summarising as he looked at them. 'They attacked a large frigate at the mouth of the harbour. But they were fired on by troops from the shore, so they fled.' Tapping at another letter, he glanced at her. 'Twice the corsairs have raided a trading post to the east. On the second raid they took nothing. It was empty.' He paused to drink, and again his eyes settled on her. 'It seems that Capitán Draque has caused much inconvenience but achieved very little.'

Ellyn looked at him. She had no idea of Drake's strategy, or why he had been harrying shipping so far to the east; she thought Drake had wanted the treasure that the mule trains brought from Panamá. But where was he now? Where was Will?

She fanned herself briskly.

'I am glad that no alarm has been caused here in Nombre de Dios.'

Bastidas nodded and smiled wryly.

'I think the people of Cartagena were not too concerned. Your friends were driven away by the fire of cannon, then, possibly, they went to find the supplies they had left on some of the islands nearby.' He flourished a letter embellished with the remains of a large seal. 'Your friends would have been vexed. Their provisions were found by us. Of course, we took everything.'

She speared a piece of fruit, anything to appear unconcerned.

'You cannot know those stores were Captain Drake's.'

'We found more . . .' He waved the letter and eyed her sharply. 'The wreck of a ship. You are interested?'

Ellyn tensed. Had Drake's fleet suffered a catastrophe? Had one of the ships struck the reef? She put the fruit in her mouth and swallowed uneasily.

'The coast must be littered with wrecks.'

'This was English, we know, though it had been burnt.' His voice rose. 'It was one of Capitán Draque's ships.'

She looked at him incredulously. How could he know? She supposed there would signs by which a ship might be identified, but was he telling the truth? She stared at the letter in his hand.

'I do not believe you.'

Bastidas stood and walked round to her. Then he spoke quietly as he put the report by her place.

'See. You can read.'

He hovered near her, despite her turning her back to him. Still she felt the touch of his look, making her skin tingle where she was most exposed; she shivered in the heat. Her gaze was drawn to the report, but she resisted the urge to pick it up. She tried to make sense of it where it lay, because, thanks to Marco, she now knew enough Castilian for simple reading in the language.

'What does this mean?' Bastidas asked, close beside her. She was already troubled by the same question; she could see that the report seemed to accord with what he had been saying. She shook her head slowly. Out of sight, in her lap, she crushed the napkin into a ball. Suddenly she felt something run over her shoulders, light and quick. She shuddered and recoiled, wheeling round as Bastidas stepped back. What had he done? She raised a hand to her neck while he returned to his seat, but he turned his head quickly to watch her again. The feel of the touch lingered on like a burn. Probably he had done no more than draw his fingertip over her skin. But she felt sullied by the thought. Was he trying to show her some intimacy? She was loath to pass remark lest he enjoy hearing her protest. Had she imagined it? She looked round. There were moths and insects flying about; one of them could have been the cause. She kept silent.

Bastidas hunched his shoulders and peered at her.

'Your friends had problems; that is what the report means. They could not sail two ships and their boats. Perhaps some men wanted to go back to England. Perhaps Capitán Draque did not.'

Ellyn picked up her knife again; it was something to do. Her mind was spinning. She did not eat.

'You are only guessing, believing what you want to . . .'

'There are things we would like to believe that are now clear. No one has seen the English corsairs for two months.' His voice dropped as he smiled. 'Maybe they have gone back.'

'Maybe,' she responded, her hopes sinking, aware of something flickering past her and throwing a moving shadow around a candelabrum: one of the moths. The creature fluttered erratically close to a flame. The next moment it dropped, landing stunned on the tablecloth.

Bastidas glowered and raised his knife in his left hand; then abruptly he stabbed down. The thud made her jump.

'You say that but you do not think it,' he continued softly. 'You think they will return for you. They will not. I can tell you.'

She stared at the knife. He had pinned the moth on the blade. As he pulled the knife up she saw its wings quivering in a blur. She shivered.

'How can you be sure?'

He held the knife before his eyes, examining the death throes of the creature with an air of mild curiosity. Slowly he extended his arm, bringing his knife towards a candle until the moth touched the flame. She watched because she could hardly believe he would do it. Only in the small flare of light did she flinch and look away, catching the trace of a slight hiss, and a whiff like scorched hair. He did not answer her. When he spoke it was to put another question, as if about nothing of any consequence.

'Does your Capitán Draque have hair that is red?'

Her answer was curt. He was tormenting her, and she was revolted by what she had witnessed.

'You know that he does; you have met him.'

Bastidas leafed through the pile of papers.

'There is another report: a frigate was attacked by English corsairs not far from this city. The corsairs were . . . beaten away. One of them was killed – a musket ball to the head. Another was shot in the stomach.' He clenched his hand into a fist and pressed it against his waist. 'The wound was mortal.'

He tossed the papers towards her.

She sat rigid.

Bastidas poured himself more wine.

'This man had red hair.' He raised his glass, and the gems in his rings gleamed and sparkled. He smiled. 'But you must not be sad. The fleet from Seville is with us soon. We will have music and dancing. You must be happy.'

She struggled to show no concern. But what if Drake was dead? What if the ships had sailed for England and Will had gone back with them? She could not reason clearly.

She made herself look at Bastidas.

'I would like to leave now. I insist you let me go.'

Bastidas raised his thick brows.

'But you must finish your meal.'

'Friar Luis will take me back. He will not allow you to keep me here. If I do not return to him soon, he will seek my release. He may already be with those in authority . . .'

'Ah, yes, Friar Luis,' Bastidas interjected. Then he stretched out his arms and picked up a trencher on which some twisted baked dough lay coated with sugar and crystallised fruit. 'Please try this,' he said mildly. 'It is *Roscan de Reyes*, our Epiphany bread. You will find it delicious. Here.' With his knife he cut a thick slice and placed it in a bowl that he passed to her.

Ellyn stared at the slice, reluctant to touch it, wanting only to leave. But she supposed that the dinner would have to be concluded first. She prayed that the mention of Friar Luis would help her.

Bastidas cut another slice for himself.

'We have a tradition; in the bread things are hidden. If you find a bean, you must pay for the bread.'

He broke off a piece with his fingers, and began to eat. Then he examined what he had left. 'There, you see?' Eyes widening in a show of astonishment, he held up a bean. 'Now I must pay for this. But what have you found?'

Ellyn poked at the dough, anxious to end the farce of searching the bread. She exposed something tiny and as hard as a tooth. It was carved out of bone. She felt sick.

Bastidas leaned forward.

'Surely I do not need to tell you what it is?' He made a mockery of any surprise. 'The baby! Whoever finds the baby is king of the fiesta. But you, *señorita*, must be queen. I salute you.' He raised his glass. '*Feliz Navidad!*'

The toast was interrupted by a rapping at the door. He scowled and stood, marched over and wrenched the door back.

'*Sí?*'

Ellyn saw one of the guards bow low before delivering a clipped report. Bastidas snapped a reply and returned to the table looking pleased. He did not sit. He held up his glass.

'The fleet has arrived!' He drained his wine and beamed at her. 'You may take the baby with you.'

Ellyn remained motionless though she supposed she could go. She stared at her bowl where the miniature bone carving lay in a pile of flesh-coloured crumbs.

Bastidas moved to her side. With a start she heard him whisper as his breath brushed her ear.

'You are *bella* even with no smile.'

Will blinked and drifted in the no-man's-land before waking. He was lying in gloom, looking between the poles of a tent-shaped shelter, and what he saw was trampled sand-bleached white by burning light. Beyond was an awning where skittles and archery butts lay in a dusty heap, along with bladderballs and roperings. No one had the inclination for games any more. Men lay beside him on low trestle frames, and some snuffled in their sleep while others moaned, gripped by fever. But Will's head was clearer than it had been for days, and he was content for a while to listen to men talking, though he sensed wretchedness in their voices, and he wondered whether they were deliberating on sailing for England again. That was the subject of most furtive conversations: going back while they still could.

His gaze returned to the trampled sand, and the triangular

stockade of the fort, with its scavenged planks from a wreck still stained black with caulking. When had he last worked with tar, or done anything much except fight illness and frustration? He rolled his head and squeezed his eyes closed, and then opened them again to see a face like a wraith's: a death mask cast in wax – the surgeon's boy, wasted by illness. Would he live? The surgeon was dead, together with patch-eyed Simon and over half the crew – so many that they had re-named their base 'Slaughter Island'. And though some, like John Drake, had lost their lives after skirmishes, most had succumbed to the same vile malady, like the Captain's other brother, young Joseph, and that loss had changed them all. Twenty-eight men had died together in one week. Awareness made Will long to drift, as he had when he was sick, his mind floating in numb oblivion. For weeks they had kept to the coral islets, a day's sailing from Nombre de Dios, east of the headland called the Cativas, lying low in the reef. But if many more died, would any ever leave? How could he reach Ellyn on her island and then take her all the way to England? With the return of some of his strength, he longed to get back to her. She had been left alone for too long and he felt answerable for her plight. He turned to gaze at a patch of sky, seeing frigate birds flying by, and he yearned to be with them, moving freely, heading westward over the sea.

Clambering out of the shelter, he stood unsteadily in the sun, feeling the sand scorching his soles. The metal bands around the water bucket were baking when he touched them. It was empty inside, save for the reek of damp decay. A loud rumbling made him turn. There was a Cimaroon at the gate, rolling a barrel over rattling boards. As Will watched he remembered the *Jesus*, the ship he had sailed with General Hawkins: the carrack that had carried a cargo of men in her hold. Now Negroes were their friends, and the first slave who had joined them remained with them still: Black Diego, the man who had brought a warning during the attack on Nombre de Dios. They had all sworn alliance through Diego's intercession – a pact born of the same hatred, uniting Englishmen and runaways.

The sound of splashing drew Will closer as the Cimaroon unplugged the cask. Will's tongue was dry, but he eyed the water in the light, noticing it was brownish and foaming while he cupped his hands under the spurt. He was parched, yet he hesitated. Had the water made them ill?

'Good day, Will.' The voice was Drake's. Will turned to see the Captain drinking deeply beside him. Will brought his hands to his lips and did the same.

'Come with me.' Drake strode off to the gate.

They walked along the beach and looked out to sea. Stretching to the horizon were countless coral islands topped by mangroves and palms. The *Pascoe* was almost invisible, covered by foliage and with her masts down.

Drake slowed but did not stop. He frowned.

'What are the men saying?'

Will understood; he answered truthfully: 'Some of them say, perhaps we should go back. They fear disease more than the Spaniards.'

'So, do we quit?'

Will bowed his head, unsure how to answer.

Drake sighed.

'Aye, perhaps we should, while there are still enough of us left to sail the *Pascoe* . . .' There was defiance in his voice though not his look. He strode on. 'But to leave with nothing, after so much sacrifice . . .'

He lapsed into silence, and Will noticed the slight limp in Drake's gait as he trudged over the sand. By the sea all the scrub had been cleared. It was possible to circuit the entire island without leaving the shore. Will wondered whether Drake was intent on doing just that. He seemed thrown into a mood that Will had not witnessed in him before: sombre and bleak.

Drake turned.

'What have we achieved?'

Will looked from Drake to one of the corners of the fort; the rest was largely hidden behind mangroves and brush. What could he say? The truth was they had achieved little, but brooding on that would do no good. He sought to dispel Drake's melancholy; there was not much else he could do to be of use. He seized upon every triumph he could think of.

'We have put the fear of God into the Spaniards, attacked where they thought they were impregnable, terrorised their trade routes, captured many prizes . . .'

'Ships with cargoes of no real worth. Am I to go back to the Queen and present her with trifles? She will not thank me for beans and flour . . .' Drake drew breath. 'The whole of the Spanish Main is on the alert. Nombre de Dios has been reinforced, warships patrol the seas around Cartagena and after six months of opportunity I have less than half the men I came with, and no riches of any account.' He looked away, as if only the sea could understand. 'I have not had my vengeance. That is . . .' He shook his head slowly. 'That is *failure*.' His voice dropped until it was close to a whisper. 'My brothers are dead.'

'They died bravely.'

Drake craned round and looked Will in the eye.

'Joseph died like a dog that has been kicked over and over. He died wretchedly, in my arms, spewing blood.'

'Even the best soldier cannot fight disease.' Will tried to offer some comfort. 'We have been beset by mishaps, through no lack of courage. Consider the catastrophes that have afflicted us, yet we have endured them – Raunce parting from our venture—'

'Raunce left because he had not the nerve to carry on. That was no catastrophe.'

'But we have endured much worse: sickness like a plague, the loss of the *Swan*—'

Again Drake cut across him.

'No,' Drake said, still walking. 'Losing the *Swan* was no accident.'

'What then? I thought . . .'

'You thought the *Swan* sank because she had sprung a leak and we could not bail her out fast enough.'

'We did our best to save her, toiled a full day at the pumps, both your brother's crew and the *Pascoe's* . . .' The memory of the disaster was still raw in Will's mind. He did not want Drake to suppose that their efforts had fallen short.

Drake shook his head.

'I ordered holes drilled in her hull. I had them covered over so they would not be noticed. Only the carpenter knew.'

'Why?' Will grasped Drake's arm without thinking. His voice rose. 'In the name of God, *why?*'

'The *Swan* had to go.' Drake's answer was firm. He looked at Will's hand, and Will released his hold. Will would not have dared touch him if he had thought about what he was doing, but then Drake had never before been so forthright. Will drew breath. It was for him to listen, not question. He supposed the Captain had few left to confide in who might not threaten his authority. Leaders could not easily be friends. But that made the truth no more bearable. He clenched his jaw as Drake carried on.

'The men had to be committed. I did not like what was necessary. My brother loved that ship. She was John's, and I took her from him. Even command of the *Pascoe* was no recompense. He died without knowing what I had done . . . for this venture . . . for a greater cause.'

'We all swore an oath to see this venture through.' Will could not disguise the edge in his voice, however much he wanted to show his loyalty. He could barely contain his grief. 'Did you not trust your own men?'

'You have heard them talking.' Drake looked again at the sea. 'There could be only one ship able to get back to England. One ship to hold us all to the venture. But now . . .' He turned back, and Will saw a depth of sorrow beneath the blithe confidence he was used to. Drake raised his chin. 'I thought it could be done.'

'And I,' Will murmured and sighed. The anger had left him. Drake's decision had been made long ago. Nothing would be achieved by questioning it now. He needed Drake to be strong. 'We have come so close. There was a king's ransom within our grasp at Nombre de Dios, and only ill luck stopped us seizing it.'

'No'. The denial was soft, and perhaps, Will supposed, Drake was thinking of something else in his low spirits, so Will went on. 'Consider the storm that spoilt our powder . . .'

'No.'

'The ball that struck your leg . . .'

'No!' Drake was vehement. 'We were never close. There was nothing to take.'

'But yes, if not in the Treasure house, then certainly in the Governor's house. Remember all the silver . . .'

'There was none.' Drake lumbered on. Will caught him up.

'You saw it. "Silver enough to fill our ships", you said – more than we could carry.'

'There was no silver.'

Will stopped, stunned.

'But why did you say otherwise?'

'The men had to believe that the treasure was close.' Drake snapped and carried on. 'They had to have faith.'

'Faith in treasure?' In a few long strides Will drew level with Drake, challenging him with the question, repeating it, because he could not make pretence of his reaction. He had never believed Drake to be so ruthless. By his own admission Drake had destroyed his brother's ship; he had lied about the silver. How else had he used those sworn to his endeavour?

'They are men of fortune. You know them.' Drake's voice dropped. 'Perhaps I expected too much. I thought a river of bullion flowed through Nombre de Dios, and it would be an easy matter to dip into it with daring: strike the Spaniards where it would hurt them most, divert their riches and be avenged.' He drew his hand over his brow. 'I did not expect the river to run dry.'

Will glanced down. He had given Drake his trust, and now he knew where that would lead: to one end, and one end only. Drake would let nothing deflect him. The enterprise was greater than anyone, mariner or brother, man or woman. Drake would only help Ellyn if that did not interfere with his purpose, and he would not readily sail for England without achieving his goal. They had to succeed. Will turned to him.

'The bullion will flow again. The Cimaroons have told us the treasure fleet has arrived. Once the fleet docks at Nombre de Dios, then the mule trains come from Panamá. Ellyn confirmed as much before we left her.'

'Do you believe that?'

'Yes.'

Drake looked grave.

'I cannot rely on what the Cimaroons say. They mean well, but they want to please us. They tell us what they think we hope for. Treasure means nothing to them; the silver trains are of no significance.'

'Ellyn understands what is at stake.' Will paced beside Drake and eyed the sea. 'She was certain: the mule trains begin moving after the fleet reaches Nombre de Dios. The convoy was expected around Christmastide. If it has arrived, the timing would be right. She has a keen intelligence.'

'Aye.' To Will's surprise, Drake voiced no reservation. 'She does. I've sent Ox in the *Lion* to scout for sight of the Spanish ships.'

They had almost reached the point at which they had started, and the talk of Ellyn made Will long to comfort her with a message: to let her know she had not been forgotten. She would be wondering what had happened to them. He no longer trusted Drake to ensure her safety, at least not before seizing the treasure he wanted. Will stared at the reef. His gaze shifted to the horizon and the small lumps of scattered islets. Then, slowly, the square of a sail came into view.

Drake shielded his eyes.

'Well there is our *Lion*. We may soon know more.'

Will could see that the *Lion* had a capture. There was a frigate further out. If the treasure fleet had arrived, they might yet have another chance. He studied the pinnace. The *Lion* was driving ashore with prisoners aboard, rich merchants from the look of them. He saw everything more clearly as the *Lion's* oars brought her in. A mariner jumped into the shallows and raced up the beach. Will strode with Drake to greet him.

'There are above a score of ships . . .' The man gasped as he neared. 'In Nombre de Dios . . . The fleet from Seville . . .'

Drake smiled broadly, eyes twinkling as he clapped Will's back.

'Rouse the men, Will. We have a venture to finish!'

That night the air was still. The sound of honing and stropping made a continuous sharp swish; voices were muted. The heat was trapped. As Will walked through the fort, he caught the smell of resin and tallow. Someone was bent over a longbow, waxing the yew. By the light of the half-moon he made out more.

'Are you ready, Morrys?'

'Aye, Will. Keen to get goin'.'

'I feel that too.'

Will could sense the urge to be gone in every wan face that turned towards him, and in the remarks as he passed.

'Sleep easy.'

'God keep you.'

In one of the corners of the fort, a candle glimmered behind a screen. The shifting shadows revealed huddled forms. Drake would be in counsel with Black Diego and Ox, deciding how eighteen Englishmen and thirty Cimaroons could best attack a mule train loaded with bullion and under guard. With so small a force they would need the advantage of surprise, a plan of daring and much courage. But every man in the enterprise was eager for some action at last.

Will spotted Hix sitting with his back to a post. His friend had no reason not to be sleeping; he had been chosen to command those left guarding the *Pascoe* and the fort, but Will sensed what he would be feeling: envy and frustration. He had known those feelings, too.

'Fare thee well,' Hix said, and nodded as Will strolled on towards the gates. Perhaps Hix understood something of Will's mood, just the same; he did not question why Will walked out onto the beach.

In order to think Will needed some space. He began the same circuit around the island that he had made with Drake only hours before. In the dark he could make out footprints that the tide had left untouched; some might have been his. The sea shone, and the rippling lines of surf made a luminous verge to the silvery sand. He walked fast and breathed deeply, taking in the aroma of sap and brine. Away offshore, strange greenish patches glowed, bobbing on the waves. One of the mysteries of the sea was that it sometimes made its own light. When most things were obscured, a few became clear. The night revealed stars.

He was worried for Ellyn – more worried than he had ever been since leaving her near Nombre de Dios. 'She will be safe,' Drake had assured him, but that was when he had seen her last, over half a year ago. 'Trust me,' Drake had said. But did he trust Drake now? If the attack on the silver train succeeded, then their fortunes would be made. But all would be lost unless they were able to escape. What if they failed? Whatever the outcome, Ellyn's position would be more precarious. Will picked up a pebble and threw it far over the sea, watching light shimmer where it sank. He had to face what he knew. His conversation with Drake had helped open his eyes. He could not rely on the Captain to safeguard Ellyn at any price. He could not comfort himself with the notion that seizing Spanish bullion would help her. It might put her in worse danger. He would have to find her, and take her away from the reach of the Spaniards. But when? How? What if she was no longer on the island where she had been left?

His feet sank in the loose sand. He ploughed back towards the spume. He could not go to her before the attack; if he tried to and was caught, then the Spaniards would discover Drake's intent, and all those with him would be trapped. But he must go to Ellyn straight afterwards. He must find a way, even if that meant defying Drake, and in the meantime he would send her a message. She had to be on the island when he got there. She had to be ready, and not in the city.

He reached for another pebble and hurled it away with all his might, and again he saw a faint burst of pale greenish light. The waves sparkled against the shore. How could he get a message to her?

He stooped down once more and picked up a shell.

18
Heart

'If thy heart fails thee, climb not at all.'

—Words written on a window pane by Elizabeth I, in response to those marked on the same pane by Sir Walter Raleigh: 'Fain would I climb, yet I fear to fall' (as recorded in Thomas Fuller's Worthies of England*)*

Ellyn had been shut in the same room for hours, long enough for the heat to become intense, and for the slivers of light to mellow and widen. She knew she was in the garrison where Bastidas had once questioned her, somewhere high, under the roof. The wooden ceiling was sloping on one side, and occasionally, in the distance, she heard musket shots and orders. From the window came the sounds of people below. She was sure that, if she could look out, she would see the plaza and the government buildings, but the shutters were bolted closed, just as the door was firmly locked. So she stared at the light because there was little else to look at, except for the gecko, inert on a beam.

The room that imprisoned her was small and hot, empty of furniture save for the chair on which she sat. There was a guard outside who coughed and shuffled. She pinched a fold of her skirts, feeling the weave of the worn fabric, and wished that she'd had time to clothe herself more carefully. Soldiers had taken her from her island even before she was properly dressed; then she'd been ferried to the city, marched in soaked skirts through the streets and confined in the garrison without any explanation.

She ran her fingers through her uncombed hair, tidying it as best she could. 'You are *bella*,' Bastidas had said when they had dined together on Twelfth Night. How long ago was that? She could not reckon it clearly. Perhaps seven weeks had passed since she'd been with him last, and then he had seemed intent on flattering her in his own peculiar way. Yet his aims must have changed. She recognised a cloying scent like ambergris in the room, powerful and sharp. The smell was his.

She would not despair. She thought of the message she'd received that had been hidden in a shell. It had been delivered only a few days before, given her by the Cimaroons who often brought her fish. She had come to trust them. The giant with the scars had handed her the shell, holding it to his ear before pointing inside its lip. She had found the slip of paper coiled into its folds. The message had been unfurled as she now smoothed out her skirts; then she had committed the words to memory:

We are very close. Be ready. I will come for you soon. Burn this after you have read it. Your voyager, Will.

Could Bastidas have found out? Yet how? She had done as Will had asked. No trace of the message remained. But perhaps the Cimaroons had been followed. It was always possible they had betrayed her. She shook her head. She would not believe that.

The Cimaroons could tell her little except that the message had come from 'the English of the Dragon', and not '*el inglés de la luna*' or 'the Englishman of the Moon'. Drake was known as the Dragon, so this confirmed what she hoped. But she had no idea who the other Englishman was who was said to be marked by the moon, and she did not much care, since Will was not with him.

She stared at the slivers of light. 'We are close', Will had written, and she took hope that he might find her, despite the manifest difficulty that he could not know where she was. 'Your voyager', he had signed himself, and she clung to those words: he was on a voyage to reach her – her ordeal would end soon. She could even hear footsteps. Her heart raced. But the striding outside was surely too crisp to be Will's. Then she knew. Even before she heard the guard stand, she knew Bastidas was at the door, and when she turned, there he was, dressed austerely and armed with dagger and sword.

Bastidas closed the door and paced slowly around her. When he spoke his tone was cold.

'I am trying to think why not to send you to Spain – for examination by the Holy Office.' He stopped and looked at her. 'The Inquisition,' he added quietly.

Ellyn tensed, though she tried not to show it.

'I am not a heretic.'

'You have lived as one for years.'

'I attend Mass with the good people of Nombre de Dios. Ask Friar Luis—'

'Friar Luis does not speak for the council of this city.' Bastidas stepped towards her. 'There are many here who believe you should be made to account.' He moved around to her other side. '*Inglesa*.' He moved closer. '*English* woman.'

She kept still.

'It is not a sin to be English.'

'No?' Bastidas began to stalk around her once more. 'You are stained with the sins of your friends, the corsairs.'

'No more now than I have ever been.' She watched him, certain that something must have changed. Suddenly she was desperate to know. 'Has there been news of Captain Drake?'

Bastidas continued to circle her, back straight and head down, hands clasped behind him.

'I was hoping you would tell me that – to spare yourself.' He veered nearer and stooped, just enough to bring his head level with hers. 'Tell me,' he murmured. 'It would be sad for such beauty to be lost. You know what the Holy Office can do.' He spread his right hand in front of her. 'Perhaps they begin with your fingers . . .'

He reached out to her lap, and she willed herself not to recoil. She would show no fear of him. She stared at the hair around his knuckles as he brought his hand towards hers. He touched her fingers.

She looked up.

'I have heard nothing.'

'Truly?' Bastidas raised his brows. 'Then let me tell you.' He resumed his pacing. 'Capitán Draque has attacked a silver train on the Royal Road. You know what I am talking about?'

She was conscious that he was studying her, assessing her

reaction. She guessed that by a 'silver train' he meant one of the pack trains carrying bullion from Panamá to Nombre de Dios. She stared at the shutters.

'His corsairs with some *cimarrones* marched across the land,' he went on. 'They got almost to Panamá. Then they set a trap by the road. They did this near a little town: Venta de Chagres.' Bastidas circled her in measured steps. The floorboards creaked with each shift in his weight. The light flickered across his legs. 'The Treasurer of Lima was with the next mule train. It is clear the corsairs knew. Capitán Draque probably thought the Treasurer would ride straight into his arms. But no. The Treasurer sent on a *caballero* – a horseman. This man saw one of the corsairs. He gave warning.' From behind her, Bastidas drew back her hair. The sudden contact made her start. His breath brushed her ear.

'*Así*, when Capitán Draque attacked the pack train he found only what was sent for him: a little silver and food. The Treasurer rode back to Panamá with his gold and his jewels.'

She turned, but at that instant Bastidas stepped away, with his fist to his chin in an attitude of contemplation. He resumed his pacing.

She looked at the gecko and breathed steadily.

Bastidas snapped, making her start. 'Your friends are fools and they are cowards!' His voice rose. 'They only have audacity because they are in league with the Devil and black savages.' He paced closer. 'Not satisfied with the mule train, they attacked the little town. They came across some holy fathers: Dominicans with a guard. Capitán Draque refused to concede. "For the honour of the Queen of England, I must pass", he said. Pah!' Bastidas gave a hollow laugh. 'What honour?'

'The honour of a sovereign,' Ellyn answered with as much composure as she could.

'England is nothing!' he snarled. 'Your countrymen are filth!' Sweeping his fist from behind his back, Bastidas held it clenched tight in front of her.

Ellyn shrank back, her eyes drawn helplessly to the gem-embossed rings that flashed towards her.

'Their answer was to shoot. They fired at priests. One is dead!'

Ellyn bowed her head, but Bastidas grabbed hold of her chin forcing it up until she looked at him.

'Then this band of corsairs and savages swept with war cries upon the town, to plunder . . . to burn . . .' He unsheathed his dagger left-handed. The blade gleamed, only inches away from her face.

She tried not to flinch.

'Now tell me, *señorita*, why I should not show you the same courtesy as did your Capitán Draque. There were women and children in that town.'

'I am sure he would not have hurt them.'

'There were ladies in convalescence after childbirth.' Bastidas squeezed her chin painfully. The blade shimmered before her eyes.

She managed to speak.

'Treat me no differently.'

He swept the blade aside and strode behind her. Her skin filmed with sweat. His footsteps stopped. She turned her head, seeing nothing, wanting to run, though there was nowhere to go. She was poised to rise the moment he struck. The blade hit the back of her chair; its impact shuddered through her. She jumped up and straight into his grasp. With his hands round her neck, he pressed with his thumbs.

'"Trust me", said Capitán Draque.' Bastidas brought his face closer until his mouth almost touched her brow. He repeated the words while he bore down on her. '"Do not resist and you will not be harmed."'

Ellyn spluttered, choking. Bastidas was so close she could smell his bitter breath. She tried not to look.

'"Do not resist",' Bastidas murmured, and she felt him relax his hold. But he kept his right hand on her neck while with his left he stroked her breast, first through her clothes, then forcing his hand beneath her shift. He kneaded and pinched her soft flesh. His breathing quickened.

She opened her eyes, blurting out, trying to distract him.

'Did Captain Drake get away?'

Bastidas gripped her breast hard.

'He has left.' Bastidas squeezed harder. 'Gone back with his little booty.'

She ground her teeth. She would not cry out. All the while he dug deeper. The sound that came from her at last was half-wild: a tortured keening she could not suppress.

He was breathing fast.

'So now for you, *señorita*. When the fleet sails for Spain, do I send you with it?'

She felt faint. The shadows were swimming. He tightened his hold. She made herself speak.

'When does . . . the fleet sail? How long . . . ?'

Suddenly he drew back, snagging his rings on her shift. She felt another sharp pain as he twisted his hand to wrench it free. Then he caressed her face.

'Six weeks maybe. No more. In which time you may come to know me better.'

She slumped forward with a groan and crossed her arms over her chest.

'I can be *dulce*,' he said, stroking her cheek. 'I could make you a Spanish lady.'

Glancing up, she met his gaze. She had to gain some control. Keep him away. Not beg. Not weep. She fumbled to re-arrange her clothes. The next instant he grimaced. She looked down at her bodice and saw the red of fresh blood. A scratch from his rings, she told herself: nothing more. She covered the spots with her shawl. He had to desire her.

Bastidas stroked her hair.

'You should stay here, in Nombre de Dios.'

She stared ahead. The light sliced like wire over the floor. In an abrupt shiver of movement, the gecko on the beam scurried to vanish into a crack. She glanced at Bastidas. Let him believe his mastery excited her. Imagine it. She was drawn to him. He was good looking, after all. He could help her if he chose to.

'I must first return for my things . . . and for Marco.'

Allow Bastidas to suppose he was courting her; he seemed to think that he was. If he would give her the chance, she might go to him willingly. Let him believe it. 'There is much . . . I need to do.'

He continued to toy with strands of her hair. He brought his face nearer.

'Go, then. Fetch the boy and your things. Prepare as you wish.

See how I am kind. My men will take you back, and I will return for you the next day.'

Then he kissed her, pressing his lips against hers, and she suppressed the urge to shrink back while shock froze her mind. Only when he pushed up her skirts did she raise a hand and pull away.

'Tomorrow, then . . . I shall leave now.'

At that, he released her. She was numb. Even so, she heard him.

'*Mañana*. I shall think of you.' He kissed her cheek. 'I shall wait.'

Ellyn gestured for Marco to go quickly. 'Leave that for the workers.'

'Where?' The boy blew out his cheeks as he struggled with a basket full of fruit.

'On the beach.' Ellyn gave another wave. 'I want nothing left to rot in the house.' She knelt by a chest and tried to force down the lid.

'*Sí, señorita*.' Marco's piping continued behind her back. 'What of the goats? I tie them and leave also?'

She leant on the lid, and still the hasp would not fasten. 'Why will this not fit? It must do. Help me, Marco.' She contemplated sitting on the chest while reflecting that her father's armour was crammed inside.

'Look,' Marco babbled. 'You have something stuck.'

'Oh, no!' The thing that she stared at looked like the tip of a thumb. She jerked the lid back and the contents overflowed. She picked up a gauntlet, badly crushed: her father's glove. With a pang of remorse she rubbed at the leather, before replacing it in the chest and repacking the rest with more haste.

Marco edged away.

'Now I go . . .'

'Where?' Ellyn frowned. Had Marco said he was going? Then she remembered; he had been asking about tying up the goats, and she could not bear to imagine their fate if they were left helpless on the beach. 'No, I will free the goats.'

'But they will eat everything!'

She made a decision.

'Take out all the fresh food and leave it where it can be seen. I shall be back soon. And hurry, we must be ready tonight.'

Marco watched with his faint brows raised high, and on impulse she hugged him, cutting short further talk. Her freedom would end the next day, but her thoughts kept returning to events hours earlier, and she could not speak about them. So she took the path to the fields, but drifted back in her mind to the shuttered room in the garrison. While the last shafts of sunshine set the foliage glowing in the trees, she remembered how Bastidas had circled her, asking questions, the blood on his hand, his fingers inside her slip, until what she recalled finished blank like the end of a nightmare. The shame was much worse than the ache she still felt. She crossed her arms over her chest and hunched as she stumbled, almost crashing into the goat pen before she recognised where she was.

The sun had gone down. From the rise, facing the sea, she noticed clouds that were tinged red, the colour of blood over a bruise. And if there was ever beauty to a scene that she would never see again, then she could not find it as she looked but saw instead that she was trapped, since she had no boat, and no means of escape, and the sea all around her was like a vast immuring moat.

With an effort she opened the gate, so numbed that every action required a huge focus of will, and the dun kid that nuzzled up to her induced the urge to cry out loud. He was her favourite, and she embraced him, not caring that he nibbled her apron while she pressed her face against his coat. She tousled the curls between his horns, and in the slits of his eyes she saw the shape of open doors. Let him live, she thought. Let everything go. She took off his collar, and smacked his rump to make him run, then watched the other goats springing after him, bleating as they fled.

They were soon lost to her sight, no more than ripples in the dusk, but she remained standing, staring at the trees around the pen. The vegetation shook, though there was no breeze. She could hear snapping and rustling, but there was no wind. Rubbing her eyes, she put her hands to her ears, conscious of a ringing inside her head that made her moan in dismay. There was too much to do and her reason was failing. She settled her sight on the sea to try and clear her fogged mind. There stood the palms by the bluff, her tiny coral-stone shelter and the beach. Nothing had changed – except that there was also a boat. Or was there? Something like a small galley was drawn up on the shore. She could not be certain, the light was too weak, yet there were surely men moving about, disembarking and dispersing. In that instant of realisation a dread certainty chilled her heart: Bastidas had come – his soldiers were close and seeking her out. She wheeled round and ran.

Her steps faltered in the gloom. She lurched and slipped but raced desperately for her life. She was not ready to face Bastidas, lose her freedom or endure any more. He must have released her to taunt her – returning her to brief liberty only to maliciously cut it short. He would enjoy the chase. He was hunting her down. She ran as hard as she could, dragging her skirts past barbs and thorns. She would not offer herself up, or meekly submit. There were men coming nearer, crashing behind her through the brush. Someone was close, calling out. But she hurtled on, stumbling blindly. She had to escape. She would not stop.

Something caught at her shoulder. She wrenched violently away. Her breath came in gasps. Her legs shook as she tired. She slowed and was seized. Her arms were pulled back. She was pinned against a man who locked her tight in a hold. She could only shriek and slump down. But he held her.

'Ellyn! It is I, Will!'

She wrestled to break free, beating at his chest, though the first glimpse of his shadowed face was enough to burst open her heart. And when he pressed his face next to hers, her tears would not stop. She shuddered as she leant against him, feeling his hand stroking her hair, his beard by her cheek and his deep voice as if already within her, sounding in the core of her being.

'I am here, and I am not leaving you.'

She buried her face against his shirt, surrendering to his strength, his body like a rock, conscious of the tang of leather and salt, and that his touch was tender, so tender she wept afresh.

She could barely see, but she heard sounds that alarmed her. Men were shouting in the distance. She shrank back, twisting round. They were coming nearer very fast.

Will ran his hands over her shoulders.

'You are shivering like a lamb. What has happened to you? Why so frightened?' He raised a hand to her face that was bandaged about the palm, and she flinched when he touched her, though his questioning was soft. 'What is it?'

'Bastidas . . .'

She clutched at Will and looked about. There were men with bows emerging like black phantoms from between the trees. Her eyes darted wildly from where they were massed to where they were not, searching for a gap, a place to flee. Their whole appearance was sinister, yet she guessed they were Cimaroons, and when Will addressed them like friends she let out her breath.

Will waved them away.

'Go back and wait for me.'

He held her arms gently.

'Bastidas. You mean the captain in charge of the garrison?'

'Yes.' She shook in remembering. 'He is coming. You must get away . . .'

'When is he coming? Tonight?'

'Tomorrow. Perhaps at daybreak. Please . . .'

He embraced her again.

'Hush. We will be gone before he gets here. The wind is westerly and that will help.'

He glanced up, and she followed, seeing the pale disc of a rising moon and the faint glimmer of stars. He seemed satisfied.

'We will sail through the night. Are you ready to go?'

'Yes.' She began to move away and he kept close by her side.

'There is only Marco,' she murmured.

'The boy we saw heaping bananas on the beach?'

'Yes, I asked him . . .'

Will took her hand and led her on past the fields.

'He cannot come with us. He would have no life back in England.'

She felt the stiff strips of his bandage, and looked ahead into a void. The path was like a tunnel where it dropped down through the trees.

'I know,' she said quietly, and wiped at her eyes.

Two Cimaroons were at the doorway; they moved aside to let Ellyn pass. She entered her house to find Marco with a pike: the same great weapon that her father had once used. His posture was threatening though his mouth gaped open. Everywhere she looked, articles and clothes were strewn in chaos, and for a moment she was shocked, until she remembered how she had left them.

She stepped forward.

'Oh Marco, put that down! These are friends . . .' She glanced behind her. 'Did you leave all the food on the beach?'

'Yes, Mistress Ellyn.'

Marco answered politely, even attempting a small bow which sent the point of the pike thudding down.

'Tell our friends they may help themselves,' she said gently.

The boy frowned and set the pike by his feet. He edged slowly past the Cimaroons and then pelted away through the door. The two men laughed and took hold of her father's chest, raised it with a grunt, and followed him into the night. That left her alone in the midst of her possessions, scattered like flotsam washed up from a wreck. She found the purse of pearls Will had left her and pushed it in her pocket; then she stooped by the remaining chest and began cramming in the nearest things: a blanket cloak and pewter cups, a kirtle and stockings.

Will joined her quietly, kneeling by her side.

'How have you fared? I have thought of you every day. You seem . . . anxious.'

She saw that his face looked haggard despite the shine in his eyes. But while she took this in, she was folding a chemise very carefully, doubling it over and over. She only realised what she was doing when he placed his hand upon hers.

'You were not afraid of Bastidas when I saw you with him last.' He pushed down with his fingers until their hands were intertwined. 'What has he done?'

Silently, tears rolled down her cheeks to land in dark splotches on the chemise. She picked it up and all the folds fell out at once. While she tried to refold it, she felt Will push back her hair. She looked up into his eyes, and his gaze was searching.

'What has happened?'

She could not hold her feelings back. She felt her face crumpling and there was nothing she could do. Her tears fell as Will held her, kissing her hair, soothing and steadying, loosening her shawl as he stroked her neck.

Then he stopped and pulled back.

'What is this? Have you been hurt?'

Pushing the shawl off her shoulders, he looked down at her bodice to see, just as she did, the spots of blood that stained her clothes. Straight away she covered herself up, grasping at the shawl to hide what was there.

Will sighed and bowed his head, leaning forward until his brow touched hers.

'Has Bastidas done this?'

She touched Will's hands.

'I will kill him,' he muttered. He pulled back and looked at her. 'Why?' Slowly he shook his head. 'What sense could there be in it?' He looked into her eyes. 'What did he want from you?'

She hugged him and whispered, 'I gave nothing.'

'My message . . .' Will was talking as if to himself. 'Did he? . . .'

'No.' She leaned back on her heels. Will needed to know what Bastidas had told her. 'He believes that the "English corsairs" have sailed away. He said you tried to ambush a mule train on the Royal Road. Then you attacked a town. You killed a friar . . .'

Will gave a nod.

'So he hurts you. And that is just?'

She huddled against him, and he stroked her hair.

'The friars were with soldiers who fired after we gave warning. We had no choice.'

Was that right? She no longer knew. She turned her head against his shirt.

'Take me away from here.'

His reply was a kiss, on her head, then her brow, her temple and her cheek, one kiss after another, slow and then quick.

'I will never leave you and never forsake you. I'll never again let you go.'

He kissed her next as he had kissed her at first, when, over two years before, on an autumn night in Plymouth, she had leaned from a window to find him waiting in the cold, and slipped into his arms as she now fell into his embrace. The touch of his lips carried her with him without drawing away, taking her on and on, until at last she opened her eyes.

She saw the hollows that made his face look gaunt, scratches and bruises.

'But what of you?' she asked. 'Where is Captain Drake?'

'Gone west to find gold if he can. He wants a ship full of booty; more than that, he still wants a silver train. He's determined on another raid.' Will smiled and ran his fingers through his thick fair hair, and even that appeared changed to her, darker and rougher. 'Ox has gone the other way to try and find provisions. Whatever happens we'll be leaving soon. I had to get you back. There are a few of us left at Slaughter Island . . .'

'Slaughter Island? What name is that?'

She watched a crease deepen between his brows, one that she had not noticed in his face before.

He looked aside.

'Many have died. The Captain has lost his two brothers.' His expression hardened as he went on. 'We have gained few riches to draw the sting from that.'

She took hold of his bandaged hand, beginning to imagine what he must have been through.

'You are hurt, too.'

'A little cut that will soon heal.' He spoke lightly and grinned when she pressed his hand to her face.

She kissed the bandage with care.

'Let this help it.'

'Now it is better.'

Delicately she probed the stiffened strips of frayed cloth, aware that whatever was beneath was almost black with dried blood. The wound must have been deep. It looked like the cut of a sword.

'You will have a scar.'

He kissed her again.

'And that will please me because it will remind me of this night.'

She met his gaze.

'Then I hope it never fades.'

'It will not.' He smiled wryly, pressing his bandaged hand

against her cheek. 'It will be a lasting mark, like my brother's.'

She frowned, wondering whether he expected her to know what he meant.

'Kit has a scar on his palm like a sickle moon,' he explained, 'burned by a horseshoe in the smithy. A lucky mark, so our father said, though it did not protect him from the Spaniards.'

Turning her head, she let the bandage brush her lips. Will must have loved his brother deeply. He was talking about him again. Kit had a scar *like a sickle moon.* The words jarred in her thoughts. She looked up and away, staring at the little shell on a barrel top: the one in which Will's message had been delivered, brought to her by the giant who had told her about the 'Englishman of the Moon'. Who was he?

'Kit . . .' She breathed the name. Could the man be Kit? She clutched at Will's arms, on the point of spilling out her suspicions. But what if she was wrong?

'He might . . .' she began.

What if she told him? Will would seek Kit out, of course, and Drake was preparing to leave having lost many of his men. What if Kit could not be found? It could finish far worse; Will might die in the attempt.

'He could . . . still live,' she said haltingly.

Will pressed her against him.

'I cannot believe he does not.'

She hugged him, and shivered.

'And I never believed you would not come back.'

For a moment they clung to one another, but then he released her.

'We must finish here.' He turned to the chest. 'Shall I close this?'

In a daze she looked round. Heaps of possessions remained strewn about, and most were things she had once thought precious: bolts of kersey cloth and her pen and ink, a hat Marco had woven for her, but at a stroke they were all unimportant.

'Yes . . . no.' She picked up the shell. 'Put this inside.'

The rest could be left. Then her eyes alighted on her old worn shoes: the pair that had been Thom's, that she had worn when she had played the boy – though playing was all it ever could have been. She had kept them for use like clogs in the fields. She picked them up as Marco came back. She held the shoes out.

'Here, Marco. I want you to have these.'

His face brightened, and his gratitude showed in the flash of his smile, but that soon faded as he turned his head, first to the chest and Will standing beside it, then towards all that was left in disarray about the house. When he looked at her again his brown eyes widened.

'You are going without me.'

She went up to him and held him.

'I have to. Stay here and go back with Friar Luis. When the soldiers come tomorrow, tell them—' She felt his slight frame stiffen and sought the words to prepare him best '—that I have left with some *cimarrones*,' she said, struggling to keep her voice steady. 'You do not know where.'

Sounds of banging and shuffling made them both glance round, to see two Cimaroons in the process of lugging out her chest. They were the same men whom Marco had threatened earlier.

'You must say I have left with the *cimarrones*,' she repeated.

Marco hung his head.

'This will be true.'

She bent and put her love into a kiss, whispering intently, making an earnest request, one only he could hear, knowing that this would be the last thing she ever asked him to do.

'Wait for the fishermen, the ones who brought me the shell. When they come, tell them this . . .' She gave him her message: news for the 'Englishman of the Moon', and if that man was Kit, then she prayed he would heed it.

Marco nodded and she held him, unable to bring herself to let him go until Will gripped her shoulder and the boy's as well.

'Come now.'

Will led her away towards the sea, past a group of goats, just visible in the moonlight, busily feasting on bananas by the beach.

19

Alliance

'. . . As the pack-trains engaged in the overland traffic of this realm were proceeding under guard . . . from this city to that of Nombre de Dios, with gold and silver belonging to Your Majesty and to private persons, to be laden on board ships of the fleet, when they had arrived about a league and a half from that city, there came forth . . . a certain number of English, French and *cimarrones*, who are negroes who have run away from their masters, and advertise that they have allied and confederated themselves with the English and French to destroy this realm, a thing not until this year ever seen or imagined . . .'

—From the report of the Royal Officials of Panamá to King Philip II of Spain dated 9th May 1573

Will clasped the little bells in his fist. He did not want them jingling as he brushed by to enter the hut. He could see Ellyn was asleep. So he edged inside; then he settled on a chest from where he could watch her quietly. She sat with her head down, neck arched and turned to one side, eyes closed, lips parted. He took off his cap. He would share a moment with her, and the Cimaroon outside would make sure they were not disturbed. The fort was noisy but, in the place that gave her some privacy, a sense of calm made the hubbub seem less. She had only been on Slaughter Island a few days, and in that time she had hardly relaxed. He was glad to see her resting. Whatever trauma she had been through, rest would help in healing. He was content just to be near her; he would never tire of that.

The pleasure he took in being with her was like waking up in summertime in England, beneath a bright, cloudless sky. She was a landscape entire. Her body was curved like the coombes and there was promise in her folds. He thought of soft paths through meadow grass leading to field-strips of barley. He looked at her lips, red as poppy petals: lips he had kissed and would kiss again. Merely the imagining was enough to stir him. She was the heartache of home – yearning and joy all rolled into one.

He gazed at her face. No other woman could be as lovely. His blessing was to be with her as she was at that moment, in a time that was his, without sense of its passing. Asleep, her face moved. Her eyelids quivered and her lips curled slightly. She gave a little shudder and took a quick breath. He wondered where she was in her dreams; whatever the place, he would have liked to have joined her. She frowned, rolling her head, and he reached out to calm her. Suddenly she was awake, eyes open and fixed on him.

'Will! What are you doing here?'

'Considering you.' He smiled. 'Thinking how fair you are.'

'Flattery will not excuse you. I prefer to invite people into my house.' She frowned, plainly flustered, and brushed back her hair. 'What did you see?'

'You were asleep.'

'I was pondering.'

'You were pondering with your mouth open just so.' He made a little 'O' with his lips as if he was blowing a bubble, but he had only mimicked her for an instant before she slapped her hand over his mouth.

'Will Doonan, you are a heartless, mocking jackanapes. How could you think me fair if I was pouting like a fish?'

He pulled her hand away and kissed it.

'As easily as I think you fair when in truth you are dark.'

'So I am not fair?'

At that he reached for her and pulled her to him on his lap.

'No, not fair at all; so unfair that I expect no justice. You wrong me, sweet maiden.'

'*I* wrong *you*!'

'Yes,' he said, kissing her, 'you do.' He did not try to put his feelings into words; he doubted that he could, and he feared that if he did then she would only pick whatever he said to pieces. He simply kissed her again.

His reward was her laughter, and her arms around his.

Ellyn took up a shoe and traced the outline of a blood-smeared hole, imagining the agony of each step without protection where the skin was broken. 'Your work could make the difference between life and death, Mistress Ellyn,' so Drake had said. But why did the mariners need shoes now? She could guess the answer from what Will had told her. On the long march inland, the one that had led to the failed attack, the men had returned so footsore and weary that many had to be carried on the backs of the

Cimaroons, so Will had told her. Handling their shoes gave her more understanding. She assumed Drake was planning another trek. Why else would he want shoes repairing? And in a way that pleased her, because of the message she had left with Marco; she had always supposed Drake would venture inland again – Will had said Drake still wanted a silver train. But she was also fearful.

On Slaughter Island there were few able men left. She looked up at empty shelters inside the walls of the fort, and then at her own tiny hut: the one that the Cimaroons had made for her in the week since her arrival. She scanned the trampled sand where hog bones and corn husks attracted flies in small clouds. She knew where the men would be: aboard the frigate that John Oxenham had seized, fitting her out as a man o'war, moving the ordnance from the rotting *Pascoe* where the Spaniards from the captured ships were now held as prisoners. With the bounty from Oxenham's prize, she had seen how the mood had changed. Drake's men had been restored, their bellies filled, fortified by wine and roused afresh by fighting talk. They were clamouring again for vengeance, and now Drake was plotting another strike. The sudden arrival of French corsairs had emboldened him even more; they had forged an alliance. But where did that leave her? She was labouring like a cobbler without really knowing what to do, cutting soles from a leather bucket since there was nothing else to use. She was trying her best, despite the pain in her hand from piercing holes with an awl, and the pricks of the curved needle, and the cuts of the waxed thread. But she would much rather have been helping to prepare for a voyage back to England.

The French alarmed her. They were Huguenot freebooters who

outnumbered Drake's men, with a much larger ship that was far better armed. Where would a pact with them lead? Drake had only thirty men left, and a good number of those were unfit to fight. She had seen men too weak to stand, wasted by fever and with terrible wounds. Men had died on every one of Drake's raids, and no doubt more would die on the next. Where would it end? With her fingers inside a shoe she felt the mould of a man's toes – someone who might be alive, or could be dead, and she had no idea who would wear the shoe next. The shoe could be for Will. She glanced up again and wondered where he was.

Only one man was near: a burly Cimaroon picking at fishing lines and hooks. It had not escaped her attention that while Will was hardly with her, the Cimaroons were never far from sight. At night at least one of them would be stationed somewhere outside her hut. She smiled at the man and looked back at her work. It was as if she had been assigned a constant guard. But did she need one? 'I will never leave you,' Will had said. But of course he would; he would be leaving on Drake's trek. 'I will never forsake you,' he had promised. She wanted to believe him, but what did that mean? They were not betrothed. He had not asked her to marry him, or involved her in his plans, or even said that he loved her. She shook her head and jabbed with the awl.

Will's conduct could be explained; she tried to calm herself with reason. To preserve the general harmony it was better to behave as if nothing lay between them. If Will kept his distance, and she did not openly favour anyone, then no one could be put out: she would be no object of envy, and cause no resentment – there would be no rivalry when the men were preparing for another venture. Will would have other matters to think about and better things to do. Or was that just an excuse: an explanation she had devised to spare herself the truth? She struggled to push the spike deeper. Then the crunch of footsteps made her start. Her hand jerked back and the spike slipped out. She yelped with pain and sucked her thumb quickly; it was badly pricked, and she had seen Will approaching.

'What have you done?' Will stooped to her with knotted brows. His eyes flickered as he studied her face. 'Let me see.'

'Oh, nothing,' she said, though her thumb was throbbing, and the slip had upset her. 'I was careless.'

Will eyed the pile of roughly mended shoes.

'You have been working hard. But come with me now. The French captain has asked for you.'

She stood, brushing down her skirts with her uninjured hand.

'For what reason? Does he also have shoes in need of repair?'

Will took her arm and kissed her hurt thumb gently, smiling as he straightened.

'Not Le Testu. I believe he has shoes fit for a royal audience. He is a distinguished navigator who has impressed our own Captain with his skill in drawing maps.' Will told her more as he guided her through the gate. 'He has made a fine cosmography of the world based on his voyages to Africa and the Americas.'

In brilliant sunshine Will led her to a little boat, and the effect of his company was like balm over everything; she felt instantly soothed.

'Get in, and I will row you over,' he said. 'There is a meeting in Drake's cabin.'

She smiled at him happily, unsure how she could be of any use though her uncertainties paled.

'What is the meeting about?' she asked, after settling herself in the stern and watching him take up the oars.

Will sculled the boat away, glancing over his shoulder at the two ships in the roadstead, before settling into a rhythm, pulling hard with each stroke. But while his body moved, he kept his eyes upon her.

'Le Testu was a confidant of the Admiral of France,' he said at last. 'But the Admiral is dead. There was a massacre in France on St Bartholomew's Day last year. Le Testu has told us. Most of the Huguenot leaders were murdered. Thousands of Protestants have been killed.'

'But why?' She blurted out the question, shocked by the news, and still none the wiser as to why Le Testu had asked to see her.

Will continued to row steadily, bringing his face closer, and then pulling back, so that she found herself fixing on each detail of his strong features: the line of his stubbled chin, and the pale creases by his deep-set eyes, with an intensity compounded by his constantly shifting. Coming towards her again, he spoke.

'The Catholics feared them. Catherine de Medici turned her son, the king, against them.' Will heaved on the oars. 'The wars in France grow worse. And now you know why Le Testu is here.' He leaned forward again. 'He wants to join us in striking at Spain.'

'For the Protestant cause?'

Will eyed her and grinned.

'For freedom.'

Freedom. She thought of what that meant as she looked at the ships: the captured frigate and the French ship newly arrived. The activity all around gradually became clearer as they neared. Men were on the ratlines, and balanced on ropes under the spars, working on the rigging, winching up barrels and crates. They were scaling rope ladders, carrying up weapons and provisions. She noticed the gun ports cut in the sides of the smaller frigate, the little boats nearby and the pinnace roped alongside. She was free: free from Bastidas and the island and everything that had once constrained her. If she was asked to do anything for freedom, then she would.

'How can I help?' she asked.

'Le Testu wants to know what you have seen of the silver trains.'

Apprehension unsettled her, and she wanted to prepare. Her recollection of the mule trains was hazy, and she supposed the questioning would be severe. If she could picture Le Testu, she might anticipate what she faced. She had already conjured up an image of him as a vigorous swashbuckler, dark and lithe.

'What is he like?'

Will's answer was no help at all.

'Brave,' he said, and smiled.

Drake was puffing on a smouldering leaf, ruddy-cheeked and clearly at ease. There was a fug of collusion in the air, in the way the smoke wreathed and curled, drifting in the sunbeams slanting through the arched stern windows. Ellyn imagined some sort of bargain must already have been concluded. She saw complicity in the way the men sat close: mariners and Cimaroons alike were all hunched around the captain's table until, as she entered, one by one they raised their heads. She recognised wiry John Oxenham and Ellis Hixom with his hideous scars. They faced two fearsome-looking Africans, and a swarthy seaman whom she knew but could not name. With his back turned towards her was a white-haired gentleman wearing a faded blue cape. This man was the first to rise, and when he greeted her she was amazed, for he was Le Testu, slight and stooped with age, gracious and softly spoken, with a manner more suited to a scriptorium than a warship.

At Le Testu's invitation, Will made a place for her to sit. Then a silver cup was pushed into her hands.

'Would you care for some *eau de vie*, mademoiselle?' Le Testu asked. Her bewilderment probably showed. 'I believe you call it brandy wine,' the Frenchman explained, while his face crinkled like an old dried leaf.

She held the cup near her lips. A trace of strong spirits caught at the back of her throat, along with the reek of weed-smoke and tallow.

'Thank you, Captain. It is a long time since I partook of drink such as this.'

Le Testu cocked his head.

'Ah, yes. You have lived here for well over a year, I am told, on an island near Nombre de Dios, under the nose of the Spaniards with little charity from them to sustain you.' He smiled, blinking rapidly. 'So please drink with us. This is the finest *eau de vie* from Armagnac; it preserves youth and makes the wit lively.'

'Then I shall be glad of it.'

To please him she sipped, and someone chuckled as she gasped.

Le Testu raised his cup.

'*A votre santé*. You must be pleased to be with your countrymen again.'

'I thank God for that.'

'And my countrymen are your friends also. Did you notice how many there were on my ship?'

She looked around the table, puzzled by the question, but no one else seemed surprised; they all drank or smoked, scratched or examined their hands. Ellyn frowned.

'A good number, sir. I should say about forty mariners were above decks.'

'Excellent. And in the mast tops, were any men there?'

She hesitated. An image of the French ship formed uncertainly in her mind, culled from what she had glimpsed when she had been rowed across from the fort, though then she had been concentrating on Will and what he had said.

Le Testu fixed her with his pale eyes.

'I wonder, can you tell me how many mast tops you saw on my ship?'

'Tush, sir! Do you not know your own ship?' She bridled, suddenly aware that she was being tested, and affronted by the implication. 'You have a carrack with a main, fore and mizzen, and fighting tops on them all. I believe I saw a man at the top of the foremast.'

A sound like a hand-slap made her turn towards Drake. His shoulders were shaking while a suppressed smile creased his face. Someone cackled and coughed.

Le Testu raised a gnarled hand.

'I am pleased you are so observant. Now tell me of the mule trains if you will. You have seen them entering Nombre de Dios?'

'Yes, they come in most days now from Panamá, and that will continue until the treasure fleet leaves for Spain.'

'Do you know when that will be?'

She was aware that there had been noise in the cabin only when it stopped, and then what she heard was the slow creaking of the frigate's timbers. The men around the table were all completely still. She answered with conviction, as best she could.

'No later than mid-April, when the rains start, and the Royal Road becomes impassable.'

A murmur rippled and gathered strength.

'So we only have a few weeks?' Oxenham demanded. 'The fleet may already be underway.'

'What then?' someone asked, and voices were raised.

'God's teeth!' Hixom snarled.

Le Testu broke into the clamour and asked, 'Are you sure of this?'

He looked at her. They all looked at her. She tried to explain, thinking back to Bastidas and the things he had said, through memories of the degradation she had sought to forget. She glanced at Will and saw the strength that she needed.

She took a deep breath.

'In the third week of February, I saw Captain Bastidas, the Commander of the garrison at Nombre de Dios. He said that the fleet would sail in six weeks.'

Will nodded.

'That would be the beginning of April.'

'We are near the end of March now,' the swarthy mariner broke in. 'We might be too late.'

'We might be rich very soon, Master Sherwell.' Drake silenced the muttering that ensued. 'The most precious loads will be carried last. The Spaniards will not risk leaving the King's gold for long in that Treasure House, not since our attack.'

'The most precious will be the best guarded,' Le Testu said

softly. 'Could you describe the escort for the mule trains, mademoiselle?'

'In the main, they are light.' She thought of the barefoot guards she had seen marching into the city. 'The Spaniards still fear an attack by sea, not along the road. I have seen trains of about fifty mules guarded by a dozen men, mostly slaves armed with bows. Sometimes they carry firearms, but these are often old.' Her gaze was drawn to Drake's Cimaroon friends. She took in their proud faces and muscular shoulders. She saw pieces of armour, and bracelets of leather and teeth. The men looked menacing, but she would be truthful. 'Since the Cimaroons do not use firearms, and the Cimaroons are perceived as the principal threat, these weapons are considered sufficient.'

The Africans scowled, while Hixom's mouth twisted into a wide, ugly grin.

'We'll rout 'em.'

'It's as we thought,' Oxenham said.

'Aye,' someone growled and others followed.

Ellyn sensed the eagerness swelling in the hearts of the men. Even Will's eyes were flashing. The mood caught like wildfire but it left her untouched. They could not know what they faced.

'The mule trains usually travel in convoys of two or three,' she said. 'The largest may have two hundred mules and be guarded by fifty men.'

Will nodded.

'Some of those might be Spanish horsemen: *caballeros* – armoured and carrying matchlocks. We have seen the kind.'

'And bested them,' Hixom added.

'Together we can better fifty!' Drake slapped the table and gave a triumphant smile. 'Near the city, at the end of their long journey, their vigilance will be less. This is where we should strike.'

'Aye!' Oxenham and Hixom led the chorus, and the Cimaroons soon took it up. 'This is a good plan.'

Le Testu leaned forward.

'Such an attack will depend on surprise.'

Drake stroked his beard and looked from the Frenchman to the Cimaroons.

'The Cimaroons will help us. They know the forest trails. We will round the headland of the Cativas and sail west for eleven leagues. There is a river called the Francisco that is within a day's march of the city. It should suit our purpose well. Our pinnaces can take us to a landing place upstream.'

'You say "us",' Le Testu interposed. 'Am I to have the honour of being included in this venture?' His manner was reserved but Ellyn felt his zeal. His gaze settled on Drake.

'Most certainly,' Drake gestured with open palms. 'But I would rather have a few good men than an army not up to the task. I can count on fifteen in my own company: strong men of courage, experienced, fit and ready.' His bright eyes scanned the faces of every Englishman around the table: Oxenham, Hixom, Sherwell and Will. One by one they all showed their commitment. Then he looked across at Le Testu. 'Can you match that?'

The French captain smiled, and with good reason Ellyn thought, since his forces were plainly greater, but he answered respectfully.

'I have seventy men and, since our fortunate encounter, most are now restored in health.'

His men had arrived in a parlous state. Ellyn remembered how they had been desperate for both water and food, but their recovery had been swift.

Drake gave Le Testu a knowing look.

'Twenty will be sufficient, yourself included, but pick only the best, and we will have Cimaroons enough to balance us in numbers, since the success of our venture will depend equally on them.'

He turned towards his old allies and she saw them conferring, but she could tell from Drake's expression that he never doubted their support; it was given by a warrior with tattoos across his brow.

'We will join you.'

Drake drew on his leaf and half closed his eyes, then he exhaled, blowing smoke towards the low ceiling before turning to Le Testu.

'Have the rest of your men get your ship ready for a long voyage.' Suddenly his tone became strident. 'We may need to leave quickly!'

Ellyn noticed the change as the men broke into broad smiles.

Hixom stood, swayed and held up his cup.

'I'll drink to that.'

'To victory!' Le Testu followed.

All at once the men got to their feet, pitching their voices in deep accord. Ellyn alone was left seated, until she rose with the awareness that she had almost been forgotten.

She spoke up from her heart.

'I pray for that, too.'

'Thank you, dear lady,' Drake kissed her hand before giving the order to prepare. 'We must be ready at dawn!'

While the men began to move, Will gestured for Ellyn to go first.

'Four more days,' he murmured from behind her. 'You won't have long to wait. Then we'll all leave together.'

The stranger was a giant. Kit watched him approach, surrounded by a growing crowd as he passed through the village. The man towered above most. When the man came close, Sancho rose and challenged him, and even Sancho was no taller. After they had spoken, Sancho turned to Kit.

'This is Gibad,' Sancho said. 'He comes as a friend, with a message for you.'

'Welcome, Gibad.' Kit raised his hand in greeting, taking in the man's impassive face, and the length of cloth that he wore like a robe, wrapped about his hips, then draped over one shoulder. The garb was curious. The *cimarrones* usually wore clothes that were stolen.

Kit beckoned the stranger closer.

'What is your message?'

As the man strode forward, Kit noticed the puckered scars that ran in lines down his chest. The man looked at him uncertainly. He stopped a pace away, then he dropped down on one knee, speaking to Sancho who interpreted for him.

'He asks to be shown the mark of the moon.'

Kit understood and held up his hand. The visitor bowed, reached out, and pressed Kit's palm to his brow in a way Kit had witnessed countless times before. He did not resist.

The man spoke again, and then waited for Sancho to explain. 'He says he has been told there will be Englishmen near the road.'

Kit tried to show no reaction. He had learnt to keep hope contained. 'Where, near the road?'

The man answered and looked at Sancho.

'He is not sure,' Sancho said. 'The message was not clear. He was told to tell you that Englishmen are expected near the road to Nombre de Dios. He can say no more.'

Kit nodded. The man had delivered the message freely. Why would he have kept anything back?

Kit caught the man's eye.

'Who told you?'

'The boy of the Englishwoman of Bastimentos. The message came from her, though she has left the island now.'

An Englishwoman? Kit had heard rumours of an Englishwoman on an island, but he had never before believed them. Perhaps they were true. But, if so, then how had she come to be there? Where was she now? He looked from Gibad to the food laid out by the fire, set ready for the evening's feasting. He gestured to it.

'Eat with us, and accept our thanks. We like to know what passes on the road. We like to learn of pack trains that might carry things we can use – weapons and tools. If you hear of such traffic, then please tell us more.' He smiled and stood. 'What is ours is yours.'

Sancho drew the man away as Kit walked to the edge of the clearing. From the hilltop he could glimpse the sea. He drew a deep breath. Looking over the treetops he saw the distant stretch of water that led eventually to the ocean. A rustling made him turn, and he saw Ololade drawing nearer, hips swaying, leaning back. She was heavy with child, and he knew the child was his. Behind her were the thatched roofs of the village, greyed by smoke and the low, fading light. He could hear the soft chant of singing, the beat of drums and babbling voices – smell the cooking and the earth, sense the warmth leaving the forest. Ololade walked up to him and pressed her swollen belly to his side. He put his arm around her and closed his eyes. The laughter of children took him back to his own childhood in England, and a memory of chasing around corn stooks with Will. Then, the sound of the church bell had rung clear across the valley, but in his mind that soon faded, displaced by the evening riot of jungle noises.

Ololade snuggled against him.

'The stranger has troubled you,' she said haltingly in the English she was still learning.

'Yes.' Kit sighed. He had hoped not to alert her, but she knew him too well.

She leant her head on his chest.

'You want to find your countrymen.'

'Yes.' He could not keep it from her. 'But the Spaniards control the road. It would be dangerous for us to go there. And for what? For nothing that will help us.'

'For you.'

Kit buried his face in her hair, inhaling her cocoa scent, feeling her heat.

'I cannot take anyone with me. Even if I find a ship bound for England, I cannot leave, except alone. There is no one of your kind who is free in my country, only a very few Negro page boys who serve in rich households. You could not come with me as my woman.'

'I understand, yet your birthplace is across the sea. You have the chance to go back and you will not rest until you do.'

He felt her shaking and knew she was crying. What could he do? Should he try to forget what the messenger had told him?

She pressed his hand to her hard belly.

'You must go.'

Kit held her tight, conscious of the new life under his scarred palm and that though her words were few, her perception was great. He could not remain forever an outcast; neither could he take her with him, and still less raise their mixed-blood child in England. The *cimarrones* were her family now – her people, but not his, not truly. Sancho would look after her, shelter and comfort her, protect the child she was carrying. He hugged her and kissed her, over and over, then stroked her forehead gently and felt the wet of his own tears.

She looked at him bravely, cupping her hands under her stomach.

'A part of you will be always with me.'

'My love,' he said, turning aside as he wept. 'Tell the others I have gone hunting.'

Ellyn crossed her arms and hugged herself as she paced along the beach. 'Only two more days' was the thought that cheered her, and provided the excuse for another little squeeze. Four more days was what Will had said, and two had already passed since he had sailed off with Drake. Then, when Will came back, they would leave together as he had promised, no matter whether he returned with riches or nothing at all. They would sail for England, away from Slaughter Island and the Cativas, and Panamá and the Spanish Main. Drake would have to embark on the homeward voyage or miss the favourable currents and risk being caught in storms; and, anyway, the fleet would soon be on its way to Spain taking with it the treasure that was all Drake wanted, so there would be no reason for him to stay any longer.

Then, throughout the crossing, she and Will would share stories. They would fill in the time they had missed, he in her life, she in his, until they each knew the other as if they had never been apart, for as far back as memory served, and nothing would be hidden or left overlooked. They would share their thoughts and ideas. They would reveal every incident that had shaped their histories, or given them pleasure, or stayed in their hearts, and grow together in the telling, like vine stems intertwined. She gave a small skip and glanced round, noticing a Cimaroon watching her from the shade beside the shore. Let him see. She took two quick steps, a small leap, and twirled about. Then her pace slowed and she continued head bowed. She would return without her father – her mother would be distraught.

Ellyn hugged herself again, but for reassurance, not for joy. How would she explain? Her mother's grief would be immeasurable. The loss would seal her in seclusion as if her door had been boarded over. Ellyn clutched at her sides imagining her distress. But surely her return would bring some solace? She walked more quickly. In the midst of her mother's sorrow she could give a little sweetness; her mother would come to know that Will was to thank for bringing back hope. Then perhaps she would again take some pleasure from picking up her sewing, and maybe begin a fresh design, and work it in bright colours, and when that happened then Will might speak . . .

What would he say? Ellyn studied a mangrove plant growing straight out of the sea: no more than a few arched roots, and a single thin stem with two leathery leaves. How had it grown there? She shook her head and walked on with lighter steps.

How would Will show himself worthy if he was to ask for her hand? She had considered the question so often she could not conceive it might not arise. She had no reason to suppose Will would ever be truly wealthy. Perhaps he might return with a few more pearls and silver, though even that seemed unlikely considering Drake's recent failures. But once she was in England, those small riches would be unimportant. He would have delivered her home safely. He would have proved by his conduct that he was beyond compare as a suitor. Her love for him would dispel doubt, and with the faintest of smiles, and a word barely whispered, her mother's blessing would be given and their happiness made complete. Ellyn raised her skirts and took five steps: the beginning of a galliard. Then, with a little jump, she began turning circles along the shore.

She half-closed her eyes, seeing only shadow and light, imagining Will in the dance, and the music of lutes, viols and flutes. His cape was thrown back, and in his handsome face there was pride. He was holding her for the lift, taking quick, springing leaps, supporting her with ease as she leapt for the *volta*, and she supposed his hands were on her hips, lifting her high, whirling her round. Then she was turning as he lowered her, seeing those looking on by the oak-panelled walls: her mother and Old Nan – they were smiling as she laughed. Lettie and Jane – let them see her with her love. Peryn Fownes and Godfrey Gilbert – she was content for them to gape, knowing that for all they had expected, she had made her choice regardless of fortune. She was with a man who was the best, beyond compare, without equal – and she loved him. She loved him. She carried on dancing over the beach, skipping and leaping, spinning round and around.

And when she slowed, out of breath, then the sea and the mangroves, the fort and the sun were all turning about her, and the Cimaroon was dancing, too, and drifting by in the water was the little shoot with two leaves.

Kit pushed past creepers and tangles of thorns. He followed paths that no Spaniard had ever used, looked up beneath trees that spiralled to the sky, and ferns that arched heavenward like great feathered fans. His sight was keen as he peered into the forest, scouring the furthest reaches for any movement near the ground, any flash of colour other than green, looking for something he could barely believe in, though for years the hope had persisted. Yet this was reality. This was his world waking up: the warm, damp forest glistening with spangles of light, ringing with whoops and shrieks – and what he searched for were Englishmen as the messenger had told him: Englishmen near the road.

He quickened his pace, ducking under spiderwebs as dense as wool, brushing aside leaves as huge as barrow wheels, straining to hear in an animal bedlam. He stopped and caught his breath. At times there were pauses in the racket: lulls that he tried to explore, alert for the trace of voices, signs of people – the crackle of footsteps through the forest.

Kit listened. In the next interval there was only haze: a barely audible fuzz, and then three notes – a beginning: birdsong that reminded him of mornings in the past, beautiful and liquid, full of freshness and promise. Then the memory was gone, overlain by a howl. He wiped at his eyes with the back of his hand. He carried on walking.

Slashing with his machete, his progress became faster, he ran when he could, bounding down gullies in drifts of dry leaves, thinking of another sound that was autumn and everything it evoked: beechmast and acorns and windfalls in wet grass – charging with Will along comb lines of stubble. Then all that fell away, driven to oblivion in the heat.

He stared ahead. In the distance there were leaves and fronds, and more of the same in all the spaces beyond. He ploughed on regardless, ignoring the thorns and mosquitoes, and the sores on his feet, impelled by another sound, very faint but unnatural. Then he recognised what it was.

He pulled up and crept forward. He had no idea of the source of the ringing, whether it was moving or almost still, approaching or receding, near or far. But he realised that the sound of the mule bell could only have come from the road. He also realised what it meant.

There were Spaniards passing by.

20
Attack

'. . . Certain English and French corsairs, together with a number of *cimarrones* . . . attacked certain mule-trains conveying gold and silver from this city to that of Nombre de Dios, . . . amongst this being 18,300 pesos of fine gold which came for Your Majesty from the jurisdiction of Popayan . . .'

—From the report of the Audiencia of Panamá to King Philip II of Spain sent 4th May 1573

The Royal Road, near Nombre de Dios, the Americas

April 1573

They were coming. Will could sense it: a faint vibration in the earth rising through the grass sweating beneath him. He looked between stalks, below flowers and seed-heads that were buzzing with busy insects, seeing a sultry sky, and faraway trees, with nothing to suggest any interruption to the peace. But he could hear them. He could hear mule bells behind the thrum, and a slight rustling as Morrys turned. Will met his eye then peered ahead. A tiny wisp of smoke rose from the lock of his caliver, and he cupped his hand over the pan, guarding the primer from the match. The smouldering was slight, and the acrid whiff of saltpetre would be lost in the meadow's sweetness; it would not be noticed from the road. He was ready – calmer than he had ever been before any action on the venture, but tense, even so, knowing that this would be the last.

He moved his hand to the trigger guard and prepared to take aim. The tinkling became louder, along with the swish of tramping through grass, a ripple of laughter and the low voices of men. The sight of them came with a shout: Drake's voice.

'Yield!'

Will lurched to his feet as a shot cracked out, and suddenly Drake was bellowing above the whinnying of a horse, 'In the name of Elizabeth, Queen of England! . . .'

A roar overwhelmed everything. Will joined in the battle cry rising from the others breaking cover, sighting on Spaniards so close he could see their teeth as their mouths opened. A few were quick to react. An arrow streaked overhead. Another whipped into the grass.

'Fire!' Drake yelled, levelling both of the wheellock pistols that had been a gift to him from Le Testu. Will saw flame stream from their muzzles at the moment he was deafened by a blazing volley: a barrage of bullets and bolts that drew screams from behind smoke. Then Drake's men charged, running at a pelt for the Spanish vanguard, all fifteen, except for him. Will had his caliver trained on a horse: a small bay jennet that almost fell then reared up, dismounting a *caballero* before galloping across the pasture. The man was dragged behind, caught by a stirrup until his boot was torn loose. Will held his aim. He swept round his matchlock, keeping the jennet in his sights. He could not let the horse escape. They were too close to Nombre de Dios, perhaps an hour's march for a man, but much less for a bolting horse. He braced for the recoil, finger on the trigger, but the horse collapsed before he had fired. Its legs thrashed, and then stilled. Around the place where it had dropped, men sprang up from the ground. The Cimaroons emerged like phantoms from the scrub, and from the cut in the bluff where the city road left the floodplain. Like burning over paper, they swept south in a wavering line.

Distant gunfire made Will turn. The smoke had thinned and he saw the convoy: the line of mules so long that it stretched back out of sight, men running alongside and drovers cowering. Others were taking flight, making for the riverbank. An armoured Spaniard splashed lumbering downstream. Will fired without waiting for the man to come closer. What mattered was the convoy: stopping the mules, securing the road. He barely paused to see the man falter. He was already in a lope and dashing after Drake.

His focus was on a skirmish where he could hear the clash of blades. Rushing past mules, he shouldered his firearm, feeling the strain in his legs of the past day's hard marching. He breathed in gasps while gnats rose in clouds and stuck to his sweat. Yet his spirits soared as he ran. The mules were kneeling down. One by one the mules slumped to the ground, snorting and champing, each taking down the next. This was the plan unfolding, the design playing out. The muleteers were surrendering: black slaves with rolling eyes who crouched low with their hands raised.

Will drew his sword to a Spaniard who turned tail and fled.

'Let them go!' someone called. But he was already bounding on, leaving those trying to escape to the Cimaroons who gave chase, whooping and firing arrows.

At the rear of the next mule train, animals were milling in a tangle of reins. Will heard Ox shouting, 'Bring down the lead!'

Close to sprinting, Will ran along the line, aware that a few men were following, and that, one after another, the mules were settling in the grass. But he was looking ahead, searching for Drake, his fear catching up. He stared at the high ground at the end of the pasture. Traces of smoke drifted above a winding paved road. The road led from a pass. The French had taken position there, ready to block the retreat once the convoy descended. He had expected to spot the Huguenots at the foot of the far rise. Yet the only Frenchmen he could see were those rushing towards him. They fell on loads, tearing at bindings, dragging away saddlebags, calling excitedly.

'*Argent . . .*'

'*Silver!*'

'Gold!' one of Drake's men roared. 'There's gold in lumps – quoits a handspan wide!'

Will pushed on, half-sprinting, half-striding, passing mules and the Cimaroons who were rushing up to halt them. Across the riverbed, at a distance, men were scrambling north the other way: the remnants of the Spanish escort, wading through the shallows, trying to escape. Will slowed to a fast walk. His breathing was hoarse. He was drenched in sweat. How many mules had he overtaken? A hundred and seventy? Maybe more, and all loaded with treasure as far as he could tell. Only at the end of the line could he see the high ground clearly, and the evidence of a struggle on the slopes beside the road: glimpses of baggage in the vegetation, mules that had broken free and a few men prone. Straggling over the pasture were Frenchmen in ragged groups. They appeared from between the trees, out of thickets, rising from the grass – some shuffling, others racing. He dodged between them. He could see people on the bank, near the place where the paved road ended. He broke into a run. One of them was Drake.

Will caught up. Drake made for a huddle around someone injured: a man with bloody hands – Will noticed when the others moved. Then apprehension shot through him when he saw the man's white hair: he was Le Testu.

Drake sat down next to Le Testu quietly. Will squatted on his haunches nearby. Le Testu made a sound as if there was liquid in his throat. Drake's response was to take off his jerkin and push it like a pillow under the old man's head. Then Drake took one of the wheellocks from his belt.

'These pistols are fine pieces.' Drake secured back the pistol's hammer, extracted the little ramrod from under the barrel and proceeded to clean out the bore. 'They made the Spaniards skip away prettily. I thank'ee for your gift.'

Will wondered whether Le Testu could hear. His pale-lashed eyes were almost closed, and he was quiet for a while save for the bubbling in his windpipe. One glance at his wound had been enough to make Will blench. It was easier to fix on the old man's face. His lips were drawn back in a grimace. Will hoped Le Testu was stunned, but then, in a drawl, he began to speak.

'We have stopped . . . the silver train?'

'Aye, all three lines of mules.' Drake carried on scouring out the barrel of the pistol, tipping the handgun upside down, and knocking out the residue inside. He turned to Le Testu, and did not look away. 'Beasts for half a mile, and carrying enough gold and silver to buy a small kingdom. You led your men well, my friend.'

Will saw a smile begin to play on Le Testu's lips, but then he winced.

'No better than you. Now you must go. Take the treasure while you can.'

'Therein lies a happy problem.' Drake raised his eyes to the lowland spread before them, and Will saw, just as Drake must have done, the long, long lines of kneeling mules and scattered loads, with men amongst them still unroping packs, tearing open saddlebags, and piling up trophies that flashed and glinted in the sun.

With a click Drake opened the pistol's priming pan.

'We have more than we can carry.' He spoke while he cleaned out the pan. 'I would say that we can only bear away a tenth on our backs.'

'You cannot use the mules?'

'Not by the way we came. The forest is too thick. To clear a path for the beasts would delay us.'

Le Testu gasped.

'You should at least take the gold . . .'

'Certainly.' Drake returned his gaze to the pasture and the mounting heaps of booty. 'There must be over half a ton, which leaves us with a prodigious quantity of silver; I'd say maybe fifty times as much.'

The old man's breath rattled to a gurgle, and the half-dozen Frenchmen around him began to shuffle forward. But Le Testu raised a blood-smeared hand, and no one moved between him and Drake.

'Take what you can,' Le Testu whispered. 'And when the Spaniards return, they will want to pick up their treasure, and not chase after you.'

Drake turned the pistol muzzle-up, took a small twist of paper, and tore a hole to release the charge. Carefully he poured the powder inside the barrel.

'Aye.' Drake inclined his head. 'But I would like the Spaniards to find their treasure gone completely. I want them to *feel* its loss. Let them think that with the help of the angels we have swept it clean away.' He popped in the paper after the charge, and then a small lead ball which he rammed tight with the rod. 'I thought we could hide it.' He smiled, and cast a quick look at Le Testu.

Will knew the old man was listening. Le Testu held his hands to his stomach, and the pulp of fabric and tissue through which his innards glistened.

'It may be possible . . .' he muttered, 'if you are quick.'

Le Testu beckoned to one of his mariners and spoke urgently to him in French, pointing with a bloody finger towards the islands in the riverbed.

'My men will bury what they can . . . over there.' The mariner was already sprinting down towards the river. 'I am sure you will find other places. Later . . . you can dig the treasure up.'

Drake nodded as, with a little spanner, he cranked round the shaft of the pistol's firing wheel.

'We will leave as soon as the bulk is concealed.'

Will heard the wheel lock into place, taut against the mainspring.

Le Testu slumped back.

'I will rest . . . and then follow.'

'Rest well, my friend.'

Drake primed the pan and shut the cover, then he pulled back the dog-hammer with the piece of pyrite in its jaws that would, on a pull of the trigger, strike the wheel set spinning and release a shower of sparks.

'Here's a faithful dog come back to stay with you.' He wrapped Le Testu's hand around the pistol butt. Then he looked up at the two Frenchmen who were nearest. 'You will guard over him.'

It was a statement, not an order. They murmured their assent: '*Oui, Capitaine*.'

Though the old man's eyes were staring at the sky, Will saw his fingers slowly slide over the trigger.

Drake bent and kissed Le Testu's brow.

'*Adieu*.'

He stood and marched down the slope. Will followed him at a stride. Within a few paces they were running.

'Some of those crab burrows should make good hiding places – and no need for digging!' Drake's speech came in jolts as he swept his arm towards the river. 'And those tree trunks, under the roots. See to it, Will, and remember where everything is put.'

Will scanned the terrain. He could see the crab holes that Drake meant, and the huge creatures scuttling near them, some blue and some grey, waving pincers like fists, and the dark pits beneath the tangled roots of washed-up trees that would make excellent nooks for secreting their haul.

'Aye, Captain. Just the silver?'

'As best you can.' Drake ran towards the end of the last mule train. 'We've not the time for much sorting. Leave the gold and I'll split up the loads.' He clapped Will's back, and bounded off at a tangent.

Will ran along the line, between the mules and the riverbank.

'Bury the silver! Hide it!' Shouting, he signed for the men to follow him. 'Over there! Bring the bars! We're going to feed the crabs!'

The men were nervous. They twitched and cowered, glancing around furtively. Kit could not tell whether they were English or Spanish. They wore the loose slops of mariners, and they were alone, without any slaves, but their jabbering made no sense to him. He edged closer through the undergrowth, sliding around rocks, keeping silent.

Peering out from the forest, he saw the backs of the men, only steps away from him, and the grassland before them, dipping steeply to the river. There were scores of mules in the pasture, mostly bunched up in strings, though packsaddles and crates lay scattered around them. But what drew his attention was the bundle near the men. It was a body, he realised, when he focused on the shape: a man injured, and not dead, who raised blood-stained fingers to flick feebly at the gathering insects. What had happened to him and all the mules left abandoned? Had there been an attack? One of the jittery men waved at the flies, but a moment later he turned to stare across the lowland. Suddenly, with a guttural cry, he pulled his friend down into the grass. Kit could hear snatches of their agitated conversation, enough to convince him that they were neither English nor Spanish, though their way of talking stirred distant memories. Then he realised the men must be French, having come across their language in Plymouth years before. So he kept still and quiet, and let the ants crawl over his skin.

The wounded man made a gurgling noise but gradually that faded. He did not answer when the Frenchmen spoke to him, and his hands were limp when they raised his arms. Were they going to carry him? Kit thought that they might until they darted away down the slope. After that, he supposed the wounded man was dead. The Frenchmen ran off into the forest, heading east.

What he saw next almost made Kit run as well.

There was movement: a dark ripple in the distance that suggested a crowd was approaching, and dust above it making the details hazy. Kit crept in shadow towards a gap in the vegetation. He looked along the valley; then he was certain. There were soldiers marching south from the direction of the city: men carrying pikes and lances – a troop led by a horseman. No Englishman would have a horse. The soldiers were probably Spanish. He should flee, but something held him. He searched for signs of the possibility he could not dismiss – that Englishmen might be linked with what he could see of a recent attack. He kept silent and peered out.

The horseman cantered past the milling strings of mules. He rode straight-backed and proud. He was a *caballero*, Kit was sure; he caught sight of the man's helmet: a curved and plumed morion, his cuirass and slashed sleeves. Behind him was an army of footmen, maybe a hundred soldiers, many of them with firearms. The *caballero* dismounted and cut at something in the grass. What? Kit strained to look. The soldiers trooped on. One of them raised a lance. Impaled on it was a head. The horseman pointed east, bellowing orders, sending half of the footmen at a fast pace into the forest. The rest spread around the mules, collecting up the baggage.

Kit crouched motionless. All at once he heard the rumble of hooves. He turned to see the *caballero* emerging from the valley side. The horseman galloped towards him and charged past, only slowing when he reached the wounded man. Kit ducked down. The Spaniard reined round his horse and dismounted merely paces away, near enough for Kit to see the thick, black line of his scowling brow – a line without break over the Spaniard's nose. Then the scowl transformed into a smile. The smile broadened as the Spaniard gave the wounded man a kick.

Was he alive? Kit stared. The wounded man lay inert, but Kit thought he could hear a faint gurgling, the same kind of sucking he had noticed before. The *caballero* took out a handkerchief and held it to his mouth. As he spoke he poked at the man with the pointed toe of his boot.

'*De dónde viene usted?* Who are you? English? *Vous êtes Français?*'

The wounded man wheezed.

The Spaniard raised his boot, and then brought it down hard onto the wounded man's belly.

'Your friends. Where are they? *Dónde están?*'

Kit shut his eyes, but he could hear. The Spaniard was shouting, 'Where?' *Dónde está el tesoro? Où est-il?*'

Kit could hear squelching mixed with screeching, sounds that set his teeth grinding. He clutched the hilt of his machete and looked again. The wounded man's hands were waving, clawing at the horseman's boot, hands covered in blood. Kit saw them clearly above the grass, and the twisting of the Spaniard's foot.

'The treasure. Where is it?'

Kit swallowed bile and crouched lower, unable to get away because a horde of soldiers were advancing, rushing up and crowding round. He could see the sweat on their glowering faces. One of them turned his way. Kit shrank back.

The soldier approached.

When Kit peered out again, he glimpsed the wounded man's white hair through a curtain of thorny creepers. The nearest soldier had turned aside. Further off were others. He caught sight of men pulling at a rope, gabbling and panting, marching on up the hill. With trembling fingers, Kit parted the spiny stems before him. He saw the soldiers more clearly, and the *caballero* giving orders. They formed the semblance of a column that proceeded almost to the forest edge. At the end of the rope was a man, noosed by the neck, hands tied behind his back. Soldiers were goading him, poking at his buttocks with halberds and pikes. He was one of the Frenchmen; Kit recognised his loose slops. The soldiers marched nearer. Kit tensed. Only feet away from his hiding place, the prisoner was dragged beneath a tree.

Kit watched; he could not get away without attracting attention. The *caballero* shouted, bellowing questions as before, and though the wounded man was silent, the man under the tree began to shriek, gabbling at the top of his voice.

'*La rivière. La rive. Non! Pitié!* . . .'

They must have heard him, known he was French, understood what he was saying, though the man could not point. He could do nothing with his arms because they were being pulled over his head, still tied behind his back, bound at the wrist. They were being yanked up and up by a rope looped over a branch, and Kit could hear his bones cracking once the man's feet were off the ground, and his shrill screams and garbled pleading. Yet the lifting went on. It continued until the man swung, dangling from bulging joints, and he had vomited and soiled himself, and Kit could no longer look. He clutched at the creepers and clenched his fists over the thorns, turned his eyes to the white-haired wounded man, and hoped he was dead.

But he was not.

While the *caballero* carried on shouting, the wounded man moved his hand. Kit saw his fingers twitching in the folds of his cape, all red, slick with blood. The screams rose in pitch. Kit glanced back to the torture, in the shadows very near. The *caballero* yelled louder. Kit grasped his machete. The screams cut into his thoughts, cleaving his sense. He could not reason beyond where he was: trapped in a horror he had to bring to an end – act fast and move. The wounded man was spluttering. Blood sprayed from his mouth. He drew a pistol from under his cape.

'*Bâtard!*'

Kit was poised to charge the moment the pistol fired. He froze. The *caballero* staggered back, falling heavily against his men. Through the thinning smoke Kit saw him clutching his arm, and he understood next what the *caballero* must have said, though he could not have heard. The Frenchman never stopped screaming until the rope was lowered and someone severed his throat. Then a soldier with a broadsword marched over to the wounded man, slashed down twice, and held up his head.

Men were running. Kit recoiled, vision swimming. He groped

through the undergrowth, heedless of the noise he was making. Who would hear? Soldiers were scrambling down the slope and spreading out across the pasture. Kit saw them from between the trees. They stumbled down the riverbanks and around the gravel islands, digging and delving, churning up the sediment, burrowing in the riverbed like maggots over meat. Before long they began prizing out bars from the sludge: heavy ingots caked in thick red mud. But Kit looked away. He had spotted the *caballero*.

The *caballero*'s right arm was bound with a cloth. He handled the reins in his left, but his back was straight. Kit willed him to lose his limb and die by slow degrees, but the way the man rode gave no sign that was likely. Behind him marched three lancers each bearing a spiked head: one was a Negro's and one was white-haired; the other was that of the Frenchman whose body now lay in quarters.

Kit brought his hands to his face. They were bleeding and shaking. He looked.

Another horseman was approaching, coming down from the road and proceeding across the pasture. He advanced before a large crowd, mostly slaves as far as Kit could tell: servants in rough clothes. The new horseman was dressed finely with a silk sash across his chest. When he reached the *caballero* he did not dismount first, but waited for the *caballero* to walk over to him and bow; only then did he alight.

Kit could not follow their talking; they were too far away. The noises he heard were of frantic digging mixed with splashing, cries from the work across the riverbed, and the rushing in his ears from the pounding of his pulse. But he saw. He saw the wounded *caballero* stand rigid while the man with the sash pointed to the severed heads behind him and then reached for the *caballero's* sword. No one opposed him. The lancers did not move. The sword was taken, angled against the ground, firmly trodden on and levered until it broke. Kit supposed the *caballero* had been stripped of rank. Kit prayed the man's punishment would be worse. He watched as the hilt was returned with a stilted flourish, first to the *caballero's* right hand, then to his left. The man had to be helped back on his horse. When he rode away, only the three lancers followed him. They passed through the crowd, heading north towards the city.

Kit shuddered and let out his breath. He clutched at his sides, and rocked back and forth. He turned to sink his sight within the deep forest shadows. He wanted to escape inside. Disappear into the shade. Go back to Ololade. But he would discover the truth. Had Englishmen been by the road? And if they had, would they return?

Whoever had buried the bars would be back for them.

21
Fear

'. . . No time now to fear, but rather to hasten to prevent that which was feared! If the enemy have prevailed against our pinnaces, which God forbid! Yet they must have time to search them, time to examine the mariners, time to execute their resolution after it is determined. Before all these times be taken, we may get to our ships . . . !'

—From the speech of Francis Drake, 3rd April 1573, on finding the Spanish in command of the mouth of the Río Francisco, where he had arranged for his land force to be picked up by English pinnaces, as reported in Sir Francis Drake Revived, *compiled by Philip Nichols*

'Where are they?'

'Gone . . .'

'This is the day agreed?'

'Aye, but they're not here.'

The men were still carrying the saddlebags. They stood in a

thicket on the ridge, gazing from the mangroves to the river mouth, muttering as Will joined them, and their stink was such that Will caught his breath. It was the stink of men who have sweated through two days on the run, soaked by storms, deprived of sleep, mired in the forest, each burdened by a load at least half his own weight. No one smelt good.

He stared at the water like everyone else, scanning the whole of the quiet creek, deserted save for a crocodile drifting slowly downstream. Then he felt the weight on his shoulders as if he was being dragged down by hands, but he stood doggedly and stared out to sea.

'What's that offshore?'

'Not our pinnaces,' someone answered.

'Spanish shallops.' Ox edged forward, and room was made for him since his eyes were keenest. 'Six or seven vessels, maybe half a league away: a fleet riding outside the reef.'

'Shit.'

'Sweet bloody Jesus.'

A piping whine rose above a groundswell of oaths: 'What if they come searchin' for us?'

Will pointed to the mud beside a near stretch of river.

'Look at those prints. I think the Spaniards have been here already.'

'They won't come back?'

Will shook his head. The way the ground was disturbed convinced him that the Spaniards had reached the place first: the banks of the Río Francisco had already been combed, and the question the men kept repeating was the one that screamed in his mind.

'Where are our boats?'

There was no sign of them. Drake had two pinnaces left, and they should both have been waiting.

'Taken!' someone cried out. 'The Spaniards have come looking for us and found them.'

'God 'a mercy.'

'Keep easy,' Morrys said steadily. 'Our boats may not yet have got here.'

Men began dropping their loads and falling where they stood: French as well as English, even the stolid Cimaroons. Whatever had happened to the pinnaces, they were not at the river mouth as planned. Will turned to see a mariner cursing and rubbing his eyes, a great strong man with thick dirt-stained fingers. Those nearest him looked away; others slumped down. Some hunched together, their fears magnified in the echoing.

'If the Spaniards have taken the pinnaces, then they'll make the men talk.'

'They'll find our ships.'

'We'll never get back.'

Will looked for Drake and saw him standing apart. He was alone, facing the river and Will supposed he was best left to his own quiet thoughts. Will pushed his hands under the straps that were digging into his shoulders, and only then wondered why he had not set his burden down. He took off the saddlebags, but felt no relief. In a burst of intense sunlight he watched steam rising from his clothes. His back and chest were at once cold. His legs ached, but he did not sit. He stared again at the river. He could not believe it – after so much toil, so much lost, after they had won the greatest victory, beaten the Spaniards and taken enough gold for every man to make his fortune. He had never considered that they might not escape. After the success of the ambush his confidence had been complete – he would return to Ellyn. He would show her the gold. His reward would be her delight. It was everything he had fought for. Throughout the hard marching his spirits had been high, never far from exultant, buoyed up by the conviction that the best prize awaited him: greeting Ellyn with the gold, the promise of wealth and rank, and that made all the sweeter for knowing his brother had been avenged. And there would have been even more satisfaction in proving his father wrong, showing he was worthy – in answering that last, hate-filled question: 'What hast thou brought back?' He would bring back gold. Now, at a stroke, he would be lucky to get away. He felt a rush of sudden dread. It could be even worse: the Spaniards might find Slaughter Island and get to Ellyn first.

He became aware that his thoughts were wandering, that he still stood while his friends sat. Then once more he picked up voices, though they were few and subdued.

'There must be another way, even without our pinnaces.'

'Aye, Slaughter Island is close to the mainland.'

'It's a whole day away by sea, perhaps more if the wind's opposed. Remember how long it took getting here.'

Will squatted down.

'We can't walk. It's too far. To cut a trail would take weeks.'

Hix swore.

'I can't go another league.'

'Nor I,' Morrys added.

'We're done for,' someone else broke in loudly.

'We're not!'

Will recognised Drake's bark. He glanced up to see the Captain striding purposefully towards them.

Drake was frowning, but his eyes shone.

'We have time. We don't give up. God forbid our pinnaces have been seized, but if they have, then the Spaniards will need time to discover anything, then to decide what to do, then act on their plans. In all this while we can reach our ships. We can do that by sea with the wind blowing westerly.'

'How?'

Will could not see who had asked, but he sensed the incredulity in all those listening. How by sea, if not by boat?

Drake put his hands on his hips and grinned.

'We build a raft.'

'With what?' The remarks followed thickly, sceptical and weary. 'A raft won't be big enough.'

Some of the men began to stand. The rest sat up. Will kept quiet and watched intently.

Drake took position where all the men could see him: English, French and Cimaroon. While he spoke, he gestured, miming out the substance of what he had in his mind.

'All we need is to get a few men to our ships – a simple raft could do that – one that I'm prepared to sail. I'll return with the craft to bear everyone away, and every last bar, quoit and coin of our treasure. Do you think I would leave it?'

Drake waited for the murmurs to die down, and that was done cleverly, Will thought. The men would fear being left behind, though none would admit it. But they would understand the lure of the treasure. If Drake left without them, they would trust the gold to bring him back.

Drake pointed to the river.

'See these trunks washed down?'

They were clear to Will. The riverbed was strewn with trees uprooted and carried seaward. Many must have fallen in the storms following the attack.

Drake gave a sweep of his arm.

'God has sent us the wood.' He pulled at a bag by his feet and held up an empty biscuit sack. 'We have the stuff for a sail, and the wind is in our favour. It can be done.'

'Aye,' Will concurred under his breath, and most of the men were muttering just the same.

'You'll have to get past the Spaniards,' Hix said.

Drake made a show of appearing surprised, which produced yet more laughter, and Will knew then that he had won his way.

'I'll keep inside the reef,' Drake answered blithely. 'They'll be on the look out for ships, not a puny raft.'

He waved the sack over his head as if it were a flag flown in conquest.

'Who'll come with me?' I want three lusty men who can swim like fish – I want no one petrified of a drenching. *Comprendez?*' He yelled while the chuckles were still flowing. '*Comme poisons!*' And to one bad parody he added another, swaying his hips, while holding his hands to his sides in a way Will supposed was meant to resemble fins.

Will looked round. Most of the English could not swim, but nearly everyone was laughing. Several of the Frenchmen were clamouring to risk their lives.

'*Oui, j'irai.*'

'*Et moi aussi . . .*'

Will had already decided what he would do.

'I will go. I can swim.'

Drake beamed.

'So you can, Will. Good.' He pointed to Will and two of the Frenchmen, and then made it clear he had no need of more.

He beckoned to the river with a rousing shout, 'Let's build our ark! Lash those trunks together. Find a straight tree for a mast, a small one for a rudder. I want a raft ready in an hour – nothing pretty; it only needs to float . . .'

Will pushed after him, seeing men rising and rushing forward who moments earlier had been in the grip of torpor.

'God preserve us,' someone muttered.

There was no escape from the sun, the rip of the wind or the sting of the sea. Will clung to the raft, feeling it twist and give beneath him, no more than a tangle of trunks and branches that might at any moment break apart – so low in the water that his legs were awash – so flimsy it pitched like a mad bucking horse. They were drenched when anyone shifted, or Drake leaned on the sapling he was using as a rudder, though Will had no faith that the raft could be steered truly. They were at the mercy of the wind but at least it was blowing east. They could only pray it would hold, and not drag them far out or smash them on the reef. So Will prayed. And to balance the entreaty he silently gave thanks – at least the Spaniards had not followed them.

The roaring never stopped: of the sea pounding the coral-heads, and the wind tearing past everything, making soaked clothes flap until they cracked like whips. It wrenched at vines and rope, bark and sacking, setting all that was above the surf screeching and groaning. Will's skin was blistered, and his lips were split. His hands smarted from the cuts of branches and fibres, rubbed raw over hours of hanging on for his life, until the sun was no longer blazing white over his head, but glowed like a fireball above the horizon behind him. And the sky was burning, but his body was cold, and still the mangroves slid by for league after league, swamps and inlets, palms and beaches.

Another wave broke over them, and Will gulped for breath before his head went under. Then he was up, stomach lurching, eyes streaming, spitting out water over a tongue that was swollen with thirst. But ahead was a point where the mangroves ended. He could see the headland of the Cativas: the place where the shore finished and the sea opened out. Drake was pointing, and the two Frenchmen were staring, scanning the skyline, shading their eyes. If they went on past the point, they would be committed to a crossing with night falling fast. The dark strip narrowed as the land levelled out, dwindling from hills to a ridge, and then a margin of sand, one that was visible from the wave crests, but lost in the troughs, and finally reduced to a streak where the combers rippled black. But there was something else: two boats. Will could see the lines of their masts, and the spume around their bows. Neither were under sail; they were both manned by oars. Drake was shouting and signing, and most of what he said was lost to the crashing sea but, in the midst of the pounding, Will heard a single word: 'Ours!'

The boats were pulling towards shelter in the lee of the point, and Will knew he was watching the pinnaces, though they held to their course. He took off his shirt and waved it wildly above his head. Still the two pinnaces drove on, making for the other side of the headland; their masts disappeared behind the top of the ridge. Drake swung the rudder to run the raft hard aground. They had no choice. Will close-hauled the sack-sail, and they were swept up by the next breaker to smash against the sand. Then a wave thundered in and almost sucked them all back.

'Come on!' Drake stumbled up the beach, and Will followed, clutching his shirt. They scrambled up the bluff and the Frenchmen struggled behind. From the top they could see the pinnaces at anchor below.

Drake leant against a palm trunk, bent and caught his breath.

'A pleasing sight, Will, but let's not show it.'

The wind had dropped as the sun went down. Will realised what had happened as he chased after Drake: the wind that had blown their raft eastward must have stopped the pinnaces from sailing west – that was why the boats had not been at the river as planned. But with dusk, the wind had calmed.

Will could hear Drake yelling as he crashed through the gloom, careering down the leeward slope towards the boats near the shore. He waved his shirt and shouted as well. And though the land was almost black there was a gleam over the sea, enough for him to spot that there were men wading ashore. While Drake staggered on, the crew from the boats rushed to greet him, and some ran to Will, bearing him along in the throng. So he glimpsed something of the way Drake doubled over and clasped at his waist, then withdrew a gold quoit and flaunted it in triumph. And though he could not see it, he was sure Drake smiled; he could sense a grin in what Drake said.

'Our voyage is made! Every one of you is *rich*! Now come with me. Our friends are guarding the booty – Let's fetch them all back!'

Ellyn saw the pinnaces without warning as she was walking along the shore: the *Bear* and the little *Minion*; she had no doubt about what they were. The boats were quite close. They must have sailed in and around Slaughter Island while she was taking food to the captured Spaniards. Her heart leapt. Her grip tightened around the bowl she was carrying, then she let go. The bowl fell. It did not matter. She quickened her pace. Men were spilling from the fort. She almost ran as the pinnaces drove up onto the beach. Drake's men began disembarking, Cimaroons were shouting and a cap was thrown into the air, and another, and another. There were cries of jubilation. Men streamed along the shore, more rowed over from the ships. Some of the wounded limped closer. Her ears rang as she pushed through the throng. Frenchmen and English were roaring together. Someone waved a pennant that became draped over heads and shoulders. A drum began beating. The Cimaroons were dancing. She saw Drake carried aloft, ruddy-faced and beaming. No one paid her any attention as she squeezed a way through, making for a man in the midst of the ferment about whom all else appeared to slow.

Will stood tall, with his shirt in tatters, and a broad-brimmed hat shadowing his sun-burnt face. When she neared him she saw the blisters, his cracked lips and peeling skin. His eyes narrowed as if the light was blinding. She could only be sure of where he was looking when she drew very close. Then she looked at nothing else but returned the gaze that he fixed upon her.

The clamour became louder, and next it seemed remote. In

the midst of it, she stilled. She felt the touch of his hands, rough and callused, strong and gentle, and though men shoved and jostled her, she barely noticed them at all. Will embraced her freely, and she let him kiss her unabashed, as if what she felt made a screen through which no one could pry. And as she held him the rest receded: the din and the crush. She was secure at the pivot around which everything turned, drawing strength from his warmth, with the smell of him close, and her arms around his waist, aware of little but his breathing and his body against hers. She wanted not to move, yet too much was going on. Quietly, she took Will's hand, and she saw the happiness in his smile.

They left the men offloading bags, and carrying them in lines through the gates of the fort. They passed those gathering around Drake, mariners singing and swigging from wineskins. Someone called out noisily from a group sprawled in the sand.

'Share a drink with us, sweet lady.'

'Aye. Down a draught to piss on the Spaniards!' Whoever had spoken laughed raucously. Will led her away, but the banter carried on.

'Will can afford you now, Mistress – says his riches will soften your heart.'

'And your dowry will pay him back!' The comment was muttered, and almost smothered by loud cackling, but Ellyn still made it out. Other voices followed, gravely and slurred.

'I've got riches, too, if you'd like some more from me.'

'Give the beauty some more, eh, Gillon? I could alright.'

'And I . . . Give her a sackful . . .'

The blood was rising to her face as Will suddenly turned on the men. He kicked hard at the sand, sending it spraying over their faces.

'Show respect, lads, and pipe down.'

Will turned back to Ellyn, leaving the men spitting and protesting. He was grinning.

'They're half cut and witless. I hope you'll ignore them.'

'I couldn't hear them very well.'

'Good.' He spoke quickly and patted her back. 'Better you didn't.'

They made for her palm-thatch shelter, though it was not much quieter inside; the commotion carried on. They held one another again, but she felt him sway and drew him down to sit. There were two palm-bole stools in the hut. He settled on one.

'Will you have some wine?' she asked, and was reaching for the jug and cup even before he replied. He gulped the drink down, and she poured out more.

'You must be tired. Are you hungry? I have some cooked fowl and corn.'

'No.' He raised his hand to her. 'Sit with me.'

She did so, and his weariness was like a weight that she felt as she looked at him.

'Tell me about the venture. I want to know everything . . .' She noticed the deep shadows over his drawn features, and wondered whether the carousing hid some price paid for victory. 'Has everyone come back?'

'Let us not talk of that now.'

'But you won? We can return to England?' She asked excitedly, already thinking of the long voyage homeward, and her spirits began to soar, like a bird loosed from a net.

With a wry smile he nodded, drained his cup and set it down.

'There is a question I must ask that I could not ask before.' He took hold of her hands. 'I had to be sure of your answer.'

She was puzzled, but his hands were comforting in her clasp. She squeezed them, smiling, wondering whether he would next put the question just as she had always supposed. Yet what could have changed to affect her answer? In her mind she was certain, just as she had been before he left, but she still wanted him to ask.

'Can you be sure of my answer now, if you were not before?'

'Yes.' He answered firmly, without smiling back. 'It is what I have now that makes the certainty.'

'Certain enough not to ask?' She made the challenge playfully, hoping he would put the question soon.

His expression remained sombre.

'I must ask your mother when we return, but what I have makes me sure of her answer, too – and that is a fortune, sweet Ellyn.' His voice rose. 'Enough to buy a manor and a title, enough for her to want to welcome me into her family.' He gripped Ellyn's hands firmly. His eyes never left her face. 'So tell me how this pleases you.'

With a few quick movements he reached inside his shirt and produced a large disc of gold that he held gleaming in front of her.

'What is mine will also be yours.'

She hesitated.

'But you have not asked . . .'

He pressed the quoit into the palm of her hand.

'With this, do I need to?'

He smiled then, and his eyes brightened, but she felt chilled by a sudden disquiet. The drum beat louder and the singing rose to bawling. The words of the drunken mariner rang again in her thoughts: 'Will can afford you now, Mistress – says his riches will soften your heart.' She was upset without reasoning why, though she knew deep down it was all to do with the gold.

'Yes, with this.' She pushed the quoit back. 'Most especially with this.'

Will grasped her hand.

'Then answer me and let's be done with it.' He met her eye. 'Will you marry me?'

She pulled her hand away, leaving him fumbling to stop the gold from falling. Her heart thumped faster. Was she to be bought like a whore? Why was gold so important? She looked at the quoit that was gleaming in his hand.

'You favour me in asking, but I would like to consider since I am not ruled by gold.'

'Consider?' He stared at her, breathing heavily. Then all the pleasure drained away from his face. 'Consider what?' he whispered as he stood, though she reached out to stop him.

'Please, Will . . . Have something to eat . . .'

It was all she could think of to say, but he turned and wrenched at the sacking over the door.

She called out, and he ignored her. Without a backward glance he walked away.

Will marched past the men who had settled in the open. Ellyn had refused him, and the hurt of it smothered everything. He had been conscious of hunger, but suddenly he felt sick. He was not going to plead with her or entreat. If she did not want him without reservation, then he would not persist in the asking. Though he now had a fortune, she still needed to 'consider' whether to accept him. He had never supposed she might have doubts.

He paced on, hearing friends calling for him to join them, but he made straight for Drake. He had seen the Captain by the fire at the centre of the compound, with a group clustered before him ready to listen to his tales. The drum banged on, and a crowd of dancing Cimaroons added howls and clapping to the stamping beat. It pulsed in Will's head as he picked his way through, stepping around men already drunk, and a few lying senseless. Laughter and curses rose everywhere he trod. Someone was singing a crude ballad, and he wanted to kick the man hard to make him shut up. He got nearer to Drake, and shoved a Frenchman out of the way. Just behind Drake, he squatted down, seeing the fire over the Captain's shoulder spitting sparks into the dusk.

He spoke in an undertone as soon as Drake paused to drink.

'Captain.'

'I hear you, Will.'

'We'll be going back for Le Testu and the rest of the booty?'

Drake gave a nod while keeping his face turned aside.

'Aye,' he answered in a low voice, 'but there'll be much jeopardy in that. I'll send only a few: those who are able and willing, and only when they're ready.'

Will clasped hold of Drake's arm. He would prove himself worthy, whether Ellyn wanted him or not.

'Count me as one of them.'

Ellyn stared at shadows. She had no desire to move. It was an effort even to lift her hand and reach out to the little shell on the barrel by her bed. But the fumbling for it was too much. So she sat listlessly and picked the shell up, then ran her fingers over the spiral ridges, tracing all the intricacies of its shape. What lay ahead? Perhaps she might dine with Will in a few hours but, if she did, his behaviour would be reserved, as though there had never been anything special between them, and whilst being cool he would be courteous, addressing her with manners that could not be faulted. It was enough to unnerve her completely.

She squeezed the shell in her fist. It was a dainty cone, marked in chestnut-coloured ripples, and within the lip of its mantle was the place where she had seen the note: the one with the message that had once filled her with hope. 'I will come for you soon,' he had written, 'Your voyager, Will.' Well, he had come, and brought her to safety, and now she had distanced him with her words. He must have thought she did not love him – that she believed she could do better. Did he suppose she had misled him? She touched the edge of the slit, feeling the pearly smooth lining of the spiral passage inside: the space that was empty because the message was gone, burnt as he had ordered. Destroyed.

What had she done? She must have seemed callous. Will had rescued her from danger and offered her all he possessed, yet the gold had spoilt that for her. Had she been wrong? She returned to the issue that had tormented her for days. Surely he should have asked her first, and not assumed she would marry him because he had come by a fortune? But she had not told him of her love, and she accepted that was her failing; she thought that he knew. Then the damage had been done. She had rebuffed him without meaning to and that had left them divided. But if he really did love her, why had he allowed that to happen? Why had she?

She worked the shell in her hands, turning it over and over, tracing the ever-decreasing rings at the base of the cone. She was with Will, but apart. Their association together was a shadow of what it had been. She pushed her finger into the shell. What was lost could not be found. How could she approach him and try to explain? What could she say, when she only saw him in company, and otherwise he kept away from her? Should she shout out that she loved him: scream it before the world – tell him now, before it was too late?

She pressed the shell to her lips. Will was one of the few who had been chosen to try and retrieve the hidden treasure and bring it back with the French captain: a venture so dangerous that even Drake was not chancing it, too. She squeezed her eyes shut. Soon Will would be gone on that mission. Had she driven him to it?

He might not come back.

With sudden resolve she got up and walked outside, intent on observing the pinnaces, though she had already satisfied herself at daybreak that the boats were still moored up. She ignored everything else: the men carrying stores, busy with nets, picking at rope. What concerned her was beyond the gate. If she kept her attention on her purpose, then the hurt of not being with Will was less. She moved briskly to the shore and saw one of the pinnaces at anchor, with the ships in the roadstead and a few small tenders nearby. The sea was calm, a limpid turquoise blue, with barely a wave showing white on rolling in towards the beach. But the sand around her was churned up. Then she caught her breath.

The other pinnace was gone.

22
Love

'. . . and all for love, and nothing for reward . . .'

—The Faerie Queen *by Edmund Spenser, Book 2, Canto 8*

The floodplain was a wasteland of mashed plants and mud. Little remained recognisable of the scene of the attack, though in the dark of a cloudy night Will had expected it to look different – but not like this. He remembered an expanse of lush pasture; what remained was devastation: a morass of earth turned over and trees uprooted. Between the collapsed banks of the riverbed, thin streams trickled round islands of silt. There was no firm ground left, only sludge. He was knee deep in it, digging up slush mixed with stones and other things that crunched. After hours of labouring he was plastered in filth, and so were his friends: Hix, Ox and Sherwell. Every man was slick-black as if coated with pitch. Cimaroons and English, all looked alike. Of the score who were digging and the Cimaroons keeping watch, most were lost in the gloom, and even the nearest he could barely make out. Only by their voices could he tell them apart. But caution stifled talk.

On the riverbed, they were exposed. Even without speaking they were making much noise, though there'd been no sign of any Spaniards or any lookouts left stationed. So maybe Drake was right. Will glanced round quickly before making his next throw, chucking dirt onto soil where it was less likely to splash. Perhaps in the days since the ambush the Spaniards had lost interest – perhaps they no longer believed there was any treasure left.

But he could still pinpoint almost exactly where the booty had been buried, and their efforts had not been fruitless. They'd recovered some gold, and more than a dozen bars of silver, though that was small recompense against the news they had heard. According to the French mariner found wandering near the Río Francisco, Le Testu was dead – the man had seen the Spaniards riding away with Le Testu's head. Will dug down deeper. Now all he could do to claim some success was find the remnants of the treasure that Ellyn had shunned. He dug with a vengeance though his whole body ached. He did not care. The pain in his body was pain he could cope with.

Sherwell muttered close by.

'Here be another.'

Hix cursed, breathing heavily, sloshing towards them.

'Under two feet o' shit-swill water.'

Will thought he heard Sherwell again; all were shadows in the dark. He recognised Ox next. In the absence of Drake, he had the snap of authority.

'Dig, you coxcombs, and quit mewling.'

Men stumbled and splashed about.

Will looked round.

'Quiet. Something's moving. See it there?'

By the fringe of the nearest bushes he had glimpsed a figure bobbing down, perhaps a Cimaroon on watch, except that next a whistle rang out, one they had agreed upon as a warning. Ox and Hix drew their swords. Wading through the shallows, Will took cover behind a tree trunk. He could see the shapes of men. They were creeping closer at the foot of the bank. He was sure they were Cimaroons when the whistle was repeated. Then they stopped. No one spoke.

Will pressed flat, hugging the earth. Slowly he raised his head, peering out between grasses, seeing the indigo sky above the black of the land, and the shine of mud in the churned-up pasture, and the bushes looming large where he had thought something was moving. Then he saw it again: a man, he was certain, someone running erratically through the scrub, drawing nearer.

Suddenly there was a shout, a strained wavering cry: 'Eng-lish!'

How could he be English?

'Eng-lish!' The man cried again and ran.

Will stared into the darkness. Would the cry trigger an attack? He wriggled higher, pulse thumping. Nothing had changed. Then he saw the man clearly, much closer, bobbing into view near the edge of the riverbank.

The same cry rang out, louder but less certain. It was silenced with a groan. Will heard thuds and grunts, and the slap of something falling, landing heavily in the mud. He crept along the bank, glimpsing bodies writhing in the darkness, listening to squelching and splashing – the noise of a struggle. He caught sight of swinging arms and heard the thwack of punches. He pushed closer, feet sliding, aware of his friends not far behind, and that there was still nothing to suggest that the man was not alone: no shouts or shots, or hint of others rushing out.

When he reached the man, he was spreadeagled. Two Cimaroons had him pinned down in the mud. One of them yanked up his head by a lock of his matted hair. Even plastered with mud, Will could tell he was not African. The man was gasping.

Sherwell and Hix held their swords to his neck.

Ox questioned him first.

'Speak quiet and we'll do you no harm. Is anyone with you?'

'No . . . For pity . . .' The man coughed and croaked, and the whites of his eyes caught a faint gleam of light: wide pale eyes.

Will reached out his hand as his friends withdrew their blades. He was in shock; the man's halting speech had shot through him like a dart.

'I was with Hawkins. From Plymouth . . .' the man spluttered.

'Zounds. He *is* English,' Hix growled, taking hold of the man's arm. 'Bear him up!'

The man swayed. Sherwell grasped his other arm. They all staggered in the mud, and Ox cupped up water to sluice the filth from the man's face.

'Get this muck off him.'

With a few hasty splashes he was washed down roughly. Hix took off his jacket and put it over the man's back.

'With Hawkins? When?' Ox demanded, standing in front. The man's head was lolling; he seemed on the point of collapse.

Will strained to see more of his face, needing to know who he was, because there was something in his voice that had set Will's mind racing, yet he did not dare believe what he thought he had heard.

He gripped the man's arm.

'Were you at San Juan de Ulúa?'

The man started, plainly bewildered.

'What? . . . It cannot be . . .'

'San Juan de Ulúa,' Ox repeated. 'Were you there?'

'Yes . . .' The man slumped against him. 'On the *Jesus* . . .'

Sherwell gasped, shifting position to hold the man up, and whispered, 'How long ago was that?'

'More'n four years,' Hix muttered, with a hiss between his shattered teeth.

Everyone moved to help. Will put his arms round the man's shoulders.

'I was held hostage,' the man mumbled. 'Taken . . . sold in Mexico. A galley slave . . . worked for gold. Escaped . . . I came. I was told . . . there would be English. I was waiting. Waiting . . .'

Will took hold of the man's head and pressed his face close, cheek to cheek, because he knew, even before Ox asked, 'What's your name?'

'Christopher Doonan,' the man answered, stumbling, eyes closed.

'Kit,' Will murmured as he hugged him.

'God's blood!' Hix cried. 'He's Will's brother!'

'Devil take us!' Sherwell gulped. 'What have we done?'

Will looked astern from the little *Minion* to the Spanish fleet in their wake. Then he looked ahead at Drake's frigate, riding at anchor off the reef. If Drake was ready, they should be able to escape, quit the Cativas for good and leave the Spaniards behind – *if* the frigate was prepared, with everyone aboard and ready for the voyage. But of that he was not sure. He had seen a small tender tied up alongside, and perhaps that meant the frigate was still provisioning, or some of the company were being transferred. So maybe others had not yet left Slaughter Island, and God help them in that case, because there would be no time left to fetch anyone else.

Again he glanced round. Most of the Spanish fleet remained distant, though one vessel was close, but the rest would soon catch up once the *Minion* reached Drake's ship. The wind would help the Spaniards when the pinnace furled her sails. Will hauled on one of the sheets, channelling anxiety into gaining speed, working as one with the rest to race the *Minion* to the east. They had sailed through the night, never far from the shore, yet the Spaniards must have spotted them: they were being pursued.

Will saw Drake's frigate looming large beyond the bows. Then he noticed Kit crouched ready with a mooring rope in his hands. Kit's long hair was blowing about his pinched and eager face. He had the look of a fugitive, wearing the garb of the Cimaroons. There had been no time for much talk, no chance to fill in the years. All that he knew of what Kit had been through was what he could guess from what he saw: a boy turned a man, his brother grown up, the softness gone from his battered angel features, a survivor clinging on. But though he was spent, he was trying to help.

'Turn about!' Ox bellowed the order.

The *Minion* swung round, sending Kit stumbling with the roll of the deck. Will watched him in snatches, and every look they exchanged bridged the past each had missed. They would make up for that once they were on their way to England. The frigate was abreast. They only needed to cross over, weigh anchor and set sail. He prayed that Ellyn was aboard. He had asked Morrys to stay with her. They both had to be with Drake.

Shouts rang out: 'Stand by!'

The rubbing-strakes ground, and with a jolt the vessels joined. Hawsers were thrown and ropes made fast. The hulls shuddered. Clamouring rose. Men clambered from the *Minion* to the frigate, lugging across booty. Drake shinned down the other way, hailing the Cimaroons.

Will moved beside Kit, putting a hand against his back and yelling above the noise, 'Go on. Get aboard!'

Kit gripped his arm.

'Not without you.'

Will raised his eyes. Most of the mariners had scaled the frigate's side. Drake was climbing back. The Cimaroons were settling in the pinnace and preparing to row away.

Drake beckoned from the gunwale.

'Hurry!'

Will jumped for the frigate's chains, landing on the running plate as the ship pitched in the waves.

He called up to the Captain, 'Is everyone aboard?'

'Almost, but for you two. Get up here.'

'Is Ellyn with you?'

'The Cimaroons will fetch those left. They know what to do.'

'I'm going with them.'

'No, Will! She'll reach us no faster.'

Will jumped back into the pinnace, and grabbed hold of Kit.

'Get onto the ship!'

'Not alone.' Kit struggled to pull free.

'You have to go!' Will yelled, and called to the Cimaroons. 'Help get him aboard.' He shouted back to the frigate, 'Throw down a rope.'

'God's death!' someone cursed, and a rope was thrown near, but Kit was writhing as if possessed; he could not keep a proper hold.

Kit elbowed him and cried out, 'I'm staying with you.'

'We can't dally,' bellowed Drake. 'You've brought the Indies fleet on your tail.'

Will wrestled with Kit but his brother was strong. The Cimaroons were no help, and he was not going to board the frigate unless Ellyn was on the ship.

Drake's voice rang out again: 'God save you both.'

More ropes were thrown down. But then Will realised the frigate was casting off. Within moments the hulls had parted. A wave smacked between them, and Will heard the billowing of sails. The Cimaroons struck up a chant and pulled hard against the sweeps. Whatever cries came from the frigate were lost to the keening wind.

Kit staggered and Will pulled him down, putting his arm around his shoulders; he could feel Kit was shaking. Then Will turned and looked away.

He had seen the tears welling behind the bruised lids of his brother's eyes.

Kit heard Will calling, 'Row hard! There's a galley cutting ahead.'

The Cimaroons were rowing fast. Kit took up an oar and set to matching their stroke. He would help Will if he could. The galley was close. He narrowed his eyes, seeing the spume in the galley's wake as it powered through the waves. It was driven by about thirty oars, with a striped sail bearing the Spanish cross, and a forked pennant at the masthead.

Kit hauled on his oar, yelling into the wind,'The galley's faster but not attacking.'

'Bastidas,' Will called back, holding the tiller. 'He's making for our fort. He must have seen it.'

'Who's Bastidas?'

'A petty tyrant: commander of the garrison at Nombre de Dios.'

Will looked worried, staring ahead. Kit faced him in the stern, labouring in rhythm with the Cimaroons. He called out in snatches, 'Describe . . . this man.'

'Short and strutting, with brows that meet without a join.'

Then Kit was certain – Will had described the Spaniard he should have killed. 'I saw him where you found me. He tortured an old, injured man . . . and another – a Frenchman. They were beheaded.'

Will winced.

'Did the old man have white hair?'

'Yes.'

'Le Testu.' Will clenched his jaw. 'He was our ally. What did Bastidas do to him?'

'Trod on his wounds . . . while the other man's arms were pulled from their sockets.'

'God!' Will looked aside, eyes burning. 'The wind's not helping us.' He bellowed at the Cimaroons, 'Faster!'

Kit glanced over his shoulder. The galley was edging in front, and before it was the fort on an island that the Spaniards were not far from reaching.

'They've more men at the oars.'

Will shook his head, hands tight on the tiller.

'Heaven forbid that Bastidas gets to Ellyn first.'

'You love this lady?'

'Yes, and she's still on that island.'

So the woman was Will's motive, and Kit understood. He would have turned back for Ololade if he had believed she was in danger.

Will hunched forward.

'Bastidas must have reasoned she might be left till last in our fort.'

'She will be guarded, surely,' Kit yelled.

'Only by a few men.'

'Bastidas is wounded,' Kit told him, wanting to give his brother some comfort.

'How?'

'Your friend had a pistol . . . he used it when he could. The Spaniard has a bullet in his arm.'

'Good.'

'And his sword was broken by another Spaniard . . . I think an officer of higher rank.'

'So he's been humiliated.' Will grimaced. Then a look of anguish shadowed his face. 'He'll be full of hate and hell-bent on revenge. He's hurt Ellyn before. He'll stop at nothing if he finds her now.' Will threw back his head and roared. 'Faster!'

Kit looked round.

'The galley's almost at the island.'

'Jesus, no!' Will crouched, shaking, like a beast ready to spring. 'After them!'

Arms folded, head bowed under her crumpled hat, Ellyn paced along the beach. She had been left on Slaughter Island with just two of Drake's men. Even the Spaniards from the captured ships had drifted away in the rotting *Pascoe*. Though she supposed they would not get far in the old hulk with its tattered sails, yet they had gone, just like the French. The Huguenots had lost faith that their captain still lived, so they had quit with their share of the spoils. Most of the Cimaroons had abandoned the island as well, after burning the pinnace Drake had left them, taking only its iron. Of the things Drake had offered them, they had accepted very few: silks and a precious sword – tokens of Drake's gratitude, since their loyalty had brought him triumph.

But where had that left her?

She was isolated and neglected, with Will on a desperate venture about which her worries formed persistent nightmares, and a deep rift between them she did not know how to bridge. She looked up without focus. The dancing light on the water spangled like stars before her eyes. She paced again. No one wanted her. She had not yet been invited to board Drake's frigate, and she was sure she knew why: because she would get 'in the way', because if the Spaniards came searching, and there was any action at sea, then the mariners would not feel easy fighting with a woman on the ship. It was all very well for Drake to say he wished to spare her – save her from waiting in cramped quarters while provisions were loaded. But wasn't she waiting now – waiting for the men to return from searching for Le Testu – waiting for Will to come back? For years she had been waiting, and she couldn't bear any more. She should not have said what she did to push Will away. She was wrong. She repented. Bring him back safe. Let him ask her again. Yes. *Yes.* He could ask whatever he liked, and if he sought her consent, then her answer would be *yes.*

The clouds blazed. Everything was bright. She should try to live and not brood – delight in what was around her: the warm sand beneath her feet, the smell of the mangroves and the sea. She turned to the odd-shaped fort that had become her home. One of the corners of its triangular wall was just visible behind the trees. For all its shabbiness, she had grown fond of the place. She could hear blithe freedom in the laughing cry of the gulls. Open her eyes. She turned again and watched the ripple of the waves, from the foam of those gently breaking, to the flowing lines further out. And as the dazzling light receded to pinpoints of perfect clarity, she saw the spray around the bows of the galley that was approaching, and another boat some way behind.

'Get back!'

She turned as she was seized. Someone pulled her away: Will's friend, Morrys the archer. But she needed no urging, she had seen the sail and forked pennant. The galley would be carrying Bastidas. She knew he was coming. She dashed with Morrys for the gate. Inside the fort, a few Cimaroons were arming: five men – all that were left to guard the base. They stuck arrows in the sand, ready to fire from the loopholes. Shots cracked as the gate slammed.

Morrys snatched up his bow.

'Hide!'

She turned as something kicked up sand very close, hearing a report and next a cry, 'Go!'

She darted into her hut and grabbed her father's sword. She would do what she could to help, and not cower like a weakling. At the doorway she looked out. The Cimaroons were firing from the walls, loosing arrows through the slits. Some were on a platform, shooting over the top of the palisade. One man slumped and fell. She looked from the body to something that streamed over the wall: a grappling hook trailing rope. It hit the ground, then jerked back and caught. Another landed with a thud. A helmeted head appeared above the palisade. Suddenly soldiers were scrambling over, too many to stop.

Morrys knelt, aimed and fired, took a fresh arrow and fired again, but a Spaniard rushed for him. Next he was running, drawing his sword. Their blades clashed. The Spaniard thrust and Morrys staggered. Two Cimaroons rushed at one of the soldiers. But more were at the gate, dragging it open. She glimpsed Morrys doubled over, and then a Negro reeled past. In the African's hand was a great machete. It swung in an arc, shattering the helmet of a soldier who crashed against her shelter. Above the yelling she heard a scream. The Negro turned, drenched in blood. She flinched, stunned, at first too shocked to move, but then she charged straight out of the hut wielding the sword in both hands. Making for a soldier bearing down on Morrys, she aimed a strike at his side. The blow made her shudder. The Spaniard twisted and collapsed, but the sword fell from her grasp. Pain coursed through her arm. She only sensed what had happened when someone grabbed her from behind. She turned, shrieking, to look into staring eyes below a single dark brow, while the wet warmth of her own blood seeped down under her sleeve.

Bastidas held his dagger to her throat.

'Viper. You have been waiting for me – Remember?'

Will led Kit and the Cimaroons away from the gate of the fort. He pelted across the beach and then along a track through the mangroves. They were soon by the palisade, and the sounds from the other side made him want to try and scale it bare-handed – claw at the wood – beat it with his fists. Will signed frantically to the Cimaroons. 'Up! Climb one another!'

There was no other way, and they did as he ordered, pulling the lightest onto the strongest and standing on each other's shoulders – they made a human tower against the sheer defences. But even while it was forming, some were trying to use it to get over.

Will pushed Kit back.

'Stay here!'

Kit shrugged him off, and Will tensed, preparing to leap. But in a movement so quick Will could do nothing to stop him, Kit sprang past and jumped, scrambling up the living pyramid then clambering over the wall.

Will braced himself and followed.

Arrows shot past. Will saw Kit vault onto a shelter, land on the roof, bounce near the ridge and crash down heavily as the palm thatch gave way. Will jumped for the same place, hearing the twang of bowstrings behind him as he hurtled through the air. Then he smashed into branches and next he was plummeting amidst dust, colliding with something that gave way beneath him – a mattress on a frame. He stood quickly, blood racing, drawing his sword, seeing Kit.

A shot cracked and Kit weaved, striking out with his machete. Will made for his brother, glimpsing men wounded and dead, running and fighting, but nothing of Ellyn or the Spanish captain. The Cimaroons whooped, venting their fury. They dropped down from the palisade and charged at the Spaniards. Kit battled in a blur, hacking like a madman. A soldier thrust at his back. Will struck as Kit wheeled, hearing the clang of snapping steel the instant the man hit the ground, seeing a broken rapier flying up, to fall back on the soldier's chest. Kit sprang clear, and Will saw someone by his feet, eyes staring and sightless, hair trailing in blood: Morrys. His arm was outstretched, holding his bow.

Will dashed for Ellyn's hut.

Bastidas had her pinned down. Will saw his armoured back, his bandaged arm, the signs of a struggle in a small space – the dagger at Ellyn's neck, blood on her dress, her skirts pulled up. He heard her cries.

Will crept in, sheathing his sword, though his impulse was to drive it straight at the villain's guts. He had to get the dagger from Ellyn's throat, grab Bastidas by his wounded arm: his right – that might help him – disarm the man before he could kill her, move while he was distracted. The man was fumbling and grunting. Will struggled to hold back – stay quiet – take the steps: focus on the arm he had to seize.

Then he lunged. He grabbed and wrenched, pulling Basitidas to his knees, twisting round his wrist, forcing a cry of pain from the Spaniard the moment Ellyn screamed,'He's left-handed!'

Will jumped back as a blade flashed by him.

Bastidas struck, still kneeling, whispering as he smiled, 'Dog.'

Will reached to unsheathe his own sword, feeling a sting over his chest and hearing a roar from behind: the howl of his brother's wrath. He glimpsed Kit rushing past as Bastidas jabbed, fast as a snake, stabbing at Kit, drawn to the attack. Will lunged in a surge of strength – a desperate thrust while Kit closed – seeing the rapier in the Spaniard's hand, aiming round the man's breastplate, under his arm. The rapier shivered. Will wrenched his sword from the Spaniard's flesh the instant Kit's machete smashed into steel. The blow caught Bastidas full over the chest, cleaving the armour, bedding deep.

Ellyn screamed. Bastidas swayed, staggered back and lurched towards her. Will ran at him then, driving his sword under the Spaniard's chin, sending him crashing against the table and falling to the ground. Will bent so she would not see how he hastened the man's end.

Kit took Will's arm, and he stood.

Will reached for Ellyn's hand.

She clung to him. Will's grip was certain in the midst of chaos. She ran beside him, not really feeling the cut in her arm, or the bruises from her struggle. The bodies of men lay bloodied in the dirt: Spaniards and Cimaroons – men who were her friends – both of the mariners whom Drake had left with her.

'Morrys!' She pulled towards him, but Will held her back.

'He's dead. I'm sorry.' Will held her briefly very tight, wrapping her in his arms and pressing her face against his shirt. His blood smeared her cheek, for he too was hurt. But then the wild man with fair hair took her arm and urged her on.

She ran as best she could, through the gate and onto the beach, feet sinking, splashing through surf. The Cimaroons dashed for the boat. Those ahead scrambled aboard. The wild Englishman climbed in front, reaching down to help her up. Before she took his hand she saw the scar on his palm, and the shape that it made, like a thin sickle moon. Will lifted her over the side and then clambered up behind her.

As she found a place with them both in the stern of the boat, she asked the question of the wild man that suddenly burst from her mind: 'Who are you?' The man looked like Will – he had helped them both.

The wild man smiled.

'The *cimarrones* call me *el inglés de la luna*.'

Will clapped his shoulder.

'This is Kit, my brother.' He took up an oar and began to row.

'Kit!' she cried out, and squeezed her hands together, only stopping to hold on as the boat pitched through the waves. 'I sent you a message.' She wiped tears from her eyes.

'*You* did!' Will exclaimed.

Kit bent to rowing as well.

'That message led me to Will. I cannot thank you enough.'

'You brought Kit back!' Will looked hard at her; then he shook his head.

'Marry me?' he asked, and his look of entreaty made her want to throw herself upon him. 'Marry me!' he shouted.

'Yes,' she replied as she had longed to, crying out her answer for everyone to hear. '*Yes!*'

They were leaving. All was receding, spattered by sunlight and spray: the fort, the mangroves – from the stern of the pinnace they seemed to be sinking into the waves, while before her Will was rowing, driving the boat out to sea. She sat by the helmsman, a wounded Cimaroon, feeling the surge of the boat as he called out the stroke. She gazed from Will to his brother, taking in Kit's gentle battered features; then she noticed a ship near the horizon.

'Look!' Her shout was lost beneath a boom: a rippling blast that shook the air, and another, rumbling away like thunder. The ship had fired a broadside. She tried to make out more as the men glanced round, but they all kept on rowing.

'Drake!' Will yelled and grinned. 'He must have led the Spaniards away and doubled back through the reef.'

The helmsman quickened his chanting. The men hauled harder. The pinnace swept north.

She called out against the wind, 'Can we reach the ship?'

There was no answer, but she was not surprised; no one was listening. Then she pointed.

'Look at the ship!'

Will was too busy rowing, and so was everyone else, but she could see the streamers flying above the fading drifts of smoke. From the top of the mainmast fluttered the flag of St George. Silk banners rippled from every yard, sprit and spar. And from every masthead flew fine-coloured pennants that were light, thin and long enough to dance over the sea.

Epilogue

Through starry nights and long hot days, Ellyn planned and dreamed after she and Will were betrothed, their hands clasped before Captain Drake, their vows made to wed on their arrival back in England. In her optimism for the future all difficulties fell away: the need for her mother's consent, the reading of the banns without objection, the arrangements for the festivities and the recognition of Will as a worthy successor to her father's business. So it proved. It was as if Will's love made everything possible, and the elements of her life, for so long conflicting, all at once slotted together like an inlaid design. Her happiness overflowed, touching everyone she knew. And perhaps Captain Drake had much to do with the ease with which her wishes took shape, or perhaps it was simply that fortune smiled upon her because she was smiling upon everyone else, but the fact was that one fine golden morning near the end of September, less than two months after their victorious return to Plymouth, and over two and half years since she had first left aboard the *Swan*, she found herself in her mother's chamber, kneeling for a special blessing on the day she had often longed for, with the sound of merrymaking outside from the townsfolk gathered to follow her bridal procession to church.

The colours she wore were blues for purity in varied hues from dark to light. Her sleeves and underskirt were of azure brocade; her gown and bodice were soft indigo velvet. A silver pomander full of garden herbs hung from a sky-blue ribbon around her waist, and the loveliest lacework enhanced her clothes, from her high-backed collar to the line of her stomacher across the swell of her breasts. This stomacher was one her mother had embroidered with strawberries and ladybirds amidst blue-tinted leaves, while pinned to her bodice and free-flowing hair were sprigs of rosemary with silken bride-laces: streamers of blue and fresh sap green. She felt more beautiful than she ever had before, or ever would again, yet never more humble than when she bowed to receive the press of her mother's hands on the crown of her head.

'Go, my sweet,' her mother whispered in her breathy voice. 'Return with your man, and may my love strengthen your union.'

Ellyn rose to kiss her, grateful beyond words for her mother's forgiveness – forgiveness for her leaving and her father's death, though, God knows, she had laboured to save him; her choice of a man against her parents' first wishes; all the mistakes she had made in the course of her long absence, only to come back to find the same unconditional love that had comforted her as a child. Tenderly she embraced her mother, as Lettie and Jane witnessed when they came to the door, and though they both smiled broadly, their eyes were wet with tears. Outwardly Ellyn remained calm, aware of change too profound for show of emotion, knowing that she was leaving as a daughter and would return as a wife. She would weep for joy later and for everything past; this parting would be forever remembered as now.

Memories came with her as she passed through the house: of her father in the parlour, calling for his stick – and her brother, Thom, jumping down the stairs – of her home as she had known it, seemingly larger years ago, though never brighter than at that moment, decked out with broom and alder sprigs. Outside was noise and celebration, and Drake's page, Diego, the Captain's faithful Cimaroon, waiting with a pretty palfrey fitted out with a side-saddle. Diego helped her mount, then the singing became louder, and she was escorted to St Andrew's Church, to the pounding of drums and bawdy verse, with Old Nan on a donkey, plodding behind, and Lettie with Will's journeyman who had wed her that year, and Jane making eyes at the gangling youth who had once been Will's apprentice boy, and now walked afterward bearing the bridecup of honeyed fruit.

News must have spread that the Captain would be attending because all around St Andrew's the crowds were packed and roisterous. Ellyn could not believe the people were cheering for her; Drake's fame would have drawn them, and his favour with the Queen after presenting her with riches enough to fill her coffers for months. But it gladdened her to see the good folk of Plymouth rejoicing together on her special day, whistling and whooping as she reached the lychgate, waving greenery and hats, pressing forward for a glimpse of Drake striding to meet her, gloriously attired, with goffered ruff and damask doublet, and the sun glinting on the silver of his scabbard and sword hilt.

'Dear lady,' he said, giving her a ruddy grin and helping her alight with his hands at her waist. 'Allow me to lead you to safety.'

With a flick of his fingers, his men stood back either side of the path, their rough faces at odds with their lace-collared clothes. As she advanced, trumpets sounded and, one by one, these brave men bowed. They were all her friends: swarthy Thomas Sherwell and wiry John Oxenham; Ellis Hixom, with his shattered mouth – she remembered each from their adventures, and others, too: her dear slave boy, Marco. Where was he now? Morrys the archer, who had died protecting her; patch-eyed Simon with his winning smile; the Captain's two younger brothers: stolid John, her island guard, and the other, Joseph, of whom Will had told her; and Captain Le Testu, the most gracious of allies. Along with her father, they were all with her in spirit as she passed the survivors, with scenes from the trials and triumphs they had been through flickering like shadows in the fire of her mind. Yet awareness of their absence only touched her heart more, for the joy of her love and for being alive, walking towards the man who meant more to her than the world. Her Will, tall and strong, magnificently dressed in burgundy and crimson, who turned towards her when she entered the church with the passion of desire in his clear blue eyes – eyes that sparkled like sunlight on the sea. Beside him stood Kit in a soft leather jerkin, fair hair shining, flashing her a smile from his still-tanned face. Oh, they were so handsome! A chill rippled through her at the sight of the brothers together.

Then Captain Drake led her forward, and she walked down the aisle, passing friends and acquaintances, colleagues and neighbours, merchants who had once been her father's associates, mariners and maids, rich and humble, and those who would soon be her new relations: Will's father and sisters, reconciled with him at last after Kit's reappearance, still keeping a distance and apart from the others, but there, standing stiffly and dressed in their best. She recognised admirers and erstwhile suitors; Richard Dennys regarded her smugly, holding a ridiculous hat like a brightly feathered shield. Perryn Fownes caught her eye, chubby and beaming, his hand in the grasp of a simpering maiden with a look as vacant as an empty byre, and Ellyn knew he would be happy, and that only strengthened her sense that all would be right. Godfrey Gilbert hunched his shoulders and lowered his brows, glancing at her from under them with a lipless smile. Let him shift and squirm. She did not fear him, though she felt a tingling round her neck, as if from the jewelled choker she had given him back. They had never been promised, and he had betrayed her father's trust. She hoped he was stewing in guilt for mismanaging the family business; only Will's prompt action on their return had saved it from ruin. Raising her hand to her throat she touched a necklace of pearls made from those Will had given her on the island long ago. She looked straight ahead. Will was her choice; and when the Captain drew her close, letting go her hand, and the parson began speaking, she could not look anywhere but at Will's honest face.

'An honourable estate,' said the parson, 'instituted of God in paradise . . .'

She drank in the sight of him to the music of those words.

'If any man can show just cause,' the parson went on, 'why they may not lawfully be joined together, let him now speak . . .'

She held her breath and dared a peek back at Godfrey Gilbert. His mouth opened wide as if in mime of shouting out. But he would not, surely . . . She watched in sudden horror, turning back to Will, and noticing Drake raise his hand. Then, as if on order, the

Captain's men moved forward at the wings from the door, and Ellis Hixom joined Master Gilbert, favouring him with a ghastly smile.

Master Gilbert's mouth snapped closed.

A hush settled. The parson resumed, asking the same question of her and Will. In the silence she felt relief like a loosening of heavy chains, because they *would* be married, and Will would love her, comfort and honour her for as long as he lived.

'I will,' he said, and so did she; they took each other by the hand and pledged their troth as husband and wife.

Will took the gimmel ring he had worn since their betrothal: a ring matching her own that had been found in the Spanish haul, and he gave it to Kit who placed it on the parson's book. Then she watched Kit step aside and her heart went out to him – Kit, who had suffered much: years of imprisonment and slavery, only surviving as a fugitive, who, in the end, had to leave his love behind. Would he ever find her again? Would he one day wed in happiness such as hers? Let it be so, if ever there was justice. Kit smiled at her shyly, placing more gifts on the prayer book, tokens of gold and silver.

'From the men,' he whispered.

Next, Captain Drake stepped forward, producing a large battered quoit with a grandiose flourish and placing it on the book as well.

'From Her Majesty,' he announced, and the gold was so heavy, the parson almost let it fall. The Captain chuckled, and the parson recovered, giving the ring back to Will to place on her finger, saying words in turn that filled her to glowing: 'With this ring I thee wed: this gold and silver I thee give: with my body I thee worship . . .'

This gold and silver – what a story lay behind it, and now it was the gift and seal of her marriage. They were wed; the bells rang out, and she and Will stepped outside to a soaring ovation. Arm in arm they proceeded, as Drake's men lined up, drawing their swords to form an arch, and sending Peryn Fownes stumbling in momentary panic. Through this arch they walked, showered with sugared grains and petals, with a flurry of white from the doves that were released into the sky.

'A kiss,' the people called, and Will bent to kiss her tenderly, until the Captain intervened, clapping his hand on Will's shoulder.

'That's no kiss for a mariner,' Drake declared, pushing Will aside. 'Here, let me show you . . .'

Drake made ready to kiss her to hoots and whistles. His merry face came closer, red and whiskered, and she would have made no objection because of the regard in which she held him, but Will took hold of the Captain and bodily pulled him away.

'No, Captain.' Will embraced her again, more firmly now, with the kind of hold that no one could break. 'Let *me* show *you* . . .'

She could not hear any more for the cheering of the crowd.

Author's Note

On 9th August 1573, during a sermon at St Andrew's Church in Plymouth, the news spread that Francis Drake had docked in the harbour, and one by one the entire congregation crept out to greet him, until the preacher was left quite alone – so the story goes . . .

Drake and his men returned to a hero's welcome, their fortunes made, with a haul amounting to a significant proportion of Queen Elizabeth's annual revenue – some estimate as much as a fifth. Of the seventy-three adventurers who had left Plymouth over a year before, no more than thirty-one arrived back, but Drake had established his reputation, and dared strike a blow for independence and religious freedom against the might of imperial Spain. The success of the enterprise heralded the beginning of the Elizabethan Golden Age, and set the course for the rise of England as a great maritime power.

I expect you will now be wondering just how much of this story is true. The answer is: a good deal; Drake's activities in the Caribbean between 1570 and 1573 took place much as I have described them in *Mistress of the Sea.* Insofar as the novel concerns well-known real-life figures, the story accords with the generally accepted facts. Drake really did mount several attacks on the Spanish bullion supply in Panamá and eventually succeeded after many failures – he did raid Nombre de Dios, ally with the Cimaroons, lose many of his men to yellow fever, capture a mule-train loaded with gold and other riches, escape on an improvised raft and return to England victorious but without two of his younger brothers who died during the venture. The rout of the English fleet at San Juan de Ulúa in 1568 is also a well-documented event, and the duplicitous behaviour of the Viceroy of New Spain during this incident – treachery, as Drake saw it – was the spark that ignited his hatred of the Spanish and a determination to exact vengeance which continued for the rest of his life. Of course, he famously had the ultimate retribution after the period covered by this novel, with the defeat of the Spanish Armada in 1588.

The setting for *Mistress of the Sea* is supported by such sources as there are, principally the reports of Christopher Ceely, Ellis Hixom and other members of Drake's crew, on the basis of which Drake's chaplain, Philip Nichols, compiled an account which was annotated and approved by Drake and dedicated to Queen Elizabeth for presentation to her on New Year's Day, 1593. This account was later published as *Sir Francis Drake Revived* by Drake's nephew (also Sir Francis Drake) in 1628. In conjunction with this, I have made use of the Spanish first-hand accounts which were translated by Irene A Wright and published in 1932 by the Hakluyt Society in *Spanish Documents Selected from the Archives of the Indies at Seville*. The degree of consistency between both English and Spanish accounts gives credibility to much of the story of Drake's 1572-3 venture as set out in *Sir Francis Drake Revived*, even allowing for some fairly flagrant elements of exaggeration and dissembling.

For the evidence of what really took place at San Juan de Ulúa I have consulted the eye-witness reports of the gunner, Job Hortop, and the page, Miles Philips, which first appeared in Richard Hakluyt's seminal work: *The Principal Navigations, Voyages, Traffiques and Discoveries of the English Nation* first published in 1589. Also in this collection was John Hawkins's own account of his 'unfortunate voyage' of 1567-8. All three narratives are excellent not only for the information they contain, but also for giving the reader a real feel for the mindset, language and habits of these Elizabethan seafarers from diverse social backgrounds. Again, I have looked at the Spanish sources, and back in 1961, Rayner Unwin wrote a superb description in *The Defeat of John Hawkins.*

But this novel is not faction; it is not primarily concerned with dramatising and retelling the known and probable history. *Mistress of the Sea* is unashamedly fiction; the characters of Ellyn, Will and Kit are all imaginary, and their adventures are products of my own invention, set within the framework of the evidence for what actually happened at the time, so far as I have been able to ascertain it.

Francis Drake and John Hawkins were giants of the age, and I have tried to be faithful to the historical records concerning them both as regards what they did and said, and as regards their characters. Some of the things Drake says in *Mistress of the Sea* come directly from the early sources, for example, several of

Drake's responses to the Spanish 'gentleman soldier' on the Isla Bastimentos, after the failed attack on Nombre de Dios, are taken from *Sir Francis Drake Revived,* an account that Drake presented as his own. He may well not actually have made any remark to the effect that, before he departed, 'He meant to reap some of the harvest which they [the Spaniards] get out of the earth, and sent into Spain to trouble all the earth!' (meaning the gold and silver), but there is little doubt that this is the kind of remark Drake felt he *should* have made.

Drake, the man, as I found him described in the first sources, was not quite the avuncular hero who has come to be revered as Drake, the icon. He was a man of superhuman achievement, from humble beginnings, but the Drake I got to know was quintessentially ruthless. This was a leader who, by his own admission, scuttled his brother's ship in secret so his men could not sail back home, then watched his brother labour in vain to try and save it, who almost certainly lied about the treasure he had found at Nombre de Dios (we know from the Spanish accounts that it was most unlikely there would have been any bullion left in the city at the time of the raid), and who later infamously hanged two innocent friars in retaliation for the mortal wounding of a black messenger boy after the capture of Santo Domingo, and then threatened to execute two prisoners a day until the murderer was punished or surrendered (the culprit was eventually hanged by the Spanish). The Drake who came alive for me in the accounts would stop at nothing to get what he wanted – and he would never give up. This is the Drake I portrayed in *Mistress of the Sea*: the kind of man who would always put the success of his venture before any individual concern, but who inspired absolute confidence and devotion.

Amongst the many non-fiction books about Drake and his ventures, some of the most useful I found were: *Sir Francis Drake* by John Sugden, *Sir Francis Drake, The Queen's Pirate* by Harry Kelsey, *The Pirate Queen* by Susan Ronald and the nicely illustrated and compact *Sir Francis Drake* by Peter Whitfield.

There are other characters in *Mistress of the Sea* whose names appear in the records, but about whom little is known: those such as Ellis Hixom and Thomas Sherwell for example. With these players I have envisaged them almost from scratch. Others, such as Capitán Gonzalo de Bastidas, are inventions derived from just a smidgen of fact. There was no officer in command of the garrison at Nombre de Dios by the name of Bastidas, but there really was a Rodrigo de Bastidas (the grandfather of Capitán Bastidas in the story) who sailed with Christopher Columbus and then led his own expedition to the New World and discovered Panama, as well as claiming much of the Columbian coastline for Spain (and how could I resist a name like that?!).

A book I found invaluable in tracing the early colonial history of Panamá was *Old Panama and Castillo Del Oro*, published in 1914 by CLG Anderson (and read in one sitting at the British Library). For the Elizabethan history of Plymouth, I would recommend *A History of Plymouth* by CW Bracken (1931) (bought second hand from a bookshop by Sutton Harbour), as well as *Plymouth – An Illustrated History* by Crispin Hill, and I still keep referring to Liza Picard's wonderful *Elizabeth's London* for information on daily life for townsfolk in the era. Of the numerous reference works I consulted on sailing in the Age of Discovery, probably the most helpful for my purposes were: *Galleons and Galleys* by John F Guilmartin Jr (lavishly illustrated), *Sailing Ships of War 1400-1860* published in 1979 by Dr Frank Howard, *Spain's Men of the Sea* by Pablo E Pérez-Mallaína and also *The Mary Rose*, a gem of a little handbook, from the Mary Rose Exhibition in Portsmouth. This brings me to the guides and maps, the notes and museum displays, the Elizabethan House run by Plymouth Museum and Art Gallery, Panamá la Vieja, the remains of the Camino Real and Las Cruces Trail in Panamá – the resources that bring the sensory experiences of time and place that much closer – because for me these are just as important as the text books.

As soon as I had the idea of writing a story with Drake's raid on the Spanish bullion supply as a backdrop, I was determined to get to know the places involved, to walk some of the unspoilt terrain that my characters would have covered, to understand the climate and gain a feel for what it would have been like to be bitten by sandflies on a shadeless, oven-hot beach, or trudge up and down mountains, heavily burdened, through thick rainforest in near hundred per cent humidity. In this respect there was no better guide for me than Michael Turner's *In Drake's Wake: the Early Voyages*, because this series faithfully traces Drake's journeys over sea and land in superb pictorial and topographical detail. '*Espero que encuentres lo que quieres*,' Michael wrote in the flyleaf to his book in my possession, now extremely battered after numerous treks and thumbings. Well, I did find what I wanted, and his book was a huge help; for anyone interested in following in Drake's footsteps, I would heartily recommend it.

Did a woman ever accompany Drake on one of his early Caribbean voyages? There's no evidence that this happened – and there's no evidence that it did not. For me, it would perhaps have over-stretched credulity to construct a story on the premise that a woman sailed aboard the *Pascoe* or the *Swan* in 1572 when that voyage is so well documented, but there are hardly any records relating to the two earlier Caribbean voyages that we know Drake made. What if a woman had been aboard then? . . . What if? . . .

'What if?' is how many a story begins . . .

Glossary

Ambergris – A wax-like substance used in making perfume, secreted by the sperm whale, and often found floating in the sea

Arquebus (also harquebus) – A muzzle-loaded, long-barrelled handgun, which was a precursor to the musket, often supported on a rest

Astrolabe – An instrument used to measure the altitude of stars and planets as a navigational aid

Black powder – Gunpowder (though 'black powder' was descriptive at the time)

Bladderball – A ball made from an inflated animal bladder

Bowsprit – A large spar projecting from the bow of a vessel on which the foremost stays are fastened

Bo'sun – A ship's officer responsible for the crew and equipment aboard, effectively the deck foreman (from a contraction of 'boatswain' or 'boat man')

Breech (of a gun or cannon) – The closed part furthest away from the muzzle. (The best cannon were cast in bronze, which was called brass; cast iron was much cheaper, but if the casting was not skilfully done then the firing chamber could burst at the breech)

Bride-laces – Long ribbons of lace used to bind the sprigs of rosemary traditionally worn by a bride and her party

Bridecup – A cup or bowl full of sugared fruit or spiced wine which would be handed round at the wedding feast

Bulwarks – The raised sides of a vessel above the level of the deck

Caballero – A Spanish knightly gentleman or mounted soldier

Caliver – An improved form of arquebus, being light enough to be fired without the support of a rest (originally of standard calibre and deriving from that word). (Calivers were the principal firearms used in Drake's Caribbean voyage of 1572-3)

Carcanet – A jewelled collar or necklace

Caravel – A light and fast sailing ship, used by the Spanish and Portuguese, typically with a broad beam, moderately high deck at the stern and lateen rig, i.e. triangular sails

Carrack – A large and potentially cumbersome three or four-masted sailing ship used by the English and others sailing in the Baltic and Atlantic. It had a high forecastle and sterncastle, and was usually square rigged on the foremast and mainmast (i.e. with square sails) and lateen rigged on the mizzenmast (i.e. with triangular sails at the stern). The equivalent Spanish ship was the *nao*

Caulk – To pack the seams between the planks of a hull with waterproof material, typically oakum sealed with pitch, to prevent leakage

Cawle – A cap or net for the hair worn by women

Churl – A peasant

Cimaroon (Spanish: cimarrón, plural: cimarrones) – A runaway slave, typically of African-Negro origin, who banded together with other fugitives and lived in the mountain wilderness (probably from Spanish for summit: *cima* and dirt: *roña*). (The Cimaroons allied with Francis Drake and gave him invaluable support in his attacks on the Spanish)

Coif – A close-fitting cap

Coxcomb – A vain and foppish man (from the cap, resembling a cock's comb, worn by a jester)

Cresset – A metal basket, mounted on a pole, filled with flammable material such as wood and pitch and set alight for illumination

Cuirass – Armour consisting of a breastplate and backplate fastened together

Culverin – A large cannon with a length of about 10-13 feet, capable of firing shot weighing 17-20 lbs fairly accurately

Duenna – An older woman acting as a chaperone to a girl or young lady, especially in Spain

Farthingale – A framework of hoops, usually of willow or rope, worn under a woman's skirts to extend and shape them

Fore (mast or sail) – A mast or lowest and largest sail at the fore or front of a ship

Fighting top – A large platform on a mast equipped with guns designed to fire down at the decks of enemy ships. (Typically, masts were made up of three sections, and a basket-style platform or 'top' would be at the upper end of the first section)

Forecastle – A raised structure at the bow of a ship, originally castle-like and providing a high base for firing at the enemy

Frigate – A relatively small and fast sailing ship

Fustian – A kind of coarse woollen cloth

Galliard – A quick and spirited dance characterised by leaps and jumps

Gibbet – A structure resembling a gallows on which the bodies of executed criminals were left hanging as a warning to others

Gimmel ring – One with several hoops or links that fit together to form a composite ring, typically used in betrothals where the engaged couple would wear one hoop each and rejoin them as a wedding ring

Goffer – To press wavy pleats into a frill or ruff using heated irons

Gorget – A piece of armour protecting the throat

Grapple (in warfare) – To secure with a grappling iron, i.e. a hooked claw or grapnel at the end of a rope

Gun carriage – A mobile support for a piece of artillery, typically with two heavy wheels at the front and a wheel-less wooden trail at the back. English gun-carriages used aboard ships often had four small wheels, or 'trucks', with ropes allowing for recall after firing and repositioning.

Gunwale – The upper edge of the side of a ship or boat

Halberd – A weapon like a spear and battleaxe combined, having a long shaft with an axe blade and a pick topped by a spearhead

Hautboy – An early form of oboe

Hawser – A thick rope used for mooring or towing a ship

Hornbook – A teaching aid usually displaying the alphabet, the ten digits and the Lord's Prayer, mounted on a wooden tablet and protected by a thin plate of horn

Hose – Male clothing for the legs consisting of 'upper hose' or breeches (typically short padded 'trunk hose' or loose 'slops'), and 'nether hose' or close-fitting stockings, usually made out of wool, which could reach down to the ankles or cover the feet as well

Huguenot – A French Calvinist or follower of the minority Protestant Church in France

Hulk (ship) – The body of a dismantled unseaworthy ship retained in use as a store-vessel or for other purposes

Jackanapes – A cheeky person (deriving from a man whose behaviour resembles that of a tame ape)

Jennet – A small Spanish riding horse

Journeyman – A worker who could charge for each day he worked, who had completed an apprenticeship and was competent to practice a trade or craft, but who had not yet been admitted as a master to a guild (from Old French for a day or day's work: *jornee*)

Kirtle – A woman's skirt or outer petticoat

Lackey – A servant or hanger-on

Lawn – Very fine linen fabric

Lee – The side or part that is away from the wind (hence 'leeward': on the sheltered side)

Lighter (boat) – A flat-bottomed boat used for transporting cargo especially in loading or unloading a ship

Lychgate – A roofed gate to a churchyard

Main (mast or sail) – The chief mast or sail of a ship, between the fore and mizzen masts of a three-masted ship, and usually the largest

Mantilla – A large light veil or scarf worn by Spanish women over the head and shoulders

Marry! – An expression of surprise or outrage (from Mary, the mother of Jesus)

Mastiff – A breed of massive, powerful, short-haired dog, usually fawn or brindle with a dark mask. The dogs were prized for blood sports such as bear and bull-baiting

Match cord – A length of hemp or flax cord treated to make it burn slowly

Matchlock – A mechanism for firing a handgun in which a piece of smouldering match-cord held in a clamp on a lever is used to ignite priming powder in a flash pan and thence the main charge in the gun barrel. The word can also refer to a gun with this type of firing lock

Medlar – A small bushy tree with brown apple-like fruit, which are only edible after they have begun to decay

Mizzen (mast or sail) – A mast or lowest and largest sail aft or behind the mainmast

Morion – A curved brimmed helmet without a visor usually having a crest from front to back

Nosegay – A small bunch of sweet-smelling flowers

Oakum – Loose fibre from unravelled old rope used for caulking ships' seams

Palfrey – A light docile saddle horse much favoured by women riders

Palisade – A fence of wooden stakes forming a defensive enclosure

Pallet – A crude bed, often having a straw-filled mattress

Partlet – A woman's covering for the upper chest worn when the bodice had a low neckline

Pinnace – A boat, typically with sails and oars, carried aboard merchant and war ships to serve as a tender, or for scouting and raiding. (Drake took three pinnaces on his 1572-73 venture, which were carried disassembled and in pieces in the holds of his ships; they were put together and made seaworthy in a matter of days)

Placer – A deposit in the bed of a stream or river containing particles of gold or other valuable minerals (probably from Spanish for pleasure: *placer*)

Plate corselet – Protective armour comprising metal plates covering the upper body

Primer – Gunpowder placed in the pan of a firearm to ignite a charge after itself being ignited by a spark or friction

Quoit – A lump of crudely processed gold or silver formed into a rough disc that was thickest in the centre and tapering towards the edges. (Much of the bullion from the mines in Peru was transported by the Spanish in these disc-shaped ingots as well as in the form of bars and coins)

Rapier – A thin, light sharp-pointed sword used for thrusting

Rubbing strake – A projecting line of planking extending from stem to stern along the side of a ship which acts as a crude bumper

Saltpetre – Potassium nitrate: a crystalline substance typically found in decayed manure from old stables and chicken coops

Scriptorium – A room set apart for writing, especially one in a monastery where manuscripts were copied

Scut – A term of contempt for a person, probably deriving from its other meaning as the short erect tail of an animal in flight

Shallop – A light sailing boat used mainly for coastal fishing

Sheet (nautical) – A rope attached to the lower corner of a sail for securing or extending the sail or changing direction

Slops – Thick loose breeches, reaching to the knee or below, often worn by sailors

Sluice – A trough with grooves through which a current of water is directed in order to separate gold from the ore containing it

Spar – A thick, strong pole used for supporting the sails of a ship

Stanchion – An upright support

Sterncastle – A large raised structure at the stern of a ship

Stomacher – A V-shaped piece of decorative cloth, worn over the chest and stomach

Stooks – Sheaves of grain stood on end in a field

Tallow – A hard, fatty substance made from rendered animal fat used for making soap and candles

Tapir – A nocturnal, hoofed mammal native to the forests of tropical America, resembling a very large pig, and having a flexible snout

Tender (boat) – A boat used to ferry people and supplies to and from a ship

Tholes – The pins set upright on the gunwales of a rowing boat to serve as a fulcrum in rowing and against which the oars press

Trencher – A flat piece of wood or other material on which food was served and cut

Trunnions – The supporting stubs on which a cannon barrel pivots up or down

Tussie-mussie – A small bunch of flowers or aromatic herbs

Waxbill – A finch-like songbird having a bright red bill resembling sealing wax in appearance

Wheellock – A firing device that was a development on the matchlock using a rotating steel wheel rubbing against a piece of pyrite to provide the spark for ignition of the charge. The word can also refer to a handgun with this kind of mechanism.

Yard – A cylindrical spar slung across a ship's mast from which a sail could hang

Acknowledgements

I wish to thank all those who have helped in any way with this book: my wonderful agent, Jonathan Pegg, for his mentoring and unfailing encouragement; my terrific editor, Gillian Green, for giving me the chance that all new writers dream of; Caroline Newbury and Ellie Rankine for their help with publicity; Emily Yau and the rest of the team at Ebury Press; Donna Condon for her expert work in copy-editing the text; Emma Djonokusumo for her careful proofreading; my mother and first literary guide, Maureen Hall; my sister, reader and ace-typist, Caroline Duffield; my daughter, Emma, for her excellent observations; my family for standing by me and not complaining (much!). Thanks also to Verulam Writers' Circle for listening to me read over many evenings at the *Goat* and *White Hart* and giving helpful feedback with generosity and good humour; particular thanks to VWC Chair, Ian Cundell, reader-buddies, Tim Blinko and Cheryl Alleyne, and everyone at *Get Writing*. Thanks to the Historical Novel Society and especially its founder, Richard Lee, for his really useful comments and morale-boosting endorsement when I was close to rock-bottom; thanks to friends at HNS Conferences in the UK and US, the London Chapter of the HNS and the support of all HF devotees at the *Zetland Arms*, and thanks to Michael Turner, founder of the Drake Exploration Society.

Thanks to the Romantic Novelists' Association and the many friends from the Cambridge and London Chapters, Summer Conferences and meetings who have kept my spirits strong and hopes high; warm thanks to the only other members of the St Albans mini-Chapter: Barbara Alderton and Gail Mallin. Thanks to Melanie Hilton for all that she does for the New Writers' Scheme, and thanks to my readers under that scheme for twice giving invaluable critique on this book. Huge thanks to Elizabeth Hawksley and Jenny Haddon. Thanks to all at the Festival of Romance, particularly the members of the Reader Panel.

Thanks to everyone who has ever shown an interest in my writing. If you want to know how the book's going – here it is, thanks to you.